MY SiSTER'S
KEEPER

MY SiSTER'S KEEPER

Bill Benners

McBRYDE PUBLISHING
New Bern, North Carolina

McBryde Publishing
United States of America

MY SISTER'S KEEPER - Copyright © 2007 by Bill Benners.

For information, McBryde Publishing, 108 Dogwood Lane, New Bern, NC 28562. info@mcbrydepublishing.com.   877-830-0759

www.mcbrydepublishing.com

ISBN 10   0-9758700-3-3
ISBN 13   978-0-97-587003-7

Library of Congress Cataloging-in-Publication Data

Benners, Bill, 1949-
  My sister's keeper / Bill Benners. -- 1st ed.
      p. cm.
   ISBN 978-0-9758700-3-7 (pbk.)
   1. Brothers and sisters--Fiction. 2. Invalids--Fiction. 3. Family secrets--Fiction. 4. New Bern (N.C.)--Fiction. 5. Domestic fiction. I. Title.
PS3602.E664425M9 2007
813'.6--dc22

                                  2007010566

3 1967 01007 0855

First Edition: May 2007
Manufactured in the United States of America

For Dorrie

Acknowledgments

A HALF-CENTURY AGO my third grade teacher, Mrs. Price, planted the seed from which the writer in me would develop. She introduced me to the "theater in my mind" where the feature NOW PLAYING was produced instantaneously in my head by reading a book. But that seed lay dormant waiting for the right conditions to germinate. For that, I thank my wife Dorrie, to whom I owe the most. She gave me the time, space, and encouragement to do it and never once doubted I could. I love you, Angel.

To those who have probed the many versions of this novel as it developed over the last decade, a heart-felt thank you. I especially thank Trish Corlew, Natalie Thompson, Linda Winfield, Donnie Benners, Jimmy and Peppermint Jones, Susan Myers, Toni Marrese, and Arden Lindsey. I stand and applaud you. Your feedback has been instrumental in shaping the final version of this book.

To author, publisher, and editor Eddie Ellis, thank you for your priceless guidance and suggestions. I will forever be grateful.

To Laura Brown, editor supreme and lawyer, thank you for your insight and knowledge of North Carolina law.

To my dearest friend and fellow writer Skip Crayton, we've been best friends since the day we discovered that inside each of us was a writer begging to get out—dreamers who refused to let go of their dreams. Thank you for the years of daily phone calls, long discussions on writing theory and authors we've read, and the brainstorming we did for our works. What a great pleasure it has been having your eyes looking over my shoulder, having you always challenging me, and sharing this adventure. You have been a source of constant support and invaluable advice. No other resource has contributed so much and made the process so enjoyable. Thanks, man!

And a special thank you to my mom and dad and to my children, Natalie and Lucas, who have loved me regardless.

MY SISTER'S
KEEPER

Bill Benners

T HOMAS WOLFE WAS RIGHT. You can't go home again. And I
wouldn't have had it not been for my sister's *accident.* I flew
back to Wilmington, North Carolina, and sat vigil over her for
weeks listening to the beeps and clicks of the machinery that
kept her alive, pleading with her not to die. Martha was the one
person in this world that had always been there for me, believed in
me, looked up to me, and never failed me. And I, Richard Charles
Baimbridge, could not survive without her.

She kept me sane.

Even in the darkness of her hospital room, I could see beyond the
bruises on her face to the whimsical little girl with auburn hair and
bright eyes that had grown up alongside me. The curious
perfectionist turned investigative reporter who would not let go of a
thing until she'd figured it out. Like the time a girlfriend of hers
showed up with a Rubik's Cube. Martha was only eight at the time,
but she'd spun and twisted that thing relentlessly—practically that
entire summer—until finally she woke me early one Sunday morning
holding it out in the palm of her hand. All the colored squares were
in perfect alignment and there was a look in her eyes I've never
forgotten to this day. I was twelve and had given it a serious shot
several times myself to no avail. That was the first time she'd beaten
me at something, but it wouldn't be the last.

That moment established a pattern for her life. In some backward
way, I became her motivation—her *inspiration.* If she saw me give up
on anything, regardless of how insignificant—forgetting a phone
number, finding the right nut to fit a bolt, or fixing a broken toy—

she'd go after it with fanaticism and would not give up until she'd figured it out.

Being better than me challenged her and when she succeeded, it fulfilled her. I was proud of her, but not like Dad. Dad *loved* it. It seemed the more she outdid me, the more *he* liked it. And when she did beat me, he always cast that malevolent glare from the corner of his eye that cut deep and made me feel as though I'd stepped in something foul and tracked it into the house. By the time I left home at eighteen, there was a gap between my father and me that an ocean couldn't fill.

The connection between Martha and me, however, only grew stronger. I envied that spark she had, that do-it-or-die attitude, and the way my father thought she could do no wrong. But his praise never seemed to mean much to her, and maybe that's why she got so much of it from him. It *mattered* to me, though, and he knew it, and he manipulated it to cut out my heart. Ironically, she craved *my* praise instead of his and I gave it to her in heavy doses. It felt fantastic to be needed by somebody for something and I used it against him. Maybe that's why he hated me so much.

God! If only I'd turned on her, belittled her, or ignored her, maybe she wouldn't have ended up in her current state.

Though we'd talked on the phone weekly, it had been more than a year since I'd seen her. Her hair was shorter now, and she'd lost that baby fat that had lingered long past high school. Her eyelashes were long and thick—the envy of the whole family. Her cheeks were high and her lips were wide and thin like mine—typical of Dad's side of the family.

I pulled a chair up next to her bed, took her hand, and studied her fingernails where tiny bits of pink polish lingered—reminders of a time when her life had been full of hope, ambition, and romantic dreams. Dreams that were going to die hard.

Until the accident, things had always gone incredibly well for Martha. When she decided she wanted to go to college, Mom—somehow—had scraped together the money. "An anonymous scholarship," she'd said. Martha graduated summa cum laude, took a job with the local paper, then landed the one she truly wanted; investigative reporter for the Raleigh *News and Observer*.

I'll never forget that day. We talked on the phone for hours. She was ecstatic! Twenty-four years old, armed with a Master's in communication, and craving that one big story with which to prove herself.

A few weeks later, Martha received a tip that a thirteen-year-old girl had been dragged to the top floor of an abandoned warehouse in Wilmington, raped by two men while being videotaped by a third, then bound, gagged, and thrown in the Cape Fear River to drown, and knew she'd found her story. It was a story I would come to hear Martha tell *over and over...*

"A FRIEND FROM WILMINGTON CALLED and told me about the rape. She said the little girl had survived and that Sam Jones— a detective I'd gotten to know well while working for the Wilmington Star-News—had been assigned to the case. After a two-hour drive, I planted myself in Sam's office and hounded him relentlessly until he finally agreed to let me have a look at the place where the rape had supposedly taken place. He told me to meet him there when he got off at 5:00 p.m.

"It was Halloween and a cold front was moving in. The temperature had dropped fifteen degrees since noon. I arrived a few minutes early, pulling my Toyota into the dirt lot next to the abandoned plant, and parked facing a sagging eight-foot steel-mesh fence surrounding the property. Railroad tracks crisscrossing the grounds all led into a huge four-story corrugated metal building set back along the river's edge. Among the tall weeds around the perimeter lay stacks of creosote-coated wooden railroad ties, rusting steel wheels, and bent rails. To the left of the building, a rickety dock jutted out into the Cape Fear River. Across the river, the trees were showing a hint of fall color.

"Knowing what had happened to that girl, I was afraid to turn off the engine. And when I finally did—after looking in all directions—the silence was nerve-wracking. I could actually hear my own heart thumping in my chest. As I waited, I envisioned that helpless thirteen-year-old being snared off the street, fighting against the strengths of three men—her cries smothered, her breathing obstructed by a powerful hand clamped over her face. I felt her terror as they whisked her across that barren yard to be held down, stripped, tortured, and raped in a night of horror from which she was not supposed to survive.

"A black crow abruptly landed on the hood of my car rattling me back to reality, leering at me with its yellow eyes. I honked the horn to frighten it away, then wished I hadn't, looking around to see if anyone had noticed.

"The street was deserted except for a group of trick-or-treaters crossing at the next intersection with their parents protectively tailing them fully aware of the dangers that lurked in the shadows of their young lives.

"I checked the clock on the car radio. It was 5:47. Sam was late. I dialed his cell number, but only got his voicemail. I hung up without leaving a message and began making a detailed description of the property and a list of questions I needed to answer for the story. Finally, as the sun melted into the trees on the far side of the river, I wondered if Sam had forgotten about our meeting. I called him again and this time left a message trying to sound relaxed and professional. 'This is Martha Baimbridge,' I said. 'Just calling to confirm that we're still meeting at the warehouse. I'm here now and...waiting.' I hung up wishing I hadn't sounded so unprofessional.

"To fill the time, I jotted down notes on how I might package the story and a few angles to explore in the articles that would follow. I closed my eyes and imagined the panic that must have been going through that thirteen-year-old's mind and what could have been going through the sick minds of those bastards that raped her. What is this need some men have to have sex with little girls? Don't these monsters realize that they are children? That they will be scarred psychologically for life? Do they care? And why would they videotape it?

"A child's shrill scream abruptly pierced the darkness peeling the skin off my nerves leaving me feeling raw and exposed. I extinguished the interior dome light and searched the darkness around me sensing a thousand eyes out there watching me. Looking back at the railway yard, I noticed a flicker of light in the highest window in the building, but could not tell for sure if it was a light or a reflection.

"I tried Sam's phone again, and again I got his voicemail. 'Mr. Jones, I just heard a horrible scream and I think I can see light coming from a window in that warehouse. Please hurry.' After hanging up, I just sat there staring at that window horror-stricken that another young girl could be in there at that very moment having her youth savagely ripped away—perhaps even fighting for her life—and realized, Sam or no Sam, I had to do something.

"I took a deep breath, opened the door, and stepped out. There was a chilly breeze blowing in off the river and an oily, tar-like stench mixed with the fishy smell of the Cape Fear. As I pulled on a navy blue windbreaker, I made a mental note to keep a flashlight, running shoes, jeans, and an old sweatshirt in the car for future times like this. I switched my phone to vibrate only, crept along the fence toward the river, and found a break in the wire. Pausing one last time to check for Sam, I squeezed through the gap and crouched in the grass gathering enough nerve to go farther.

"Then, zigzagging around piles of scrap iron, I ducked into the shadow of the giant warehouse and laid an ear to the cold metal exterior. Hearing nothing, I crept along the edge of the building testing every door and window, but it wasn't until I pressed against a wooden hatch near the ground that I found a way to get in. Dropping to my knees, I shoved it inward breaking loose its rusty hinges and crawled into the opening to get a look inside. I listened for a full minute, but heard nothing. Figuring my imagination had gotten the best of me, I chuckled at myself and started to back out when I heard a whimper inside and cold terror seized me.

"Panicked, I retreated to the outside, ran to the corner of the building checking for Sam, then dialed his number again and left one last message. 'There's something going on inside that warehouse, Sam. For God's sake, hurry! I'm going in.'"

2

I N THE SOLITUDE OF MARTHA'S HOSPITAL ROOM, my mind drifted back to that summer day when a sixteen-year-old neighborhood bully named Jimmy Lassiter pulled a switchblade and tried to rob us. I was fourteen at the time and Martha was ten. Without hesitation, she snatched up a broken chunk of brick and hurled it, permanently blinding him in his right eye, and scarring me internally for the rest of my life. *Coward!*

Why couldn't I be more like my sister?

As I watched over her and prayed for her life, I promised God that night that if he'd let Martha live, no matter how badly she was injured, I'd take care of her for the rest of her life if needed. I hadn't kept many promises I'd made to God, but that was one promise I *did* intend to keep.

When Martha finally did emerge from her coma and I realized how much rehabilitation she was going to need, I went back to New York City, packed up my Tribeca photography studio, and hauled it down to Wilmington so I could help with her recovery.

After four months in the hospital, she moved back home with Mom and Dad and things got easier. In addition to helping with Martha, I set up a studio downtown and got involved in the local theatre. That was three years ago.

The events of that night at the warehouse cost Martha a kidney and left her paralyzed from the waist down. She's gotten used to the pain, the limitations, and the prognosis of a future alone, but I don't think she'll ever get over not being able to have children.

Although the police had a solid set of fingerprints and even some DNA evidence, the case still had yet to be solved three years later. Two more girls had turned up floating in the river and another two disappeared without a trace. The police feared they had a serial killer on their hands and—although confined to a wheelchair—finding the owners of those fingerprints had become the focus of Martha's life.

And mine, too.

I wanted her to go with me. I told her we'd go anywhere she wanted, but until this thing was resolved, she wouldn't leave—and neither could I. I was her legs.

When the police exhausted their leads, Martha talked Sam Jones into giving her detailed copies of the three sets of fingerprints they'd found in the warehouse. She ordered a fingerprint kit along with computer hardware and software on the Internet, and read every book she could find on how to collect, store, and interpret them. She became an expert.

I pushed her around town and took her places she couldn't go on her own so she could secretly lift drinking glasses, forks, and knives from seedy bars and restaurants from which to get fingerprints to scan at home.

Her scrapbook grew to contain more than seven hundred prints catalogued with notes identifying where they came from, when, and to whom they belonged—or most likely belonged. She even took to getting possible suspects to help her with her wheelchair just so she could get their prints off the handles.

That's all she had to go on. That and the name "Jack." But that's all she needed. She'd *never* give up, and had started to make *some* people very nervous.

Then she found something.

I had stopped by to pick her up for another outing and leaned in her bedroom door. "How'd we do, Babe?" I asked.

She was comparing two images of fingerprints on her computer screen. Her shoulder-length hair was pulled back in a short ponytail exposing her freckled forehead and thick Brooke Shields eyebrows. Through frameless eyeglasses resting on the end of her nose, she squinted at the screen. "I think we can finally rule out Jackie...Wilkes," she said. The lisp in her speech was now gone and the hesitations were waning. I stepped in and kissed the top of her head.

"Good. Maybe we can move on to someplace else. *Mickey's* is starting to give me the creeps."

"But...take a look at this," she said rolling her wheelchair to the side.

Leaning forward, I examined the images on the screen. "What?"

"See that faded print to the right of the dark one?"

"Got it."

"Now compare that to this one." She touched a few keys on the keyboard and the image on the screen changed. "This is number three from the warehouse, the one they found on the window sill." I looked back and forth between the prints. There was a scar in the shape of a slanted cross in them that seemed to match.

"Jesus! What was this on?" I asked.

"A cigarette butt. Do you know what…this means?"

"Print this out. We need to show it to Sam."

"It means the man was there."

"You're getting close, Babe."

"We have to go back."

Mickey's Pub and Rib House was a fancy name for a trashy hole-in-the-wall that probably hadn't served a rack of ribs since sometime back in the '80s. Patrons consisted mostly of bums off the docks, drifters, and drug addicts. The only regulars seemed to be the girls that hung out there shifting from lap to lap looking for enough money for a fix.

"I've got a busy day tomorrow. I won't be free until at least four and I don't think it's a good idea to be there after dark."

Mom leaned in the door. Pearl—as she was known to her friends at church—was Bette Davis in a size 16 dress with a southern drawl and a hint of white fuzz along the sides of her chin. It was her heavy, sad eyes that did it.

"You had dinner, Richie? How about some black beans and rice?"

It was tempting, but I was not in the mood for another round with my father so I lied. "Thanks, but yes I have and I swear I can't eat another bite."

"You ought not to let the things your daddy says bother you, Richie. You know he doesn't mean anything by it. He just doesn't know how to say things right."

I didn't reply. It was an argument nobody wins. "I'll see you tomorrow, Babe." I squeezed Martha's shoulder and kissed Mom on the way out.

The next day we stopped first by Sam Jones's office and showed him the printout. I was relieved, myself, when he told us to stay away from *Mickey's*—that they'd had a complaint that we were driving away his business. Sam said he'd stop in and see what he could find out.

But Martha didn't want to turn it loose. She wanted to *at least* watch the place for awhile and get photographs of those coming and going. I wanted to do like Sam said, to stay away, but I was ready for this thing to be over, too. With Dad constantly snapping at my heels reminding me of why I left Wilmington in the first place, I'd decided that just as soon as this case was wrapped up—as well as the play I was directing—I was out of there. Martha or no Martha, I was leaving. New York. Atlanta. Cleveland. *Anywhere*, but Wilmington. A place with a good theatre community. Everyone needs a hobby. Mine is directing theatre. It would be my career if I could figure out how to earn a living doing it.

With the Azalea Festival only days away, the streets downtown were ablaze with blooming azaleas and dogwoods. As we headed for my studio to get camera equipment, Martha was quiet, lost in deep thought, then broke her silence.

"Sister Hazel's going to be at the...festival Sunday," she said gazing out at the street decorations.

"What does she do?"

"It's a rock band I...saw once." Her voice was heavy, thoughtful.

"Oh? I figured you to be more of the Carrie Underwood type."

"They were at Lincoln Theatre in Raleigh."

"Oh yeah?"

She wiped a tear from her cheek and drew a deep breath. "It was at that concert that Todd asked me...to marry him."

"Oh, Babe. I'm sorry."

She turned her face away and wiped her nose with a tissue. Marrying Todd had been her dream since high school. After the accident, he stopped by only once. We rode the rest of the way to my studio in silence where I picked up a digital Nikon, a high-powered telephoto lens, and a pair of binoculars.

"Can we go to the beach this weekend?" she asked as I turned off Market Street and headed into the older part of the city near the docks.

"It'll have to be early on Sunday."

"That's okay. It's been three years since I've seen the ocean."

"It hasn't changed."

She didn't laugh.

The neighborhood we drove through hadn't changed since we were kids either. Even the posters plastered on all the vacant buildings announcing the Cole Brothers Circus was coming to town looked the same. As we drove along, the trees thinned, the streets got dirtier, and the color faded to gray.

We pulled around to the back of a row of abandoned stores across from *Mickey's* and parked behind a hollowed-out brick shell of a building with the doors and windows missing.

I eased her wheelchair through the rubble to a spot inside from where we could watch the comings and goings at *Mickey's*. I clamped a bracket on an exposed water pipe to steady the camera and zoomed in on the entrance to the bar.

A short time later, a pair of city detectives walked into *Mickey's* and during the next five minutes, I photographed close to twenty patrons as the place emptied out. Martha watched through the binoculars while I captured images as fast as the camera would go.

Neither of us heard the two come up behind us until one spoke.

"What the hell do we have going on here?"

3

T HE LAST THING I EXPECTED was to be accosted by a couple of women. One was blond with dark eyebrows, the other had dark hair piled high in a bee-hive with a tattoo on her neck—some kind of Chinese symbol. They wore jeans, t-shirts with the sleeves and midriff area ripped off, and metal studs in both their navels and lips—like many of the women you'd run into at Wal-Mart. I saw Martha's hand moving slowly toward her cell phone.

I cleared my throat. "We're working undercover here. You'd better run along if you don't want to get in trouble."

The blond smacked a wad of gum and pointed a finger at Martha. "Just keep your hands where we can see them, Sweetie. And you," she said looking at me, "what did Sam Jones tell you, Baimbridge?"

Sam Jones? "He—told us to stay away."

"Right. And he don't like it when you don't listen."

"We...just—"

"You are endangering the lives of every officer down here. If you don't want to be charged with interfering with an investigation, then do as you're told."

Martha and I said little on the way back to Mom and Dad's. We'd had the hell scared out of us and agreed that in the future we needed to take along some kind of protection. Next time, it might not be the police.

When we arrived back at the house, Mom was loading her car for what she called her *missionary work*—a visit to some shut-in's to deliver food and see to it that they had everything they needed.

She saw that our plans had changed and begged us to go.

Twelve miles southwest of Wilmington she turned up a dirt road, passed two abandoned doublewides parked in what appeared to be a makeshift trash dump, and stopped at a small farm up on a hill.

I'd been here before—dozens of times going back to my childhood. I think this was Mom's favorite case. She'd stopped doing for most of the others, but not this one. The man that lived here was named

Winston. I'd always liked him. He was younger than the rest and treated everybody special.

He'd been burned horribly in a fire. His skin had melted like a wax doll set too close to the stove. His nose and his ears were mostly gone, just enough left to show where they'd been. His eyelids always looked tight and red, and he blinked all the time. He had no hair anywhere that I could see except a tiny patch on the right side of his head. No eyebrows. No eyelashes. And no lips.

Martha and I thought his mouth looked like it belonged on a fish. I had nightmares about him that went on for more than a year after seeing him for the first time. But now I hardly notice.

He made his living raising livestock for the local meat markets. Cattle, pigs, goats, and chickens. He smoked Borkum Riff tobacco in a pipe, an aroma I could still smell in my clothes long after we were gone. To this day I love to smell it.

It had been at least ten years since I'd been there. He welcomed us in as he always did and seemed genuinely pleased that Martha and I had come. He wanted to hear all about what we'd been up to since he'd seen us last and acted like he truly cared. He was thoughtful, positive, inspiring, and way too generous. I think Mom usually took home more than she brought, but maybe having someone to talk to was more important to him than the food.

He had a quick sense of humor and was the most intelligent person I'd ever met. I don't think I ever went there that I didn't leave glad I'd been.

I think Mom cared a lot about Winston, too. She always cried when we left. Sometimes for days.

After a couple of hours, he and Mom went for a walk and it was obvious why she'd kept coming back all these years. It was good to be respected, needed, and appreciated.

When I arrived back at my home, I reached across a counter of dirty dishes, seized the last clean glass in the cabinet, and splashed dinner into it from a bottle of scotch.

I kept thinking about Winston and my mother. I'd never noticed before how different she was with him. She was relaxed and charming. She smiled the whole time and laughed often. I had no idea it had been so long since I'd heard her laugh. And how I do love to hear her laugh.

All that adversity and still he made others laugh. He must have been one hell of a man. I wish Dad could have been a little more like Winston.

Stepping out the back door, I took a long swig and gazed out over the hundred-acre lake behind the house. Surrounded by aging boat docks, weathered purple martin houses, and a dampness that still lingered from winter, it never failed to calm my nerves and soothe the beast within me. One more thing I was going to miss after I left.

Storm clouds moving in from the west were transforming the sky into something dark and menacing. The breeze coming off the lake died and left the air hot and muggy.

Yes sir, just as soon as this thing is over with Martha—and I finish the production I'm directing at Thalian Hall—I'm out of here. Just thinking about it was enough to lift my spirits. That and the approaching storm. *God, how I do love a good storm.* Especially when I'm depressed. I love the feel of it, the sound of it, and all its special effects. Some storms come up so rapidly you barely have time to get out of their way. This was the kind of storm that crept in slowly, that displayed its splendor a piece at a time like an orchestra tuning up. Maybe that's what I like about storms. The lights, colors, sounds, and intensity. The drama of it. *Nature's theatre.*

That's the only thing in life with which I truly am in harmony. The arts. Theatre. When I step through those massive doors into Thalian Hall with its grandeur, history, and ghosts, it's like walking into another dimension—another universe completely separate from this one. It's a magical place where anything is possible. You only have to imagine it for it to be real. And when the intensity is high, it's the most real place on earth.

But my father says that the theatre is a refuge for queers, drug addicts, and dreamers, and that any man that works in the theatre is a loser. So I don't *work* in the theatre. I do it as a hobby—one I take very seriously. And that's what I'm going to miss most about Wilmington. The house, the storms, my Mom, and great theatre. My father can go to hell.

Lightning streaked across the sky on the other side of the lake. Mrs. Winslow, my overweight, snoopy backdoor neighbor around the lake to my left was folding deck chairs and putting them in a weather-beaten tool shed built decades ago by her late husband. No matter what she's doing or how she's standing, she always seems to have one eye on me. By now you'd think she would have realized I don't have friends over, I don't throw parties, and I certainly do not bring women into my house. Strange or not.

Leaves swirled into the air and the neighborhood abruptly came to life. Trees swayed and thunder broke the sound barrier. I closed my eyes and rolled my head in a circle as the vibrations rumbled through my body and out my extremities. It felt good to be touched by something. *Anything.*

As the wind rose and drops of rain began to spatter the deck, I chugged the rest of the scotch, went inside, and turned on the six-thirty news. Evening quickly turned to night and the flickering TV became the only light in the room. With a fresh scotch in hand, I stepped to the floor-length windows just to watch the storm. It was beautiful and passionate. Delicate and gentle one moment, violent and savage the next. Like a relationship. Like sex.

I sipped the scotch. *What sex?* I haven't been in a serious relationship in years. There's something about me that women don't like. Something they're able to sense right away. Some flaw in my character. Maybe I drink too much. Maybe I don't call often enough when we're not together. Maybe it's just too much work for a man that's as busy as I am.

Lightning turned the night back into day and thunder exploded above the house with enough force to rattle the foundation and knock the power out. For a moment, everything stopped. It was spectacular.

Nature's theatre indeed.

The power flickered back on and the refrigerator returned to its endless humming, but the TV stayed off. I slid my glass up next to the liquor bottle and was considering whether to pour another single or go for a double when the doorbell rang an odd chime.

I started for the front door, but spotted the silhouette of a woman standing on the back deck. As she struggled to keep an umbrella over her head, I realized I'd never heard the back doorbell before. I switched on the deck lights and cracked the door enough to get my face wet.

"Yes?"

4

" **M**ISTER BAIMBRIDGE?"
The woman at the back door held a black umbrella against her shoulder and struggled to keep her balance as she braced herself against a mighty gust of wind. She looked to be in her early twenties.

"Yes?"

"My name is Ashleigh Matthews. I live in Dr. Hardesty's pool house next door. May I come inside for a minute?"

There was a pained look on her face that reminded me of the loneliness I often felt. The kind of loneliness that gnaws a hole in your chest, steals your youth, and makes you *vulnerable*.

I parted the door just enough to allow her to get past me without letting in the whole storm. "Sure. Of course. Please come in."

"Thanks," she exhaled dashing by me. As I closed the door, I caught sight of Mrs. Winslow gazing at me from a window. I gave her a two-finger salute and flipped on the kitchen lights.

"I'm sorry to impose on you on a night like this," the woman said folding down her umbrella. She wore a pea-green raincoat over a white cotton shirt and faded jeans soaked from the knees down. Her lips were a bit too large for her face, but, still, she was extremely attractive.

"It's no problem, really. What can I do for you?"

"Well...two things actually." She looked around as if to see if I was alone. "My lights have gone off—"

"Oh? You could have a circuit breaker that's tripped. I'll be glad to go over and take a look if you like. Would you like to sit here until the rain slacks off a bit?"

"Yes. Thank you. That would be great." Her blond shoulder-length hair had six or seven strands of multi-colored beads woven into it hanging off the right side that clinked when she moved.

"And the other thing?"

"Well..." She rotated the umbrella from one hand to the other and wiped the bottom of her chin on the back of her hand. It had been so long since I'd had a guest in the house, I'd forgotten how to treat one.

"Oh, here, let me have that." I reached for the umbrella. "And the raincoat, too."

As I removed her raincoat, I caught the scent of her perfume. It was as out of place in my house as the aroma of a good home-cooked country dinner. She shook droplets out of her hair and the beads jangled. "That's some storm, huh?"

I balanced the umbrella in the sink and hung the raincoat on a cabinet door handle. "Yes, isn't it?" A smile spread wide across her face, but her eyes failed to hide her worry. "Would you like something to drink? Ashleigh, is it?"

"Yes. Ashleigh. A little wine would be nice—if you have any." I opened the fridge and was relieved to discover an unopened bottle of Zinfandel that had been tucked in the back some time ago for just this type of occasion. I reached in for it as her eyes roamed around the room.

The house had been nice in its day. Built in the 1920s as a hunting lodge by a man that owned a railroad. It had high ceilings, wide crown molding, polished oak floors, and glass paneled doors separating the downstairs rooms. But the place had eventually fallen into the hands of heirs who couldn't agree on whether to keep it or sell it. So for decades it remained unoccupied as the neighborhood grew around it. I got use of it from one of Martha's doctors, a great-grandchild of the builder, who just gave me a key figuring it would be better to have someone in it for free than to simply let it continue to deteriorate. I did not pay rent, but I'd made a good many repairs and renovations to it, especially to the kitchen. It not only brought the house back from the dead, it kept my mind and hands occupied when I wasn't working on a play or running Martha around town.

"It's nice in here," she said brushing a strand of wet hair from the corner of her eye.

"Thanks." I uncorked the bottle then opened the dishwasher more out of habit than actual expectation and was surprised to find a clean stem of crystal. I poured the wine then circled the counter holding the glass out to her. "You said there were two things you needed, didn't you?" As she took her drink, I noticed her hand trembling, so I stepped into the den to light the gas logs in the fireplace.

"Yes. The other thing is..." She followed me and sat on the edge of the love seat nearest the fire holding her glass with both hands.

"I'm trying for a part in a Brad Pitt movie they're going to be shooting here..."

I waited to see if there was more as I crossed back to the kitchen for my drink. "And—"

"I'll need some photographs for that."

I topped off my scotch. "Great. Seems simple enough." The wind rose and there was a sharp crack and a loud thump on the deck outside. Ashleigh jumped to her feet as if expecting something to leap through the glass.

"The regular head-shot for an agent?" I asked crossing back to the den.

She sat again slowly. "Actually... What I really need..."

I sat on the couch and waited.

"What I really need..." She rolled the glass in her hands. "...is something a little more..." She took a sip of wine and cleared her throat. "...a little more..."

I'd seen this before. I knew what she couldn't say. "Something sexy? Risqué?"

"Well..."

Lightning struck nearby and thunder rattled the dishes. "If you can't say it, Ashleigh, how do you expect to be able to do it?"

She walked to the window taking her glass. "Oh, I can do it," she said, her voice sounding confident. But the color in her face suggested a different answer. "I have to do it."

She kept her eyes off me, but I couldn't keep mine off her. Her neck was long and her breasts just barely pushed the front of her shirt out. She was definitely intriguing. A flicker of lightning illuminated her face as she gazed out the window. "You need nude photographs to get a part in a movie these days?"

She cut her eyes toward me. "He wants them."

"I'm sure *he* does." I inhaled deeply. "But, Ashleigh...if you walked into McDonald's looking for a job and the manager asked if you had any nude photographs of yourself, you'd probably knock his block off and call the cops. So what makes this different?"

Her voice was quiet, almost dreamy. "Brad Pitt."

"Brad Pitt wants nude photographs of you?"

"I get to do the nude scenes with him." Ashleigh finished the wine in a single gulp, crossed back to the love seat, and flopped her petite figure onto it.

"Don't they use body doubles for that?"

She set the empty stem on the coffee table, sat back, dropped a loafer, and tucked her left foot up under her right thigh.

"That's the part I want."

"Why?"

She picked a painted fingernail at a spot on the seat cushion. "People tell me I look a lot like Julia Roberts. She's the female lead. So, I think I have a good chance to get it. I heard you're a photographer and since you're right next door, I just thought..."

"You'd do this just to be able to rub bellies with Brad Pitt on a movie set?"

She looked at me as if she thought every woman would. "Well, yeah."

"You know there will be about twenty-five other people standing around watching, don't you?"

She flipped a thread of hair off her face and stretched her right arm over the back of the love seat. "That's okay."

What is it with young people these days? They don't have time to do groundwork, build a foundation, or climb anything. They want to jump right into a world of fame, fortune, and adventure and don't mind mortgaging their morals to get it. That's nothing, the way they see it.

Thunder rumbled in the distance. I stood and lifted my glass. "Look, I don't mean to throw cold water on your dreams. Anything's possible. Why don't we go take a look at your fuse box? Would you like some wine to take with you?" I waited for her to respond. When she didn't, I moved into the kitchen, pulled another bottle of scotch from a cabinet, and cracked the seal.

"You don't think I'd get the part do you?" she said. I could tell her feelings were hurt, but I refilled my glass and drank from it without answering. "Seriously, you don't think I'd get it, do you?"

I turned to face her. "Well, how would I know, Ashleigh? I don't know you. I don't know them. I don't even know what the movie's about."

"You're a man, aren't you? You're about his age aren't you?" Lightning lit the room.

"Brad Pitt?" I sighed. "He's—a little older, I think." As I took a gulp, she stood and began unbuttoning her shirt while I choked back the scotch.

"Wh-o-o-o-a! Hey! Hold on there. Wait just a minute."

She ignored me, jerked the shirttail out of her jeans, and worked the rest of the buttons free.

5

"STOP!" I SHOUTED. Ashleigh looked up, her hands frozen on the last button. "I'm sorry, Ashleigh," I said. "Call me drunk. Call me stupid. Call me whatever you want. I'm as red-blooded as any male and you're the best looking woman I've had in this house *ever!* But you just don't need to be doing that. Please, just call the studio in the morning and make an appointment." Her gaze remained locked on me even as another heavy branch fell on the deck. Her shirt lay open exposing her bra. It was tempting. *God, was it tempting!* I turned away. "Please, Ashleigh." The telephone rang and broke the impasse. I reached for it immediately. "Hello?"

It was Mom. "Richie, can you run over and help your dad move Martha's bed?"

I closed my eyes and drew a slow breath. "Move it where, Mom?"

"Is something wrong?"

"No, nothing's wrong. Move it where?"

"Just turn it so she can see the street out the window."

"Okay. Sure. I'll stop by in the morning on my way to work."

"Thank you, Baby."

"You're welcome, Mom."

"Did you get something to eat?"

Thunder rattled the house. "I've got to go, Mom."

She paused. "Is something wrong, Richie?"

"No. I'll call you later."

There was a short pause. "Is someone there?"

"See you in the morning, Mom. Bye-bye."

I set the phone back on its cradle and looked up at Ashleigh. She reminded me of the way my dad often looked at me. *Arrogant and pompous.* I spoke gently. "Think about what you're doing, Ashleigh. You're extremely beautiful, sexy as hell, and certainly don't need me to tell you that." She remained motionless. "Just call the studio tomorrow. Okay?"

She flipped her hair back, exhaled sharply, and began fastening the buttons. "Yeah, sure."

"And we'll go see what we can do about your lights." I tossed down the rest of my drink, found a pad of paper, and made a note to remind me to stop by Mom's in the morning. As I propped it by the coffee pot, Ashleigh drifted toward me jamming her shirttail back into her jeans. Her eyes were downcast and her shoulders slumped. I lifted her raincoat off the cabinet knob and held it open for her. She slipped her arms into it, pulled the collar high, and buttoned it. She kept her eyes low and said nothing.

I snared my windbreaker, pulled it on, and retrieved a flashlight from a drawer next to the back door. "Please don't take this personally—"

A clap of thunder rocked the house and the lights went out. Ashleigh screamed and threw her arms around me. The scent of her shampoo and the heat of her breath on my neck brought back long-forgotten feelings. I should have pushed her away. Instead, my arms folded around her and my lips brushed her forehead. "Shhh. It's just thunder," I whispered. For a long moment we held each other and, for that moment, she was all mine and I ached for more.

As the lights flickered back on and the microwave beeped, she raised her face, closed her eyes, and puckered her lips. I hesitated, then as my lips touched hers, my heart stopped and I relived my entire life—falling in love all over again and making love a hundred times—before releasing her and turning away.

"I'm sorry," she whispered.

I cleared my throat, gripped the doorknob, and wiped a tear from my eye. "Don't be. There are things in this world that frighten me too." I drew a breath. "You ready?" She nodded and I opened the door holding it for her to step back out into the storm. I felt like a fool—like a failure. *Coward!*

It was a short walk to her front porch. I held the light while she unlocked the door then followed her into the darkness panning the light about the room. The place smelled of perfume and potpourri and reminded me of a weekend cottage with a breakfast bar separating the living room and the kitchen. She took my arm and led me across the room saying, "The fuse box is over here."

Luckily the "fuse box" turned out to be a circuit breaker panel. I shined the light on the switches as Ashleigh stood closely behind peeking over my shoulder.

"See anything?" she whispered into my ear.

The main breaker was off. Not tripped, but switched off. I flipped it on and the room filled with light and the hum of appliances. A second later, an ancient console television fizzled to life showing an old black and white Greta Garbo movie. Ashleigh leaned on the counter next to me and planted a hand on her hip. "Well, if I'd known it was that simple, I wouldn't have bothered you."

"Oh, it's no bother," I said scanning the rest of the switches.

"Can you stay a few minutes? I'd like to talk about the photos."

"Well, I..." The rain pounding the roof caused me to hesitate.

"Please? I have some scotch," she said. "Would you like a drink?"

I closed the panel box and turned off the flashlight. "I—think I'd better go."

"Couldn't you at least have one drink so I could show you the pose I had in mind? Please?" Ashleigh lifted a tumbler she had waiting, opened the freezer door, and dropped a few ice cubes into it. "I promise I won't keep you long." She broke the seal on the bottle of scotch, screwed the cap off, and held it poised over the ice. "Please?" Her smile was soft. Her eyes had that sparkle children get when they're excited and as she moved, the beads in her hair clinked against one another. She was much more relaxed here than she'd been in my house and I really didn't have any reason to rush home.

"Well, okay. Just one."

She poured the liquor, placed the glass on a small square napkin, and handed it to me. "Just make yourself comfortable and let me get set up."

"Thanks." I sipped the whiskey and couldn't help but smile as she scurried through the living room into the bedroom. There was a time when I, too, had wild dreams and unrealistic expectations.

Some of the furniture reminded me of my grandmother's and the rest had a Pier One look. I lifted a framed 5x7 photograph off a buffet behind the front door and studied it. It was a portrait of a teenaged Ashleigh with a woman, a man, and a boy—probably her family.

Over the couch hung a large portrait of her and a cat. It wasn't bad, but I would have done it differently. As I stepped closer to the portrait, a longhaired tan and black cat stood up on the couch and stretched. It had blended so well with the pillows I hadn't even noticed it, but when I reached out to stroke it, it vaulted to the floor. I didn't mind. Normally, I wouldn't have even offered. It looked back at me and I noticed it had one blue eye and one brown one. As far as cats go, this was a pretty one.

I drifted to the closed door Ashleigh had vanished through, leaned against the doorframe, and could hear her fiddling around behind it.

"Ashleigh?" I called.

"Not yet. Just a second."

I felt like a teenager playing some kind of childish game. It was delightful, even sensual. I chuckled and sipped the scotch.

"Okay," she called. "You can come in now."

6

I GRIPPED THE DOORKNOB, turned it slowly, and pushed the door open. Except for a pair of white stockings from mid-thigh down, Ashleigh was stark naked. She lay amid a mountain of pillows with her arms thrown back over her head and her legs cocked outward at the knees. Half a dozen lighted candles scented the room and provided the only light. The sight of her took my breath away. She looked like a movie star—Julia Roberts in person, naked.

My internal control system changed gears and my movements slowed.

She raised a Polaroid camera high and giggled. "Take my picture, Mr. Photographer."

I snickered. "You're not going to get much of a picture with that thing."

"I don't care. I just want to see what it looks like."

I sipped my drink, set it on the dresser, took the camera, and stepped back. My heart thumped hard in my chest as I framed her in the viewer. She puckered her lips and cut her eyes at me.

"Don't try to look sexy," I said. "Just relax." Her face softened and her eyes smiled. "Bring your chin down just a little. That's it." I rose on my toes and pressed the shutter release. The camera's tiny strobe blasted the room with light and a motor pushed the undeveloped photograph out the front and left it hanging there. She pushed the pillows aside and patted the bed next to her. "Now, take one for me. You don't have to be naked, just get up here with me."

"I don't think so," I said, pulling the self-developing photo from the camera and tossing it on the dresser.

"Please. The two of us." She rolled onto her side. "Just this once."

I could hardly hear the thunder for the blood rushing in my ears. "Why would you want a photo of me with you like that?" I placed the camera on the dresser and picked up my drink.

Bounding off the bed, she grabbed the camera and poked a finger into my chest. "What's the matter, Mr. Photographer? Don't like having your picture taken?"

I stumbled backward trying not to spill the drink. "Not like that, I don't."

"You're a famous director. This could be important to me." She poked me again.

I laughed and juggled the drink. "I'm not a famous director and even if I was—" She pushed again and I got annoyed. My voice sounded dark and evil inside my head. "Ashleigh, stop that! You're going to spill my drink."

She lowered her head and rolled out her bottom lip. In that light, with her eyes sparkling and her beads dangling and her breasts jiggling and my head spinning, she was bewitching; almost irresistible. "I'll tell you what. Put something on and we'll take one."

Throwing an arm around my neck, she kissed my cheek and at that instant, the camera went off with another blinding blast of light.

"Oh, no!" she groaned turning it over to check the number on the back. "Thank goodness. There's four more." Tossing the wasted picture on the dresser, she set the camera on the foot of the bed, slid into a robe, and left the front of it hanging open. "Better?"

I sighed letting my eyes travel down to her breasts. "Well..."

"Man, this is more than I wear to the mall."

Drums were beating a steady rhythm in my brain. I was getting weak. "All right."

I lifted the camera, downed the rest of my drink, and wrapped my left arm around her clasping the front of her robe together. With rain pelting the bedroom window, I turned the camera lens toward us, placed my thumb on the shutter, and stretched my right arm out as far as I could.

"Ready?"

Lightning flickered. "Ready."

Again the flash dazed me the instant it went off and Ashleigh shoved me backward onto the bed falling on top of me, tickling my ribs. Sliding up and down me, she teased me, daring me to touch her. With her beads slapping the side of my face, she brushed her lips lightly over mine and kissed me ever so gently. It was sweet and natural. Her fragrance filled my head and I felt as if I was suspended in some other place in some other time with a chorus of male voices holding the same note for what seemed like minutes.

Normally, the more selfish and demanding a woman is, the more distance I want between us. And she was way too young to be interested in me. At least, she should have been. Yet here she was—

naked, squirreling around on top of me, and holding my hands to her breasts. Something inside told me there was something *wrong*.

I tried to roll her off me, but she flattened against me and held me down. The music in my head changed to harsh noises. My strength was gone and my limbs tingled. I raised my head and whispered, "Please, Ashleigh."

"What's with you? Are you gay?"

I saw my father's eyes glaring at me and felt the same heaviness in my heart that I always feel explaining myself to him. I shook my head from side to side, but no words came. My skin felt cold and the bed began to turn. My heart hammered against the walls of my chest and sweat ran down my neck. I threw my head back and gulped air.

"Are you okay?" she asked.

"I think...I need...to go." I tried to move, but fell back against the bed.

"Do you want another drink?"

The bed spun faster and my eyes rolled back into my head. I tried to raise my hand, but my arm wouldn't co-operate. *Damn. How much have I had to drink?*

"Ashleigh," I whispered. "Can you...help me up?"

Straddling me on her hands and knees, she lifted my left eyelid and studied my pupil. "Don't worry, Richard Baimbridge. You'll be just fine." She licked my cheek and that's the last thing I remember until I awoke with a splitting headache around 3:30 a.m. laying on the deck outside my back door in a cold rain.

7

B UMBLING TO MY FEET, I stumbled into the house, groped the medicine cabinet for ibuprofen, swallowed three capsules, and downed a full glass of water. Weaving my way to the den, I flopped onto the couch and passed out again. My sleep interfused with images of Ashleigh. Ashleigh straddling me laughing and flirting, her beads pressing against my neck. Ashleigh in white thigh-high stockings with snakes crawling all over her naked body. Ashleigh's lips against mine. Ashleigh biting a hole in my cheek.

At 6:30 a.m., I awoke trembling. My clothes were still wet and every inch of my body ached. The last thing I could remember was passing out on Ashleigh's bed. *God, what must she think of me?*

I tripped up the stairs, toppled into the shower, and stripped away my clothes. There were scratches on the back of my right hand. I wondered how I'd gotten them, how I'd gotten home, and if I'd made a fool of myself doing it. I turned the water on and lay under it for twenty minutes waiting for it to wash away the cobwebs and strange images, then cranked it up as hot as I could stand it and cleaned up.

Dressing for work, I noticed the deep gash stretching along my left jaw from ear to chin. Upon closer examination I found a second, smaller cut above my right eye. I poured antiseptic into the cuts and shaved. Descending the stairs, I found the note reminding me to stop by Mom's on the way to work.

MY PARENTS' TWO-STORY ROW HOUSE had been gloomy and forsaken back when I grew up in it and it appeared no differently now. The back door was unlocked and Dad sat at the dinette table reading *The Morning Star* in a faded plaid housecoat. His thin gray hair was combed straight back and lay flat against his head. His eyebrows were thick and grew together in a single line that made him appear to be in a constant state of disapproval.

He and I had never seen eye to eye on anything. Nothing. Not ever. I gave up trying to win his affirmation a long time ago. I just tried to stay out of his way and not give him any excuse to come down on me. Mom set out a fresh cup of coffee for me as I came in.

"Thanks, Mom." I kissed her cheek.

She took my jaw in her hand and twisted it to the side squinting those Bette Davis eyes at me. "What happened to your face?"

"Scratched it in the bushes last night," I sighed throwing a leg over a chair and sitting across from Dad.

"Where you been?" he grumbled without even looking around the newspaper. "I thought you were coming early this morning."

Mom flashed me her "Don't Say Anything" look and pursed her lips. I reached for the sugar. "I said I'd come by on my way to work. I'm on my way to work."

He popped the paper to straighten it. "I just don't understand how come a boy who ain't even got a job is always running late."

Mom sighed. "Now don't go starting in on Richie, Gus. He came by to help you with that bed. Now let him be."

"Why is that, boy?" he asked.

I lifted a spoon and stirred my coffee. "I'm self-employed, Dad."

He rattled his paper again. "That's why you ain't got no wife. A woman wants to see a paycheck every week. Somethin' she can count on."

"For Heaven's sake, Dad. Are you ever going to get over the fact that I work for myself?"

"You kids today don't know what work is. I was on that car lot at seven o'clock *every* morning. The early bird catches the worm, I tell you. Thomas Jefferson said that. People's known it for a long time."

I lifted the coffee cup. "I think it was Ben Franklin, Dad."

The paper jerked away and his open hand smacked the side of my face with a loud crack. My coffee cup bowled across the table spewing its hot contents over the table and me. "Always the smart-ass, ain't cha?" he glared.

As I came up out of my chair, Mom clutched her arms around me from behind. "Stop it!" she screamed. "Both of you!"

I snatched the towel from her shoulder and dabbed at the hot coffee burning through my pants. "Jesus! You want my help or not?"

Dad crushed the paper against the table. "Go on to work! I don't need your help."

I threw the cloth on the table, wrenched out of Mom's hold, and left the room. The head of Martha's convalescent bed was raised and her hands skimmed back and forth over the laptop sitting on a stand in front of her. She had a pencil tucked behind an ear and a pair of glasses perched on the end of her nose.

She sensed I was there, but didn't look up. "Hi."

I tried to hide my anger. "Morning, Babe."

Her fingers continued dancing over the keyboard. "Just need to get this thought down."

I crossed to the window and looked out. It was not much of a view. A tree. The street. The houses across the street. This had been the dining room when we grew up, but the only time I remembered dining in here was at Thanksgiving every other year. I moved to her side and sat on the edge of the bed facing away from her. "What are you working on?"

"It's a surprise." She finished with a flurry of keystrokes and lowered the screen. "It's a novel. Give me a few more days. Then I'll let you see it. I'm dying to get your thoughts on it." I flopped back and lay next to her staring at the fake chandelier hanging from the ceiling. "Gosh, what happened to your face?" she asked.

I shook my head. "I don't know. Scratched it."

She raised her body off the mattress and winced as she slid down to get more comfortable. "Mom said you had a date last night. Did she do that?"

"It wasn't a date. It was the woman next door asking if I could help her get her power back on."

"Is she married?"

I cut my eyes at her. "No, she isn't married, and she's way too young for me."

"How young?"

"Twenty...something."

"So? Girls like older men."

Dad slumped into the room, gripped the foot of the bed, grunted, and lifted it off the floor. "Let's get this done. Ain't nobody going to keep a man that shows up late for work."

I rolled off the bed and moved to the headboard. "I work for myself, Dad. I'm not going to fire myself."

He dropped the foot of the bed. "You want to do this or not?"

Martha groaned from the jarring.

"Hey! Take it easy, will you?"

Dad had short, thick legs, a barrel chest, and a day-old gray beard. He leaned his wide body over the foot of the bed and grabbed hold again. I must have taken after the men on Mom's side of the family. Tall and slender.

We raised the bed and shifted it around so Martha could face the front window.

"That's it. Right there," she announced. "Hey, would you look at that?" She aimed a finger at the window.

From behind her I had a clear view of the sidewalk and the houses across the street. "What?"

"That bird."

A red and black bird hopped along a branch to a nest under construction in the maple tree a few feet from the window.

"It's a Cardinal," she said.

"This where you want it?" Dad asked.

"Oh, yes. This is perfect."

"Anything else you need, Darling?" he asked.

"No. This is great, Daddy. Thanks."

He kissed her forehead, then cut his eyes at me as he left. I moved the roll-around cart with her lamp and laptop back within reach of the bed. She grabbed my arm. "Don't let Daddy get to you like that." Her voice dropped to a whisper. "He's going through a lot right now."

"Like what?"

"They told him he needs by-pass surgery."

I pulled my hand from under hers and circled the bed. "Well, that doesn't give him the right to—"

"He's not going to do it, Rich."

I lowered myself back onto the bed facing her. "Why not?"

"He's afraid."

"Him? Afraid of what?"

"Afraid he'll die on the table."

"Well, that still doesn't give him the right—"

"Would you stop thinking about yourself for a minute? He needs your support."

"Yeah, right. If he's stupid enough not to have the surgery, then he deserves what he gets."

She rose on her elbows and glared at me. "Richie! What's gotten into you today?"

I didn't like the tone in my voice or the disappointment in her eyes and I certainly didn't want to say or do anything that would drive a wedge between the two of us. "You're right. I'm sorry." I slid off the bed and headed for the door.

"Richie, wait. Please don't go yet." Her head dropped back against the pillows. I stopped at the door and looked back. She shifted her position on the bed and I could see that it was painful. I stepped back to her side. "You okay?"

She raised again off the mattress and grimaced as she repositioned herself. "It—just hurts a little."

"You want something for it?"

She closed her eyes and rocked her head slowly. Her voice dropped to a whisper. "No, not yet. I don't like to take it when I'm writing." She squeezed her eyes shut, pressed a hand to her side, and panted.

"You sure you're okay?"

"I've been having a lot of pain in my lower back lately. I hope it means I'll be getting some use of my legs back."

"God, wouldn't that be wonderful?"

She couldn't hide the pain in her voice. "If I don't have the pain to go along with it."

I patted her arm. Seeing her in pain was hard to tolerate sometimes and I had to leave. "I'll see you later."

She opened her eyes and forced a smile. "Forget her age. Take that girl out again. You need a wife."

Truth was, if I could find a wife like my sister, I'd marry her *today*—wheelchair and all.

At work, the projects were routine and uneventful—typical for a Monday, but I couldn't get Ashleigh out of my head. *Why doesn't she call?* I passed a mirror in the hall, stopped, and backed up. *What would a girl like that see in me?* There were dark splotches under my eyes. My skin felt tight and drawn. *My God, is that a patch of gray hair?* Where does the time go?

I wanted to call and apologize to her for last night and see if we could get her shooting scheduled, but I couldn't find a listing for her and decided if she didn't call, I'd knock on her door after I got home. By noon I was feeling much better. By late afternoon, more like my usual self.

When I arrived home that evening, the street was crowded with police cars and trucks. There were so many I couldn't even tell which house was involved. I eased through all the vehicles, pulled into my garage, and let the door close the world out behind me.

I'd just poured myself a scotch when the doorbell rang. As I approached the door, I could see three men crowding the porch. Sam Jones was one of them—the gumshoe that let my sister down. I unlocked the door and pulled it open. Sam looked up. He had dark brown skin, the beak-like nose of an Indian, and a patch of white flesh that covered his right eyelid. I'd always wanted to ask about it, but it never seemed the right time.

"How's Martha doing these days?" he asked.

"She seems to get a little better each day."

"I'm glad to hear that. Do you know a young lady by the name of Ashleigh Matthews?"

My heart dropped into my belly and I could feel the blood draining from my face. "She lives next door. Why? Has something happened?"

"May we come in?"

8

I LED SAM AND THE POLICEMEN into the kitchen as Sam introduced the two with him—a skinny white man named Melrose with the wide lip-less mouth of a lizard, and Crabby Staten, an older black man with gray sideburns and a thick scar across his nose. The heavy-set one, Staten, stood next to me with his arms folded like a nightclub bouncer. Lizard Lips set a black satchel on the breakfast table and stepped closer. Jones fished a small writing pad and mechanical pencil from his shirt pocket.

"What's going on, Sam?" I asked. "Something happen to Ashleigh?"

"When did you see her last?" he asked, flipping through the pages of the notepad.

I felt as if all three of them were watching me a little too intensely. The muscles in my neck knotted as I considered the reaction I'd get from my answer. "Last night." That struck a chord and all three of them shifted in unison—like dancers in a Broadway production. Jones widened his stance as he made a note on his pad. Staten adjusted his thick leather belt and Melrose raised his foot onto the bottom rung of the barstool next to me.

"Last night?" Jones asked, his words dripping with insinuation.

"She came over during the storm. Her power was off and she thought I might be able to get it back on...and wanted to talk about some photography she said she needed. Why? Has something happened to Ashleigh?"

Jones made another note. "Photography?"

I sighed. "Yes. She *is* okay, isn't she, Sam?"

Staten arched his back and his leather equipment belt squeaked. "You the same Baimbridge with the place downtown?" he asked.

"Sam? What's going on?"

Sam hung his head. "Just answer the questions."

"Yes. The photography studio on Market, down near the river."

Jones's eyes studied me. "What time was she here, Richard?"

The room suddenly felt warm and my palms became slick. "Oh...
seven-thirty or eight."

"How long did she stay?" Melrose asked in a thick Harkers' Island
accent—a cross between the local dialect and 17th-century English.
He kept flicking his tongue out the corner of his mouth like a kid at
the carnival waiting in line for cotton candy.

"She was here...half an hour?"

Detective Jones rubbed a finger over his white patch. "Do you
normally discuss business with customers in your home?"

"Well...no. Not *normally*."

"Did she seem *upset* in any way?" Staten asked, pressing his
thumbs into his back and stretching up on his toes. The questions
were coming faster now, as if they had a routine.

"Upset?" I thought back. She had seemed a little edgy. "No, not
especially. She seemed to be afraid of the storm...and her power was
off. Would you gentlemen like to sit down?"

Detective Jones continued without looking up from his pad. "Did
she say anything that might lead you to believe that someone was
threatening her?"

Threatening her? I dropped onto the barstool behind me. "What's
going on here, Sam?"

He still looked down as if he wasn't prepared to look me in the
eye. "Just answer the question, Richard."

"No, she didn't say anything about anybody *threatening* her or
anything like that. She was—" The street was swarming with police
cars. It was obvious something had happened. Something terrible. I
stopped to think about what I was saying.

"Was what, Richard?"

"She acted a little nervous and kept looking out the window. I just
thought she was afraid of the storm. Should I call a lawyer?"

"Do you need one?"

"I don't think so. I haven't done anything."

"And you said she left around eight-thirty?"

"Something like that."

From behind me Lizard Lips asked, "Did she go straight home
when she left?"

I drew a deep breath, "Yes, she did."

"How can you be so sure?" Staten asked.

"I went with her—to get her power back on."

Jones looked up. "You went to *her* house?"

"Well, of course. How else was I going to get her power back on?"

Lizard Lips' tongue rifled out and back in. "Around eight-thirty?"

"Yes! Eight-thirty or nine. Why can't you tell me what's
happened?"

Staten propped one fist on his hip and placed his other hand on the counter behind me to balance himself. "Maybe you could tell *us*."

"Me?" I felt the heat rise in my neck and cheeks. I swallowed. "There was nothing wrong when I left."

"And what time *did* you leave?" he asked.

"I wasn't there too long, but I'm not exactly sure what time I left. Probably nine-thirty or ten, but she was fine when I did."

Jones chewed the inside of his cheek. "So you were there about an hour and a half?"

"Oh no, I don't think I was there that long." I scrubbed my palms on my pants. "I told you, I'm not sure what time I left."

"So you got her power back on?" Lizard Lips asked.

I turned sideways to see him. "Yes. Just a circuit breaker tripped."

"And that took an hour and a half to reset?"

"No. She wanted me to stay. She fixed me a drink and we talked some more. And...she changed and showed me a pose she wanted to do for a movie production. I don't think I was there more than thirty or forty minutes."

Officer Staten sighed wearily. "How often did you see Miss Matthews?"

"Last night was the first time I've ever seen her. I didn't even know anybody lived in that little house back there. You can't really see it from here unless you look through the bushes."

Jones squinted and cocked his head. "Could you tell me how you happened to get that scratch on your face?"

The fingers on my right hand went to my cheek. "I—I don't know. I told you I had a lot to drink last night. I swear this has never happened before, but...I passed out over there."

Sam Jones looked up drawing his eyebrows into an owlish look. "Richard, I need to ask you if you mind if we take DNA samples?"

"DNA?" I wanted to rise, but the circle around me was too tight. Perspiration slid down my sides inside my clothes. "I didn't do anything but get the girl's lights back on, have a drink, and take a picture she asked me to take. That's all. Nothing else. If anything else happened over there, it happened after I left."

Jones put his pad away. "Then it'll clear you. You should be thankful. You mind?"

Squeezing between Sam and the Lizard-man, I walked to the back door and looked out toward Ashleigh's house. All of Hardesty's floodlights were on. Through the trees, it looked like they were having a party except for the yellow and black tape stretching from tree to tree around the pool house—and all the little red flags stuck in the ground. Two boats moved about on the lake behind her house with men in yellow waist-high wading boots holding lights out over the water probing with poles. A camera flash went off inside her house. It seemed more like a movie than reality.

"She seemed like a nice kid," I said. "I can't imagine anyone wanting to hurt her." I turned back to face the men. "Is she okay?"

Sam and I had been through a lot the past three years. It hadn't always been cordial, but he'd always been professional and understanding of our situation. He lowered his voice and spoke to me like a friend. "If you're innocent, Richard, you should have nothing to fear from DNA testing. You should do everything you can to eliminate yourself as a suspect."

"I'm a suspect?"

"Everyone's a suspect right now."

"Jesus, Sam. I don't even know what's happened."

Sam set his jaw and flared his nostrils. "If you refuse...and you have the right to do that...we'll just get a court order and come back." I watched the way the white patch on his eyelid grew larger as he blinked, then almost disappeared when his eye opened again. It gave the illusion that his eye rolled up in his head when he blinked instead of closing. He blinked several times while waiting for me to respond. "Are you refusing?"

"No, of course not. I'd just like to know what the hell happened, Sam. That's all. I think I have a right to know *something* about what I'm being accused of before I submit to any damned thing."

"Just relax, Richard. No one is accusing you of anything. This is routine. You were in her house for Christ's sake. This is for your benefit more than ours."

Moisture trickled down my neck. I felt dizzy. I lowered myself back onto the stool as the events of the previous night played through my mind. Words and images flashed by. Ashleigh standing in the rain fighting to steady the umbrella. Ashleigh naked on her bed. Ashleigh's lips against mine. I gasped. *Oh God, please don't let me be accused of rape.*

"Yes or no, Richard?" he insisted.

"I was there. I told you I was there. My DNA is bound to be there."

"Yes or no?"

I exhaled loudly. "Go ahead. Do it."

Lizard Lips yanked open his black case and pulled on white latex gloves.

"Where is Ashleigh now?" I asked.

Staten snickered, but nobody answered.

"What does that mean?" They watched me like referees looking for a violation—whistle at the ready—afraid if they blinked they'd miss something. As Lizard Lips snipped hairs off my head and placed them in a glass vial, it dawned on me. My knees buckled. "Oh God, no!" Sam Jones raised his thick eyebrows as I dropped back onto the stool. "Jesus Christ!" I whispered. "You don't mean—?"

I felt sick in my stomach. What must they be thinking?

"Was there anyone else in the Matthews house when you were there?" Sam asked.

"No."

Lizard man stepped in front of me holding a long cotton swab. "Open your mouth."

I did and as he wiped the swab along the inside of my cheeks, Sam continued. "Did you see anyone else coming and going from there?" I rocked my head to indicate I hadn't. "How long have you lived here?"

The room felt small. My mouth tasted cottony. I needed air. "About three years."

I pictured Ashleigh on the love seat. So young. So hopeful. So *alive.*

My stomach turned sour and the blood drained from my face. Sweat dropped off my chin. I rested an elbow on the counter and laid my head in my arm. My skin turned ice cold.

Detective Jones dragged a stool out and sat in front of me. "You don't look too good, Richard. Are you all right?"

I drew in a slow, cleansing breath. "I'm sorry. I just need a minute." Sweat beaded on the end of my nose and hung there.

Staten stepped away. "You mind if we have a look around, Mr. Baimbridge?"

I raised my head and wiped the perspiration off my nose. "You know, I've got nothing to hide here, and I've answered every question as best I could, but I think I need to consult with an attorney before I let you go any further."

Sam folded his pad shut and jammed it back into his breast pocket. "All right, Richard."

Lizard Lips gathered his samples together and they showed themselves out leaving me feeling like a flat tire. I saw that nosy Mrs. Winslow scrutinizing the situation from her back deck and wanted to close the blinds, but just didn't have the strength.

I tried to reach my attorney, Joe Forrester, at his home and on his cell phone, but got no answer. I turned the lights off, spent a moment at the window watching the police at work, then collapsed onto the couch. My body trembled and I couldn't stop it. *What in the hell could have happened at Ashleigh's last night after I passed out?*

I don't know for whom I grieved the most—Ashleigh or myself. My emotions catapulted back and forth between being *furious*—and being *terrified.*

9

T HE NEXT MORNING I was dressed and downtown by 7:30. Like my mood, the weather had turned cold and blustery—not the best for Azalea Festival Week. I pulled my collar up against my neck for the short walk to *Tripp's Ham and Eggs* still stunned by the events of the night before. Inside, I tracked to the same table with the same five other guys I join for breakfast most every morning.

Sappy Talton was doing his customarily splendid job of getting our waitress Sheila flustered and confused. Sappy and I had been best friends since eighth grade when we stole a pack of Lucky Strikes and a can of Miller's Beer from Smith's IGA, which started a summer of wildness that cemented our friendship forever.

A burst of laughter spread through the group as I took a seat. That's what I like about these guys. They're relaxed and fun to be around. No heavy burdens allowed.

Besides Sappy, there was Fred Gorman, a salt and pepper-haired fishing guide who'd lost two fingers off his left hand to a winch. Next to Fred sat Bob Bennett, an accountant with black horn-rimmed trifocals and buckteeth. George Reason, the bald-headed and goateed past-president of the Chamber of Commerce sat next to me. And my attorney, Joe Forrester, sat on the other side of George.

As I took my seat, Sappy reached across the table and slapped my arm. "Hey, that girl they think got murdered day before yesterday? Wasn't that over in your neck of the woods?"

I exhaled. "She lived next door."

Sheila slid a cup of coffee in front of me as she walked past without even slowing down.

"You have anything to do with that?" Sappy asked, his usual smart-alecky smirk plastered across his face.

"Actually," I tore open a packet of artificial sugar and dumped it in my coffee. "I might have been the last person to see her before it happened."

They all got quiet and turned their attention to me. Fred massaged the nubs of his missing fingers with the heel of his right hand. "You know her?" he asked.

I stirred my coffee. "She came to my house during that storm Sunday night. Her power had gone off and I went back to her place to help her get it back on."

Their faces could not hide their surprise. Joe shoved a copy of *The Morning Star* at me. "You seen the story in today's paper?"

"No, I haven't." Taking it, I saw that Ashleigh had made the front page.

"Which house did she live in, Rich?" Fred asked.

My eyes drifted over the story. *Single female...twenty-three years old...* "She lived behind Dr. Hardesty in his guest house." *Violent struggle... blood-spattered walls...sexual assault...*

Sappy wagged his finger. "I told you to get out and date more." A collective chuckle rose from the table. According to the paper, it appeared she'd been murdered although her body *has not been found. What?* I read the line again: *Her body has not been found.*

I read the entire article, then, as I folded the paper and handed it back to Joe, he asked, "Have the police talked with you about it yet?"

"Oh yeah. They came last night." I sipped the steaming coffee and could feel his eyes burning into me.

"What'd they say?"

My hand trembled slightly as I sat my cup down. "They mostly just asked a lot of questions. What time I went over there. What time I came back."

"That was it?"

"And they took hair and blood samples."

Joe's face deflated. "Why didn't you call me?"

"I did. I couldn't get you."

"Last night? Oh, we went to a movie."

"Besides, I have no idea what happened over there. They just wanted to know if I knew her, when I saw her last, what time that was. I had nothing to hide. I hadn't done anything. Then, when I realized how serious it really was, I tried to get you, but there was no answer."

"Damn Rich!" He lowered his voice, but his eyes were intense. "They don't take DNA unless they consider you a suspect."

A shiver snaked through me—a familiar feeling I've grown accustomed to when talking to my father, and my response probably sounded overly *defensive.* "I probably am a suspect. At the top of their list, but I still didn't do it."

Bob tilted his head back and eyeballed me through the lower part of his lenses. I set my coffee down and gave them the abbreviated version of the story. When Joe grasped his head in his hands, my chest tightened. "I was trying to help her. What would you guys have done?"

"What did she look like?" Sappy asked.

Sheila returned carrying an armful of plates and began dealing them around the table. "She was cute," I said. "You would've stayed the night."

"Damn right I would have. Let me see that picture again?" He reached across the table and took the paper from Joe.

George flipped a napkin across his lap. "So what happened at her house?"

"I just got her power back on and—left."

"No you didn't," Sappy pressed. "I can tell by the sound of your voice. Something happened. What?"

I ripped open a single-serving tub of butter, scooped it into my grits, and leaned forward. "Okay, you want the truth?" The five of them leaned closer. "After I got her lights back on..." They were frozen in place as if I'd hit the pause button on the VCR. I spoke softly, slowly, and distinctly. "...she went in her bedroom, lit a bunch of candles, stripped stark naked, and tried to get me in bed with her."

George's mouth dropped open as his left hand wiped across the top of his bald head.

"You wish," Sappy quipped breaking the yolk on a fried egg along with the tension. "I know you," he added. "You wouldn't have done it if she'd let you."

Ouch! The truth hurt. But, thank God I didn't do it. No telling what problems that could have caused. The conversation around the table drifted away from Ashleigh into a debate of why none of the North Carolina teams made the final four in college basketball this year. I sliced my eggs, stirred them into the grits, and wondered why they hadn't found a body. Joe remained quiet the rest of the meal and pulled me aside as we were leaving.

"This thing could turn out to be a serious problem for you, Rich," he said heaving an overcoat over his shoulders. "If I were you, I'd get an attorney right now."

"Can't you handle it?"

"You need someone that knows criminal law, Rich. That's not what I do."

The look in his eyes and the sound of his voice gave me the jitters. "You think it's that serious, huh?"

"How'd you get the scratch on your face?"

"Swear to God, I don't know."

"Swear to God, I'd get an attorney." He slapped my arm as he walked away.

I trailed after him. "But I didn't *do* anything."

"You need a good attorney *more* if you didn't do it than if you did."

"Okay. Then who?"

"Let me check into it. In the meantime, don't talk to anyone else about this. Not a peep! Do you understand?"

"Yes."

"Good. If the cops want anything else from you, make them get a search warrant. I'll call you later."

10

A LL I COULD THINK ABOUT for the rest of the morning was Joe's admonitions and how he'd acted. My creativity was gone and I couldn't concentrate. I made it through my first appointment on pure instinct. My eleven o'clock was an on-site conference with the younger sister of a girl I dated back in high school. Pulling into the parking lot of the *Deagan Dance Center* a few minutes early, I parked next to a black Mazda van lettered with the school's logo. I'd driven by this place thousands of times, but had never paid much attention to it. The grounds were well-kept and framed with gigantic oak trees budding with new life and dripping with long strands of Spanish moss.

I entered a spacious lobby plastered with dance-related posters, informational signs, photographs, and three large TV monitors high on one wall each showing a different empty classroom. Long wooden benches lined three sides of the lobby, and there was a receptionist center on the fourth with shelves of trophies behind it that covered the walls all the way to the ceiling. There was no one around. Just the steady rhythmic beat of music deep within the building, the melody constricted by the walls.

"Sydney?" I called.

"Just a minute. Be right there," a voice replied. Out of the corner of my eye, I glimpsed a figure cross one of the monitors and disappear from view before I had the chance to get a good look. An instant later she entered the adjoining room and for a second I would have sworn I was looking at her older sister Jewell. Though a few years younger, Sydney had always flirted with me whenever I'd showed up at their house. There was a definite resemblance, but as she drew near I could see that Sydney had grown into a far more beautiful woman. She had the same auburn hair and large blue eyes as Jewell, but somehow it had all come together better. It could have been the sparkle in her eyes, the way her personality livened her face, or just the fact that I was seeing a familiar face I hadn't seen in a long time, but the sight of her set my heart to dancing. She was taller than Jewell and seemed to float across the floor as she moved toward me with that fluid motion that only dancers have. Her hair was back in a ponytail and hung down the back of a dark green dress that laid softly over her slender figure.

"Sorry, I didn't hear you come in," she said coming toward me. "I was taping a floor." Her voice was rich and deep, like a tenor sax crooning the blues; luscious and *unique*. A spark flashed across her eyes as she extended her right hand. "Richard Baimbridge, it's *so* good to see you again. Thanks for coming."

She'd called and asked if I'd photograph her students. It wasn't the kind of photography I normally do, but I agreed to come and take a look. Seeing her now brought back memories I hadn't thought of in years. "Wow! Look at you." I held her at arm's length. "Sydney Deagan all grown up."

Her face was soft and warm. Her smile genuine. And there was a hint of pride in her voice. "On my own with responsibilities and everything—just like a real adult." Her laugh was the same squeaky laugh she'd had as a little girl. It gave me chills back then and it gave me chills that day. My thoughts were momentarily disoriented as I relived a few laughs from the old days. Finally, I spoke.

"You really look great, Sydney."

"So do you, Richard. I see you every once in a while around town. You haven't changed much."

"Well, you certainly have. The last time I saw you, you were swinging on a rope in your mom's back yard."

"No, the last time you saw me I was dancing in a recital. You were there with Jewell and later that night she broke up with you."

A pain shot through the back of my head. Jewell and I weren't actually going steady, but it still hurt to be told that they'd rather date someone else. "Yes, I think you're right. That was the last time I remember seeing either of you."

"She came home and told everyone about it and I stayed awake all night crying. I think I had a bigger crush on you than she did."

"You probably did." I felt strangely weak and off-balance. My pulse was running wild. I needed to sit. I drew a deep breath and looked around. "So, what's it been? Fourteen years?"

"Yes. Hard to believe, isn't it? I heard about Martha's accident. How's she doing?"

"She's...coping well. You know Martha. Nothing's going to hold her down for long." We gazed at each other evaluating each other's faces for a moment. She had definitely inherited all the beauty in her family. "So, why don't we take a look at the photography you've been getting and let me see if I can do any better?"

We stepped into her office where hundreds of photographs were stacked on her desk. I'd spent enough time in New York to know the difference between a beautiful, powerful image and one that lacked good lighting, lines, and composition. A few of them were artistic, even stunning. The majority, though, were atrocious and amateurish. I knew I could do better than that.

I asked her to show me where she wanted me to set up and followed her to a room with a door marked STUDIO B. It was forty-by-fifty foot with a rack of stereo equipment in a far corner, a mirrored wall along the right side, and ballet barres around the other three walls.

"It needs to be a really large background," she said.

"No problem."

"Like thirty feet wide."

"Fine."

She didn't look convinced, but accepted my word. "Good. Can we put it over there?" I noticed she wasn't wearing any kind of wedding or engagement ring when she raised her hand to point.

"Sure. I can attach it to the ceiling, and—"

"The ceiling?" she interrupted. "How are you going to do that? It's a drop ceiling—acoustical."

"It'll hold it. I do it all the time. Even bigger."

"It was very expensive."

Her persistence amused me. "It'll be fine, Sydney. I promise." Our eyes locked and something passed between us. Soul to soul. Trust, maybe, but something powerful. When she called me on the phone, she'd told me about all the problems she'd had with other photographers. Backgrounds that were too small, eyes that were shut, feet cut off in the photos, poor lighting, under-exposed negatives, and bad attitudes. The last one had even failed to deliver all the photographs that had been ordered and paid for.

Then she told me how badly she needed good photography for her advertising, brochures, and website and how much she liked my work. She said she'd thought of calling me many times, but didn't think I'd do it so she never called. The more she talked, the more interested I became.

As she moved about explaining how she wanted things arranged, she was charismatic, energetic, and dynamic—her voice gentle one moment and flamboyant the next. She was just as self-confident and enchanting now as she'd been at the age of thirteen and there was no way I could turn her down.

After I told her I'd do it, I received a gracious thank you and a warm hug, and was on the way out when my eye caught sight of a face in a photograph on the wall. Stepping back, I took a second look. It was a ballet pose. Sixteen girls in the same black and silver costume. And right there in the front row was a girl that looked exactly like Ashleigh. Her hair was up in a tight bun and though she was much younger and less developed, I was certain it was Ashleigh.

Sydney's voice startled me as she stepped up behind me. "Are you critiquing another photographer's work?"

I pointed to the photograph. "Isn't that the Matthews girl? The one that's missing?"

"Ash? Missing?"

"It looks like her. The police think she might have been murdered."

Sydney gasped. "Ash? I haven't heard anything about that. What happened? When?"

"Monday morning her landlord found her house open and a lot of blood inside, but they haven't found her body."

Sydney's hands covered her mouth and her voice fell to a whisper. "The studio is closed this week. This is the first I've heard."

"She lived next door to me, but I hardly knew her." I touched the photo with my finger. "That's Ashleigh, isn't it?"

"Oh, yes. That's her. A good dancer, too. I thought she'd go all the way to Broadway."

Broadway? I'd walked it often, but on the wrong side of the street. I'd carried a camera when I should have carried a script and a playbill. I thought just getting to New York would take me close enough to the action to open doors to what I really wanted— Broadway theatre. But, it's a big place and there were so many doors. I exhaled. "Maybe she'll turn up alive."

"I hope so. She's a beautiful dancer."

She gave me another hug and we said goodbye.

Seeing Sydney had definitely revved up my spirits. My emotions were flipping around wildly, diving and climbing like a kite with a short tail on a windy beach. I wanted to do the photography for her, but was going to have to keep things on a professional level if I didn't want to end up crushed when it was over.

I stopped by Barnes & Noble and picked up a copy of *Peterson's Field Guide to Eastern Birds*, then spent the afternoon shooting a new line of audio mixing boards for Barleystone Corporation's catalogue and web site. As I worked, my mind retrieved many lost memories of Sydney that made me smile. Although I'd paid no attention to it at the time, I now realized just how much of a crush she'd had on me back then and wondered how she'd taken it when Jewell and I stopped dating.

I had one more session scheduled that afternoon—a portrait of an older couple—and the moment they stepped into the camera room, I realized there was something very different about these two.

Mr. and Mrs. Jacob Ballance appeared to be in their eighties. They were frail and weathered. Yet, there was something fresh and alive within them. They touched each other as if they were pieces of heirloom crystal and their voices were soft and sympathetic. Their eyes caressed one another with the tenderness of a first-time mother with her newborn child. It was dazzling.

During the session I asked Mrs. Ballance if she remembered the first time she'd laid eyes on her husband and as she spoke about it, her cheeks flushed and her eyes twinkled. It was mesmerizing. I took a picture and the flash froze their images for a brief instant. The joy in her eyes and the love in his hung suspended for a second and I knew the photographs would be remarkable.

I burned a lot of film on Mr. and Mrs. Balance during that session. They were delightful, fun, and uncommon. I felt I was in the presence of something extraordinary. *Something sacred.* Whatever was in their hearts that day touched mine. I wanted what they had. It was going to require some changes in me, but I was determined to find it.

At home that evening, I sat on the deck watching the police activity next door and thought of Sydney, how different she was from Jewell, and the way I felt when she'd looked at me.

I fixed a scotch and headed to the den to watch the news when I noticed something white beneath a cushion on the couch. Lifting the cushion, I discovered a pair of women's panties. They were ripped down the side with a spot of blood on the waistband.

As I held them up to examine them, the doorbell sounded. Turning my head, I saw several men peering through the etched glass of the front door. Stashing the panties in my back pocket, I crossed to the door.

It was Detective Jones and his posse.

11

W HEN I OPENED THE DOOR, Sam slapped a search warrant into my hand and walked in without invitation. As a photographer followed, a knot tightened in my gut. There are times when you draw the line and dare someone to cross it, and times when you open wide and take the drill. This was a root canal without Novocain. Staten went immediately to dusting the den for fingerprints. Lizard Lips headed for the kitchen and the photographer stuck out his hand to shake.

"I've always wanted to meet you, Mr. Baimbridge. Danny Butler." He carried a fairly inexpensive digital camera with a Metz strobe. I forced the warrant into the pocket with the panties and shook his hand. "I really hope to have my own studio some day," he said, "and do the kind of work you do."

"Don't wait too long to get started," I said, my voice flat. "Dreams have a way of slipping away."

"Yeah, I've been thinking about that." He looked uncomfortable as if waiting for my permission to start. I closed the door and left him standing there. He raised his camera to his eye, aimed it at something in the room, focused, and fired. The drilling began.

I couldn't stand around and watch while they picked through my life. I had nothing to hide. It just looked so insignificant in their hands. Like the piece of driftwood on the mantle over the fireplace that I'd picked up on the beach the one time Jewell and I made love. To them, it was just a stick. I rinsed a glass and poured a drink with the intention of stepping out on the deck.

"You don't have to say anything if you don't want to," Jones said sitting at the counter.

"Good. My attorney told me not to," I said replacing the cap on the bottle. "I don't know anything else anyway." I pulled the warrant out of my back pocket and flung it on the counter. As I did, the panties fell to the floor. I lifted my glass and turned.

"You dropped your handkerchief," Sam noted flipping through his notepad.

Looking down, I saw the panties lying on the floor. With heat flushing my face, I scooped them up and stuffed them back in my pocket. "Thanks."

"Could I see the shoes you were wearing Sunday night?" he asked nonchalantly.

"I...don't have them, Sam."

His eyes raised, then he set his elbows on the counter. "You don't have them?"

"I didn't have them on when I awoke out there on the deck."

"You think they're still at Ashleigh's?"

"I guess."

"You guess wrong. What did they look like?"

"Maybe they're outside. I haven't actually looked."

"What did they look like?"

"Brown leather Bass loafers with a tassel on top."

"Like the one's you're wearing?"

"Yes, only darker."

He made a note in his pad, opened the back door, flipped on the outside lights, and walked out. I followed with the scotch in hand. The night air was cold and damp. He produced a flashlight and began searching under the deck. I gazed out at the lake and wondered if this once tranquil backdrop had been changed forever. The police tape and the colored flags would soon be gone, but would I ever feel peace here again?

I moved to a wooden chair, sat, and sipped the whiskey. A strobe flashed inside my house. I laid my head back and closed my eyes. *How could those panties have gotten under that cushion?* As Sam moved about under the bushes, I replayed Ashleigh's route through my house from the kitchen to the love seat, to the window, and back to the love seat. *She never went near the couch.*

Sam came up the steps and paused. "Don't see them. Would you mind walking me through the events of the other night again?" He lumbered past me leaving a trail of mud and went back inside. Danny's flash went off again somewhere in the house. I drained the glass, rose, and followed Sam. Carrying the empty glass, I walked Sam through the re-staging of events while Lizard Lips picked through dirty glasses around the sink, put them in plastic bags, and labeled them.

"Do you mind telling me again what you did after you went to her house?" Sam asked.

Danny followed Staten around taking photographs of anything the officer pointed out. I exhaled slowly. "I told you my attorney said not to say anything else."

"I was thinking if you could just go over the same things you've already told us."

I squeezed my fingers against my eyes. "She...unlocked the door and we went inside. I had a flashlight with me and she pointed me toward the kitchen—"

"Could we see the flashlight, please?"

I sighed. "Sure." I drained the last drops from the glass as I went to the drawer by the back door. As I pulled it open, it dawned on me that it wouldn't be there. And it wasn't. I closed the drawer slowly. "It's still over at her house."

"Could you describe it?"

"It was one of those long black metal flashlights—the kind you guys carry. Held three or four batteries."

Sam made a note. "What happened after you went inside?"

As Staten feathered a brush along the edge of the back door, black prints appeared. I figured they were mine. I couldn't remember Ashleigh touching the door. "She showed me to the box where I found the main circuit breaker switched off. I reset it and everything came back on."

"You said before that the breaker was tripped."

"Yes, I know, but—actually—it had been switched off."

"How do you know?"

"When they trip, they only go half off and have a red marker. This breaker was off."

"What happened after that?"

"She...fixed me a drink and went to her room to—"

"Bedroom?"

"Yes. To get ready for a pose she wanted to show me."

"A pose?"

"For the photographs she needed to get an audition for that movie they're going to be making here."

"What movie is that?"

"I don't know—a Brad Pitt movie."

"And then you...?"

"Well...after that, I'm not sure. Like I said, I passed out. I didn't think I'd had that much to drink, but I must have."

"Where? In the kitchen?"

"I was...on her bed."

"On her bed?"

I could still feel her weight against me as she pushed me down and fell on top of me.

"Richard?"

I looked up. "Yes?"

"You were on her bed?"

The photographer looked over at me and waited to hear the answer. I lifted the bottle of scotch and poured a short drink. "Yes."

Lizard Lips worked his way to the den and began examining the items on the coffee table.

"And where was she?" Jones asked.

I took in a breath and expelled it. "She was lying on top of me."

"She was on top of you?"

A smile passed over the photographer's face. I chugged the scotch and swallowed. "Yes."

"Are you sure it wasn't the other way around?"

I turned to the sink and filled the glass with cold tap water. "She was on top of me." I drained the glass and filled it again.

"And that was around nine-thirty?"

"I guess."

"Did you notice anything unusual while you were there?"

"Unusual?" I sipped the water. "There was nothing normal about anything that night, Sam. Even her cat had one blue eye and one brown one. What did you do with the cat?"

"We haven't seen the cat."

"It was tan and black—longhaired."

Lizard Lips lifted a pillow on the couch and looked under it. The panties in my back pocket felt like a rock. As he lifted another pillow, I ripped a paper towel off the dispenser and wiped my face.

"Sam," Lizard Lips called.

My stomach tightened. Sam stepped into the den where the two of them gazed at something under a pillow. I finished the water in the glass and set the glass on the counter.

"Richard, would you step over here?" Jones asked.

I wiped my face again, dropped the towel, and crossed to the den. Right there under the pillow on the couch was the black metal flashlight I'd taken to Ashleigh's.

And on the material under it was a long red smear.

12

I STARED AT THAT FLASHLIGHT and the red smear feeling as if I was standing before my father once again being accused of something I didn't do. *Don't lie to me!* The skin on my back felt as if it was crawling around under my shirt.

"Is this your flashlight?" Sam asked.

"It...looks like it."

"What's it doing here?"

"I don't know. I didn't put it there."

"You think Ashleigh did?"

The photographer nudged in next to me focusing his camera on the flashlight. I stepped back. "I swear to you I have no idea how it got there." The strobe went off and the camera beeped.

"Could Ashleigh have done it?" Lizard Lips asked.

My mouth felt hot. "Of course she could have. I was passed out on the deck. Anybody could have done it."

The man's tongue danced back and forth across his lower lip. "But, did she?"

My stomach soared and I burped. "As far as I know there were only two of us and I was passed out in the rain." Another burst of light from the camera's flash further aggravated my anxiety.

"And why would she come in here and put your flashlight there?" Sam asked, his eyes piercing me. They were my father's eyes. Hard. Judgmental. *Don't lie to me!*

"You're the detective, Sam. You should be able to tell *me*. I'd love to know. In fact, I hope to God you can tell me *exactly* who put it there. *When* and *why*."

Sam used his pencil to lift the other cushion. "Bag it."

"Because, Sam, the thing that scares me the most is finding out that you *can't*. And if you can't do any better with this than you did with Martha's case, I'm screwed." I crossed back to the sink, leaned, and drank directly from the faucet. Sam pulled two Polaroid photographs from an envelope he'd brought in with him and shuffled them in his hands. I took another swig, turned the water off, and leaned back on the counter. I knew what was coming next.

"You recognize this photograph?" He dropped one of the photos on the counter in front of me.

I didn't need to look, but rotated it anyway. It was the one of Ashleigh in the robe with her head on my chest. "Yeah, we took it Sunday night."

"Looks like you're a little more than an acquaintance, Richard."

"Well, I wasn't." Tearing another paper towel free, I wiped my forehead. "Sunday night was the first time I ever laid eyes on her."

"You have sex with her?"

"No sir, I did not."

He dropped the other photograph on the counter. Without looking I knew it had to be the one I took of her on the bed. "Is that you in this photograph?" he asked.

What? I leaned to look at the photo and felt a dagger pierce my chest. It was the picture Ashleigh had taken accidentally—*or so I'd thought.* You could clearly see her kissing me on the cheek and the fact that she was nude. Sweat beaded on my face and I could hear the blood rushing through my ears. "Yes sir, it is." Lizard Lips ran a vacuum over the love seat, couch, and floor. Staten took his black fingerprint brush and the photographer up the stairs. Sam just stared. Finally I said, "It's not what it looks like, Sam."

He closed his eyes and squeezed the bridge of his nose. "It never is, Baimbridge. How do you explain it?"

"When she took this picture, I thought the camera had gone off by accident and didn't even know she'd gotten us in it."

"How do you explain the fact that she was *naked*, Richard? Kissing you *naked*. Appearing quite comfortable I might add. Kissing you in a very comfortable, very *naked* manner? You need to explain that, Richard."

I spun the photograph around for him to see. "Have you noticed how *uncomfortable* I look in this photograph?"

"Uncomfortable? It looks like heavenly bliss to me."

"Well, it wasn't."

"You said you hardly knew her. How do you explain the fact that she was *naked*?"

I wiped the towel across my face. "Sam, I am a photographer. The photographs she came to me about were necessary for her to audition for that Brad Pitt movie that's going to be made here. Nude photographs. After I got her power back on, she fixed me a drink, ran to her bedroom, closed the door, took her clothes off, lit a bunch of candles, and called for me to come in. Honest. I didn't know what she was up to. When I opened the door there she was." I could see he wasn't buying a single word of it and I was becoming more and more agitated. "She asked me if I liked that as one of the poses. I told her I did. Which was *true*, I did!" I waited for him to respond, but he just stared at me. "She had a Polaroid camera and asked me to take a photograph of the pose so she could see it. So I did. Did you find that one too? Where she's laying on the bed alone?"

"No, we didn't."

"And why did you let me think that she was *dead* last night? The paper says you haven't found her body. As far as you know, she could be out there somewhere right now praying for somebody to find her. To rescue her. You got anybody out looking for Ashleigh?"

"Tell me how you got that scratch on your face."

I stamped my finger on the photograph and shrieked, "Does it look like I'd have to force her if I'd wanted it?"

Sam grabbed my face and yanked it to the side. "Did she do this?"

I backed away and skulked off. "No she did not!"

"How'd you get it?"

"When I woke up yesterday morning it was there. And these on my arm." I unbuttoned my right sleeve and pulled it up.

Sam called Danny down from upstairs and scrawled in his notepad while photos were taken of my face and hands. "Sam, I know it sounds improbable, but I swear it's the truth. I blacked out around ten and when I came to, I was lying on my deck in the rain. I have no idea what happened after I passed out, how I got home, what time I got home, or how that flashlight got under that seat cushion." Sam said nothing, just dissected me with his eyes. The clock on the microwave read 6:10 p.m. I sighed, "How much longer is this going to take? I've got a rehearsal at seven."

Sam dropped onto a stool at the counter and flipped through his notes. "You can leave anytime you want."

I wished he'd told me that earlier. I would've taken off right then. As I reached for my keys, Staten came down the stairs toting a clear plastic bag containing something white. "Sam."

Sam met him at the foot of the stairs where they discussed the contents of the bag, then brought the bag to me. "Is this the shirt you had on Sunday night?"

There were several drops of blood on the sleeve, a couple more on the shoulder, and a large stain on the right-hand cuff.

"Yes. That's from the scratches on my face and arm."

There it was. That scorn in his eye that I feared most from my father. "Well I certainly hope—for your sake—it turns out to be *your* blood."

I flinched expecting his hand to bolt out and slap my face, then turned and walked out as bile rose in the back of my throat.

13

FTER DIRECTING A SUCCESSFUL run of Tennessee
Williams' *A Streetcar Named Desire* my first year back, and
Neil Simon's *California Suite* the second, I was asked by the
Board of Directors of the Thalian Association to direct
Stephen Patterson's brilliant new play, *Laying Down the Law,*
making its world premiere that fall in Wilmington. It was the break I
needed. It would open a great many doors for me and might even
change the way my father saw me.

Unlike most directors, I insisted on longer rehearsal periods and,
since the theatre's rehearsal halls were not available yet, used my
own studio. I pushed all the equipment in the 40x60 camera room
back against the walls, arranged a couple pieces of furniture in the
center of the room, and aimed a few lights down from overhead to
simulate a "stage."

As Sam and his team pawed through my house, I headed off to
our first rehearsal. From the moment the first actor arrived, I was in
my element—stroking egos, exploring characters, experimenting with
blocking. There were even moments when it took my mind
completely off the investigation, and—considering the events going
on in my life—I thought it went quite well. Just before 10 p.m., we
wrapped for the night.

Finding the police cars still at my house, I went to my parents'
house, let myself in, and looked into Martha's room. The head of her
bed was raised and her fingers typed madly into her laptop. Riveted
on her project, she looked like the sister I'd known growing up. She
lifted her hands, then typed a bit more before laying her head back
and looking my way. "Hi."

"I brought you something." Keeping the book I'd bought for her
hidden, I moved into the room and sat on the edge of the bed, then
handed it to her.

"Oh, wow! You didn't have to do that."

"I know, but I thought you'd like it."

"It's a book of birds. Thank you." She flipped through the pages.

Leaning over, I kissed the side of her forehead and whispered, "Let's go for a walk."

"What? Now?"

"Why not now?"

"It's after eleven and—I don't know—it's dark outside."

"This street looks better in the dark. Besides, when's the last time you were out at night?"

She changed the subject. "Uh-oh. Something must be wrong. What is it? That woman you had over the other night? Is that it?"

I placed my hands on her bed and jiggled it roughly. "Why does it have to mean something's wrong every time I come to see you?"

"At this time of the night?" Her sweet laughter lifted a load off me. "There must be something wrong."

I stepped around her bed, rolled the computer stand aside, and moved her wheelchair up next to her. "You're right. I need to talk. Are you coming?"

Minutes later, with her coat secured tightly around her, a blanket tucked around her legs, and a knit cap pulled over her head, we headed out the door. Though summer was just around the corner, the nights were still cool. I rolled her down the ramp and onto the sidewalk where I abruptly dashed off speeding down the block.

"Oh, my God!" she shrieked. "Stop!"

"Hush," I laughed. "You're going to have the whole neighborhood thinking somebody's getting murdered out here."

Martha's scream reverberated back from all directions and lent an eerie mood to the night. I turned left at the corner and charged past eighteenth-century front porches heading toward the river, but it didn't take long to wear me out. By the time I reached the end of the next block, I had slowed to a fast walk with the moon trailing along behind the pecan and oak trees that lined the street.

Smoke rising from chimneys hovered around the street lamps and permeated the cool night air with the ancient scent of burning oak. Martha flapped her arms in the air as we glided past a graveyard of seventeenth century weather-beaten statues, headstones, and moss-laden trees. "Hey, this is great! Hello-o-o night-time!"

"Shhh. Let's not wake the dead or attract too much attention."

"What happened to that adventurous spirit you had growing up, Richie?"

"I got old."

"You aren't old."

"My hair is starting to turn gray, my eyes are failing, and I don't attract women anymore."

"Tell me about your company the other night."

"Actually that's exactly what I wanted to talk to you about."

"Ooooo, this sounds serious."

"It is serious, but not in the way you're thinking."

"What's her name?"

"Her name's Ashleigh."

"She sounds young."

"She is. Or was."

"Was? Is it over already?"

"Yes, I think it's definitely over, but I wouldn't call it a date."

"Oh, I thought—"

"I know, but it wasn't."

"Then what was it?"

As we moved into a part of town I'd long ago forgotten and whose charm and beauty had somehow evaded the younger me, I told her everything about Ashleigh's visit. She listened without interrupting as I told her about passing out and waking up outside in the rain, the scratches on my face and arm, and the visits by the police.

"Is that the girl? My God, Richie. It sounds like you're a suspect."

"Oh, yes. I'm sure I am. They came back tonight with a search warrant."

She caught her breath. "A search warrant?"

"And they found the flashlight I took over to her house."

"So?"

"They found it under a cushion on my couch and I think it had blood on it."

"Oh, Richie!"

"And that's not all." I pushed her up to the railing at the edge of the river, stopped under a street lamp, and bent to catch my breath. The air smelled fishy. I pulled out the ripped, bloodied panties and unfolded them for her to see. "Just before they showed up tonight, I happened to find these."

Martha's eyes studied the panties, then rose and questioned mine. There were tears in their corners. "Where?"

"Under the same cushion where they found the flashlight."

"Did you and she..."

"No."

"And you don't know how they got there?"

"No, I don't."

She held her hand out. "Give them to me."

"What are you going to do with them?"

"You don't want them to be found in your possession do you?"

"But—"

"Just give them to me."

As she raised her shoulder and stuffed them into her coat pocket, I noticed her grimace. She lifted her coat collar higher around her neck and turned her gaze to the river. Lights were twinkling up and down the opposite shore and a few moved along the river itself. The U.S.S. North Carolina Battleship Memorial was brightly lit on the opposite shore to the right. "This reminds me of the night I was thrown out that window."

"Oh, I'm sorry. I didn't think—"

"No, it's okay. I relive it every night anyway in my dreams. *Every night. Same dream.*

She didn't have to tell it again. I'd heard it a thousand times...

"CROUCHING AT THE BACK CORNER of the warehouse, I left a message on Sam's phone, then brushed aside the dead leaves and spider webs and dragged myself back into the hot, musty darkness inside that warehouse where thick chemical vapors burned my eyes and collected in the back of my throat. There were thousands of holes in the walls and roof that looked like stars and reminded me of the planetarium in Chapel Hill where I spent a lot of my time when I first moved to Raleigh.

"Hearing nothing, I'd about decided to back out and wait for Sam when the shrill scream of a frightened little girl hit me like a glass Christmas tree ornament bursting against the floor.

"I froze. For the first time in my life I was truly terrified. I wanted to back out of that hole and run as fast and as far as I could, never to step foot near that building again, but my heart wouldn't cooperate. I couldn't leave thinking there could be a child in there about to be raped and murdered.

"With my heart pounding, I slithered through the tight opening onto the stony cement floor inside ripping the knees out of my panty hose, then heard another panic-stricken cry that cut through me like an ice needles and brought me to my feet.

Sick to my stomach and hyperventilating, I groped along the wall in the darkness toward a faint glow high at the other end of the building. Stumbling over coils of steel wire and broken cement blocks, I fumbled my way to the base of a metal staircase rising toward the light and froze. At the top of the stairs I could see an open door and a room lit with a faint bluish light, but having fallen down that fire escape at the age of four, my acrophobia paralyzed me. I can't get in an elevator or even look up at a tall building without breaking into a cold sweat. I knew there was no way I could climb those stairs.

"But the child screamed again and it rattled through me as if I'd grabbed hold of an exposed electric cord.

"'No! Please, mister. Please don't do that. NO! STOP! Pleeease.'"

"Her fear was so intense, I gagged and threw up at the foot of the stairs, my lunch thick, lumpy, and sour in my mouth. I gripped the railing to keep from falling, spit nibblets from the corners of my mouth, and gulped deep breaths to calm my nerves. With tears streaming down my face, I listened to the child's terrified screams until I heard a series of hard slaps and ripping cloth.

"Rising up, I locked my eyes on the door at the top of the stairs and—fighting panic—I took a step. Then another, dragging myself upward one step at a time, trembling and gagging, holding myself up to keep my knees from buckling until, at two-thirds up, I spotted a TV screen inside the door at the top of the stairs and stopped.

"Through tear-blurred vision, I saw the image of a grown man on top of a young girl one third his size, her chin jammed against his chest, her tiny hands clutched in fists at her shoulders. Then the picture froze and spooled forward at high speed and I realized I'd been listening to the replay of a video recording rather than the rape itself.

"Closing my eyes and holding my breath, I took a step backward. Then another. But on the third step down, the metal stairs shifted with a loud clang and swung away from the wall. As panic seized me, I dropped to my knees and grasped the steel tread waiting for the stairs to stop swinging.

"'That you, Jack?' a man called from the room above.

"Holding my breath, I eased down another step, but the staircase again clinked and swayed. A chair in the room above creaked and rolled across the floor.

"'Jack?' the man called loudly.

"Reaching for the wall, my fingers hunted for something to grasp and discovered a hollow. I swished my hand through a thick mesh of cobwebs and touched something in the back of it that moved, revealing a thin line of light. I pushed against it harder and a tall narrow window swung back and I saw the moon rising over the river.

"As heavy shoes crossed the room above me, I leaned into the opening and discovered a tiny platform attached to the outside of the building. Locking my eyes on the moon, I grasped the metal frame and dragged myself out onto that rotting perch careful not to look down.

"The breeze off the Cape Fear felt icy as I grasped the sides of that tiny shelf and rotated slowly on it pulling my legs out the window behind me.

"'Who's there?' the voice commanded.

"With gravity tugging at me pulling me over the side and the sound of feet clanging down the metal stairs, I eased the window shut behind me and, grasping hold of the hinges, pulled myself up onto my feet. But just as the man's shoes clopped past the window, a blazing light beamed up at me from the ground.

"'Hey. Pssssst!' a voice called up from below. Sam had made it after all, but his timing could not have been worse.

"'Martha? What are you doing up there?' he called out, illuminating me with his light.

"As I waved him away, the window banged open nearly knocking my off the platform and a fist clutched my ankle. I screamed and kicked, clutching at the building, smashing my foot through the glass, splitting my leg open as it connected with the man's chin, screaming for Sam to help me.

"Pulling his revolver, he fired a shot into the air and shouted. 'Police! Get away from the window!'

"But the bastard ripped my foot off the platform and shoved me. I fell backward somehow managing to catch hold of the deck, but the man leaned out, punched me in the face, and wrenched my hands away.

"As I dropped toward the ground below, I saw a brilliant flash of blue light with the letter "N" and the number "3" within it. It would be the last thing I recall before crashing through a pile of wooden crates and slamming against a stack of steel rails."

"IT WAS A NIGHT JUST LIKE THIS," Martha said wincing as she gazed out at the full moon and pulled her collar tighter around her neck.

"Are you all right?" I asked kneeling in front of her.

"No," she whispered squinching with pain. "I need you to take me home now. I need my medicine."

"Why didn't you say something earlier?" Gripping the chair, I turned her around and started back toward Mom's house.

"I try to get along without it as much as I can," she uttered, no longer able to conceal the pain in her voice.

I lengthened my stride, quickening the pace. The wind was against us now and bit into my skin. "You warm enough?"

She whispered so softly I barely heard it, "Just get me home as quick as you can."

Martha never complained about anything, even when she should have. I lowered my head against the chill, covered the next three blocks in little more than a minute, and turned left onto the dim, tree-lined road that led back to Mom's street. The next four blocks were uphill. I arched my back and pressed forward. My legs began to burn by the end of the first block and my arms shook by the time we'd reached the end of the second.

"Where are we?" she asked, her voice quivering.

"Halfway," I grunted.

Martha took short, rapid breaths to ease her pain and I tried to match her rhythm. As we moved under the street lamp at the end of the next block, she twisted further around in her chair and I saw a tear slip down her cheek.

"One more block to the top of the hill," I panted.

Pain suddenly gripped me in my right side and I doubled forward trying not to slow down. Martha bit down on the knuckles of her left hand as I twisted sideways to ease my cramp. My legs wobbled and my side burned as though a red-hot iron poker had been shoved into me, but I knew it could never match the pain my sister endured every day of her life.

I could no longer feel my arms and, as we neared the top of the hill, the chair collapsed against my chest. "Almost...there," I panted.

As we crested the incline, I reached deep inside my soul and pulled out the last steps. "Just...a little...more," I wheezed.

Turning the corner, I saw several car doors fling open across the street and three men jump out. "Richard Baimbridge?"

I couldn't stop and I couldn't answer. The men spread out.

"Baimbridge! Stop right there!"

I raised my head and looked around. The men crouched twenty feet away with guns drawn. I paused leaning against the chair, but Martha looked up at me, her eyes pleading as tears rolled down her cheeks. I leaned forward and pushed.

"Baimbridge, stop or I'll shoot!"

"Please..." I gasped falling to my knees. "Please...help..."

"On the ground. Hands above your head."

Two men jumped me pressing my face to the sidewalk as they cuffed my hands behind my back. Though my wrists were small, the cuffs pinched my skin. I raised my head and saw Sam coming toward me.

"Sam, please. Get Martha home fast. She's in pain."

He took one look at her, then raced her to the house leaving me lying on the sidewalk like a trophy—like a ten-point buck draped across the hood of a 4x4 pickup being paraded around town for everyone to see. A neighbor from down the street glared at me as his car inched past. More police arrived and milled around murmuring to each other. A TV crew showed up, cranked their microwave antenna above the trees, set bright lights on tripods, and began broadcasting live from the scene. More and more lawmen came and soon there were a dozen vehicles parked up and down the street, their colored strobe lights flittering through the neighborhood. It looked like the scene of a major disaster.

Sam returned a half hour later, stood over me, and read me the Miranda rights in front of the neighbors that had gathered to see what had happened. He was so close, I could smell fresh wax on his shoes. Minutes later, they jerked me up and, with every TV station within the city now there to capture the moment—most broadcasting *live*, they shoved me through the crowd to a waiting patrol car. As they jammed me into the back seat, I caught a glimpse of Dad standing far back in the crowd.

While it was a triumphant display of force and victory for the police and a public-relations disaster for me, it was the utmost *humiliation* for my father. As we drove off, I looked back to see him turn from the crowd and head back home. The thing that hurt the most was knowing that he presumed I was *guilty*.

14

AT POLICE HEADQUARTERS, they moved the cuffs around to the front and escorted me into a room with four metal chairs, a metal table, and what I was sure was a two-way mirror. Forty-five minutes later Sam Jones joined me tossing a thick manila envelope on the table. He had a strange look on his face as he set up a tape recorder on the table and started it recording. He then sat, identified the two of us for the tape, propped his elbows on the table rubbing his face with both hands.

"I'm going to help you, Richard," he said, his voice calm, quiet. "I'm going to do everything I can for you."

"I appreciate that, Sam. So why am I here?"

He smiled the smile of a man who had the answers to the test before he took it. "I know you did it. Ain't no sense denying it."

"What the hell are you talking about, Sam?"

He rubbed his eyes with his hands. "I'm going to do everything I can for you, Richard. Your sister would never forgive me if I didn't. But you've got to do something for me."

"Sam, if you're trying to get my attention, you've got it. Now tell me what's going on."

"It's over, Richard."

"What's over?"

"Admit it. You made a mistake. You had one too many drinks. Things got out of hand."

"Oh, stop it! I had nothing to do with what happened to Ashleigh. If this is some kind of game you guys play to freak people out when you get them in here, guess what? It's working. You're freaking me out."

"Ain't no game, Richard. Everything you do from here out can work for you or against you."

"I didn't do anything, Sam. Whatever happened in that house happened after I left."

"You did it, Richard."

"I did not!"

"I told you that I'm going to do everything I can for you, but you've got to do something for me."

"What? What do you want, Sam? A confession? You want to go home the hero tonight? Is that it? You want things to be easy? Detective work getting a little too hard for you, Sam?" He dropped his hands and looked at me with tired, red eyes and I saw *pity* in them. He was looking at me in the same way Mom looked at Winston—like he really cared for me and wished it wasn't true. And *that* freaked the hell out of me. "My God, Sam. What's happened?"

He sighed. "I know you did it."

"Are we talking about Ashleigh Matthews?"

"I know you did it and you know you did it."

"You know what, Sam? You're so full of shit, it's no wonder you never solved my sister's case."

"Where is it, Richard? What did you do with the body?"

"And to think I thought police work was all about science now days."

"I can't help you if you don't help me."

"And I can't tell you if I don't know, can I?"

"But you do know, don't you?" I didn't answer him. The conversation was going nowhere. "You're not as smart as you thought you were, are you?"

I sighed. "Did you bring me down here to see if you could badger me into a confession or am I under arrest?"

"You know that blood on your shirt cuff?" he said looking me in the eye.

"What about it? I told you how that got there. I showed you the scratches."

"It ain't *your* blood, Baimbridge. Not all of it."

My brain tried to grasp the meaning of what he'd just said and when it did grasp at least some part of it, there was a momentary shutdown of my entire electrical system followed by a surge that rocked me in my seat.

"What?"

He leaned across the table and lowered his voice almost to a whisper. "Don't do that. Don't act innocent with me. I can see right through it. You know damned well whose blood it is." My mouth went dry as he unfastened the manila envelope and withdrew a form. "You're A-positive, Baimbridge. The blood from Ashleigh's is O-negative. That large spot on the sleeve of your shirt is O-negative. Now you want to tell me what you did with her body?"

"Jesus Christ," I whispered. My voice had lost its strength. "I think I need a lawyer."

He exhaled and wiped his hand across his face. "Yeah, I think you do, too. You got one?"

I sighed. "Joe Forrester."

Sam ended the interview with a few words into the recorder, turned the machine off, pushed himself up, and swaggered out the door. I cloaked my cuffed hands over my face and tried to think. Whatever had happened in that house must have happened *with me there*. But even drunk, I can't believe I could have slept through something like that.

Jones opened the door and stood there. "Forrester isn't answering. We'll have to stop until he can be here." He stepped to the side and held the door back. "Come on. A Grand Jury hearing is set for tomorrow morning. If they return an indictment, bail will be set at that time."

My chest felt as if a flying brick had struck me dead center. They fingerprinted me, took a mug shot, and let me make a phone call to my secretary Lizzy at her home. I asked her to cancel my appointments for the next day and to see if she could get hold of Joe Forrester. My voice had a strange hollow sound to it.

"Is something wrong, Mr. Baimbridge?"

"Yes, something's very wrong. I've been arrested."

There was an extended pause. "Arrested? For what?"

I bowed my head. "It's a mistake, Lizzy. I want you to keep trying to get Joe if it takes you all night and let him know where I am."

"What am I supposed to tell people if they ask?"

A hot flash rose up my neck. I was sure it was all over town already anyway. "Just tell them it's a mistake." Again silence. "And Lizzy, if you don't hear from me tomorrow, you're going to have to start canceling more appointments."

The things I was saying sounded more like lines from a script than real life. I spoke in a hushed mechanical monotone. If I'd been playing this role on stage, I would've had more emotion. But this was no act.

"I'll take care of it," she said.

"Thanks."

They took me to a holding cell on the third floor. The eyes of the other prisoners watched as they walked me in. Blacks, whites, Latinos, old, and young. They watched with sad, hopeless eyes as they removed the handcuffs and locked me in my own cell.

I thought I knew what it would be like to be in jail. I'd seen it in the movies and on TV a thousand times. But what you don't get on the screen is the smell of it. Urine, alcohol, perspiration, blood, and puke.

And fear. Fear of the unknown, fear of injustice, fear of not being in control.

Footsteps echoed around the chambers and mixed into the reverberations of men shouting and complaining, iron doors slamming, and the jangle of keys.

Sitting on the edge of a steel cot, I hung my head as my mind raced back through Sunday night over and over. So many things didn't make sense; the circuit breaker that was turned off and that photo of her kissing me on the cheek—that couldn't have been an accident. And how the hell did *her blood* get on my shirt?

The reality of what was happening slowly began to sink in. I'd never felt so embarrassed and helpless in my life. My dad was going to disown me. I expected that, but this was going to break my mother's heart. It might even kill her. And who was going to take care of Martha now?

I collapsed to my knees and wept. The eyes that had watched me so intensely now turned away.

15

P EARL BAIMBRIDGE SAT on the edge of her daughter's bed as the Channel 3 News began: *"A local photographer was taken into custody for questioning earlier tonight in the case of missing twenty-three-year-old Ashleigh Matthews."*

Pearl clutched Martha's hand. "This is going to devastate your father."

"Teresa Hedge has more in this live report."

The picture changed to a female reporter standing in front of Ashleigh's house holding a microphone.

"Police arrested Wilmington photographer Richard Baimbridge earlier this evening on suspicion of murder in connection with the case of missing twenty-three-year-old Ashleigh Matthews."

Martha had taken a Percocet that left her groggy and thick-tongued. "Oh, Richie," she moaned as they played video of Richard being paraded through a crowd of reporters and pushed into the back of a police car. Tears streaked Pearl's cheeks and collected on her chin.

As the reporter continued, the picture changed to video of the police going in and out of Ashleigh's house. *"Matthews was reported missing Monday morning after her landlord found her door open and evidence of a violent struggle inside."* The picture panned from Ashleigh's dark pool house to the left as the reporter pointed to Richard's house next door. *"Thirty-two-year-old Baimbridge lives next door to the missing woman and is thought to have been romantically involved with her."*

Martha squeezed her mother's hand. "He didn't do it, Mama. I know he didn't."

"Sources close to the investigation say evidence linking Baimbridge to the victim was found in her home and a witness alleges to have seen the two of them enter her house around nine Sunday evening. A grand jury hearing has been scheduled for tomorrow morning and is expected to return an indictment formally charging Baimbridge with

second-degree murder. Baimbridge could stand trial as early as October. Tonight, some are wondering; Is this an isolated case or could Richard Baimbridge be Wilmington's serial killer?"

Pearl clasped a hand over her mouth but it could not contain the cry that escaped from deep within her.

"This is Teresa Hedge reporting live."

With a clinched fist against her lips, Pearl's sobs became wails. Martha switched the TV to Channel 6 and caught another story about the arrest—one that showed a close-up of Richard from a photograph taken the year before when he received an award for *Director of the Year* at Thalian Hall. As another version of the story unfolded, Pearl dropped back against the headboard and wept. Gus stumbled into the room clutching his chest, staggered back against the wall, then toppled face-first onto the hardwood floor.

"Daddy!"

Pearl hurled herself off the bed and, rolling her husband onto his back, dug into his pockets. Blood dripped from a split in his lip and his eyes darted about aimlessly.

"Mama! Mama!"

Pearl screamed, "Call 9-1-1, Baby. Now!"

As Martha lifted the phone and pressed the numbers, Gus began slapping an open hand against the floor. Not finding his bottle of pills, Pearl leapt over him and dug into more pockets. When the emergency operator answered, Martha tried to speak clearly, but the operator had to ask her to repeat twice. "What is the nature of the emergency again?"

Martha spoke as clearly as she could. "Har—attack!"

"Heart attack?"

"Yes."

"I'm sending help immediately. They're on the way, Ma'am."

"Than' you."

The operator spoke calmly, "Please stay on the line."

Pearl's fingers found the tiny bottle of nitroglycerin, ripped it from Gus's pant's pocket, and dumped the tiny white pills on the floor. She'd witnessed many of her husband's attacks over the last several years, but never one as bad as this. Grasping a single pill in her fingers, she lifted it to his mouth now clamped shut with pain.

"Open your mouth!" His lips parted, but his teeth were clinched. She shook him. "Gus, open your mouth!"

"Daddy?"

Gus's eyes were hammered shut and his skin had turned gray. Pearl grasped his jaw and tried to open it, but he knocked her hands away. She slapped his face. "Open your mouth!"

Martha dropped the phone, rolled off the side of the bed, and dragged herself across the floor. "Daddy, open your mou'h!"

Pearl saw the terror of knowing he was going to die in Gus's eyes, and realized her worst nightmare was becoming a reality. Her skin flushed. With perspiration pooling in the creases of her neck, she straddled him on her hands and knees and shook him. *"Don't you die on me, you—you—BASTARD!"*

She cupped his neck, hooked her thumb in his nose, and wrenched his head backward forcing his mouth open. As Martha fell on his shoulder, Pearl dropped the pill under his tongue.

"Don't die, Daddy. P'ease don't die."

The nitroglycerin dissolved quickly and as it entered Gus's bloodstream, his blocked arteries began to dilate, and the blood began flowing past the blockages. As his panic subsided, Gus relaxed, closed his eyes, and drew a deep breath as Pearl planted a row of kisses across his forehead. Then the three of them lay on the floor until the ambulance arrived and took him away.

16

A WEEK EARLIER, I HAD SECURITY, a good reputation, and a thriving business. Everything except a woman to share my life. Then one stopped by. A woman. Just for an hour. But that's all it took to destroy everything that had taken me a lifetime to build. One hour. One lousy hour. *When will I get it through my head that women and I don't mix?*

I'd had no sleep, still wore the clothes I'd been arrested in, and was growing more panicked by the minute. *What was taking so long? Why haven't I heard from Joe?* Finally, shortly before noon, he showed up and there was someone with him.

"Scott McGillikin, Rich Baimbridge," Joe said introducing us as a guard let them in. "Scott's a criminal attorney."

Scott extended his hand and, clearing his throat, waited for the guard to leave before speaking. "The Grand Jury just returned an indictment, Mr. Baimbridge. On what are they basing that?" he asked, his eyes cold, uncaring.

"I was in her house the night everything happened and they found a spot of her blood on my shirt."

"How'd that get there?" he asked.

"I have no idea."

"You have the victim's blood on your shirt and you don't know how it got there?"

"I wish I did. It would answer a hell of a lot of questions."

Taking a seat on the end of the cot, Scott sighed, propped his briefcase on his knees, and produced a tape recorder. "Suppose you start at the beginning and tell me everything." I lowered myself next to him and for the next thirty minutes gave him the complete story. Scott's eyes were dull and piercing—like Dad's—and he didn't seem to grasp the situation at all, asking questions that seemed completely off-base. He acted as if he presumed I was guilty.

When we finished, I asked, "So, what do we do now?"

He returned his tape recorder to the briefcase and withdrew a set of papers. "First, we get you out of here. Do you have two hundred thousand dollars?"

"Cash?"

"Or equity in something."

"I have some equity in my building downtown, but not much."

"I'll have to use it as collateral to post bail. Sign these papers."

I had no idea what I was signing, but signed and dated each one. He snapped the briefcase shut and rose. "You should be out in a couple of hours." After the guard closed and locked the door, the pounding in my chest returned and panic again swelled inside me. I dropped my head against the bars and closed my eyes.

By 3 p.m. I'd been released, given my belongings, and told they were keeping my car until they'd finished with it. I was tired, dirty, bewildered, and confused. I emerged from the building into another horde of frantic reporters that had obviously been tipped off by someone at the police station. Like children around the ice cream truck, they pushed and shoved seeking a headline and a sound byte for the evening news. Scott told me to keep my mouth shut and guided me through them to his Porsche Boxster.

Arriving at my house, he had to ease through yet another caravan of news trucks and reporters, some from as far away as Charlotte. Neighbors watched anxiously from their porches as if something important was about to happen.

"The best thing you can do is say nothing," Scott said.

"Can't I at least tell them I didn't do it?"

"You can say that if you want, but no more. You'll just end up giving the prosecution rope that he'll use to hang you."

When I got out, the mob pushed in around me, knocking me off balance and yelling questions. They tripped over each other and stumbled about while keeping their cameras trained on me. A microphone swung in on an overhead boom and struck me on the forehead hard enough to break the skin. I pressed a hand to my head and there was a burst of at least thirty camera flashes. It reminded me of feeding the fish in the fountain at the cemetery where mother used to take us as kids. She'd give us stale bread to throw at them while she changed the flowers on a nearby grave and sat on a stone bench crying. The fish, some as big as cats, all fought to get to the front, rolling over each other, pushing and shoving like a pack of starving animals all wanting their piece of the kill—their mouths stretched wide like camera lenses. As we threw the bread crumbs, the water erupted in a frenzy of pushing and shoving that even splashed us. The only difference here was that I was in the fountain with them, surrounded.

"Mr. Baimbridge, what did you do with the body?" one asked.

There was a momentary silence as they waited for my response. *Did I have any crumbs to throw?* "I had nothing whatsoever to do with Ashleigh Matthews' disappearance," I said, but before I could even finish the last word, they erupted into another volley of questions. "Quiet! Listen!" I shouted, waving my hands in the air as Scott drove away. *Say no more.* I started to turn away, but pictured how guilty that would look if I were watching. It was *my* ass on the line here, not Scott's. I pumped the air with my hands to quiet them. "I am cooperating fully with the police and trust that their investigation will prove my innocence. I extend my sympathy to Ashleigh's family and pray that she will be found alive." With that, I turned and waded through them to the house.

As I've grown older, I've noticed that there are rhythms to my life. Cycles. Patterns. Times when everything is going my way, as if I have an angel on my shoulder. And there are times when everything begins to unravel regardless of whether I caused it or not. These seem to come in ten-year cycles and I realized I was *due.*

It wasn't until I'd showered and dressed that I remembered my only transportation was a '89 Harley-Davidson Low Rider in the garage that hadn't been started in close to a year. I knew the battery would be dead, so I connected it to a charger. I then called Mom to let everyone there know I was okay, but didn't get an answer and decided to run by there later.

At six o'clock, I flipped back and forth between channels to see how the media was portraying me in the news. I was the lead story on every station and they all had photos of me, video of the arrest and my leaving the police station, and my statement at the house. I looked tired, worried, and *guilty.* I only hoped Mom, Dad, and Martha weren't seeing this. I poured my third scotch and was about to call Mom when I remembered I had a rehearsal at 7 p.m.

I showered and, just before 7 p.m., pulled the bike off the charger and cranked it. After a couple of growls, the machine thundered to life and I wondered why I had stopped riding it. My favorite rides had been out in the country where I could open it up and feel the exhilaration of speed, and along the beach road on warm summer nights.

That was another thing I was going to miss about Wilmington.

I snapped on my helmet and, with the cameras rolling, goosed it out of the garage, through the mob of reporters lining the street, and headed to the studio where I found no one but Sappy waiting.

His expression was somber. "I guess they all figured you wouldn't be here tonight."

I slumped on the seat. "Great."

"This thing's going to cost you the show, you know."

I exhaled. A nighthawk beeped high above the buildings of downtown Wilmington. I looked up to see it flitting in its distinctive rhythmic pattern as Sappy dragged his shoe across the asphalt. "You've been charged with murder, Rich, and the reporters already have you convicted as the serial killer. Don't you think the board will consider that something of a problem?" The lonely cry of the nighthawk faded slowly as it headed up the river. "I suspect they're on the phone with one another right now. You need to talk to them. Soon." He slapped the back of my helmet. "Let me know what happens."

"Yeah. Okay."

"You going to have rehearsal Sunday?"

"I'll be here. Don't know about the rest of the cast." I fired the bike up, the rumbling vibrations soothing me as he walked away. Sappy was right. I needed to talk to them—and soon.

I eased the Harley forward, gunned the throttle, and rode to my parents' house where Mom threw her arms around me and sobbed like a mother burying a child. Telling her it was all a mistake made no difference. Nothing was going to calm her fears. Then she told me about Dad.

Over her shoulder I could see him sitting in the den in his pajamas and robe with his arms stretched forward like that statue of Abraham Lincoln at the Lincoln Memorial. She cried as she told me about all the tests they'd put him through and what they'd said. I put my arms around her and held her.

"Come here, boy!" Dad's voice barked from the living room. Her eyes pleaded with me not to go to him. Seeing my mother like that was unnerving, but she knew I had to go to him.

I touched my forehead to hers, closed my eyes, and whispered, "I've got to go to him, Mom. You know he'll be a lot more upset if I don't."

"Come here, boy!"

She gripped my shirt at the shoulders and cried.

"I'll make it quick. I promise. And I'll walk out if he starts anything."

I kissed her cheek, pulled her hands off me, and stepped around her. Dad raised his chin and looked through the bottom of his trifocals as I sat on the arm of the padded couch opposite him.

"Sorry to hear about your heart, Dad."

His voice was strange—hoarse. "So what the hell was that all about last night?"

I looked at the marks on my wrists. "It's just a mistake, Dad."

"That don't tell me what it's about."

"Something happened to the woman that lives next door to me Sunday night and because I'd been over there earlier, they think I had something to do with it."

"Did you?" I let my eyes travel around the room I'd come to hate. His *courtroom* where I'd been tried and convicted too many times to count. A room I'd not set foot in for years.

I scrubbed the palms of my hands on my legs and sighed. "What the hell kind of question is that, Dad?"

"I want the *truth*."

"That is the *truth*, Dad. Plain and simple. Why can't you just believe me for once?"

"Once you tell that first lie, you can't ever be trusted again."

"What are you talking about, Dad? Are you talking about that car thing twenty years ago?"

"One lie's all it takes."

"I've told you a thousand times I didn't take that car. Ten thousand times. I even proved it to you. What the hell's it going to take to get you to believe me?"

"They had a witness."

"It wasn't me! I was taking a photograph on the other side of town. I had a witness. I couldn't have been there."

His face reddened and his eyes glared. "Oh, give it up, Richard! The woman identified you in a line-up, for heaven's sake!"

The hate in his voice sent a chill through me. There was no way I was ever going to change his mind and I certainly wasn't going to confess to something I didn't do. The only thing this was leading to is another heart attack. I lowered my voice and rose to my feet. "The woman made a mistake. That happens, you know. I've got to go."

"Aren't you going to ask me how I'm feeling?"

"I can see how you're feeling, Dad, and my being here is not good for you." I started out.

"All you care about is yourself." He chuckled deep in his throat as if he was bringing something up to spit out. "A selfish *liar!* No wonder you ain't got a wife."

I stopped at the door, slapped a hand against the frame, and turned back to face him. "You're right, Dad. It's taken me thirty-two years to figure it out, but the only way to keep you from ripping me apart inside is simply not to care. So I *don't* care anymore—*Daddy.* You don't care how I'm feeling and I don't care how you're feeling. A chip off the old block!"

"Well, I'll tell you how *I'm* feeling. I go to the door last night and look out and I see the police all up and down the street—like something big has happened—like there'd been a murder. So I step out and what do I see? *You* being handcuffed and hauled off in a police car and all the neighbors and all the TV people taking it all in. How do you think I feel? Huh? It's all over town, you know."

"That's not *my* fault! I had nothing to do with any of it!"

"Liar!"

I stepped toward him. "I am not lying! What you saw was just the police trying to look like they're doing something."

"Well, how do you think I'm going to feel when I have to go back to work and face everybody? You think anybody's going to want to buy a car from me now?"

"Well, how do you think it's going to affect me? I'm the one that was spread all over the ground with handcuffs on. I'm the one that they paraded in front of the TV cameras. I'm the one that spent the night in jail! How do you think *I* feel?"

His hand went to his chest. "I would hope you're just as ashamed as I am."

I should have stopped right there and left, but I couldn't. There were things that had been bottled up inside me my entire life and they were coming out.

"You know what hurts the most, Dad?" My eyes stung and my chin quivered. "The thing that hurts the most is having to come here and face you. It's bad enough to have to face the rest of the town, but coming here is *worse*. Just once in my life I'd like to have your support on something. Just once in my life I'd like to feel that you were behind me."

His hand reached into a pocket, withdrew a tiny bottle, and opened it. "So you think I should have been proud of you last night?" He shook out a pill and placed it under his tongue.

Tears clouded my vision. "And just once in my life I'd like to have a real conversation with you, Dad. Something intelligent. Something that isn't me trying to explain some shit that you can't understand. *Or won't!*"

He extended an arm and pointed a finger at me speaking through his teeth. "Watch your mouth, boy. I can still take you down."

I'd said none of what I wanted to say, too much of what I didn't want to say, and knew it wasn't going to get any better. "I'm sorry about your attack. I'm sorry you're too stupid to have the surgery and I'm sorry I'm your son! I've got to go."

"And I'm sorry you were ever born!"

His last words pierced me like a spear and kept ricocheting through my mind all the way home. *God, please let this shit blow over so I can get out of this damned town before I do kill somebody!*

As I entered my house, I felt a sharp crack of pain in the back of my skull. My legs dropped out from under me and everything went black.

17

WHEN I CAME TO, the pain in my head was so intense I couldn't open my eyes. I lay on my back on the cold stone floor and tried to focus, but my brain wasn't ready to function. The side of my face rested in a gooey puddle and my shirt collar was wet and sticky. As I lifted my head, nausea settled over me. Holding my breath and waiting for it to pass, I remembered going to rehearsal, talking with Dad, and finding the reporters all gone when I got home. *Had someone struck me as I came through the door?*

The house was dark except for the silvery moonlight coming in the windows. The room spun around me as if I'd pulled a cheap drunk. I sat up drawing deep breaths to clear my head. My hair, shirt, and jacket were wet. I pressed a hand against the back of my head and found a lump at the base of my skull. The room seemed to wheel up on its side. I braced myself to keep from tipping over and vomited between my knees.

I was shaking, dizzy, and weak. I couldn't see. I had lost a lot of blood and I needed help. I dragged myself across the floor to the telephone and fumbled around the end table for it. It wasn't in the cradle and looking for it exhausted me. Falling back against the floor, I gasped for air.

"What did you do with the money?" a voice boomed out of the darkness.

I railed up onto my elbows. "Who's there?"

"You heard me." The voice had a thick New Jersey accent. "What did you do with the fuckin' money?"

My arms gave way and I sank back to the floor panting. My mind edged toward unconsciousness and my voice dropped to a whisper. "What money are you talking about?"

"The money you took from the girl you killed, asshole."

The room swirled and faded to gray. My head rocked from side to side. I tried to think. "I haven't killed anyone."

"The police think you did."

My pulse faded and my breathing slowed. I exhaled slowly. "The police are wrong."

Suddenly, I was floating a foot above the floor. I grabbed his wrists to steady myself and fought against the heightened urge to vomit again. His face came close to mine. He had a thick mustache, heavy eyebrows, and smelled of mineral spirits and bourbon.

"Don't...screw...with...me...man!" he shrieked, the knuckles of his fist bearing down into my chest. "The bitch stole one hundred fifty thousand dollars from me and I'm willing to bet you stole it from her. It's a lot of money, Baimbridge, but I don't think you want to die for it."

The room swirled as I dangled from his grip. "I have...no idea...what you're—" Vomit erupted from my throat interrupting my reply. He released me and as I slammed back against the stone floor, light flashed through my head and I sank into a pool of darkness.

I AWOKE TO A CONCERT of chickadees, robins, and a bright morning sun in my eyes. I tried to rise, but fell back when pain fired around my head. Memories of the previous night flooded through my mind like a dream.

I felt the sticky floor, rose to a sitting position, and discovered the blood and puke on the floor, and the open wound on the back of my head. The house had been ransacked. The nightmare had been real. I stripped out of my clothes, used them to clean up the floor, and left them in a pile. I fixed a pot of strong coffee and drank about half of it sitting naked and bloody by the windows. Mrs. Winslow pretended not to notice as she shook the dust out of her mop, but kept stealing glances in my direction.

After a hot shower, I got dressed, tossed the clothes in the laundry, and mopped the floor. By 8:30 a.m., my eyesight had pulled back together.

Picking up the phone, I got a dial tone, called the office, and told Lizzy I wouldn't be in until later. I took the bike to the emergency room at New Hanover Hospital where they put eleven stitches in my head and charged me nine hundred dollars.

I stopped on the way to work to see Scott McGillikin. We hadn't gotten off to a very good start and I thought things might be better in his office. I was led right in and waited for an invitation to sit, which didn't come. He looked rough, like he'd been up all night. I told him about my visitor, the money, and the stitches. "How do I stop him from coming back?"

He leaned back, looked over his nose at me, and acted as if even an idiot should know the answer to that question. "Give him the money."

I stepped forward, planted my hands on his desk, and leaned well over it. "Let's you and me get something straight right now." He tried to intimidate me with his steely eyes, but I didn't let that deter me. I'd seen a pair just like them too many times. "I'm being harassed by the police, by the media, by some gangster that thinks I have his money, and by my own father who wishes I'd never been born. I sure as hell don't need it from my attorney. I did not harm Ashleigh Matthews in any way and did not know about the damned money until last night. I may be the first one you've ever had, but this man is innocent and if it's beyond your abilities to treat me that way, then I want someone else to represent me. Got it?"

His expression never changed. He raised his coffee and sipped. "What did this man look like?"

I dropped into the deep leather chair in front of his desk and propped my feet on the ottoman in front of it. "It was dark. All I know is he had a thick mustache and a northern accent."

"Did you report it to the police?"

"I didn't see where that would help." Scott didn't respond, just sipped his coffee. "But don't you think it sheds new light on the case?"

"New light?" he asked.

"Let me ask you something. How does this work? Do you build your case on things you look into on your own, or do you just use what the police share with you?" He sipped his coffee. "Do you think we could find out where Ashleigh worked? Who she worked with?" He drew his eyebrows down, but remained silent. "Look, I just want to know how it works. What to expect. I've never been charged with murder before."

"I ran a check on her social security number first thing this morning. Nobody's reported any income to it in a year."

"So, what do we do now?"

"What I do is plan the work and work the plan. What *you* do, Mr. Baimbridge, is stay out of trouble and let me do my job."

"What about my car? Do they keep it or is there a way I can get it back? I need it for work."

Scott fingered a Rolodex, dialed a number, and talked with someone that seemed to know him. After a short exchange, he hung up and told me how and where to pick it up. Finally, a positive feeling about Scott. Then he told me he needed five thousand dollars cash to continue on the case.

A few minutes later I picked up the Suburban. Planning to come back for the bike, I drove to the office to load up equipment. I was scheduled to shoot digital images for the Coastline Convention Center, but Lizzy said the agency handling the project had called and canceled. I called the agent and he was up-front and honest saying he couldn't take a chance on anything going wrong that could cost him his customer. I understood his position, but it hurt nonetheless.

I was still getting work out, but these were projects that had begun before Ashleigh disappeared, and when Lizzy called to tell clients their orders were ready, they weren't bothering to pick them up.

Being at the office was fruitless and demoralizing so I called Martha and asked if she was up to going out to Paddy's Hollow for lunch. It had been her favorite place before the accident. She said she'd be ready in thirty minutes.

I cashed a check for five grand and dropped it by Scott's. Thirty minutes later, while waiting for Martha, I stood at the door leading to the living room watching Dad sleep in a chair wondering what could have ever attracted my mother to him. He just didn't seem the right type for her.

Paddy's Hollow is in a revitalized section of the historic district known as the Cotton Exchange and has the look and feel of an authentic Irish pub. The hostess recognized Martha immediately and set us up at her favorite booth where she leaned forward and confided. "I don't miss my legs nearly as much as the places they used to take me."

Although she never meant for it to, the comment hurt. I'd give anything to be able to fix her. I'd even trade places with her if I could. "Anywhere you want to go, Babe, just tell me."

She smiled, "You're too good to me."

"I mean it."

Our server recognized Martha, slid in the booth next to her, and with lots of hugs, laughter, and tears, the two of them enjoyed a boisterous reunion. With her wheelchair stowed away and her legs hidden under the table, Martha looked like the same spontaneous, fun-loving, vibrant, outgoing person she was before the accident.

After the waitress took our drink orders and retreated, Martha reached across the table and touched my hand. "Thanks. This is great."

"I'm sorry we haven't done it sooner."

"Oh, stop it. You're too busy. Besides, you do enough for me."

"I'm certainly not busy with photography anymore."

She studied me for a moment. "You okay?"

"Oh, sure. I'm under suspicion of murder, friends I've known my whole life won't speak to me anymore, and Dad had an attack that Mom blames on me."

"No she doesn't."

"Somebody broke into my house, knocked me in the head, and I spent the night on the floor."

"What?"

"Oh, yeah! About the only good thing that happened to me this week was running into Sydney Deagan again after all these years."

"Somebody broke into your house and hit you in the head?"

"He wanted the hundred fifty thousand dollars back that Ashleigh had stolen from him."

"What?"

"I told him I didn't know anything about any money."

"Rich, there's something else going on here. Something big. And I think we're just seeing the tip of the iceberg."

Our drinks came and Martha ordered a shrimp Po-Boy. I ordered a corned beef on rye. She lifted her soda. "Did you call the police?"

"No. Do you think this changes anything?"

"Well..." She sipped from her frosted glass. "If she *did* steal that money, then there's somebody out there who definitely had a *motive* to kill her."

"*And* who now believes that I took it from her and so has a motive to kill *me*. Hell yes..." I lifted my beer. "...it definitely changes things."

Martha stared at the table thinking as she pushed her fingers through her hair. "What I don't understand is...what was all that about night before last?"

"They found Ashleigh's blood on the shirt I was wearing that night."

Her hand moved from her hair to her mouth and her voice quietened. "Are they sure?"

"Well, her *type* anyway. O-negative."

"But how could that be?" Martha asked.

"I was hoping you could figure it out." I took a sip and caught sight of two women across the room whispering with their eyes cocked toward me. I tilted the mug and guzzled the rest of my beer.

Martha leaned closer. "Ashleigh has a brother. His name is David."

"How did you find that out?"

"I...did a little investigating on my own."

"Martha!" My voice carried and heads turned toward us. Leaning forward, I lowered my voice. "Are you crazy? These people are dangerous. Just look at my head. I got eleven stitches in it this morning."

"What? You didn't tell me you had stitches."

"You can't see them?" I turned my head to the side.

She examined the back of my head. "Well, now that you mention it."

"Listen to me. If something happened to you, I'd never forgive myself and Dad would absolutely kill me." I exhaled sharply, then considered what she'd said. "So how'd you find out about the brother anyway?"

"I googled her name on-line and this story popped up about how her parents died."

"What did it say?"

"Just that there had been an explosion on their yacht, that her mother and father had been killed, and that her brother had been severely burned."

"When was that?"

"About six years ago."

"So how can the brother help?"

"He might know who could have killed her."

"Don't you think the police would have looked into that?"

"If they can find him."

The waitress brought our sandwiches and by the time she stopped gabbing with Martha, I was nearly finished. Martha lifted her sandwich. "Thank you, Richie. I really needed this. It's great!"

I smiled, winked, and took a sip of her soda to wash down the last of my sandwich. "Any information on where David is now?"

"He was at the Burn Center back then, but I doubt he'd still be there. We might need to find someone that has stayed in touch with them. Like his doctor."

"Ashleigh used to take dance. I saw a photograph of her the other day at Sydney Deagan's studio."

"Oh, yes. You mentioned seeing her again. How'd that go?"

"It was interesting and—in a way—strange."

"Well, at least it's someplace to start."

"Start what?"

"Start looking for Ashleigh."

"Oh. Yes."

Martha visited with more of the staff while I paid the tab then, on the way home, asked me to take a detour by the abandoned warehouse. I pulled up near it, stopped, and turned the engine off.

"It looks pretty much the same, Babe."

She sat for a long time without saying anything. Finally, she took a deep breath and wiped a tear from the corner of her eye. "It's like there's something in there drawing me back, something I missed. And lately, it seems to be calling me all the time."

"There's nothing in there, Babe. I've looked. Nothing but a bunch of old railroad cars and scrap steel."

"I know that if I could go back in there, I'd find something the police overlooked. None of those cases have ever been solved, you know."

"I know."

"A few weeks ago, when I was feeling pretty good, I rolled down here and just sat and watched the place."

"Martha! Don't you ever do that again. You hear me?"

"Don't tell me what I can and can't do."

The last thing I wanted to do was to make her feel she couldn't do things on her own. "What the hell do you think you're going to see down here?"

"I'm hoping to see that light in the window again."

"Those guys are long gone, Babe. Too much attention has been focused on it."

"Not anymore. No one ever mentions it anymore."

"Well, if you feel like you have to come here, let me know. I'll come with you. It's just not safe to be down here alone. Especially at night." I started the car and pulled away.

She sighed. "I wish they'd bulldoze the place so I could get it out of my head."

I knew how she felt. I'd been thinking about getting another look inside Ashleigh's house. I dropped her off and headed home.

18

A FTER DARK, I slipped into the laundry room and lifted a slat in the blind to get a look at Ashleigh's house. The place was dark. I visualized the inside and tried to recall anything she'd said that might be a clue, but nothing came to mind. I located another flashlight, slipped into a dark windbreaker, and stepped out into the night. It was cave black.

The darkness was alive with a thousand sounds. Endless rhythms and patterns of drumming, chirping, buzzing, rustling. Nature's symphony. The sounds of life. Sounds one would rarely hear locked away in prison.

I squeezed into the row of bushes at the back of the lot and emerged about thirty feet from Ashleigh's steps. There was a large seal on the door that hadn't been there Sunday night. Otherwise, it looked exactly the same; potted plants hanging along the edges of the porch and a pair of dirty tennis shoes sitting by the entrance.

I moved forward, lifted the police tape, and started to step under it when the backyard floodlights burst on around me. My heart leapt into my throat and I dove back into the bushes from where I saw Mrs. Hardesty at her kitchen window looking left and right. She disappeared briefly, then reappeared at the sliding door. The outside lights went off and she stepped out onto her back porch.

Holding her robe off the ground with one hand and carrying a flashlight in the other, she tiptoed across the yard to the pool house and under the police tape. Inching farther back into the shrubs, I watched her peel back the seal on the door and—with a key—enter the house.

Jumping the police tape, I crept around to the back of the house and, through a window, saw Mrs. Hardesty standing at the foot of Ashleigh's bed, her light slowly moving over the blood-splattered walls. It looked like someone had poured a bucket of red paint on the bed and tried to stir it with a chainsaw.

Suddenly her light shined directly into my eyes. I tore from the window, leaped the barrier tape, and smashed through the shrubs. The screen door banged behind me and I heard Mrs. Hardesty call "Who's there?" as I ran into Mrs. Winslow's backyard.

From behind a rotting shed, I watched Mrs. Hardesty search the bushes with the light. My neck pulsed with the beat of my heart as I watched her cross into my yard and aim her light at my back door.

"Mr. Baimbridge?" she called, her voice quivering.

She moved her light in a slow circle and shined it along the line of bushes separating our houses before heading back to Ashleigh's house.

I sat up and had just leaned back against Mrs. Winslow's shed when her back porch light blasted on in my face. Lurching forward, I dived into the shadows under her deck as her door opened and she stepped out ten feet from me. Lugging a weighted plastic bag, she crossed to a rubber garbage caddy, lifted the lid, and dropped the bag in. Edging to the back of the deck, she leaned and gazed through the trees toward the Hardesty's.

"What in blazes you s'pose that woman is doing in that girl's house?" she asked. Holding my breath, I cowered against the deck siding. "What was it you was seein' over there just now, Mr. Baimbridge?" Not sure I'd actually heard what I thought I'd heard, I lay perfectly still and didn't answer. "I know you's there," she said. "I seen you. I seen you when you snuck over to that girl's house, too."

I sighed and stood up. "You don't miss a thing, do you, Mrs. Winslow?"

She lifted the apron hanging from her waist and wiped her hands on it. "I gener'ly try to keep an eye on what's going on 'round here."

"I've noticed you do."

"Yes, I do. And I seen you jest now lookin' in the window of that girl's house, too."

I looked toward Ashleigh's. I could hardly see the house. "How'd you know it was me?"

"I just knew. That's all."

"Do you know who's in there right now?"

She leaned forward clutching the front of her robe and whispered, "'T'is that uppity Mrs. Hardesty."

I whispered, too. "And do you know what she's doing in there?"

"I 'spect she's looking to steal something."

"What else do you know about the goings on in that house?"

She straightened tall and cut her eyes down at me. "Oh, I knows more'n people think."

"Mrs. Winslow, did you see who went in there Sunday night?"

Hearing the screen door at Ashleigh's house squeak open and slam shut, Mrs. Winslow shuffled back inside and cut off the outside light.

"Wait!" I whispered squatting by the deck. In the darkness I heard the sound of Mrs. Winslow's door jingle shut and a security chain being hooked on it. I waited for Mrs. Hardesty to get back inside her house, then jumped onto the deck and tapped at Mrs. Winslow's door. When it cracked open, I noticed there were no lights on inside.

"Mrs. Winslow, did you see who went into that house Sunday night?"

"I seen you."

"Did you see anyone else go in there?"

"Didn't see nobody else."

"But somebody must have gone in after me."

"Didn't see nobody."

"Did you see me when I left there?"

"I seen you laying in the yard."

"Do you know how long I was there?"

"Least an hour."

"Did you see how I got there?"

"Only other thing I seen was the girl leaving."

"What girl?"

"The girl. Her."

"She left? What time was that?"

"While you was layin' outside. She just walked away carryin' some kind of bag."

"Walked?"

"Just walked off."

"Did you tell the police?"

"They didn't ask me that."

"What time did she come back?"

"Didn't."

"Where do you suppose she would have gone at that time of the night? On foot?" Mrs. Winslow shook her head, then closed the door. "Wait!" I whispered tapping on the door.

She didn't answer and despite my determined knocking, she didn't open the door again. I finally made my way around my house and entered through the front door. I was wet, cold, and trembling. It took another double scotch to settle me down. *Could Mrs. Winslow be mistaken? Could it have been another woman?*

19

FIRST THING THE NEXT MORNING, I called Scott and left a message on his voicemail telling him what Mrs. Winslow had said about Ashleigh walking off later that Sunday night. The way I figured it, that changed everything. All my appointments for Friday had been canceled and the phones were silent all day. I set up prices for Sydney's photo packages, ran off twelve hundred order forms, and dropped them off at the dance studio on my way home. The lobby was crammed with moms gabbing noisily and tending to babies while keeping an eye on the monitors.

Sydney was teaching, so I left the forms with the receptionist. I did, however, see Sydney on one of the monitors. She and her class were moving in complete unison like a school of fish darting here and there changing directions at the same instant, controlled by the same remote. She was dressed in a black leotard with a short sheer skirt and her hair was back in a ponytail. Even on that monitor I could see the joy on her face and the love and respect the students had for her.

The place was teeming with energy and reminded me of being backstage before a live theatrical production. It was intoxicating, but the conversations around me gradually lapsed and the moms began to whisper among themselves and I could feel their gazes. I took one last extended look at Sydney and left.

The news crews were back at my house and prodded me for remarks as I drove through them. I hadn't been inside long when I spotted Ashleigh's cat on my back deck. But when I opened the door, it ran off. Searching the pantry, I found a can of tuna, spread the contents on newspaper, and left it outside.

There was nothing new about Ashleigh on TV so I turned it off, fixed a drink, and sat in a chair staring at a photograph of me and Jewell taken at the beach and realized Sydney was right there in the photograph with us. Jewell and I had gone surf fishing for croakers and had allowed Sydney to come along to get her out of her mother's hair for the day. I'd looked at that photograph hundreds of times and had paid little attention to the skinny kid in the yellow bikini squeezing in between Jewell and me.

I don't remember what was said when that photo was taken, but from the looks on our faces, it must have been hilarious and I'm sure it came from Sydney. She always made us laugh. Even then, Sydney's personality outshined her sister's.

The doorbell interrupted my thoughts. I expected it to be just another reporter and considered not answering it. When I looked out, though, I saw a young boy about ten years old standing on the porch. Beside him sat a brown and white collie and out in the yard, a man waited for them. The reporters had gone. I turned the outside lights on and pulled the door open.

"Mister, you seen my bike?" the boy asked timidly.

I stepped out and pulled the door shut behind me. "Well, I don't know. What does your bike look like?"

"It was my dad's old bike. It's got fat tires and a bell on the handlebars."

I shook my head. "I don't remember seeing one like that recently."

He shrugged his shoulders. "Somebody must've stole it. My dad's pretty mad, too, 'cause he says it was a Columbia *Thunderbolts* and he spent a lot of money fixing it up."

"Sorry, I wish I could help."

"Okay," he sighed. He hung his head, descended the steps, joined his dad, and turned toward the next house with his dog trailing.

I started to go in when something occurred to me. "Excuse me," I called. The man and boy turned around. "I was just wondering how long the bike has been missing."

The three of them stepped back and the man extended his hand. "Hi. I'm Tom Frederick."

"Richard Baimbridge."

"My boy says it was gone Monday after he got home from school. Why?"

"Just wondering. Where exactly do you live?"

"We have the house with the brick driveway in the next block."

"Oh, yes. I know the house."

"The bike was a rusted old hand-me-down that became mine when I got old enough to ride." He kept a hand rubbing the boy's head. "I hate to lose it, if you know what I mean. You don't see bikes like that anymore."

"No, you don't. Sorry I couldn't help." As the man, his son, and the collie headed on down the street I lingered at the door and watched. That was a part of life I'd missed out on so far—being a dad.

Later that evening, I noticed the tuna fish was gone, set another can out, and sat awhile in the kitchen watching for the cat, but it didn't come back. It must have known I wasn't much of an animal person, but solitude had been taking a toll on me lately and I'd come to hate being alone. If I didn't like it then, I surely wouldn't like it later in life. I fixed another scotch and stepped out on the deck just as the moon was getting above the horizon. One thing I've noticed about the moon. It can be rising behind moss-draped cypress trees with a lake under it or ascending through skyscrapers in a city with smog dying it red. Either way, it's beautiful. And tonight it was as beautiful as ever, and huge. Why is it you can only watch a great movie once or twice, rarely more than that, but you can watch the moon come up night after night for a hundred years and it's always as picturesque as the first time you ever experienced it? Why is that?

A chilly breeze blew in off the lake hinting that summer was still six weeks away. I turned to head back inside when I thought I caught sight of Ashleigh's cat.

"Come here, girl," I called. "Kitty, Kitty, Kitty." I moved down the steps toward the line of shrubbery and heard a tapping coming from Ashleigh's. I moved closer. The house was dark, but the door was open and I could see a man inside with a flashlight standing on a table that had been moved to the center of the room. He was in his early twenties with short blond hair spiked to stand straight up and a large John-Boy mole on his right cheek. He wore straight-legged blue jeans, a Black Sabbath T-shirt, and latex gloves. He had his head up in a heater return vent in the ceiling and was shining his light in all directions, but must not have found what he was looking for. He stooped, closed the vent, jumped down, and moved the table back to its rightful place. He then came out, closed the door, reset the police seal, stripped the gloves off, and moved down the side of the drive toward the street. I followed at a distance and watched him get into a black late model Chevrolet Corvette parked a few doors down.

I wondered what this man was doing in Ashleigh's house and if he'd had anything to do with her disappearance.

Deciding to follow him, I sprinted back to my house, chose the bike over the car which had my business name displayed all over it, snapped the helmet on over my bandaged head, and pressed the starter. The engine chugged, but didn't start. I worked the gas throttle back and forth and tried it again. It coughed twice and backfired twice before coming to life. I clicked it into gear, pushed off, and spun away in search of the black Corvette. Four blocks later I eased up behind it at a stop sign.

20

I HADN'T HAD TIME to get a coat and the cold air was almost unbearable as I trailed the Corvette through town. The helmet's interior support straps dug into my stitches and tormented me with every bump. I took down the man's license plate number and was about to head back when he made a left turn toward Wrightsville Beach and I decided to stay with him a little longer.

He crossed the bridge to the barrier island and turned north where the air got much colder and tasted heavily of salt. The moon accompanied me, its reflection sparkling like diamonds off the ocean.

Many of the homes in Wrightsville Beach had been built in the first half of the twentieth century. One-story wooden white structures with colorful shutters and screened porches that sometimes wrapped completely around them. The vegetation was minimal and most driveways were sand, shell, or rock. In summer, there would be cars parked all around the cottages with surfboards on their roofs or leaning against the buildings, flags flapping in the wind, and men and women in flip-flops and sandals walking everywhere.

As we rode farther up the island, the houses got newer and larger. Finally, the Corvette slowed and turned into the drive of a well-lit elegant three-story residence sitting high on pilings overlooking the ocean.

Slowing, I turned up the driveway of an unoccupied weekend rental on the opposite side of the road, parked the bike under it, and lifted the helmet off.

Across the road, the car slid up under the beach house and extinguished its lights. John-Boy got out, leapt up the wide front staircase to the main floor, and disappeared inside.

Outdoor lighting burned brightly around the house and I doubted I'd be able to get very close until it was off. Leaving the bike, I hiked up the road, cut through a vacant lot to the beach, and drifted back toward the house.

An icy breeze blustered off the ocean and the flags up and down the shore popped and clinked on their metal poles. Waves crashed onto shore and pushed almost to the dunes before receding. With sea foam blowing past my feet, I stuffed my hands under my armpits and proceeded on toward the brightly-lit house. Sand, carried by the wind, stung my face and collected in my eyes. I lowered my head and ploughed forward. As I drew nearer, I spied two giggly young women on a patio behind the house wrapped in blankets passing a joint back and forth. I wondered who these people were and if Ashleigh had spent time there, and if she could be there now. *Alive.*

The house looked like something out of *Architectural Digest* with large windows, unusual portals, and ornate colored glass. There were porches on all three floors running the entire width of the house with stairs joining each level to a dock-like walk that connected the house to the beach—humped in the middle to rise over the dunes.

I dropped into the sea oats on a sand dune next door and waited for the lights to go out. Around 1:00 a.m., the girls disappeared inside and the outside lights went off. Soon after, lights inside began going out and eventually the last of the lights on the third floor went off.

I waited another twenty minutes before crawling over the dunes into the back yard. Immediately, the floodlights snapped back on and my heart did a double slam in my chest. I held my composure, acted a little tipsy, and continued on hoping the lights had been turned on by an automatic sensor and not by security personnel.

As I passed the side of the house, I ducked under a set of stairs, held my breath, and listened. The pounding of the surf made it impossible to hear if anyone was coming, so I pressed back into the shadows and waited. The raw wind off the ocean swirled around me and robbed me of heat. My body shivered, my teeth chattered, and sand stuck to my skin. Pulling my knees up, I wrapped my arms around them, jerked my shirt up over my nose, and breathed into it to capture the warmth.

At 2:00 a.m., the outside lights went off again. Ten minutes later I prowled from my hiding space and inched up the stairs to the first level.

The porch held a dozen white rockers set in ghostly motion by the steady ocean breeze. There were a few shrubs and ornamental trees in stone planters. Gazing over the top step, I could see little more than the moon reflecting back at me off the sliding glass doors. I squeezed in behind a recently manicured square bush and crawled up to the house under cover of a budding Ficus tree. The moon passed behind a cloud and darkness closed in.

I shielded my eyes against the salt-glazed glass and stared into a dark room. The moon reappeared and I could make out a giant-sized TV screen, walls lined with videocassettes, DVDs, and speaker grills, along with plush couches and chairs neatly arranged to face the screen. It was a private movie theater.

As the moonlight again faded, a sliding glass door rumbled open at the other end of the porch. Hidden behind the tree, I watched as a young woman stepped out onto the deck and gently closed the door behind her. She strode barefooted to the stairs and down a few steps where she pulled her thin robe tightly around her and sat less than a dozen feet from me facing the ocean. She lifted a cell phone from a pocket, flipped it open, turned it on, and pressed the lighted number pad. I could hear the various tones as she touched each one. It sounded like *Mary Had a Little Lamb* with a note too high at the end. She held the phone to her ear, covered her mouth with her hand, and waited. Finally, she whispered something I couldn't hear then raised her voice a little.

"Bobby, it's me, Angie." She turned her head and looked back at the dark house. The moon reappeared and lit the porch like a floodlight. I remained motionless watching her through the budding tree.

"No, I'm still here," she whispered, turning away and tucking her head down. "I don't know—tomorrow maybe. Something's happened to one of the girls. Everything has been crazy."

A light came on in the room behind me and Angie hopped down a couple of steps, bent lower, and twisted around surveying the activity inside with frightened eyes. I dared not move. I would now be a silhouette against the bright room to Angie and easily visible through the glass from the inside. *I was trapped.*

I could hear my heart pounding and resisted the instinctive urge to leap over Angie and flee for my life.

"I've got to go," Angie whispered. "I love you, too. I'll call you later." She turned the phone off, dropped it back into her robe pocket, and hunkered lower on the steps. Her reddish hair was pinned up behind her ears and her face was covered with freckles. She couldn't have been more than eighteen and looked closer to fifteen. She slid backward another step and clasped the neck of her robe closed. She suddenly gasped and flailed backward nearly losing her balance as her bright blue eyes discovered me.

21

S TANDING MOTIONLESS in front of the window, I held my breath and waited to see what Angie was going to do. Her eyes pleaded with mine and mine with hers. The two of us stayed fixed on each other until the lights in the room went off whereupon she bolted across the porch back toward the door from where she'd come.

"Wait," I whispered, spanning the deck behind her.

"Please don't tell," she pleaded as I got closer. "I'll do anything you want." She let her gown fall open and as the wind whipped it out like a sail, I saw that she wore nothing underneath. "Please?"

I stopped a few feet from her. "I don't work here. I'm just trying to find out what happened to a girl that's disappeared."

She pulled her robe closed clasping it at the neck and waist. "I—I don't know anything about the others. I just started last week."

"What do they do here?"

She looked inside her room then back to me and whispered, "Who are you looking for?"

"Ashleigh Matthews."

As the chilly wind pressed her thin robe against her naked body, she struggled to keep it closed. "I've never heard that name."

"What do you do here?" I asked again.

A sliding door rolled open one level above us and hard leather shoes scuffed the porch above our heads. The door closed with a bump and as the shoes crossed the deck and started down the stairs, Angie pulled me into her darkened room closing the door behind us. Through the misty glass I could make out the shape of a heavy man in his 50s or 60s as he continued down the stairs and disappeared.

"That's creepy Fat Albert. He walks around all night, but the girls say you can get anything you want from him if you do him favors. Don't let him see you."

I took her arm and swiveled her to face me. "Tell me the truth, Angie. What goes on here?"

She ripped her arm out of my grip and stepped back into the darkness. "How did you know my name?"

"I just heard you say it on the phone."

"Please. Leave now before you get me in trouble."

I whispered gently, "Listen to me. This girl could be in a lot worse trouble and I need to find her."

Her voice grew fainter, "I told you I've never heard of her."

I shuffled blindly toward her voice and spoke softly. "A blond man from here was in her house earlier tonight looking for something. When he left I followed him here. He drove a black Corvette and had a mole on his face. Who is he?"

I could hear her breathing through her mouth. "That's Greg. He works here, too."

"Doing what?"

"Whatever they want."

"On the phone you said things were crazy around here. What did you mean?"

Her breathing became more rapid. "Someone took some money and they're trying to find it. They questioned us and searched our bags."

I bumped against something with my left leg and moved more to the right. "When?" I asked.

Her breathing became more rapid. "Don't come any closer. I mean it."

I stopped moving. "When did the money disappear?"

"Sunday or Monday," she sounded panicked. "Now will you please go?"

"I will if you'll tell me what they do here, Angie." I could hear her breathing and lowered my voice to a whisper. "Please tell me what they do here."

Her voice was so low I almost missed her answer. "It's an adult website."

Moonlight suddenly illuminated the room and I could see Angie a few feet in front of me—a cornered animal clutching a lamp like a baseball bat, ready to strike. I took a step back. "Was Ashleigh Matthews involved in this?"

"I don't know. I've only met a few of the girls, but there's lots of tapes with different names on them."

"They might have called her Ash?" I added.

"Sometimes they use fake names here, but everyone has tapes in the screening room just down the hall."

I backed away. "Thank you, Angie. I'm sorry if I frightened you."

"Just don't tell them I helped you."

She was definitely afraid of something. "I won't. I promise." I cracked the door to the hall, but could see nothing more than the outline of the doorway to the screening room.

The stirrings of the house were masked by the distant rumbling of the surf, the snapping of the flags, and tinkling of their metal clamps. Easing through the door, I stole across the carpeting into the dim light of the screening room and scanned the wall of video cases, but there was too little light to read the hand-written labels. I tugged one off the shelf, opened the cassette, and read the label inside. *Lindsey 11.*

I replaced the cassette, moved farther along the wall, removed another, and read that one. *Madison 15. They're in alphabetical order.* I stepped to the beginning of the row and opened a case. It read *Ashleigh 1.* I removed the cassette and was about to return the empty holder to its place on the shelf when the glass sliding door behind me rolled open.

As the roar of the ocean filled the room, I ducked behind a padded chair fumbling the empty black case out onto the sand-colored carpet just as Fat Albert stepped into the room gliding the door shut behind him. Scrunching as low as possible behind the chair, I forced my lungs not to breathe. They revolted in spastic jolts and my arms and legs went numb.

As Fat Albert crossed the room, I crept backward around the chair. Passing right over the cassette, he continued into the next room and pulled open a refrigerator door spilling light into the room and over the cassette case lying between us. Withdrawing a carton of milk and leaving the door open wide, he stepped back toward me, opened an overhead cabinet, pilfered a glass, and filled it.

The black cassette case lay on the floor six feet in front of him. As he cocked his head back and drank, I thrust an arm out and snatched the case. He drained the glass, wiped his mouth with the back of his hand, poured another glassful, turned, and set the carton back in the refrigerator. When the door closed, the house returned to total darkness. I listened as he shuffled across the kitchen, then heard nothing but the muffled sound of the wind and surf. I didn't know if he'd left the kitchen or not. I slid the empty case back into its rightful place on the shelf, tucked the videotape into the back of my trousers, and covered it with my shirttail. With sweat dripping off my chin, I nudged the sliding glass door open and the sound of the surf again thundered in. Squeezing through the crack, I eased it shut behind me and vaulted down the stairs.

My damp clothes turned icy stiff as I scooted down the driveway toward the road.

A voice from the front porch called out. "You there!"

Although my body jumped, I pretended I hadn't heard it and continued down the drive acting a little drunk.

"Hey," the voice shouted. "This is private property! You come through here again and I'll have you arrested. Or worse!"

I staggered around to face the man on the porch and executed my best drunken-Englishman accent, "Truly sorry. Won't happen again." It was Fat Albert. I bowed clumsily and stumbled on down the drive, my knees so weak I feared they'd give out on the next step.

"I won't be so sociable next time," he called behind me.

"Right-o. Sorry, ol' Chap," I shouted back over my shoulder staggering forward. As I reached the edge of the highway, I heard a car engine crank, looked back, and saw a man running down the drive toward me. As the car's lights popped on and it squealed from under the house, my heart leapt into my throat. I bolted across the road and up the opposite drive, tossed the cassette in the saddlebag, hopped on the bike, and cranked it to life. The car picked up the man running, then sped across the highway and was right behind me as I spun out the backside of the property, crossed another sandy lot, and fled out a different road. I pushed the bike to speeds of over 70 M.P.H. with my helmet flapping off the side and the sedan swerving back and forth across the road just a few car lengths behind me.

Managing to get my helmet on, I cut through another sandy lot back to the beach road hoping for more cars, but summer was still officially two months away and traffic was light. I passed one slow moving vehicle, but the sedan also cruised by it and got even closer. As I neared the next car, it made an abrupt left turn causing me to skid on the sandy pavement and bounce off a blue and white 50s-era Chevy parked on the shoulder of the road. I smacked the pavement and got hung up under the bike as it made a 360-degree spin on the roadway and skidded into the deep sand of a beach access ramp.

Pain flared through my left leg as I wriggled out from under the bike and strained to lift it. The sedan slowed, its tires squalling, then swerved and headed straight for me.

Throwing my leg over the bike, I rammed the throttle and—with the back tire spinning in the loose sand—wobbled up the slippery wooden ramp and clunked onto the beach. As the bike hit the sand, it lurched forward just as the sedan came crashing into the sand behind me and stopped dead. I heard their engine racing and their tires spinning freely in the sand as I sped off down the beach.

22

B ACK AT THE HOUSE, I discovered the cassette had been crushed in the collision. Finding an unopened blank videocassette in the entertainment center, I transferred the tape from the smashed cassette to the new casing and, after a frustrating scuffle, managed to get the cassette closed and screwed back together.

Inserting it into the VCR, I pressed "play" and stood back. The tape squealed and the video fluttered as the machine dragged the crumpled magnetic ribbon over the tape heads. Through the static and distortion, the silhouette of a woman quivered on the screen. Wobbly music with a heavy beat began to play and the woman seemed at first confused and embarrassed, but then began dancing and posing for the camera in what appeared to be some sort of amateur audition.

I pressed "fast forward" and the jerky images scrolled by as the camera panned slightly to the right and zoomed in past the woman to a man hiding in the shadows. I stopped the tape and ran it forward slowly—a frame at a time—to see if I could get a better look at his face, but could not. When I resumed normal play, the sound and picture struggled as the camera pulled back to again show the girl prancing about teasing the camera. She wore a red sequined dress, long black gloves, and black high heels.

I couldn't see the face well enough to tell it was Ashleigh, but neither could I rule her out. In fast-forward, she danced around at high speed, discarded the dress, removed her black lace bra, and wiggled out of her panties. The camera again zoomed past her to the shadowy face of the man who stood motionless, watching from behind. Again I pressed the "pause" button and moved forward one frame at a time until a strobe burst on and I got a fairly clear image of his face. He had heavy eyebrows and a thick mustache and could have been the same man that slugged me in the head.

I pressed "play" again and the tape quivered and squealed once more. The strobe pulsed and in slow-motion freeze-frame, the young woman danced about nude as the camera slowly moved in on her face. Although the hair was longer and darker, it was a face I recognized. There was no doubt now. Ashleigh Matthews was connected to the house at the beach.

Suddenly the man swooped out of the shadows like a lion attacking its prey and in the frozen pulses of the strobe, I saw the petrified face of terror—the kind that can't be faked—as he savagely attacked her—beating and mauling her. It was appalling, disgusting, and repulsive. As she kicked and clawed and fought back screaming, crying, and pleading, I dropped to my knees and screamed with her. And when she fell mercifully unconscious from his brutal assault and the vicious rape began, I turned it off and wept.

THE NEXT MORNING, Saturday, I ached and throbbed from the back of my head to my ankles. I took three ibuprofen tablets, bandaged an open wound on my leg, and called my attorney, I told him about last night and the video, and he told me to take it to him.

As I pulled away from the house, I saw the Frederick boy on an old style bicycle heading up the street toward the house with the brick drive. I followed him and found Mr. Frederick pushing a wheelbarrow loaded with limbs and pine straw toward the street.

I lowered my window glass. "I saw your son riding down the street. Was that the missing bike?"

He plucked the gloves off his hands. "Yep. Turned up yesterday."

"Would you mind telling me where you found it?"

"Sure. You know where those big boats are docked on Oleander?"

"By that little bridge?"

"Exactly. Well, it was leaning against the side of an old shed down there. Someone spotted the classified ad I ran and called me. Mighty glad to get it back. It means a lot to me."

I thanked him and—on a hunch—went back to the house for the newspaper with Ashleigh's photo in it. After dropping the videotape off at Scott's office and filling him in on the house at the beach, I drove to that bridge on Oleander and turned down the dirt drive that led to the old shed.

The scene was like a picture on a jigsaw puzzle and probably hadn't changed much in the last half-century. There was a run-down bait house sitting next to the water's edge surrounded by abandoned crab pots and nets. At least fifty boats of various sizes from work skiffs to sleek schooners and banged-up trawlers were moored to dry-rotting docks built decades ago and now strewn with bits of netting, crab pots, and empty oil bottles.

I rolled into the dirt parking lot, cut the engine, and got out. The place smelled of gasoline and fish, and the greasy water along the shoreline had a coating of yellow pollen. The creek widened here and the banks were checkered with boathouses, docks, and marshes with patches of towering cattails and dying cypress trees. From the water's edge I could see a half-mile up and downstream.

I strolled to the bait house, pushed in the door, and stepped inside. It smelled of dead fish, insects, and smoke from an antique pot-bellied wood heater standing in the center. The single room shack was lined with cages of live crickets, two bubbling 20-gallon aquariums of minnows, and shelves with cardboard containers of worms and a few cans of pork 'n beans. An old rusty freezer marked "ICE" tilted where the floor sagged on the left side and a glass-top horizontal Pepsi box hummed behind the door. The place had never seen a broom.

A white-haired, leather-skinned old-timer sat on a cut-off tree stump mending fishing net and didn't look up. "Morning," he said, his coastal drawl making it sound more like 'marning.' "Somethin' I kin do for ya?"

"Good morning, sir." I pulled the newspaper from my back pocket and opened it. "I'm looking for a girl. Blond hair, early twenties. Was wondering if you've seen her around here recently."

He didn't say anything, just kept working a wooden tool attached to a heavy cord over and through the net repeatedly with the speed and accuracy of a mechanical weaver. I held the paper in front of him and continued, "I think she could be in a lot of danger. I'd like to find her."

He still didn't look up. "You her papa?"

"No. A friend."

Without a word, he continued with his work, his tongue sliding back and forth along his bottom lip. I pressed on. "I get the feeling you've seen her, but you don't know whether or not to tell me."

"Don't cha read them papers, Mister?"

"More this week than usual."

"Then ya ought-a know she's dead."

I watched his hands working in perfect harmony with each other making their way along a single cord like a machine. I sighed, "Everyone seems to think so."

"But you don't?"

A cold breeze whistled through a broken window in the shed. I zipped my jacket to my neck and backed up to the heater. "No, I don't. I think maybe she got herself into something she needed to get out of, concocted a plan to fake her own death, stole a bicycle, and ended up down here early Monday morning." He looked up at me on the word "bicycle," then back at his work without comment. "Where it goes from there," I said stepping back closer to the heater, "I was hoping you could help me fill in."

His tongue again worked back and forth along his bottom lip as if it was doing the thinking for him. "Why you int'rested in that girl?"

"The police think I'm the one who did it."

His eyes looked up and studied me while his hands kept going on their own. "Why they think that?"

"She planned it that way."

He tied off a knot and cut the cord with a small well-honed curved blade stationed on a weathered bench next to him. Then his hands walked along the net and started another repair. I dragged a log stump closer to the heater and sat down stuffing my hands into my jacket pockets. I waited quietly, but didn't have to wait long.

"She first come by Tuesday last week. Just hung 'round a spell...lookin' at the boats. Then, the next day, she come back and asked how much to rent one. Said she wanted to go 'xplorin.' Wanted to keep it fir a week, she said." His eyes stayed on his work. "Paid for it in cash and give me a extra two hundred."

"So, she got it Wednesday?"

"Well now, that's the *strange* part. I gassed it up and give her the key on Wednesday. Then she showed up T'ursday, and took it out most all day. Then brung it back, gassed it up again, and just left it. Ain't never come back."

The heat was too hot on my back. I stood up and moved around trying to get some of the warmth down into my legs. "Can I see that boat?"

"Well, that's another *strange* thing. Somebody stole it."

"When was that?" I asked.

"It were here Sunday when I left, and gone Monday morning when I come in at five. I figured she took it 'til I seen her picture in the paper and learnt what happened. That's when I called the law."

"What did it look like?"

"Just a old workboat. Had a 85 Merc'ry outboard on it. Run good. That's it in that yonder picture." He pointed his chin over his shoulder to a four by six color photograph thumbtacked to a wooden cabinet door. It was a picture of the old man standing in an open Boston Whaler holding a string of giant-sized trout. There was a cockpit in the center with a steering wheel and gauges, but no windshield.

"When was this taken?"

"Shoot. You don't find trout like that 'round here no more. Probably twelve or thirteen year ago."

"Where'd she say she went with it?" I asked.

"Didn't say."

"How long was she out on Thursday?"

"She come 'round 10 that morning. I seen her load a ice chest on it and then hightail it outta here like her hair's on fire. She didn't have no fear of it neither. Know'd what she was doing. Next I seen her was half past four."

"How far could she have gotten in that time?"

"Depends what way she went and what the wind was doin'."

"You got another one you can rent?"

"Well, ain't none here now. Folks got 'em all out. You want one in t'morning?"

"Yeah, I do. What time do you open?"

"Five every day. And I'm here 'til they all come back."

"Put me down for one. Richard Baimbridge. I'll be here when you open. Five o'clock."

"Baimbridge."

"Right."

"You got it."

23

I PICKED UP A FEW THINGS I'd need for the outing: a laminated nautical chart of the waterways from Wilmington to Little River, fresh batteries for a radio, a waterproof flashlight, cans of food with pull-open tops, bottles of Pepsi and water, and a couple of cans of tuna. By the time I got back to the house, my left leg was twice as large as normal and the skin felt like it was splitting open. I pulled myself up the stairs, cleaned the wounds, applied an antibiotic ointment, and wrapped the leg again.

I looked up the phone number for *Screen Gems'* Wilmington studio and dialed it. The operator reeled off a list of movies in production or about to commence, but said she didn't know of any Brad Pitt movie scheduled for Wilmington. I thanked her, hung up, unfolded the nautical chart, and laid it out on the dining room table. The Cape Fear River actually runs south from Wilmington and empties into the Atlantic Ocean some thirty or forty miles downstream. But Wilmington is only a few miles west of Wrightsville Beach, which is also on the ocean. It's as if Wilmington sits atop an ice cream cone-shaped peninsula; the Cape Fear on the left side and the Intracoastal Waterway on the right. These waters meet each other about twenty-five miles to the south.

Ashleigh rented the boat at Bradley Creek which flows due east and dumps into the Intracoastal Waterway right behind the barrier island that is home to Wrightsville Beach. From there you could take the waterway north or south, or go into Wrightsville Beach. I didn't think she would have gone to Wrightsville Beach unless she had someone meeting her, and if someone was going to meet her, why not meet them somewhere she wouldn't need a boat? Besides, to leave Wrightsville Beach by car, she would have come right back through Wilmington. My guess was that Ashleigh was on her own and headed either north or south.

The phone rang and I picked it up without taking my eyes off the chart or considering who it might be. "Richard Baimbridge."

"Richard, this is Sydney Deagan." There was that voice again—musical and unique. I sat back and the tension inside me mellowed.

"Hi."

"Martha called me and asked if I knew where Ashleigh's brother was staying. So I checked with a few of the girls and found out that he's living with his aunt and uncle, Henry and Doris Jackson, on a farm about twenty miles from town."

"Do you know how to get there?"

"Well, that's why I called you instead of Martha. If you're thinking of going out there, it might be best if I go with you."

"And why is that?"

"I was told he won't talk to anyone. He may not talk to me either, but he might if he remembers me. Ashleigh used to bring David to the studio years ago and he'd hang out during her classes."

"Okay. When can we go?"

"I can go right now if you want."

"Which way do we head?"

"Toward Lake Waccamaw."

THIRTY MINUTES LATER, I was sitting at the new Wal-Mart watching for Sydney's van. Everywhere I looked there were couples walking hand-in-hand laughing and teasing, hugging and kissing— even folks that looked like they'd been married half their lives acting like newlyweds. Have these people always been out there, or is it just spring fever? *God, how I missed being in a relationship.*

The passenger door abruptly snapped open and Sydney hopped in wearing a dark gray cowl-neck sweater with a silver ballerina pin near the collar, black jeans, black sneakers, a three-quarter-length gray suede coat, and sunglasses. Her hair was pulled back in a looped ponytail and a wide smile spread across her face. I whiffed the light fragrance of her perfume and realized being around Sydney for an entire week and *not* falling in love was going to be difficult.

"Hi," she said.

I took a deep breath and smiled. "Hi."

Minutes later, as we crossed the Cape Fear Bridge heading northwest, I could see her watching me out of the corner of her eye. "I guess you've been keeping up with the news this week."

"Oh yes," she replied.

"Then you must have been a little shocked when you saw me."

"Yes, I was."

"Then do you mind if I ask why you're here now?"

"I know you didn't have anything to do with what happened to Ash."

The quickness with which she answered surprised me. It just came out without a second thought. Not only did I find that comforting, but encouraging as well. "Thanks. I needed that."

She smiled. "You're welcome."

We passed a doe with a couple of fawns grazing on new grass along the shoulder of the road. They didn't even look up as we blew by.

"So, what made you decide to open your own dance school?"

"I was teaching two days a week in Myrtle Beach, two days a week in Wilmington, and one day a week in Jacksonville and just got tired of all the driving. Then a school came up for sale here in Wilmington and I really wanted to buy it, but they wanted more for it than I could afford so I decided I'd start one on my own. And I did. But I never dreamed it would be this successful. I only needed enough students to earn a living, but they kept coming. It got to the point I had to hire more teachers. Then after three years, I moved it to where it is now."

"It looks like you've got something very special there."

"Thanks."

I could see her eyes staring at me through the dark lens and wondered if she was trying to figure out if I was guilty or not. "What?" I asked.

She looked down and brushed a piece of lint off her jeans. "I was just thinking about how little you've changed."

"And I was just thinking about how *much* you've changed. Why haven't you gotten married and started a family?"

"People ask me that all the time. I've always said I was too busy and that my students are my children. But, now? I don't know. It would be nice, I think."

As we rode on, we talked about the photography I'd be doing at her school, about the old days when I dated Jewell, and the black and white Manx cat named Tux that she still had after fifteen years. The more we talked, the more comfortable we got. And the more comfortable we got, the more we laughed. And the more we laughed, the more infatuated I became.

"So what do you want from her brother?" Sydney asked.

"I've got to start somewhere."

"Start what?"

I took a deep breath. "This whole thing—her murder, or disappearance, or whatever it is—just seems a little fishy to me."

"What do you mean?"

"Like it was staged."

Her mouth parted slightly and I could sense her eyes on me. I told her about the bicycle, the boat, the guy who knocked me in the head, the missing money, and what Mrs. Winslow had said. "And if she did set all of this up, I can't believe she'd just walk away without letting her brother know what she was doing."

"I see what you mean."

"And tomorrow I'm going out on the river to see if I can find the boat she rented and figure out why she needed it and, hopefully, where she went."

She looked to her right. "Why are you doing this?"

"Why am I doing this?" I laughed and looked her way, but she wasn't laughing. "I'm trying to prove I had nothing to do with what happened to her."

"And that's the only reason?"

"Isn't that enough?"

"I thought maybe you...liked her."

"You get right to the heart of things, don't you? Maybe you ought to be the one to interview David." She slapped my arm and smiled.

As we neared Lake Waccamaw, she called out the directions and I drove right to the farm. An older man in denim coveralls and mud-caked boots answered the door. I stood back from the porch and let Sydney do the talking. She spoke to him through a screened door.

"Hi. I'm Sydney Deagan. I was Ashleigh's dance teacher a few years back and I—"

"She ain't here," the old man growled stepping back to close the door.

"Wait! Actually, I was hoping to talk to David."

"David don't talk to nobody since the accident."

"He knows me. Sydney Deagan. Would you ask him?"

"Won't do no good. I told you. He don't talk to nobody, not even the police. They came the other day and banged on his door for half an hour. He ain't been out of that room since he come here, except to see a doctor."

"We were hoping he could help us find Ashleigh."

"You ain't heard what happened?"

I spoke up from behind Sydney. "Mr. Jackson, we think there's a chance Ashleigh might still be alive."

He pushed the screen door open and squinted his eyes. "You the police?"

I climbed the steps and extended a hand to shake. "No, sir. I'm Richard Baimbridge. I live—"

"Baimbridge?" He retreated, closing the screen door. "Ain't you the one they say done it?"

I retracted my hand and stuffed it in my pocket. "I had nothing to do with it, Mr. Jackson. And that's why I need to find her."

"We don't know nothing but what the police tell us," he said.

"When was the last time you saw Ashleigh?" I asked.

"You folks best be on your way. We got nothing to say."

"Please, I don't think anything has happened to Ashleigh. I think she planned this whole thing herself and made it appear there had been foul play. I was hoping—"

"Now why would she do something like that?"

"I'm not sure, Mr. Jackson. But I believe she got involved with some people she wanted to get away from."

"That girl was smart as a whip. She wouldn't get herself messed up in nothing that wasn't proper. Somebody done her in and that's the way it is."

I noticed a curtain slightly pulled back in a window at the other end of the porch and strode toward it. "David! Talk to us! We're trying to help Ashleigh!" The curtain dropped back into place. I banged on the window with the side of my fist. "David!"

The screen door sprang open and the old man stumbled out holding a double-barreled shotgun leveled at me. Sydney backed down the steps.

"Git on now 'fore I drop you dead." His eyes were clear and his hand steady. "Don't think I won't do it."

I raised my hands and moved slowly to the edge of the porch and stepped off into a long-abandoned flowerbed. "We're not trying to cause any trouble here, Mr. Jackson."

"If you know what's good for you, Mister, you'll stay away from here. I mean it. Now git!"

I backed toward the car, cupped my hands over my mouth, and shouted, "David! Call me! Richard Baim—"

The shotgun exploded.

24

SYDNEY GOT ME INTO THE CAR, drove me home, and helped me upstairs. I was bleeding from wounds over practically every inch of the front of my body, but the shotgun shells had been loaded with rock salt instead of lead shot. Although the injuries were not life threatening, they were painful.

The house was still in disarray—"from the visitor," I told her. "If you think this is bad, you ought to see what he did to the back of my head."

She pushed my hair to the side, pulled off her sunglasses, and examined the lump and stitches. "Richard, why didn't you tell me?" she asked as we stumbled into the bathroom.

"You mean you didn't notice it?"

She lowered me onto the side of the tub. "No I didn't. You should have told me."

"You should have seen it Thursday."

She wet a cloth and touched it gently to my face. As she wiped away the blood and cleaned the salt from my wounds, I saw up close how beautiful she was.

"Who'd you say you were dating?" I asked.

"I didn't."

"Is it serious?"

"It used to be."

"So, what does he do?"

She exhaled. "He's an attorney."

An attorney? All my hopes vaporized and the energy in my body receded as she rinsed the cloth and wiped it over my face and neck once more. "Thanks," I whispered. "If you'll let me get a shower and change clothes, I'll take you back to your car."

"Are you sure you can do this?"

"I've been doing it since I was five."

"You know what I mean."

I smiled. "Yes. I'm okay."

Touching her hand to my face, Sydney started to say something, changed her mind, turned, and left me alone. Again I stripped off a set of clothes that I dropped into a pile to throw away. With a hot shower and clean clothes, I felt better. Leaving the bathroom, I saw that Sydney had straightened up the bedroom and made the bed. As I came down the stairs she was busy wiping down the island countertop. Behind her, a clean pile of dishes rested on a drying towel next to the sink.

"Thanks," I said. "You shouldn't have done that."

"I didn't have anything else to do."

"Would you like something to drink or eat?"

She folded the cloth and set it neatly next to the sink. "I'd better be going."

"But you haven't finished. Look." I pointed to the pillows thrown around the den. "There's another whole room to go."

Her fingers whisked aside loose sprigs of hair hanging in her face. "It'll have to wait until the next time you get shot."

That struck me as incredibly funny—belly-laugh funny—and laughter spilled out of me. She laughed too and although it hurt my head, it felt so good to just let loose and laugh at something silly. It had been such a long time since I'd laughed like that.

"That's a deal," I replied when I'd finally regained enough control to speak. "I'll try to get shot again first thing tomorrow morning." The laughter started all over again and it made her blue eyes twinkle. But the way I studied her must have made her uncomfortable somehow and when she turned away and rinsed the cloth again, it struck me that Sydney was no ordinary woman. She had a full life and more than her share of responsibilities and deserved someone like a lawyer. Certainly not me. Yet she seemed to need something.

I took her hand, gently pulled her to me, and put my arms around her.

"Thanks, Sydney," I whispered.

"For what?"

"For all you've done to help me today. For believing in me." Slowly, she relaxed, laid her cheek against my shoulder, and placed her arms around me. "You've really done well for yourself, Sydney, and—thanks for such an incredible day."

Her warmth seeped into my clothes and a strange force encompassed us. My insides trembled and for a few minutes the world stood still. It was exhilarating. Then she whispered, "I think we'd better go."

A minute later, we were in my car heading back to hers. We hardly talked at first, then she asked if I was involved with anyone.

"No. Haven't been in a long time."

"Have you ever been married?"

"Almost."

"What happened?"

"I wish I knew. I've been trying to figure that out for years."

The drive across town seemed to take no time at all. I pulled into the parking lot where she'd left her vehicle, parked next to it, and turned the engine off. "Thanks for going with me, Sydney, and for patching me up and cleaning the house and...everything."

"It's been a very interesting day," she said searching her purse for her keys.

"Yes, it has and I've thoroughly enjoyed it. Well, most of it."

She laughed and looked at me. I didn't want her to go. I felt as if I'd found something that I'd misplaced years ago—something that rightfully belonged to me. I wanted to spend the rest of the day with her—maybe even the rest of my life, but I knew in my heart I'd never be able to have her. She was too special, too unique to fall for someone like me. She had this other thing going with the lawyer and I didn't want to interfere. I got out, circled the car, and opened the door for her.

She stepped out, pressed the button to unlock her van, and placed her purse inside. When she turned back to face me, I leaned to kiss her, but she turned her head away.

Damn! How could I have been so stupid?

I stepped back. "I'm sorry, I—"

"It's okay. I'm just..." She left the sentence unfinished, exhaled, got in the van, and cranked the engine. I pushed her door closed and stepped away from the van regretting the way the day was ending.

She rolled the window down. "Be careful tomorrow."

I nodded. "Thanks. I'll be fine."

For a brief moment our eyes locked and I felt a surge of something. *Was that hope? Or was it pity?* She clicked her seatbelt in place, shifted the vehicle into "reverse," and backed away.

25

FTER SYDNEY DROVE OFF, I sat alone in my car not wanting the memory of Sydney's visit to fade just yet—reliving the day over and over, able to still feel her in my arms. Finally, I started the engine and drove to my parent's house. As I slipped into Martha's darkened room, she turned her head and blasted me with a radiant smile that I could see even in the faint light.

"Hi," she whispered.

"What are you doing laying here in the dark?"

"I took a Percocet. I had therapy today."

"Are you okay?"

"Fair," she whispered. "I'm glad you came by. You need to straighten things out with Daddy."

I sat on the edge of the bed. "He's the least of my worries."

She exhaled slowly. "No, you need to."

"He doesn't care about me. He's just humiliated by this whole thing and wants me to get it straightened out. Quickly."

She reached out and gripped my arm. "He loves you, Richie."

"Ha!"

"He asked me to find out what was going on; if you were all right."

I turned to her. "Why can't he just ask me? Huh?"

"Richie! What happened to your face?"

I dropped down next to her on the bed and told her everything that had happened.

"For heaven sake," she said. "It's a wonder you weren't blinded."

"I'm okay."

She shifted her weight on the bed and groaned. "You have got to be more careful." Her voice was tense. "I'm proof enough that these kinds of people can be ruthless."

I exhaled. "Yeah, I'm starting to get the picture, but I think I'm onto something now."

She wiped a tear off her cheek and sighed. "What?"

"Something tells me that Ashleigh set this whole thing up."

"She what?"

I placed an arm under my head and explained about the house at the beach, Angie, the missing money, and the video cassette. "Ashleigh is most likely the one that stole that guy's money and—if she did—might have set her place up to look like she'd been murdered in order to get away with it."

Martha slapped her hand against the bed. "Damn! Why do I have to be trapped in this bed?"

I touched her arm. "What's wrong, Babe?"

She shifted her weight again. "If those people at the beach are into porn, they could be the same ones that did this to me, that are killing those girls."

"Jesus, Babe. I never thought of that."

She laid back and dropped an arm over her eyes. "I need to get a look at this place. Check out the occupants. Get fingerprints."

"I slipped in last night and got a video cassette, but Scott McGillikin has it now. No, wait!" I rolled up on my elbow. "It got smashed. I transferred the tape. I've still got the cassette it came in."

With her arm still over her eyes, she exhaled. "I want it. But don't touch it."

"I've already touched it. I had to take it apart."

"I still want to check it for prints."

"Okay, I'll bring it to you."

"Tomorrow, when you pick me up?"

"Tomorrow? I—can't."

"Aren't we going to see Sister Hazel?"

"Oh, shit. Is that tomorrow?" She didn't answer, just sighed. "I—I'm going out on the river in the morning."

She took shallow breaths. "What's happening on the river?"

I laid back and told her about the boy, the bicycle, and the boat. When I finished, she grabbed my arm. "Take me with you, please?"

"Gosh, Babe. It's an open workboat. It doesn't have seats. It'll pound you to death. You can't even put your chair on it."

She flung her head from side to side and covered her face with her hands. "Oh God! I hate being a cripple!"

It wasn't often that I saw her like this and it hurt me just as much as it did her. "I'm sorry, Babe."

She wiped tears off her cheeks. "It's not your fault. You do more than you should. I just miss it so much sometimes...and hate having to depend on others for everything. Just be careful, okay?"

I couldn't stand to see her like this, but there was nothing I could do about it. I sat up and threw my legs off the bed. "Don't worry,

Babe. I'm not going to let anything happen to me. I've got to look after my baby sister."

She picked up a tissue and wiped her nose with it. "Why do I feel like *you're* the one that needs looking after?"

I smiled and gripped her other hand. "Because I probably do. I'll get what's left of that cassette to you by Monday."

She sniffled. "Thanks."

I rolled off the bed, brushed a tear off her cheek, and kissed her forehead. "Goodnight, Babe."

She grabbed my arm. "I love you, Richie. Be careful."

"I love you, too, Babe."

AT 5 A.M. SUNDAY MORNING, I pulled into the dirt parking lot at the boat landing. Dawn had not yet broken and the temperature had dipped to around thirty-six degrees. The cuts on my face had scabbed over and now looked like freckles. Concerned about the morning chill, I kept my pajama pants on and added a pair of insulated underwear beneath a pair of blue jeans and put two wool shirts on under a lined leather jacket. If it warmed up, I could take it all off. I also packed a rain poncho, fur-lined gloves, a red ski mask, and a tan and blue baseball cap I'd picked up a few years back on an assignment in Nassau.

The old-timer was shoving dry wood into the heater over a bed of red coals. "Might get some rain t'day," he said. "How long you plannin' on bein' out?"

"Two-thirty at the latest."

He walked away from the heater without lighting it and pulled a key off a hook screwed in the wall. "What'cha going out there lookin' for anyways?"

"I'm looking for your missing boat."

"Well, le' me know if ya find it. I ain't got no 'surance."

The wood in the heater burst into flames as I paid cash for the boat, the gas, and a bag of ice. "How far can I get on that gas?" I asked.

"Ya gots two six gallon tanks," he said counting out change from an old hand-crank cash register.

"And how far will that take me?"

"One runs dry ya gots to change to the other one and pump the bulb 'fore she'll start again. Then you'll know how far ya kin run on one."

That's the kind of wisdom people seem to have lost these days. Common sense. I smiled. "Right. Thanks." I wrote down the registration number of the missing boat and left.

Outside, the air was nippy and the horizon was just beginning to lighten. I dumped the ice over the sodas and bottled water and loaded it into the boat along with the food and a box containing binoculars, chart, cell phone, radio, gloves, poncho, and a thermos of hot coffee.

The boat rocked under my weight as I placed and secured everything in it. I turned the key and the outboard motor cranked instantly, as if it had been running all night, and warbled back and forth pulling against its steering lines. A cloud of gray-blue smoke gurgled out of the murky water behind the boat and drifted up the creek.

The sky was glowing in the east, but it was still nighttime on the creek for the frogs and crickets performing their endless songs. I untied the lines, pulled them in, and pushed the boat off the dock. The wind was calm and the water was black as ink. Grasping the wheel, I eased the gearshift forward. The transmission engaged with a grind and the boat gently advanced. Without a windshield, even the slowest forward movement brought a cold, damp breeze onto my face. *It was exhilarating.*

I loved being on the water and don't know why I had stayed away so long. The creek was narrow and unfamiliar. I'd taken a Coast Guard course about ten years earlier and will always remember their "red on right on return" rule. It means that when you are going upstream, you keep red markers on the right. I was going downstream, so I needed to keep the red ones on my left.

From the thermos I poured steaming black coffee into a spill-proof insulated cup and set it in one of those swiveling holders designed to keep it right-side-up regardless of the position of the boat. Setting the engine to putter along at its lowest possible speed, I stayed close to the center of the creek watching for blinking channel markers as the dawn light began to paint the horizon in pastel colors. The Intracoastal Waterway was only a mile or so ahead and would be laden with crab pots, nets, stakes, and traffic. I preferred to have a little more light before plowing through them.

I tuned the radio to the local weather frequency, sipped hot coffee, and thought about Sydney while the monotonous voice of a NOAA weather announcer called for a 40% chance of rain.

SYDNEY AWOKE EARLY and tossed restlessly until yielding to the realization that she was not going back to sleep. She knew Richard was going out on the river that morning and could not get him out of her mind. Throwing back the covers, she eased off the bed trying not to awaken Scott.

With a pot of coffee on, she sat quietly at the breakfast table looking out at the pre-dawn darkness thinking about Richard. The feelings she'd had for him growing up had been revived—feelings she thought she'd locked away long ago. And she couldn't get him off her mind.

She and Scott McGillikin had been together for five years and—in the beginning—he had pulled her out of the depths of emotional devastation after her break-up with a radio DJ and given her the strength to go on with her life. She had been grateful then and had felt safe with him. He had been strong, patient, thoughtful, and understanding.

Later, he helped her start her dance school. "Plan the work and work the plan," he'd say. He'd even taken charge of investing her profits and now—thanks to him—she had a sizable savings account. He was everything she'd needed...back then. But, over time, he had become less nurturing and more possessive and had begun to spend more and more time away. She'd even suspected there were other women and eventually came to hope he *would* find someone else. It would be an easy breakup. She'd fake being hurt and he'd be gone. But he'd continued to drop by every week or so. And when she tried to push them apart, he would twist things around and make her feel guilty and selfish. Now she felt trapped and alone and just wanted things to be *over*. She knew that if she wanted things to change in her life, she'd have to make changes. *Plan the work, work the plan.* She also knew that making changes isn't easy.

A tear rolled down her cheek as she lifted a hot cup to her lips. Through the window, the sun broke over the horizon and spread its warmth and golden-orange light as far as it could reach.

"The dawn of a new day," she whispered.

She wondered where Richard might be at that moment, if he was warm and dry, and if he, too, had seen and appreciated the magnificence of that glorious sunrise.

Her thoughts drifted back to the sound of that gun exploding and the shock on Richard's face and the sight of him riding back in that car—humiliated, with his clothes tattered—and began to laugh. It was an uncontrollable, cleansing, loving laughter and with it came more tears.

If you want change, you have to make changes, she thought.

26

PRESSING THE THROTTLE FORWARD, I steered the open boat into the choppy waters of the Intracoastal Waterway and turned southward into the wind. The boat bounced hard across each wave and a light spray moistened my face making it feel as if the temperature had suddenly dropped another twenty degrees. I reached for the ski mask and pulled it over my head.

The channel was no more than a hundred feet wide, but the waterway itself varied from a few hundred yards wide in places to a mile wide in other places. In the wider stretches, there were strings of islands and shallow grounds on either side of the marked channel. A mid-sized yacht with a dinghy dragging behind it approached from the south and cruised past me twenty yards to my left with a rolling wall of water streaming outward behind it. Cutting toward the wave, I slammed through it, slipped into the smooth draft behind the yacht, and resumed my southward trek.

A fisherman in a workboat much like mine pulled at a net and eyed me suspiciously as I cruised by. Pelicans nestled around him and fought over the fish he didn't keep. Occasionally, I'd spot a boat like the one I sought and would slow down, get a closer look at it, and then move on. Farther and farther I traveled southward crossing back and forth across the waterway eliminating one boat after another. As the waterway grew wider, I decided I'd check the right side going south and the other side coming back.

The hours and the miles rolled past and by 9 a.m. I'd approached the intersection where the waterway and the Cape Fear River merged. Waterway traffic going both north and south had increased to a steady stream and was especially heavy going in and out of the Cape Fear. In spite of all the layers of clothing, my legs and feet had gone numb. My hands cramped and my back ached. I was cold, wet, and hungry and decided to rest a bit before crossing the rough mouth of the river. I steered into calmer waters to the right of the channel and cut the engine.

Standing, I stretched my back and let the blood drain back into my legs and feet. I pulled the lid off a can of pork and beans and popped the top on a Pepsi. Sea gulls gathered overhead just out of reach and pelicans sailed in dropping quietly onto the water around the boat.

Fifteen minutes later I was underway again without the ski mask. As I moved into the mouth of the Cape Fear, the channel got wider and the seas got rougher. The boat banged hard against the waves and sprayed seawater into the boat as I dodged large fishing vessels heading out to sea and cargo freighters heading for the State Port at Wilmington.

I wondered if Ashleigh could have done this in the dark, or if she'd waited for the sun to come up before daring to cross. Or had she avoided this entirely and gone north? Cruising on the water at night steering blindly from flashing buoy to flashing buoy with a full moon reflecting off the water is about as beautiful as it gets, but I wouldn't want to do it in unfamiliar waters. There are just too many things floating around to chance it. But given that Ashleigh had taken quite a few chances already, she might very well have done it.

As I neared the south side of the Cape Fear, dark clouds rolled in and the wind shifted to the east forcing the boat to take each wave at a sharper angle, rocking it wildly. Water splashed into the boat more frequently now spattering my clothes and shoes, and collecting in the bottom of the boat. The cardboard boxes became soaked and lost their shape. I felt around for the drain plug under the engine and pulled it allowing the water to flow out.

There were hundreds of tiny inlets and creeks, some going no more than a few hundred feet inland, others twisting inland for miles. There was no way to check them all. Besides, it was my guess that Ashleigh would have looked for a place to blend into a crowd or grab another form of transportation. The most likely places were Southport, near the North Carolina-South Carolina border, or one of hundreds of places along the Grand Strand in the Myrtle Beach area some fifty miles farther. Southport was just a few miles ahead. From the waterfront in Southport, she could have walked to the bus station and disappeared forever.

The wind picked up as I approached the town docks and I could see rain falling to my left out over the ocean. When I'd started out that morning, I expected this to be more of an adventure. Instead, it had been miserable and uncomfortable. The temperature never got above the low 40s—unusually cool for this time of year. I reached into a box, snared the bottle of scotch I'd tossed in at the last minute, wrenched the cap off, and while taking a swig spotted another Boston Whaler between a couple of multi-million dollar Hatteras yachts moored at the yacht basin.

As a light drizzle began pocking the waters, I returned the scotch to the box, aimed the boat toward the yachts, and drew the poncho over me. Replacing the plug, I slowed and maneuvered close enough in the choppy seas to see that the boat was not the one I was seeking. This one was more disappointing than the rest. That's *exactly* where I'd expected to find it—tied and abandoned on or near a yacht at Southport. No one would have paid any attention to it. Most of these big luxurious playthings were only used a few times a year at best—not very likely in April—and some looked as if they hadn't been used in years.

I wheeled the boat around, docked at Captain Barnaby's Seafood Restaurant, covered my boxes as best I could, and huddled over a hot bowl of the best Downeast clam chowder I'd ever eaten. By the time I'd finished, a "nor'easter" had blown in and the rain was coming down sideways. Boats along the waterfront bounced about like bathtub toys and the sea had turned into vicious rolling whitecaps. The sky had become so dark that the automatic lights in the parking lot had turned on. Visibility on the river was down to less than fifty feet and I hated the idea that I had to go back out there to get home in time for an afternoon rehearsal. Sitting alone in that restaurant, listening to the thrashing rain driven by a howling wind, I wallowed in my depression.

The waitress was kind and kept bringing the coffee. "I don't believe I've seen you around here before," she noted, refilling my cup for the fifth time.

"I haven't been through here since I was a teenager."

"Picked a rough day for it."

"Well, I'm looking for someone."

She smacked her gum. "Oh yeah? Who?"

"A blond girl in her early twenties. Might have had six or seven strings of beads in her hair." I pulled out the newspaper clipping. "She would have been through here Monday."

She picked up the newspaper and popped her gum. "Yeah, she was here."

27

S YDNEY SAT ACROSS THE TABLE from Scott and stared down at her plate. She hated it when he mimicked her eating. If she lifted her fork, he lifted his. When she took a bite, he took a bite. She dropped her fork onto her plate and lifted her champagne glass. "What pleasure could you possibly get from doing that?"

He lifted his own glass. "Doing what?" His dark hair was overdue for a trim, hanging over deep-set gray eyes.

The eyes of a fox, she thought. *Or a weasel.*

Sunday brunch used to be their favorite meal together. They'd lay around in their bedclothes all morning, sip champagne, make love, eat a large breakfast around noon, and then spend the afternoon sailing.

But Scott had changed. He found more pleasure in tormenting her now and playing games with her head, making her feel stupid and clumsy, and Sydney's love had faded.

She sipped her champagne and looked away at her cat, Tux, stationed on a nearby chair—tense, ready to spring, watching. Tux knew her better than anyone. He'd been with her through the good times and the bad. *"Do it!"* he seemed to be saying, his eyes fixed on hers. She exhaled and set her glass down. Scott set his down in unison. There were moments when Scott McGillikin could be the most annoying ass on the planet. This was one of those moments.

"Why do you do that?" she asked. "Do you have any idea how irritating that is?"

Scott made a chuckling sound deep in his throat. "I think I do."

She lifted her napkin and wiped her chin. "And to think there was a time when I would have married you."

"Yeah, thank God I didn't ask, huh?" He wiped his chin.

Sydney's lip quivered. She flicked a tear out of her eye and picked up her fork. *Yes, thank God you didn't ask.*

At twenty-nine years old, Sydney was trapped in a relationship with a man she could no longer stand to be around while her youth was quietly slipping away. Outside of her dance school, her life had become empty and meaningless. *Why am I so weak?* she thought. *Why can't I tell him?*

With tears blurring her vision, she broke a piece of toast in half, held it on her plate, and scooped a bit of grits and scrambled egg on it, then ate it. As Scott did the same, she caught the arrogance in his eyes and knew the time was near. She lifted a glass of orange juice and took a long drink. As she waited for the cold liquid to calm her nervous stomach, she slid the moist glass across her cheeks, eyes, and forehead. "Scott, what happened to that interesting, sexy, intelligent guy you used to be?"

The smile in the corner of his mouth slumped into a smirk. He reached forward, dipped two fingers into his water glass, and flicked them at her.

She flinched as the droplets struck her face and glared at him.

"Can't you take a joke?" he asked.

"Yes, Scott. I can take a *joke.*"

"Good. At least I'm still funny."

She wiped the spray off her face. "We need to talk."

He lifted his fork and jabbed a bit of egg. "Let me guess. About us?"

"Yes, Scott. About us." Taking a deep breath, she tried to control the quiver in her voice. "I appreciate all the things you do for me, Scott. I do. But, I don't know what I want anymore. I need—"

"Where is this going, Sydney?" he blurted.

She closed her eyes and swallowed. "I'm...just...not happy anymore, Scott."

He exhaled through his nostrils. "So what else is new?"

Drawing a deep breath, she turned her eyes to Tux for support, then closed them and forced the words out, one at a time. "I want you...to leave."

For a moment Scott just sat there staring at Sydney, his arms resting on either side of his plate—a fork in one hand and a knife in the other. She did not look up until he dropped the utensils simultaneously onto the table and startled her. Snatching his flute of champagne off the table, he sat back, raised the glass, and drank as a chuckle sounded through his nose. When he'd drained it, he flipped the glass at Sydney smashing it against a silver candleholder knocking over a lighted candle, showering Sydney's face and arms in molten wax and glass. As Sydney vaulted from her chair, Tux bolted from his. Snatching up her cloth napkin, she swiped at the burning wax, smearing it across her face. "Thanks, a lot!"

Peeling soft wax off her burning skin, she crossed to the kitchen with Scott following.

"I'm sorry, Sydney. I didn't mean to do that. That was an accident."

Hanging over the sink, she splashed cold water onto her face and dug her nails at the hardened wax.

"Really," he said laying a hand on her back. "I mean it. That was an accident."

Sydney shifted to the side. "Just pack your things and leave."

Scott let that sink in, his head bouncing when it did. "You think all you have to do is snap your fingers and say it's over, and that's it? That you can just end everything..." Scott flashed a hand past her and snapped his fingers in her face. "...like that?"

She winced and laid the wet cloth on her face. "I don't love you anymore, Scott. You scare me."

"Oh, give me a break."

"Look, I know this seems impulsive, but it isn't. I've been thinking about it for a long time and now that I've made up my mind, I want to move on before it's *too late*."

He leaned toward her, his voice bitter and threatening. "And that's that, huh? Case closed."

Turning the water off, she moved away from the sink with hardened wax still clinging to her face. "You're hardly even here during the week anymore, Scott. Forty-five minutes at dinner—if you bother to show up—and forty-five minutes in the middle of the night every now and then when *you* feel like it. I have a deeper relationship with Tux than I do you."

"Jesus, Sydney. I'll do whatever you want. What do you want?"

Sydney didn't know how much longer she could remain strong. She knew he'd eventually wear her down if she let him. She slammed the heel of her hand on the edge of the counter. "I want you to leave!" Her jaw quivered, but she held her eyes fixed on his.

His face hardened. His eyes narrowed. "Why, Sydney? Isn't this kind of sudden?" She didn't answer. "Is there someone else?" Remaining silent, she looked away picking bits of wax off her chin. "Is that it?" he questioned seizing her shoulders, forcing her back against the counter, trying to kiss her.

"Stop it!" she screamed shoving him away.

Scott didn't like being bested—in a courtroom or on *any* turf. A jolt of pain fired through his left eye and voices shouted in his head. He grabbed her arm and pinned her in a corner of the kitchen. "Then, tell me what you want, Sydney! What do you want?" The muscle under his left eye twitched. "You want to get married? Is that what you want?" He dropped to one knee and looked up at her, his hands around her thighs pulling her to him. "Is that what you want?"

Gripping the edges of the counter to steady herself, Sydney looked away and sighed. "It's too late, Scott." Her voice was quiet. "It's too late."

He rose to his feet. "No, damn it. It's not! Let's do it. Let's get married, Sydney. I know a judge that'll do it tomorrow."

"I don't want to marry you. I don't love you anymore, Scott."

"Oh, come on, Sydney. The new boat's going to be ready soon. You said you were going to spend the whole summer on it."

"Please, don't make this any harder than it is already."

"Damn, Sydney! I ordered that boat for you!"

"The hell you did! Don't go throwing *that* in my face."

He moved closer. His voice softened. "What happened? Am I working too much? I thought everything was going along just great."

"Things have *not* been going along just *great*." As he tried to corner her again, she spun away and moved back into the dining room picking at the hardened wax as she went. "We haven't even made love in months."

"Because you're always too tired and stressed out."

She lifted her champagne glass and turned to face him. "Because I don't love you anymore, Scott." She downed the rest of the drink and a sliver of glass tumbled into her mouth. Working it around on the tip of her tongue, she spit it back into her glass. "I haven't for a long time. I'm sorry. I *tried*. Really, I did."

With a spasm making Scott's cheek flutter, he drew a deep slow breath. *Sometimes in real life—as in court—you win by appearing to concede.* He flinched as he said the words. "All right, Sydney. If that's what you want." He turned and walked out.

She'd heard the words, but didn't believe them and watched him as he climbed the stairs. *That was too easy. He's up to something.*

28

I WASN'T SURE I'D HEARD the waitress correctly. "She was here? You saw her?"

"I was outside on break smoking a cigarette when she and the guy she was with pulled up." She popped her gum again.

"Are you sure it was the same girl?"

She held the newspaper farther away and squinted. "I might not know it was her from that picture alone, but she had those hair beads."

"What kind of boat was it?"

"It was small—just a workboat." She pointed out the window. "Like that one down there." She pointed to my rental and goose bumps broke out on my arms.

"There was a man with her?"

"I didn't see him very well. He stayed in the boat. They were having motor trouble. Somebody else passing through was trying to help them."

"How old was he?"

"The man? I don't know. Young, I think."

"Do you remember anything about the helper?"

"An older couple. Gray-haired."

"What kind of boat did they have?"

"It was nice. Fairly big. I can't remember what it was, but it had an unusual name—something different. You want some pie?"

I took a pencil from her apron pocket. "What's your name?"

"Darla Pridgeon." She spelled it out for me as I wrote it along the side of the newspaper, then went and returned with a generous wedge of homemade blueberry cheesecake that I savored slowly with the coffee while waiting for the weather to clear up.

Who could have been with Ashleigh? Could it have been a boyfriend? Or David? He was supposed to be at his aunt and uncle's house. *But was he?*

It was now after 11 a.m. and I had a four o'clock rehearsal. My clothes had dried and the warmth had come back into my legs and feet. The rain didn't appear to be slacking off anytime soon, so I donned the poncho, paid the bill, and thanked Darla again pressing a hundred-dollar bill into her hand. When she unfolded it, her gum fell out of her mouth.

"You have no idea how much you've helped me," I told her.

Pulling the hood over my head, I reluctantly stepped back out into the storm. Boats along the waterfront rocked back and forth and strained against their ties as the huge waves rolled under them and crashed against the seawall, spewing water high into the air. I fought to keep my balance as I head-butted the storm, stumbled back into the boat, cranked the engine, and held the boat off the wall while untying the lines.

Jumping to the controls, I gave it some gas and nosed the bow northward trying to keep it from slamming against the dock. But just as I pulled away I heard a woman screaming, turned, and saw the waitress in a yellow hooded raincoat stumbling along the waterfront waving an arm at me.

"What?" I shouted.

Whipped by the wind and holding her raincoat together, Darla followed alongside shouting in a futile attempt to be heard. I killed the engine and heard her shout, "It's Rachel's Diamond. That's the name of the boat."

"Rachel's Diamond?"

A wave slammed the bulkhead and exploded high into the air spraying Darla. She lowered her head and held her ground. "Yes. Don't you think that's kind of sweet?"

"Yes. Yes, I do!" I laughed. "Rachel's Diamond!" Jumping to the side of the boat, I reached for the seawall to keep the boat from being slammed against it.

Darla sat down on the wall and used her feet to help hold the boat back while I cranked the engine again and aimed the boat toward home.

"Thanks!" I called.

Rachel's Diamond. No telling where it could be now. Could be anywhere up and down the eastern seaboard.

The wind had shifted to the northeast and was gusting to at least twenty knots. The river rolled with three-foot whitecaps and the boat rose and fell over each crest. The trip back was going to take longer and I hadn't allowed for much extra time. As I pulled into traffic to cross the busy Cape Fear, the rain increased to a deluge and I could only see about twenty feet in front of me. A huge wave struck the boat from the front, splashed over the bow, and flooded the bottom of the boat just as the engine sputtered, coughed, and quit. I turned the key and the engine turned over, but it wouldn't catch. I had no means of controlling the boat without the motor running. I leaned over and wiped the rain off the gas gauge on the first tank. The needle pointed to *empty*.

As I moved the gas line to the full tank, the wind skewed the boat sideways and another wave washed into the boat filling it with water. I hit the key and the engine turned over, though it still didn't start. As a foghorn blasted close by, I remembered the bulb, felt under the water for it, squeezed my hand around it, and compressed it as hard as I could. Again and again I compressed the bulb and when I felt liquid moving through it, I tried the key again. Another wave washed over the side of the boat as I repeatedly squeezed the bulb while holding the key in the start position. The engine sputtered and coughed, sputtered again, and coughed again. As another wave slammed the side of the boat, the huge gray bow of a gigantic steel freighter became visible through the mist bearing straight down upon me.

Another wave struck broadside and the boat sank lower into the water just as the engine fired to life. I rammed the gearshift forward. The engine whined, the boat lurched, water sloshed out over the stern, and I fell into the space next to the seat. Another wave washed more seawater into the boat and as the ship bore down on me, I grabbed the wheel, pulled myself to my knees, and reeled it to the left. But the boat, heavy with water and sitting low in the river, was slow to move and, although the engine was running full throttle, brushed the side of the freighter before it pulled away.

The boat was moving too slowly to pull the plug, so with the salt spray stinging my eyes, I jockeyed the boat around the river traffic and finally made it back into the narrower Intracoastal Waterway. Using my shoe, I bailed the boat while keeping it on course, and when the boat finally planed-off, I pulled the plug and let the rest of the seawater out.

As I neared the entrance to Bradley Creek, the rain ended, the winds calmed, and the sun broke through the clouds. The final leg back to the old timer's dock turned out to be the most comfortable part of the trip. I turned in the key, loaded the car, and headed for home with barely a half-hour to slip into some dry clothes and get downtown.

As I pulled into my driveway, I was met by Detective Jones and two other officers who handcuffed me, read me my rights for the second time, and hauled me, yet again, to the police station. I didn't even get the opportunity to change clothes.

I was furious.

29

OWNTOWN, THE OFFICERS AGAIN led me up the concrete ramp into the holding area. And again, as the heavy metal door slammed shut behind me, a chill squiggled up my spine. The same desk sergeant shoved the same telephone in my direction, removed the cuffs, and repeated the same line, "You only get one, so you better make it a good one."

I needed to let Scott know where I was, but doubted he'd be at his office on a Sunday afternoon, so I called Sappy. I caught him walking out the door, explained what was going on, and asked him for two favors. The first was to post a note on the back door of the studio canceling rehearsal; the second being to find Scott McGillikin and let him know I was again in police custody and in dire need of his immediate presence.

Parked in a hot room still wearing the layers of wet clothes, I became nauseous. I peeled off the jacket, two shirts, and the insulated underwear leaving them in a pile on the floor. Then waited.

When Scott arrived hours later, I blurted out, "I have great news!" the instant he entered.

He raised his hand to stop me and held it there until the escort had gone, then leaned close. "What have you got?"

"You're not going to believe this, but *Ashleigh is alive!* I found someone who saw her last Monday."

Scott set his briefcase on the table and stared at me. "You told the police?"

"Not yet."

"Then don't. Let me handle this. I'll take it directly to the D.A. There's no need for Sam Jones and his buffoons to even know about it. You understand?"

"But if Jones knew Ashleigh was alive, I'd be off the hook."

The door swung open and Detective Jones stepped into the room.

"Keep you mouth shut. Let me handle this," Scott muttered dragging his briefcase across the steel table to his place next to me.

Jones stepped over a chair and sat directly across from me dropping a stack of papers in front of him. He set a cassette recorder on the table between us and pressed the "record" button.

"Mr. Baimbridge," he started. "Tell us again what you did after you went back to the Matthews house that Sunday night in question."

I leaned forward to answer, but Scott quickly broke in squeezing my shoulder hard. "Look, Jones," he said. "For starters, turn that damned tape recorder off. Then let's you and me step out into the hallway and discuss whatever it is you think you have that gives you the right to drag my client in here in such a barbaric fashion." The muscles in Jones's jaw pulsed. He snapped the recorder off and rose from his seat.

Scott opened his briefcase and removed a legal pad sliding it to me. "I want you to write down whatever information you think you have. And don't leave out *any* details. We'll go over it after I finish with Detective Jones." He closed the briefcase, then followed Sam out.

I didn't have a pen, so I opened his briefcase and rummaged around in it to find one. As I shoved things aside, I came across a photo of a man on the beach with his arms around three very attractive young girls in swimsuits. The man had dark sunglasses, a mustache, thick eyebrows, and exquisite taste in women. Another client, I guessed.

Finding a mechanical pencil inside a compartment, I began writing out what had happened on the trip. The bicycle. The rental boat. And what Darla had told me.

As I detailed the new information I'd come across, I could hear loud voices outside the door, but couldn't make out what they were saying.

"OKAY, JONES," SCOTT SAID magnifying his exasperation. "Just what the hell is it that you supposedly have *this* time?"

"Your boy certainly does get around, Counselor."

"Your point is?" Scott held his gaze.

"The SBI report came back and—no surprise here—the semen in Ashleigh Matthews' bed belongs to Richard Baimbridge." Jones flashed a triumphant smile.

"I presume you have a copy of that report for me. If you don't—" Without looking down, Sam whipped out a copy and held it out for Scott. Taking it, Scott stepped closer to Jones and lowered his voice to an almost threatening tone. "You think this is sufficient to haul Mr. Baimbridge back down here for your amusement? I don't think so. And I remind you that my client told you—on two occasions—that he passed out. And we both know that semen can easily be extracted from an unconscious man."

Sam rolled his eyes. "Yeah, yeah, McGillikin. You forgetting the broken fingernail belonging to Ms. Matthews that had your client's skin and blood attached to it?" Sam whipped out a second set of papers. "I have him nailed and you know it."

Scott snatched them out of his hand. "You're mishandling my client and I'm going to see to it that it comes back and bites you squarely in that fat ass of yours, Detective."

Jones drew his thick eyebrows together and sighed. "If you're through insulting me, Mr. McGillikin, I'm just *dying* to hear your explanation for *this*." He waved a third set of papers in the air.

"What is it?"

"We found your client's blood type and tire tracks at yet *another* murder scene." Jones jammed a third set of copies against Scott's chest. "Like I said, your boy certainly does get around. Don't he?"

WHEN SCOTT RETURNED, he sat across the table from me, loosened his tie, and began scanning what looked to be official documents.

I slid the notepad toward him. "I wrote it all down. Everything."

"Good," Scott mumbled, clearly distracted by the papers he held.

"So, what's Jones so worked up about?"

"The semen found in Ashleigh's bed belongs to you."

"No way!" I exclaimed jumping to my feet. "That's impossible! He's lying. I did *not* have sex with that woman!"

Scott shushed me without looking up. "Careful. These walls have ears. I reminded Jones that you were passed out and that extracting semen from an unconscious man is not a complicated procedure."

"What did he say?"

Scott looked up from the papers. "He said they found your tire tracks and blood at another murder scene."

"What murder scene?"

Scott looked back at the papers in his hand. "Does Lake Waccamaw ring a bell?"

30

ROM THE MOMENT Ashleigh stepped out of that storm into my home, anything having to do with her seemed to happen in a *Twilight Zone* atmosphere. Things around her just did not look, act, or add up the same way they did in the normal world. It was as if some kind of spell had been cast on me.

"Who? The old man?" I asked.

"Both. Jackson and his wife."

I wanted to get the hell out of there. To go out and look for "Rachel's Diamond." To work on characters, blocking, and set designs. I wanted to run to my sister and scream.

"Jesus!" I said, still trying to comprehend what he'd said. "I can't believe it." He didn't answer, or even look up. I drew a slow breath to calm myself as he reached for my notes. "We need to tell them all that stuff I found out today. They need to know it."

"Quiet, Richard. Please."

I touched his arm. "All we did was go out there to talk to Ashleigh's brother."

Scott looked up. "We who?"

"Sydney Deagan was with me."

Scott's eyes narrowed. "Is...that your girlfriend?"

"No. She owns the dance school where Ashleigh used to study dance. Deagan Dance and something," I said.

"Deagan Dance Center."

"She knew David from the past and thought he might talk to her quicker than me."

He sighed. "So, was it just you and Miss Deagan?"

"Yes."

"Where did you go after you left Jackson's place?"

"We came back to my house so I could clean up and change clothes. Then I took her back to her car."

"Then what did you do?"

"I went back home and went to bed."

"Alone?"

"Yes. Do I need an alibi for that, too?"

Scott dropped the notepad in his briefcase, snapped it shut, and stood. "Sure. The D.A.'s going to say that you went back out there after you dropped her off and killed them."

"But I didn't."

"Come on. They're not going to hold you. Let's get out of here."

Scott gave me a ride home but didn't say much until he turned onto my street. "How do you know Sydney Deagan?"

"I dated her sister, Jewell, a few times back in high school and I'm shooting her students' recital photos this year. Why?"

He pulled in the drive, moved the gearshift to neutral, and turned to face me. "She's a potential witness and I don't want any surprises coming up. Are you two romantically involved?"

I exhaled. "No. Not really."

His eyes hardened. "And what exactly does *not really* mean?"

"It means we're not involved. I kissed her once, that's all."

"When?"

I looked at Scott. His jaw pulsed and the color had faded from his face. "Is this important?"

He spoke without emotion, but his hand gripped the gearshift so tightly that his knuckles had turned white. "When?" he asked again.

I unclipped my seatbelt and opened the door, pushing it out with my foot. "I'm sorry. I think I've misled you. It was a peck on the cheek—a thank you. Nothing more."

Stepping out of the car, I leaned down into the opening. He faced forward, looking out. "Women like Sydney Deagan don't find me very attractive, Mr. McGillikin. I can only dream about women like her."

He jammed the gearshift into reverse and I scarcely had time to shut the door before the car shot backward into the street and burned rubber as it sped away.

What the hell was that about?

It was nearly 6 p.m. when I lifted the bottle of scotch from the wet cardboard box and breezed out the back door. The cool, evening air penetrated the damp clothes I still wore. My eyelids weighed heavily and my limbs ached. I dropped onto a lounge chair, threw my legs up, and closed my eyes allowing the bottle to rest against the deck floor. No matter what I did, no matter how much new evidence I turned up, things just kept getting worse. The whole world seemed to have turned on me. *Even my lawyer had gone weird.* I raised the bottle to my lips and as I tilted it to drink, the phone rang in the house. *Damn! Didn't I turn that thing off?*

I jumped up, burst into the house, and snapped the phone off its cradle. "Hello?"

"I need a ride to the hospital." It was Martha. She sounded anxious.

"What's wrong?"

"Daddy's had another heart attack."

THE RECEPTIONIST IN THE EMERGENCY ROOM at New Hanover Regional Medical Center was an older woman with an exaggerated limp. Lifting her hip, she swung her right leg forward then leaned on it hard when she shifted her weight to that leg. She told us the doctors were working on Dad and that Mom was with him. She said we'd have to wait until she came out or until he was moved to a room.

The place was crowded. Elderly people bent forward at the waist waiting in wheelchairs. Children on the floor fighting over colored blocks. A woman in the corner with her hand wrapped in a bloody towel, and a nervous teenage girl who kept hopping up and running to the restroom.

"I'm going outside," Martha said spinning her chair around.

The last colors of sunset were fading to purple and a light breeze was blowing in from the south. I parked her next to a bench where I could sit with her. She pulled a pack of Virginia Slim Lights from her handbag, flipped a cigarette into her mouth, cupped a hand around a Bic lighter, and studied me as she curled smoke out the corner of her mouth. "You don't look so good."

I hadn't shaved since the morning of the previous day, nor had I changed clothes since getting off the river hours ago. "Thanks. When did you start that?"

Two columns of smoke streamed from her nostrils. "I needed something wicked in my life—something dangerous."

"You don't need cigarettes for that. You just need to tag along with me for a while."

"How'd it go today? On the river?"

I recapped the day and told her about Darla and "Rachel's Diamond" while an ambulance backed up to a loading dock and two EMTs frantically pulled an elderly man with blue lips out and rushed him in a side entrance to the emergency room.

"Richie, that's wonderful! You should be excited!"

"I was until I got home. Jones pulled me back downtown and I got more bad news."

"What bad news?"

I exhaled. "They found my semen in Ashleigh's bed." I could see the questions forming in her head as she took another drag and exhaled the smoke.

"I thought you said..."

"We didn't. I have no idea how it got there."

She watched me for a second. "That's not good, Richie."

An icy wave rolled through me as the magnitude of the situation suddenly hit me. I leaned forward with my elbows on my knees. "There's more."

"More?"

I swallowed hard. "You remember that man that shot me yesterday? Mr. Jackson?" She grunted as she drew on her cigarette. "After Sydney and I left there, he and his wife were murdered."

She coughed a cloud of smoke that hovered briefly before fading away. "You are lying."

"I wish to hell I was. And, of course, they found my blood out there so they think I had something to do with that, too."

"This is *not* good, Richie."

My stomach felt as if I'd just dropped thirteen stories in the *Twilight Zone Tower of Terror* at Disney World. I leaned back and gripped the edges of the bench. "I could spend the rest of my fucking life in prison. What the hell am I going to do?"

"Could anyone have followed you out there?"

I dropped my head back and drew a deep breath. "I guess so. I wasn't exactly trying to *sneak* out there."

Martha thumped the ashes off her cigarette. "You know what doesn't make sense to me?"

My limbs tingled and my heart raced. "What?"

"Why would Ashleigh steal money from people she knew were dangerous and leave her aunt and uncle behind in such a vulnerable position? I mean, if she cared for them, wouldn't she have tried to protect them?"

My mouth felt dry. I lowered myself onto the bench and laid on my back with one hand on my forehead and the other on my stomach. "I don't know. Maybe she didn't think they'd find out about them."

"Hey, isn't that Mom?"

I sat up and followed her gaze. From where we were we could see the silhouette of a man and a woman talking in the far corner of the rear parking lot. The woman looked very much like Mom and the man had a wide-brimmed hat pulled low over his face. "Jesus. You know who that is?"

"Winston? I didn't think he ever left that farm."

"That's who it looks like to me. The guy has no nose."

Martha took a drag on her cigarette. "You think she's having an affair with him?"

I laid back down and closed my eyes. "I wouldn't blame her if she did. At least he treats her well."

"I think she's in love with him. I saw them kissing once at the farm."

"That doesn't bother me any. She deserves a little happiness, even if it is Winston. Hell, they could probably both use it."

Martha took one last drag from her cigarette and sent the butt sailing over my head into the street. She fumbled through her handbag for a pad and pencil, flipped to a clean page, and began writing. "What was that woman's name? The woman that saw Ashleigh?"

"Darla Pridgeon."

"Where did you find her?"

"Why? What are you going to do?"

"The boat was called 'Rachel's Diamond' wasn't it?"

I sat up. "Yes." She was scribbling on her notepad and I saw that twinkle that she gets in her eyes when she's onto something. "What are you going to do?"

"I'm going to do a little investigating myself, brother dear."

LATER THAT NIGHT they moved Dad to the Cardiac Care Unit. Although we could see him through a glass window, Martha and I were not yet allowed in the room with him. He lay so still I had to look carefully for signs of life. The doctor told us he needed triple bypass surgery and they would try to arrange it for tomorrow. Mom told the doctor Dad didn't want the operation. He told us Dad wouldn't live long without it. It was difficult for her, but she still refused to sign the papers.

I tried to get Mom to go home for the night, but she wouldn't leave. Around midnight, I got Martha back home with everything she'd need for the night then dragged myself back to my house and turned the phone on next to the bed in case Mom tried to get hold of me. At 1:45 a.m., it abruptly awakened me and I fumbled to get it. "Hello?" I mumbled.

"Did I wake you?" a female voice whispered.

I sat up in bed. "Sydney?"

"Yes."

"You did, but it's okay."

"I'm sorry."

"No, really, I was dreaming about you anyway, but this is better."

She laughed quietly, then whispered. "I've been worried about you all day and was wondering how things went on the river."

"Why are you whispering?" I asked. She did not respond. "Sydney?"

"I'm sitting in a closet with the door closed."

"Why? What's wrong?"

"He's here."

"Who's there?"

"The guy...I've been living with."

I dropped my head and whispered. "The guy you've been *living with?*"

"It's a long story, but it's over. He's packing his things."

"So, the guy you've been *living with* is moving out?"

"Yes."

I pinched myself to see if I was dreaming. I wasn't. "When was this decided?"

"Today." Silence. "I wanted it over a long time ago. I just didn't have a good enough reason to go through with it. Until now."

"And what's your reason now?"

She hesitated. "It's just time. I called to see if you found out anything new today."

"I surely did. Some positive and some negative."

"Tell me."

I leaned back against the headboard and rattled off the highlights of the day in about fifteen minutes ending with my father lying in Cardiac Care. Sydney got excited about Darla and the boat people, offered sincere condolences about my father, and said nothing at all when I told her about the Jacksons and the DNA. She remained silent.

"Sydney?"

"Yes?"

"Are you okay?"

"I—" She didn't finish.

"What?"

"Why would anyone kill the Jacksons?"

"Could be the people she stole the money from trying to find her just like we were."

"But, how would they have known about the Jacksons?"

"I don't know. Is it that big of a secret?"

She exhaled softly. "I guess not."

"So how was *your* day?"

"Long. Very long. I was up at daybreak."

"Doing what?"

"Thinking."

"And what were you thinking?"

"For one thing, I wondered if you noticed how beautiful the sun looked coming up this morning."

I smiled. "Actually, I did. What else were you thinking?"

"Well...nothing in particular."

"Oh, yes you were. Tell me or I'm going to hang up."

"No you won't."

"Well, tell me anyway."

"I was thinking about you, actually."

"Sydney Deagan, don't you tease me like that."

I could hear her smiling. "Well, that's part of what I was thinking about," she whispered. "But...I know you must be exhausted, so I'd better let you go."

"Are you kidding? I'm wide awake now."

There was another pause then she asked, "Well, how are your cuts today?"

"I think some of them are infected and gangrene might be setting in. Could you rush over and look at them?"

She giggled and it felt like someone had just strummed my heartstrings. I couldn't help myself. *I was in love with the sound of that laughter.*

"I think we'd better say goodnight," she chuckled. "Before we—"

I heard the phone banging around. "Hello? Sydney?"

Then came a man's voice at the other end. "What the hell are you doing in here?"

I heard Sydney reply. "I'm just...sitting here."

"Doing what?"

"Talking to my girlfriend. Do you mind?" A door slammed, the phone rattled, and she whispered, "I better go."

"Are you sure you're going to be okay?"

"I'll be fine."

"Maybe you need to stay somewhere else tonight."

She sighed. "I don't have anyplace to go."

"You sure as hell do. You can come over here."

"I'll be fine."

I was trembling. I closed my eyes, leaned back, and sighed. "Where do you live? What's your address?"

"I'll be fine." Then her voice dropped and she whispered, "I've got to go."

The phone banged against something, then rattled around as if someone was trying to hang it up.

"Sydney?" I whispered.

I heard movement in the background, a TV far off in the distance, white noise. Silence. A commode flushed, followed by the sound of a man's footsteps approaching rapidly and a loud slap before the line clicked off.

"Sydney?"

Damn it!

31

FRANTICALLY, I CHECKED CALLER ID—*Unknown Number*—and the phone directory, but found no listing under Sydney's name. *Son-of-a-bitch!* I jumped in the car and sped to her studio hoping to find some kind of emergency number listed on the front door, but there was nothing. Back at home I lay awake the rest of the night waiting for the phone to ring again. It didn't.

I fixed a pot of coffee and sat at the breakfast table watching the sun come up wondering if Sydney might be watching it as well, wondering what kind of night she'd had.

I took a shower, dressed, remembered the shattered cassette Martha wanted, dug it out of the trash, and gave it to her when I picked her up. We arrived back at the hospital just before 8 a.m., and I noticed Winston sitting in the waiting room on Dad's floor. His hat was tipped down over his face covering his scars. I supposed he was there to support Mom.

"You think he's being a little pushy?" I asked Martha wheeling her down the hall.

"Maybe he just wants to be close by in case something happens and she needs him."

"Nice guy."

Dad was still in Cardiac Care, but was now awake. Mom sat beside him holding his hand and although she looked tired, she looked relieved. When she saw us, she came out to tell us the latest news. It was not good.

"He's had a lot of trouble breathing today and his legs are swelling which they think is because he doesn't have enough circulation in his legs to remove the excess fluid."

"Can't they do anything?"

"They put him on oxygen and they gave him something to help with the swelling, but they said it would probably get worse."

I stood at the glass and watched Dad's chest rise and sink. I wanted to feel what normal people feel when they know they are losing their father, but I felt nothing. It was as if I was looking at someone else's father. Not mine. I'd never had a real father. For me there was nothing to lose. Nothing to miss. There was no love between us and there never had been. And that's what hurt the most. *Why couldn't he love me? What more could I have done?*

A tear strayed down my cheek. Mom saw it, threw her arms around me, and held me. I didn't have the heart to tell her I was crying for *myself,* not him.

We tried to talk Mom into going home and getting some rest, but she wouldn't hear of it. We did talk her into joining us for breakfast at the hospital café. Afterward, I had the chance to spend a few minutes alone with Dad.

The room smelled of alcohol and gauze. The bed was high. The chair was low. The florescent light cold. A tower of electronic equipment next to the head of the bed beeped steadily. All so very uncomfortable and antiseptic. Then he spoke and I realized how well it fit him.

"You got that shit straightened out yet, boy?"

I stuffed my hands into my pockets and fought off the temptation to snap back. "Not yet, Dad."

"Ain't nobody ever disgraced the Baimbridge name like you done."

Here we go again! I looked away—out the window, down the hall to the waiting room. Mom and Winston. He had his hat off and I could see the burn scars from where I stood. He was holding Mom's hand. She was crying.

"Dad?"

"What?" he grunted after a long pause.

I looked at his face. There was a clear tube now wrapped around his ears with a pair of nozzles in his nose. His hair hung in matted clumps around his head. I sighed. "Why is it so hard for you to believe me?"

He pressed a fist against his chest and grimaced. The beeps on the monitor sped up for a few beats, then settled back down.

I hung my head. "Forget it. It doesn't matter."

"I believe what I see, boy. Was that you lying in the street? Was that you I seen on TV?" I didn't answer. "If you didn't do it, what are you doing about it? Huh?" The beeps on the monitor sped up.

"I've found someone who saw this woman that everyone thinks I killed. I gave her name to my attorney. So, I suppose it's just a matter of time now before it all gets cleared up."

"You make damned sure it does. You hear me? Your mother deserves to hold her head high and be respected."

"It will be."

There was a long silence. He closed his eyes and rocked his head back and forth as if he was carrying on a conversation in his mind. I stepped closer. "Dad?"

"What?" he grunted.

My voice fell to a whisper. "I'm sorry I was never able to be the son you wanted." His head turned toward me and his eyes opened, and for the first time in a long time I felt he was actually looking *at* me. As our eyes met, I realized how old and feeble he'd become since I last looked closely at him. "I want you to know that I truly am sorry that I was never able to make you proud, Dad. I swear I tried. Honestly, I did. I guess I just never had the right interests or did the right things or—"

He reached up, grabbed my arm, and pulled me toward him. His eyes bore into mine and his whiskered chin dropped open as he gasped for air. "I'm dying, Rich. My life is over. Ain't no changing what's done now."

His big body looked small, deflated. I stroked the back of the hand that clutched me. "Yeah, I suppose not."

"I wanted a son. More than anything, Rich. I swear to you, more than life itself even. A *real* son. My own flesh and blood. You just have no idea how important it was for me to have a son." His face turned purple and tears pooled in his eyes.

"I'm sorry, Dad. Really, I am. Really...I am."

He reached up with his other hand, grabbed my sleeve, and pulled on me with both hands lifting himself off the bed. He gasped between his words and the beeping on the monitor accelerated like a rollercoaster coming down the first drop. "When you were born," he said, pulling hard at my arm, his eyes jumping back and forth between mine. "You were *perfect*...and I *tried* so hard to love you. God knows I *tried*." He shook and the tears spilled down his face. "You were everything I'd ever wanted, Rich." He strangled on his own tongue. The rate of the beeping increased even further, like a drum roll. I pulled back, but he held tight.

"Dad, please. I didn't mean to start anything. We can do this later. You need to lie back down."

He collapsed against the bed, but pulled on my arm keeping me off-balance and bent over him.

"I'm so...so sorry." His chin quivered. "I just couldn't, Rich. I couldn't love you. I'm sorry."

I felt pressure in my neck and face. "I'm sorry, too, Dad."

"It wasn't your fault. Any man would have been proud to have you as a son." His jaw dropped open and his eyes reached out to me in a way they'd never done before. "Please forgive me, Rich."

I covered his hands with mine and leaned closer. A tear dripped off my chin onto his shoulder. "*Why*, Dad? *Why* couldn't you love me? What was wrong with me? Just tell me that one thing will you please?" He stared into my eyes. The beeping raced faster. My voice became thin and squeaky. "Is that so much to ask? What more could I have done?"

A buzzer on the monitor abruptly shattered the silence of the room. His head jolted back. "Promise me you will never repeat what I am about to tell you for as long as you live."

I leaned closer. "What?"

He pulled me down hard. I heard a rip and felt a button pop free. His teeth were clinched. "Promise me."

"I promise, Dad. I swear."

He fell back against the bed panting. His skin was yellow and scales splotched his face. "You—"

"What?"

He closed his eyes. "You're not mine."

I leaned closer. "What? What, Dad?"

A nurse burst through the door with a hypodermic needle. "You have to leave now."

His voice was just a whisper. "You...are...my...nephew."

"What?" I placed my ear against his lips.

The nurse inserted the needle into Dad's IV tube. "Please. Leave *now!*"

Dad's last words were nothing more than a hiss of air, but I heard them clearly. "Charlie was your father."

Then he collapsed.

32

THE NURSES GOT DAD STABILIZED and sedated while the four of us waited down the hall. Mom, Martha, me, and Winston. I had a thousand questions running through my mind, but for the first time in my life, I felt whole. *And for the first time ever I felt a closeness to Dad.* He said I was *perfect.* I broke down and wept like a grief-stricken mother mourning the death of her child. *My God! I was Charlie's son. Why hadn't someone told me?* Quivering uncontrollably, I sat there in front of the three of them and balled like a baby. They cried, too. Even Winston.

It felt so good, so *liberating*—like I'd been used my whole life to mop the floor and someone had finally rinsed me clean and wrung me out.

Dad had certainly given me a lot to think about. He may technically be my uncle, but on that day he was *my dad.* And all at once, I wanted him to live. For the first time I understood him and wanted to know the rest of the story. I wanted more time with him.

Mom took Martha home, but I hung around the waiting room until a nurse reminded me for the third time that he would not be conscious until much later that day.

I went to my office and sat alone speculating on how it could possibly have happened that Uncle Charles was my dad and no one had spoken about it. *Ever.* I could hardly remember anyone even uttering his name all these years. What had Uncle Charles been like? Who was he? *Who am I?* Is Martha my sister or my half-sister? I had a lot of questions and I wanted some answers.

Lizzy interrupted my thoughts to tell me that Mrs. Sophia Wadsworth was there to see me. She was my staunchest supporter on the Board of Directors of Thalian Hall and I had a feeling why she might be there. I greeted her warmly in the lobby and escorted her to my office where she refused a seat.

"Mr. Baimbridge, I'll not be long." She lowered her eyes, gripped her pocketbook with both hands, and pursed her lips exposing the lines of her seventy-odd years. "Due to recent developments, the Board has decided to engage another director for *Laying Down the Law* and requests that you return the scripts and musical scores at your earliest convenience."

I hated hearing it, but it didn't devastate me as much as I'd thought it would. "I understand."

"I'm sorry, Richard."

"Me, too. Thank you, Mrs. Wadsworth."

She pivoted, opened the door, and left. I'd be lying if I said I wasn't disappointed. Opportunities like that come but once in a lifetime. Yet, with all I had going on, I would not have been able to give it my best effort. I'm sure my stepping aside was better for everyone involved. I was in the process of calling the cast members and asking them to contact the theatre concerning the future of the show when Sydney called.

"All you all right?" I asked.

"Yes. Why?"

"I heard some things before you hung up last night that—worried me. I tried to find your number and call you back."

"Good thing you didn't. That would not have been good."

"It sounded like he hit you."

"I'm okay."

"Did he?"

"It's okay. I'm fine."

I drew a deep breath. "Well, be careful."

She was silent a moment, then said, "The reporters seem to think—to me—they seem to think that...you're..."

Her implication knocked the wind out of me. "Guilty?"

There was a short pause before she answered. "I'm just saying that I think that's what they think."

"What do *you* think?" I asked.

My heart was pounding so loudly, I almost didn't hear her whispered reply. "I don't know."

"Well..." I tried to make the best of it. "I can't imagine how you would, actually."

She changed the subject. "How's your father today?"

I sighed. "He's—not doing too well."

"I'm sorry to hear that."

"Yeah. Thanks. Look, have you had lunch yet?"

There was a long pause before she answered. "No."

"Would you like to run out and get something?"

There was another long pause—so long that I withdrew the invitation. "Never mind. I understand."

"Where?"

"It's okay. We'll do it some other time."

"No, really. Where?"

"Anywhere you like, Sydney. Just name it. I'll buy."

There was another beat of silence. "It would have to be someplace out of the way...that isn't too crowded."

"Well, maybe it's not such a good idea right now."

"I'd love to. Really, but—"

"You don't have to say it. I understand."

"Do you know that gazebo on the back side of Greenfield Lake?"

"Gazebo?"

"It's nice. Just follow Lake Shore Drive around the lake. You'll see it. Meet me in thirty minutes?"

"Yes. That'll be good. I'll bring the food."

"All right."

I'd taken the bike to work figuring I might not have that many more opportunities to ride it before going off to prison, grabbed my jacket and riding helmet, and headed out the door. A thin layer of high clouds diffused the sun and the temperature had risen into the upper sixties—more like the weather should be in Wilmington this time of year. I ducked into the deli next door, picked up a couple of their specialty wraps—a Burro Loco and a Hurricane Duffy—along with some chips, homemade humus dip, and a couple bottles of water. A short time later, I found the gazebo and pulled into the parking lot five minutes early.

I'd played around the lake some as a kid, but it had changed. Or my appreciation of it had. There were azaleas, dogwoods, and crape myrtles in full bloom, pines and oaks dripping with Spanish moss, and patches of manicured green lawns with white benches and this one white gazebo. An elderly man in a shaggy beard sat behind an easel working on a oil painting of the lake and a couple of young lovers cuddled in a car nearby making out.

Springtime in Wilmington! One more thing I would miss about this area.

As I removed my helmet, I spotted Sydney's van through the trees and watched as it rounded the lake to the parking lot next to the gazebo. As she parked and checked her makeup, I dismounted and grabbed our lunches. She opened her door and stepped out wearing a black leotard, sheer black ballet skirt, long white leggings bunched up at the ankles, and black dance sneakers. Reaching back into the van, she grabbed a turquoise sweatshirt that she yanked over her head.

"I had no idea it looked like this back here," I said.

"It's beautiful! Especially this time of the year," she said feeding her ponytail through the back of a blue denim baseball cap as she pulled it down over her head. "Sometimes I just come and sit back here all by myself."

"I can see why."

Sydney shook out her ponytail and closed her door. "How's your face? It looks a little better today."

"It feels a little better, too. Don't you look terrific in your dance clothes."

She smiled. "Thank you." As she stepped past me, our legs brushed against one another and a ripple of electricity shot through me awakening every nerve in my body, setting them on edge. Walking ahead of me, she stepped into the gazebo and took a seat facing the lake. Soft, filtered light reflecting back from the flowers into her face reminded me of an 18th century French impressionist painting and I wished I'd thought to bring a camera.

As I unrolled the wraps, cut them in pieces, and spread the vegetable chips, I felt her eyes studying me. "You've got to have some of everything," I said opening the dip.

She took a small piece and a napkin. "It looks delicious."

As we took our first bites, a pair of white swans sailed in low over the lake, stretched their legs forward, skied across the surface of the water, and then dropped gracefully on it. I swallowed. "I wonder if they realize how magnificent they are. How *free* they are."

"I'm sure they have no idea. They just do what they know to do."

There was a moment of quiet while we ate a couple more bites and washed it down with our drinks. "I don't care what the reporters say," I said. "Or how guilty I look, Sydney, I swear to you on my sister's life I did *not* do what they insinuate I did."

"If I thought you had, I wouldn't be here now," she said scooping a chip in the dip.

"Thanks."

"But this stuff in the news—these serial killings, it's all they talk about at the studio. They're scared to death the next one could be their daughter."

"I'm sure."

"I hope you understand."

"I do. I just hope it ends soon. It's brought my business to a standstill."

"You said your dad isn't doing well?"

"No, he's..." I sighed. "...not."

"I'm sorry."

My mind drifted. I wondered if my *real* dad had ever come here. If he appreciated the beauty of a pair of swans on a lake...or a sunrise on the river...or how beautiful a woman's face can be with soft light coming across it at just the right angle. I wondered if he'd ever been in a play, or walked on the beach at night, or if he would've thought all that to be a lot of nonsense.

"A penny," Sydney interrupted.

"For my thoughts?"

She smiled, "Yeah."

"I was just thinking about you."

"What about me?"

"Sitting in the bottom of a closet. Whispering into a telephone. Wondering why *you*, of all people, would subject yourself to that kind of—"

She looked away. "It's complicated."

"Yes, but is it worth it?"

She twisted the cap off her water and took a drink while her eyes followed the swans as they paddled along the shoreline. "It wasn't always like this. Actually, he really hasn't been around all that much this past year. And it really didn't matter that much...until now. And now, I've asked him to get his things out...and that's what has him upset."

"I wish you had somewhere else you could stay until he's gone."

"Did you bring me out here to talk about Scott?"

"His name is Scott?" I snickered. "Not Scott McGillikin, I hope."

"You know him?"

"Oh, great. Scott McGillikin is my attorney and he knows we were together Saturday. You're my alibi."

Sydney laid her head back and closed her eyes. "I told him I was helping a friend Saturday."

"Well? You were, weren't you?"

She pulled her feet up onto the bench and wrapped her arms around her knees. "We've been together for about five years, but things haven't been all that good for a long time now. I wanted him to move out a year ago, but didn't say anything until yesterday. And when I asked him to leave, he got mad. But he left. Then he came back last night to—to get a few things."

"What did he do?"

"He can be a little strange at times, but he's never been violent before."

"Damn! What did he do? Tell me."

"He—" She dropped her forehead onto her knees.

That son-of-a-bitch! I crammed the rest of my Burro Loco into my mouth and wiped my hands. My eyes burned and my forearms tightened. I grunted. "I'm so sorry, Sydney. He did that because I told me about you going out to the farm with me Saturday."

"Please don't tell him about our date today."

"Don't you worry." I washed the food down with a swallow of water, then turned to face her. "Are we on a date?"

She raised her head and wiped away her tears. "It's the closest thing I've had to one in years."

I drank another sip. "Me, too."

I exhaled, grasped another slice of sandwich, took another bite, and swallowed it nearly whole. "Who do you think that was at the Jackson's window? I don't think it was David. I think he's with Ashleigh."

"Could it have been the murderer?" she asked scooping dip on a chip.

I sipped my soda. "I doubt it. It was probably Mrs. Jackson. Ashleigh could have come for David and told them that there could be some dangerous people looking for her and for them not to take any chances."

"Then you and I show up."

"Exactly."

"Then a short time after we're there someone else shows up and kills them?"

"Right." I took a long drink. "Someone that could very well have been following me."

"You think you're being followed?"

"I don't think I'm the only one looking for Ashleigh."

"Like who else?"

One of the cars in the parking lot started its engine. "Like the guy that knocked me in the head for one."

"Do you think he'll be back to see you again?"

As the car rolled across the parking lot, I noticed a sedan parked up the road with two men in it. One appeared to be looking at us through binoculars. I turned back to face the lake. "Don't turn around. I think someone's watching us."

"What?" Sydney sat up higher, but looked only at me. "Watching us right now?"

"Scott wouldn't have you followed, would he?"

She turned her head slightly and checked the car from the corner of her eye. "The one on the road?"

"Don't look at them."

"I don't know. Maybe."

"It's probably just the police. I'm their prime suspect right now."

"What about the ones that killed the Jacksons? Could it be them?" Her eyes were wide and intense.

I laid my hand on hers and squeezed it. "When you leave here, turn right, and go out the same way you came in. If they follow you,

I'll follow them. If they don't, I'll wait a few minutes, go left, and see if I can tell who they are when I ride by them."

"I'm scared, Richard."

"Just be careful. Keep your doors locked and if they follow you, go someplace where there's a lot of people or to the police station. Just don't let them get close enough to grab you."

"Now you're really scaring me."

I looked into her eyes. "What time do you get off tonight?"

"My last class ends at 9:30. I'll probably be there until 10."

I snatched a pen from my shirt pocket, ripped off a section of the lunch bag, and wrote a phone number on it. "This is my cell number. Call me when you get ready to leave." She folded it and clutched it in her hand. "And let me have your home number." She ripped off another piece of the bag and wrote the number on it.

I read it, then tucked it away. "Okay. You ready to go?"

"I guess." She picked up her keys and water bottle as I put away the trash. I then took her hand and walked her back to her van.

"Be careful, Richard."

"It'll be fine."

She started the van and waited as I straddled the bike and strapped on the helmet. On my signal, she pulled onto the roadway, turned right, and disappeared up the winding tree-lined road. The car with the two men didn't move. I caught a couple more glimpses of her through the trees as she worked her way around the lake, then gunned the bike and eased up to the roadway. I removed my helmet, fiddled with the straps, and wasted time. The men, parked up the road to my left, seemed to ignore me. Finally, I snapped the helmet back on, turned left, and eased off toward them.

As I moved past them, they looked out at the lake to their right. They wore casual clothes—like policemen working undercover—or the FBI. Their license plate was so badly banged up, I could not read the numbers as I rolled past. I opened the throttle, roared up the road around the next bend, and pulled over.

A moment later they passed me heading in the same direction. They saw me, but made no attempt to slow down or stop as I whipped back on the road and dashed off in the direction Sydney had gone, then made a quick left, a right, and another left. I didn't see them again and figured I'd lost them.

33

I RODE TO MOM'S and I found Martha sitting in her wheelchair at the desk in the corner of her room. She was hunkered over a sheet of newspaper with all the parts to the cassette laid out on it.

"Hey, hey! How's it going?" I asked spreading myself across her doorframe.

She raised her hand. "Shhh. Mom's upstairs asleep."

"Oh, sorry."

"What are you so excited about?"

"I just had lunch with Sydney Deagan."

"A date?"

"Sort of." I browsed the bookcase in the hall, removed the oldest photo album, and carried it into Martha's room where I sat on her bed.

"Tell me everything," she said without looking up.

I opened the dark leather cover on the album. It crinkled as it folded back. "Not much to tell. I picked up a couple of wraps and met her at the gazebo on the back of Greenfield Lake."

"Mmmm. Sounds romantic."

"It really was." Each page of the album contained one sepia-toned photograph inside a thick matte with arched tops and gold embellishments. The album looked expensive. "What do you know about Uncle Charles?"

She was leaning over the cassette with a magnifier in one hand and a brush in the other. "Didn't he die kind of young?"

"I think so."

"Nobody's ever talked much about him that I can remember. I just figured he died real young and that was that. Why?"

"Just wondering."

"No, you weren't just wondering. I know you better than that. What made you think about Uncle Charles?" Martha dipped a brush in a dish of white powder and flipped it back and forth across a piece of the cassette case while peering through a magnifier.

"It was just something Dad said this morning."

She twisted around and faced me. "What did he say?"

I turned another page. "I promised him I wouldn't tell anyone."

"Tell anyone what?" Her voice was emphatic, but low.

I raised my index finger to my lips. "Shhh!"

"Don't shush me. Tell me what he said."

"You're the brilliant investigator. Can't you figure it out?"

She turned back to her cassette. "Forget it."

I turned another page and studied the pictures. She pressed a wide strip of cellophane tape to a hunk of the black plastic. "Will you tell me if I guess it?"

"Of course. Now who in here could be Uncle Charles?"

She slowly peeled the tape off the cassette. "No one. That book's too old. That's the early 1900s. There's another one where you found that one."

She pressed the tape onto a square of black paper while I stepped into the hall and exchanged the book for one that was more like a scrapbook. The photos in this one were attached to thick black pages with little black glue-on corners. Some of them had comments written under them in white ink. It was the history of my grandparents, Charles and Georgia Lynn Baimbridge and their children; Beverly, Charles Jr., and Augustus.

There were photographs of the kids as infants, as children on bicycles and ponies, at the beach, and at family gatherings. As the kids got older, there were fewer photos. When I turned the page, I found myself staring at what I'd swear was an old photo of me! A teenage boy with no shirt on, leaning back against a 1950s Chevrolet. His arms were crossed over a strong upper body. Under it was written, "Charlie's first car —1958." His hair was thick, dark, and wavy, and his eyes were deep-set like mine. I jumped off the bed and held the book in front of Martha.

"Look."

She stared at the photo a moment. "What?"

"Who does that look like?"

"Who? What are you getting at?"

She turned the next page and there was a picture of Uncle Charles with a girl under which had been written, "Prom – 1960." Martha gasped and the hairs on my arms stood on end. *The girl was our mom.*

Uncle Charles had on a white dinner jacket and Mom had on a ball gown with a huge corsage pinned to her shoulder. He had his arm around her and a lit cigarette hanging from his lips. They were standing in a line along with dozens of others dressed similarly. Uncle Charles had a mischievous look in his eye. Mom leaned against him with one arm around his back and the other on his chest.

"It looks like Mom used to date Uncle Charles," she whispered.

I didn't say anything. She flipped the last page over. There was a single picture of a crowd of people gathered around a funeral casket holding umbrellas. It was hard to tell who they were. Many held handkerchiefs to their faces. "That's probably Uncle Charles' funeral," I whispered. I found it hard to take my eyes off the photograph.

"So Mom dated Charles before she dated Daddy."

"Looks that way."

"So?"

"So, maybe they were..." I lifted the book over her head and stepped back to the bed where I laid it in front of me and studied the picture of Charles with his arm around Mom. "I wonder how he died."

"What are you saying? That maybe they were lovers?"

"Could have been." I slipped the photo of the two of them from the album and into my shirt pocket.

"Oh, my God!" Martha screamed. "Oh, my God!"

I leapt from the bed. "Wha-a-a-t?"

"Come here! Look at this!"

I left the album on the bed and leaned over her shoulder. She held the magnifier up to me and pointed at the sheet of paper. "Look! Look at this!" She bounced in the chair as I moved around her, held the lens over the print, and looked through it. I saw a partial fingerprint. She tapped a finger on another fingerprint lying next to it. "Compare it to this one."

The one on the sheet was not a complete print either, but what was there appeared to match the other one. "It's the same, isn't it?"

"Son of a bitch!" She wheeled the chair back from under the desk. Her chin quivered and her face turned red. "You know whose print that is?"

"Whose?"

Her eyes glossed over. "That print came from the windowsill at the warehouse. That bastard is still around and has something to do with that house you were in last night."

34

W E GOT THE CALL about four o'clock that Dad was awake and the three of us raced to the hospital as quickly as we could. They let us spend a little time with him separately. Mom went first, then Martha. I stood at the window and watched as he held my sister's hand and cried with her. There was something very strong between them and I realized that Dad could *never* love me in the same way he did Martha. I was not *his* child. Tears blurred my vision. A part of me was relieved that I wasn't. Yet, a part of me wished I *was*.

Later, sitting next to him holding his hand, I saw him differently. I saw him as a man instead of my father. I judged him differently.

I spoke softly. "I found a photo of Uncle Charles and Mom." He didn't say anything, just looked away and nodded. "I was wondering how he died."

"Christ, boy." His voice was tired.

"Do you know? Were you there?"

He covered his eyes with his free hand. His breath whistled out of him like a kettle just pulled off the fire. "Don't ask me to go through that. Not right now."

I squeezed his hand. "Okay."

"You straight with the police yet?"

I exhaled through my nose. "Working on it."

"You're your mom's favorite. Don't break her heart. If you don't do nothing else worthwhile in your life, please get this fixed."

"I will."

"I'd like to see it done before I die, so don't take too long. I ain't got much time."

It was odd to feel important to him, to feel something for him, to care about what he wanted. I squeezed his hand. "I'm working on it." I kissed his forehead, left the room, and took Martha for a walk around the hospital grounds. I parked her chair next to a bench outside and told her what Dad wanted. "I want to get it straight before he dies and I'm going to need some help with it."

"Sure. Anything you want." She lit a cigarette, dropped her lighter in her bag, and took a long pull on it. "But I need you to do something for me, too."

"What?"

"I want you to find out who these people are at that beach house."

"How do I do that?"

"Just go back down there and snoop around a little more. Get license plate numbers, telephone numbers, names and addresses. Whatever you can find."

I placed my hand on her shoulder and leaned closer. "What if these people are the ones that killed the Jacksons?"

"Wouldn't it be nice to have *proof* of that? Wouldn't that get you off the hook? You've got to start somewhere and you've already been there once. You just need to be extra careful."

"You make it sound easy."

"Just remember, these people are dangerous. You don't want to end up like me, or *worse.*"

"Are you trying to encourage me or discourage me?"

She patted my hand. "I don't want to lose my only brother." I laid my head against hers. *Half-brother?* We wrapped our arms around each other and stayed like that for several minutes. When I pulled back and sat up, she squeezed my hand. "So, when can you do it?"

I stood. "It can't wait. I've got to do it tonight."

I left Martha in the smoking area and crossed the parking lot to leave. Stacy Myers, a local TV reporter ran toward me with a cameraman in tow.

"Richard! Richard! Can I have a word with you?"

Her medium length blond hair had been pinned back on the sides and she was dressed in a dark blue business suit. She carried a microphone in her hand and ran awkwardly on high heels.

"Sorry Stacy, but I have nothing to say," I shouted without slowing.

She kept running alongside me. "Please, if you don't tell your side of the story, the media will create it for you." I had gone through a lot of trouble to avoid the media, but Stacy had been a roommate of my sister's after they'd graduated from college. She was a friend. I stopped and turned to her. "Just a few questions," she said as the cameraman threw his camera up on his shoulder while running to catch us.

"No, Stacy. I had nothing to do with what happened to Ashleigh."

"Then tell it on camera. Let the people see you say it."

I expelled a heavy sigh. "I can't. I'm sorry. You're on your own with this one." As I turned, the cameraman grunted and lowered his camera.

She followed. "Come on, Rich! Give me something."

I turned back. "Okay, question: Where's the body?"

"Huh?"

"Where's the body, Stacy?"

She pulled a loose spring of blond hair out of her face. "That's what I want to ask you."

"Why do you even think she's dead?"

"Well, isn't she?"

"See? You're making the same mistake as everyone else."

"What else can I think?"

"Exactly!"

She stamped her foot. "Exactly what?"

"You think she's dead because her house *looks* like a murder took place there. But what if she staged this whole thing and took off never to be seen or heard from again?"

"Why would she do that?"

"Now you're thinking!" Stacy was a smart girl, but had fallen into the trap of being too beautiful and wasn't thinking. "And that, Stacy, is the best I can do for you. Sorry."

She sighed, but didn't follow when I walked off.

Back at home, I tuned through all the local TV newscasts. Everyone was reporting the Jackson murders and my presence there. One reporter even asked the Police Commissioner why I was still free.

"We're keeping a close eye on him," the Commissioner told him.

Then the reporter asked him, "Just how long do the citizens of Wilmington have to wait for Richard Baimbridge to be locked up behind bars where he belongs?"

I didn't wait for his answer. I shut the TV off, hurled the remote against the fireplace, and hoped Mom was still at the hospital and had not seen any of that.

I poured a scotch, gulped it, and poured another that I carried out on the deck. The sun had set, but the clouds still had a bright pink glow to them in the west. Settling into a chair, I brought the glass to my lips, but before I could take a sip, my cell phone rang.

"Hello?"

"Hi." The female voice was low and depressed.

"Sydney?"

"Yeah," she whispered.

"What's wrong?"

"Everything."

"Tell me."

"The parents want me to get another photographer."

I closed my eyes and exhaled. "I was afraid something like this might happen. I'm really sorry."

Her voice dropped back to a whisper. I could tell she was crying. "I've got to go. My next class is waiting."

"Okay. I'll call you later."

"Okay."

"I'm sorry, Sydney."

"Me, too." She hung up.

My heart ached for her. I only agreed to do the photographs in the first place because I wanted to make things easier for her. Now I'd turned into a bigger problem than she'd had to begin with.

I rose from the lounge chair, slung the liquor from my glass into the yard, kicked a broken limb off the deck, and gathered together the things I'd need to go back to the house at the beach.

35

I COULD SEE THE BEACH HOUSE from a half mile away, a crystal castle rising out of the darkness. I cut through to the beach where I rode the bike along that strip of firm sand at the edge of the water, then killed the engine, and hid it in the dunes within fifty yards of the house. If I needed to get away quickly, I'd have a better chance on the beach than on the highway. I opened the saddlebag, retrieved a pair of binoculars, and settled down in the dunes to watch the place.

No one was outside. I panned the binoculars window to window, switched my cell phone off, and moved along the dunes toward the back of the house. From there, I could see into the lighted rooms on the first and second floors, but curtains were drawn across a brightly-lit chamber on the third floor. Three women were curled in chairs in the screening room watching a movie on the giant TV screen.

I made a wide arc around to the house across the street from where I could see up under the beach house. There was a black Cadillac Escalade parked under the house, but the Corvette was not there so I figured John-Boy was probably not there either. I pulled the cell phone from my jacket, turned it on, and called Martha. "It's me. I'm here. Write this down." I pulled a piece of paper from my pocket and read her a phone number.

"What's that?"

Holding the phone with my shoulder, I ripped up the sliver of paper. "It's Sydney's phone number. I forgot to leave it at home and I don't want to have it on me if anything should happen."

"Do you see a house number? I can pull up the county GIS map and find out who owns it and where they live."

"Not from here. I'll have to get closer."

"Please be careful."

The black Corvette I'd seen before came into view, slowed, and turned up the driveway across the street. "He's back."

"Who?"

"The guy I followed down here before. I'll call you later."

"Richard?"

"What?"

"Please be careful."

"I will. Got to go. I'll call you later." I turned the phone off and moved closer to the house staying out of sight. The Corvette was there, but John-Boy had disappeared. As I approached the car, a sliding door upstairs opened and two sets of shoes shuffled awkwardly across the porch above and started down the stairs. I sprang back into the shadows and watched as two men stumbled toward me carrying the body of a young woman. Her right arm dragged the cement as they scuffled toward the Cadillac SUV. One of the men was Fat Albert. The other, Latino, supported the girl's legs as they slung her onto the back seat. They closed the door, shared a private laugh, and disappeared up the steps.

I crept up to the vehicle and through the window I could see that she had red hair. Easing the car door open, I leaned in, and saw that it was Angie. I pressed a finger against her neck but, before I could find a pulse, I heard voices, closed the door with my hip, and crouched behind the car.

"Don't speed," an older man was saying to a younger man as they came down the stairs. "Don't run any red lights and don't get in any wreck." The man speaking had a heavy high-tider accent, thick eyebrows, and a thick mustache. I assumed the younger one was John-Boy, but couldn't raise up to get a better look.

"Yes sir, Mr. Bonner," the youth said.

"And make damned sure *nobody* sees you."

"I will."

"Aye'm countin' on you, Greg."

"You know I always come through for you, Mr. Bonner."

Through the vehicle's windows I saw Mr. Bonner grasp hold of the younger man's shoulder. "You're my number one."

"Thank you, sir."

The car door clicked open.

"And you come straight to my office soon's you get back," Bonner told him.

"Yes, sir."

"You're the man."

"Thank you, sir."

As the Escalade's engine started, I dropped onto my belly with the intention of hiding under the Corvette, but the car was too low and the stitches on the back of my head struck against the steel frame setting my head on fire. Pressing a hand against my skull, I furled off the cement and skirted around the back of the Corvette not noticing my phone had slipped from its holder. Bonner walked along with the vehicle as it backed out, watched the guy turn the SUV around, and then headed back up the stairs as the Cadillac turned left out of the driveway.

Running through tall sea oats, I trampled over dune after dune to the bike, jerked the helmet on, and cranked the engine as the Escalade disappeared up the beach road. With a rear tire spinning in the sand, I bounced wildly across the empty lot next door to the beach house, skidded onto the roadway, and sped off southward after the Cadillac.

HEARING THE SOUND of the motorcycle, Dane Bonner veered out the front door of the beach house in time to see the bike racing after the Cadillac. He dove down the front steps, spotted a cellular phone lying on the cement, snatched it up as he hopped into the Corvette, and brought the mega-V-8 engine to life. Tossing the phone into the passenger's seat, he squalled onto the highway and floored the gas pedal. The car rocketed up the highway.

I PUSHED THE BIKE up to sixty-five and kept it there until I had to slow for an elderly woman making a left turn. Skirting around her on the sandy shoulder, I sighted the Escalade's taillights several blocks ahead. I reached for my phone to call Sam Jones and let him know what I'd seen, but the phone was *gone!* All I could do was follow and find out what he was going to do with Angie, and then let Sam know later.

There were six or seven cars between us and traffic was moving slowly. The cool night air felt twenty degrees colder on the bike. My heart raced, my legs trembled, and the helmet cut into the stitches in my head with every bump. I zipped the windbreaker up to my neck and stuffed my left hand into the jacket pocket to get it out of the cold.

I wondered if Angie could still be alive. Life is so precious. To even be born is a billion to one shot. And then, it's too short. And can be lost so easily, or *taken* from you. Regardless of your plans and dreams, or how many there are that love you.

As I kept my eyes on the Escalade's taillights, my thoughts drifted to Uncle Charlie—*my dad!* I pictured him cruising along this road in that Chevy with the radio up and the windows down, a cigarette hanging from his lips—revving his engine when he passed a good-looking girl. I wondered what kind of person he was, if he had many friends, or if he was a loner like me. *I have to talk to Mom. She can't keep him locked up forever. I deserve to know.*

The SUV slowed, turned left into the crowded parking lot at *Lloyd's Seafood Restaurant*, and disappeared behind the building. Traffic came to a stop in front of me and pedestrians prevented me from passing. I placed a foot on the roadway to hold the bike up and kept my eye on the restaurant.

"Hey, how 'bout a ride, cutie?" a female called out. I turned to see three young teenage girls standing in front of a nightclub, giggling and holding on to each other to keep from falling over. Less than a week ago Angie had been young, adventurous, and wild. Now she might be dead.

"You girls ought to go on home and thank the Lord you're still alive."

"Screw you!" one shouted stumbling back off the road. "We'll just find somebody else to party with."

If only they knew what dangers lay in wait for them.

The cars moved on and a moment later, the Escalade pulled back onto the roadway coming straight toward me. As we passed I saw his face clearly. Greg was John-Boy. I rolled into the restaurant's parking lot and circled around back. A bright light buzzed overhead and it smelled like a city landfill. Stacks of flattened and not-yet-flattened cardboard boxes surrounded two black metal dumpsters sitting back against a wooden fence with their lids closed. A leaking water hose lay across the asphalt and a mop leaned against the building next to a rear door. I felt Angie was there somewhere, but I didn't see her.

BONNER SLOWED as he neared the restaurant, snatched up the cell phone he'd found, turned it on, and dialed 9-1-1. When the operator answered he panted wildly and shouted, "A man on a motorcycle just dumped a woman's body behind Lloyd's Seafood Restaurant at Wrightsville Beach. *Hurry! He's still there!*" He pressed the button to end the call and looked back at the restaurant when the phone in his hand rang. Feeling exuberant, he answered the call dragging his voice. "Yes?"

After a second of hesitation, a female spoke. "Richard?"

Bonner smiled. "Sorry sweetheart. From the looks of things I'd say Richard's a little busy right now." He looked back in the mirror waiting for the motorcyclist to emerge from behind the restaurant. "But I'll be glad to give him a message for you."

Waiting for the woman to respond, he chuckled aloud. Then she said, "Scott?"

Looking down, he saw the number showing in the window. *Shit!* He ended the call and tossed the phone out the window.

I SET THE KICKSTAND ON THE BIKE and charged into the pile of empty boxes tossing them aside and milling into them in search of Angie. It didn't take long for me to realize she wasn't there. Vaulting to one of the two large metal garbage containers, I hoisted one of its lids and was engulfed by the odor of rancid food. Holding my breath, I shoved the cover back and there, immersed in table scraps and rotting meat, lay Angie—her legs twisted at awkward angles and her eyes gazing through me in a death stare.

Startled, I drew back, then sprung forward, leaping onto the side of the container, reaching into the opening to touch her neck.

"Angie!"

As I leaned farther, balancing on the lip of the opening checking for a pulse, two cars skidded to a stop behind me. I bounded back from the hatchway as the doors on both police cars flung open and cops dived out of each crouching near the ground with their revolvers trained on me.

"Freeze!" they shouted in unison.

I raised my arms and, twisting, pointed toward Angie. "There's a girl in there! I was checking to see if she's still alive."

"On the ground. Now!"

M ARTHA AIMLESSLY SURFED the TV channels while waiting to hear from Richard. When the phone rang, she snapped it up immediately.

"Hello?"

"Martha, this is Sydney Deagan."

"Hey! Richard told me he'd seen you. How've you been?"

"I just called his cell phone and someone else answered."

Martha pushed up in the bed. "Are you sure you called the right number? "

"Yes!"

"He went to Wrightsville beach to do something for me."

"I know, but something must have gone wrong."

The TV station broke into their regular programming with a special report. "Hold on a second," Martha said. "There's something's happening on TV." Martha raised the volume.

"...body of a young female was discovered just minutes ago behind a restaurant in Wrightsville Beach. Police at this time have not identified the girl and are giving no other details. We have a team headed there now and we'll bring you more information as we get it."

Martha flung the covers aside ignoring the pain shooting into one ankle. "They found another girl's body. This one down at the beach. I have to go down there. Can you come and get me? I'm at mom's."

"Yes. Be there in fifteen minutes."

Martha ended the call and tried Richard's number. When she got no answer, she hung up the phone, reached for her wheelchair, and snuggled it tightly against the side of her bed. Shifting her legs as far left as she could, she lowered the bed and used her hands to "walk" backward onto the chair dragging her legs with her. Then, seized by a hot burning sensation in her right ankle, she squeezed her fingers deep into the flesh trying to work the pain out, but soon had to abandon it, pulling on her shoes and jacket, rolling out the front door just as Sydney's van arrived.

PARKING NEXT TO THE CORVETTE, Greg went directly to Mr. Bonner's office where he found him loading stacks of file folders into cardboard boxes.

"You get that license plate changed back?" Bonner asked.

"Yes, sir."

"Good." Bonner pulled an envelope from his pocket. "Here's two thousand dollars cash, a map to a place aye have in Boone, and key to the house." He lifted an old leather satchel and handed it to Greg. A small lock fastened the zipper closed. "Aye want you to take this bag and the Corvette and wait there until you hear from me."

Greg closed his fingers on the envelope. "Tonight?"

"Don't even bother to pack. Things are happening fast. Use the money to buy some new clothes and whatever food you'll need. Aye'll be there in a couple of days. And don't let this bag out of your sight until you get there." He put his arm on Greg's shoulder. "Aye'm counting on you, Greg."

"Yes, sir. No problem." Greg took the bag, stuffed the envelope into a back pocket, and walked out shifting the bag to his other hand.

Bonner paused briefly to gaze at the ocean. This had been his favorite place, but if Richard Baimbridge had been there, then the police could not be far behind. He climbed the stairs to the third floor and unlocked a panel in the production studio. Noting the time was 11:34 p.m., he set the timer in the panel to one hour and fifty-six minutes, yanked a red lever one turn counter-clockwise, and withdrew a black leather bag.

Back in his office, he locked the door, closed the curtains, and laid the contents of the black bag in front of him. A respirator mask, goggles, thick rubber gloves, and a bottle of *potassium cyanide*.

He opened a box of sleeping capsules, dumped half of each capsule's contents into the trash, and—with the respirator, gloves, and goggles on—refilled them with the deadly white powder. Forcing the capsules back together, he wiped them clean and dropped them into an empty medicine bottle.

Tossing the gloves, goggles, and respirator into the trash, he unlocked the door and located Albert on the second floor.

"Find César and send him to my office."

"Yes sir."

"And give each of the girls one of these." He handed Albert the bottle of capsules. "Make sure they take it. Aye want them to get a good night's sleep and be ready to start early in the morning."

37

S YDNEY DROVE SLOWLY up the beach highway as she and Martha scrutinized the houses along the oceanfront looking for Richard's bike. Cars backed up behind them and gunned around them when opportunities arose.

"It's got to be somewhere along here," Martha whispered. "It's not much farther to the end of the road."

An impatient driver pulled out to pass just as a pair of headlights up the road turned onto the highway facing them. But instead of pulling back in behind her, the car sped up in an effort to get around her and abruptly veered to the right cutting them off. Jerking the wheel to the right, Sydney locked the brakes, her van skidding off the highway bouncing to a stop in deep sand as the two opposing cars continued on, as though nothing had happened.

Sydney whispered, "You okay?"

Pulling on the handle above her door, Martha winced. "I think so."

Restarting the engine, Sydney tried to move the van, but the rear tires spun freely in the loose sand.

Martha pointed out the windshield. "Hello. Could that be it?"

With her foot off the gas Sydney surveyed the three-story house sitting high above the sand just up the road. "See any sign of Richard?"

"That's got to be the place. Pull up so we can get a better look."

Sydney pressed the gas and again the rear tires spun freely in the loose sand. "Haven't you noticed? We're stuck!"

"Okay, let's not worry about that right now. You need to find Richard and whatever else you can about this house. Names, addresses, license numbers, phone numbers—"

"Me? What do you want me to do, break in?"

Martha sighed. "Sydney, I swear. One of us has to do it. It's you or me."

Sydney pressed her foot on and off the gas pedal, rocking the van back and forth. "No...no..."

Martha unbuckled her seatbelt. "Then I'm going in. I just need a little help getting into that chair."

Sydney banged her palms against the steering wheel. "Wait! Please!"

"Somebody in that house shoved me off a platform paralyzing me for life, and now, something's happened to Richie. *One* of us has to go in."

"Give me a second. Let me *think!*"

"If you get caught, you can tell them we got stuck in the sand and you're looking for somebody to help get us out."

"You think they'll fall for that?"

"Well, I'm not leaving without *something*. The house number. License plate numbers. Something! *And Richie could be in there!*"

"Okay! Okay!" Sydney turned the key and the engine stopped. She grabbed a pad and pencil from her purse, took a few slow deep breaths, then trudged across a wide stretch of deep sand, crouching on her hands and knees as she approached the brightly-lit house.

With a steady wind whipping at her hair and pelting her skin with sand, she lurked in thick sea oats searching for the house number. Failing to find it, she sprinted up under the house to the rear of the only vehicle there—a black Cadillac Escalade—and with trembling hands scribbled the South Carolina license number in her notepad.

Peering in a window, she spotted an envelope on the front seat, squeezed the door handle, and—just as the catch released—heard voices and footsteps coming down the stairs. With her heart pounding the walls of her chest, Sydney leapt into the darkness under the front stairway and flattened herself behind a row of small bushes as two men appeared on the stairs carrying open cardboard boxes. As they placed them in the vehicle's trunk, the wind peeled away several loose papers and jammed them in the shrubbery around Sydney.

"I get 'em," one said with a Latino accent.

"Aye'll get them," the other man insisted. "You get the shovels."

"Si."

As the Latino crossed to a utility room within five feet of Sydney, the other rounded up the loose papers tangled in the bushes. Pressing back farther into the darkness, she tensed, ready to bolt if she was discovered. As the man drew closer and reached for a sheet of newspaper that had caught on Sydney's heel, she shook her foot and the page sailed away tumbling across the empty lot next door.

"I get it," the Latino said sliding two shovels into the rear of the car.

"Forget it. Let's go."

The men closed the back of the vehicle, got in, and cranked the engine. As they pulled away and headed down the highway, Sydney grabbed her notepad and ran for the van, snatching the loose section of newspaper from the dune fence next door on the way. Jumping into the driver's seat, she tossed the pad and newspaper to Martha, burst into tears, and started the van.

"What happened?"

"I wet my damned pants!"

"Did you really?"

"They came out while I was there." Sydney jammed the gearshift into drive and floored the gas pedal. The engine raced, but the vehicle only moved slightly.

Martha held up the newspaper. "What's this?"

"They were putting some boxes in the trunk and some things blew out!"

"This is it? This is all you got?"

Sydney pumped the gas pedal and rocked the van back and forth. "And the license number of the car that just left."

"Okay! That's more like it!"

With smoke rising from the spinning rear tires, the back of the van slowly drifted toward the road. "Come on-n-n!" Sydney screamed holding the pedal against the floor. "One of them walked right by me to get a pair of shovels."

"Shovels?"

"He put them in the trunk with the two cardboard boxes."

"My God! They're going to bury whatever's in those boxes."

"It was just a bunch of papers. Some of it blew out including that piece of newspaper."

"We've got to follow them!"

"Haven't you noticed? We're stuck!"

"Floor it!"

Sydney jammed the gas pedal against the floor again and held it there while the two of them rocked back and forth in their seats, nudging the van forward as smoke from the spinning tires drifted across the road. When headlights appeared up the highway coming toward them, Sydney turned on the vehicle's lights, but kept her foot on the gas. Back and forth they rocked as the car drew nearer. Suddenly, the rear tires found solid ground and the van lurched onto the highway directly into the path of the approaching vehicle.

"Shit!" Martha cried clutching the door handle as the oncoming car braked and skidded past them with its horn blaring.

"Sorry," Sydney said, correcting the van with the steering wheel as it fishtailed across the highway. "I was afraid it would do that."

Martha laid her head back against the seat and exhaled. "Forget the car. Let's just go see what we can find out about this license plate number."

38

A FEW MILES NORTH of Wilmington on US 17, Bonner turned into a new subdivision under construction. He rolled past numbered stakes, road-building equipment, utility connection boxes, and new curbing to where the pavement ended and the road surface turned to rock. But the rock was hard and the shovels were of little use against it. Bonner tossed his aside, climbed on a nearby backhoe, and started the engine. He fiddled with the controls learning what each does, then clumsily maneuvered the machine to the spot they'd tried to dig, lowered its giant scoop to the rock, and powered it into the dirt. The engine groaned and the machine rose off the ground and warbled against the strain, but it dug into the rocks and opened a hole in the dirt. Moving levers back and forth, Bonner raised the scoop, shifted it to the side, and released the dirt away from the hole.

"I think I got it now!" he shouted over the roaring of the engine. He swung the scoop back over the hole, dug deeper, and again dropped the dirt next to the hole. Noticing a pipe in the hole, César jumped in front of the machine waving his arms.

"What?" Bonner shouted over the rattle of the machine.

César pointed to a four-inch pipe running along the side of the hole. "Water line!"

Climbing down, Bonner saw where the scoop had scraped along the length of the pipe, but it had remained intact. He climbed back on the machine, moved the scoop a little to the right, and dug again into the street. Within ten minutes, he had opened a hole five feet deep, five feet wide, and at least eight feet long. He left the machine running and climbed down.

"Get in the hole," he said. "Aye'll pass the boxes down to you."

"Si."

Bonner brought each box to the hole and handed it down to César who nudged it into the loose dirt at the bottom. As he handed the last one down, Bonner pulled a pistol, aimed, and fired, hitting

César in the center of his back. The explosion reverberated through the subdivision and echoed off into the night. César's body lurched around and landed face up lying over the boxes. His disbelieving eyes stared back at the gun. Raising a hand, he pleaded, "Por favor no dispare otra vez, Señor Bonner. Please, no shoot."

Bonner raised the gun a second time, aimed, and squeezed the trigger. This bullet opened a small hole in César's forehead and exited the rear of his skull grazing the water pipe causing a dark geyser to spout from the man's forehead and an almost invisible misty spray of water behind his head.

Flinging the gun into the hole, Bonner climbed back onto the machine, filled the dirt in, and returned the backhoe to where he'd found it.

He gathered rocks and spread them evenly over the freshly filled hole until he was satisfied that no one would know they'd been there. It was now 12:58 a.m.

AT WRIGHTSVILLE BEACH MUNICIPAL COMPLEX, Chief Milton Simmons was trying to get things straight in his head. "So, you— Richard Baimbridge—who just happens to be under investigation in the disappearance of another girl, lose your phone and minutes later it gets picked up by someone who just *happens* to see a man on a motorcycle drop off a dead girl behind Lloyd's and uses *your* phone to call 9-1-1 and report it. Is that what you're saying?"

I didn't blame the chief for being confused. I was confused myself—and I'd been there. "I'm saying, yes, I lost my phone, and I had nothing to do with putting that body behind that restaurant although I do *know where it came from and how it got there*."

"But *you* didn't put it there."

"Do you really think I could have carried a dead body across town on a motorcycle without somebody noticing it?"

"Somebody did notice. They called 9-1-1."

"On *my* phone."

"The fact he was on your phone proves to me that he was *at least* in close proximity to you."

"Oh, come on! You know damned well that would never happen."

"I've seen stranger things than that," he said holding his gaze on me, his feet propped on a chair.

So that's where I was sitting at 1 a.m. when the door opened and Sam Jones walked in. I never imagined I could be so happy to see Sam Jones.

When I told Sam what I'd seen, he was only slightly more willing than the chief to give me the benefit of the doubt. Ten minutes later he, Simmons, and I were cruising up the island toward the beach house. They rode in front and I rode in the "cage." My hands were cuffed, but not behind my back. Two other officers followed in a separate car and the chief radioed two more with instructions to head that way. Traffic had thinned and the ride took no more than seven or eight minutes. I pointed out the house and the chief pulled up the winding drive stopping just short of going under the building. The second car pulled in behind us.

Jones and the chief left me in the cage and climbed the long staircase to the front door. The other two made a wide circle around the house. A third police car pulled onto the grass at the end of the drive and parked. Laying my face against the side window, I could barely see Chief Simmons knock at the front door and Fat Albert step out, but could hear nothing. The clock on the car dash read 1:21 a.m. I sat back in the seat and waited.

One of the roving officers—a tall, muscular black man with a two-day beard—strolled up under the house and studied a wet spot on the cement. He looked up at the source—a drip under the edge of the house—then stooped, touched his finger to it, and smelled it. He then called the other roving officer over who also stooped and smelled it. Together they shined their lights up at the underside of the house. The black officer pressed the button on the microphone attached high on his shirt and spoke into it. A moment later, Jones and the chief came running down the front steps to examine the puddle. *Something was wrong.*

I sat forward gripping the bars separating me from the front seat and watched as all four men backed away then charged up the stairs and disappeared into the house. The clock read 1:27 a.m. I pressed my head far back in the rear window, looked up, and saw lights coming on throughout the house.

One of the officers staggered out the front door carrying a limp young female in his arms followed by Fat Albert struggling to carry another. They carted them down the stairs, away from the building, and placed them on a patch of grass halfway to the road. Detective Jones and the chief together were attempting to carry a third female down the steps when a massive explosion blew the roof off the house and rattled the car knocking Jones, the chief, and the girl off the steps onto the front lawn.

A huge fireball bellowed high into the night sky carrying with it pieces of the building that shot skyward then fell back to earth, some up to a hundred feet away. Flames leapt through windows that had been blown out and cracks that had appeared in the walls. Jones shoved an officer—whose hair and clothes were on fire—to the ground, rolled him, and beat out the flames.

A section of second story exterior wall gave way and crashed down on the hood of the police car smothering it in sparks, embers, and splintered construction materials. The impact crushed the hood of the car and bounced me against the ceiling. Flames spread up the windshield and I could instantly feel the heat through the glass.

There were no door handles in the rear to open the doors. I pressed a button there to lower the window, but it didn't work. I tried the one on the other side, and it, too, didn't work. I waved my hands in the back window and shouted, "Hey! Hey!"

Smoking debris lay scattered throughout the front yard and surrounding empty lots. Two of the officers dashed up the steps and into the house. A third helped the chief to his feet and a fourth began dragging the unconscious girls farther from the inferno, one at a time.

The temperature inside the car was rising. The inspection decal on the windshield bubbled, curled away from the glass, and dropped onto the dash. With sweat beading on my face, I kicked at a side window, again and again, but the window refused to break. Another chunk of debris smashed onto the hood of the car and sparks spewed past the windows. The air was getting hot, and thick with the taste of ashes and glue. I pounded the glass with my elbow and screamed, "Get me out of here!"

Cars had begun pulling off the road and there were people running back and forth seeming not to know what to do. A man was giving mouth-to-mouth respiration to one of the girls. The plastic padding on the dash began smoking, then bubbled like boiling water. The mirror mounted to the windshield wilted, slid down the glass, then dropped off. I lunged to the floor and looked up under the front seat. There was nothing there but paper trash.

Smoke now filled the interior of the chief's car and I could no longer see the windows. Perspiration soaked my clothes, and my lungs choked on the thick cloud. The fire had moved under the car and now totally engulfed it in flames. The heat was unbearable.

My God! Is this how my life is going to end? What is Mom going to think? And Dad?

I sucked at the cooler air under the seats, gagging and choking on the smoke. Another massive crash hit the car and I felt glass scatter over me. I tried to rise up, but couldn't move. The heat was too intense to even breathe. I held my breath listening to the rumble, hiss, and sizzle of the fire. Outside, I could hear the wail of fire trucks and the shouting of the crowd, then pounding on the car.

"Baimbridge!" The pounding continued. "Baimbridge!"

I felt the spray of cool water douse my hot skin. I heard the pounding of metal against metal and more glass shattering. I felt the pressure of the water as it washed me down and heard the sizzle of it as it turned to steam. My mind was awake, but my body was asleep. I felt myself being lifted and watched as though I was a witness—as though I was outside of my body seeing myself pass through the back glass into the arms of the firemen.

I saw myself carried to the patch of green grass and watched an EMT perform resuscitation. I saw the flames leaping a hundred feet in the air and the walls of the building collapse. Then everything turned white and faded away.

39

D ANE BONNER TURNED OFF Highway 133 west of Wilmington near Kendall Chapel and guided his Escalade through thick brush along an overgrown dirt trail leading back to a nineteenth-century farm house. He'd stolen the property from a client that had gotten the death penalty for the rape, torture, and murder of an eleven-year-old boy the man had picked up hitch-hiking. Although it was located in Brunswick County, it was just minutes from Wilmington along the western side of the lower Cape Fear River—a tract he now called "The Bonner Place."

The two-story frame house had been built in the late 1800s and had been wired for electricity later with exposed cables running up and down the outside of the house. The barns and sheds had been added in the more affluent 1950s. Behind the barn, there was a bulkhead and dock on the river. He got out of his car, pulled open the front doors to the barn and parked the car inside.

Bonner lit a kerosene lantern, unbolted the front door to the house, and stepped into a narrow hallway. There were doors on his left and right and stairs going up to the second floor. The house had not been cleaned or even opened for fresh air in two decades. A hole in the roof had gone unattended for years and the air reeked of dampness, mold, and bird droppings. The wallpaper throughout the house had turned dark brown and, in places, drooped from the walls like pig's ears. Cobwebs shadowed all corners and the floors were barely visible under a chalky layer of dust. He stepped into the front room to his left and walked to a metal table placed against a dark window. The corner of the room nearest the center of the house had a fireplace set in it at a 45-degree angle that shared a chimney with a fireplace in the next room. Behind the wire grill were the carcasses of black birds and squirrels unfortunate enough to get trapped in the chimney. In the room beyond, a double window was completely covered over by a hardy sprig of poisonous *Carolina Jessamine* that had somehow managed to find its way through the floor and now sought a way out.

Bonner sat, struck a long wooden match, lit a pair of oil lamps that he pulled in close to his face, and leaned forward to evaluate his reflection in a magnifying mirror set on a wire stand.

The time was near for Dane Bonner to reclaim his body.

Dipping a cotton swab into an aging glass bottle of mineral spirits, he dabbed the solution into his thick black mustache and heavy eyebrows to dissolve the glue that held them in place. Slowly the gum released the pieces of his disguise and he peeled them off one at a time, being careful not to rip the skin. Still the glue irritated his face and left a rash above his lip and eyebrows that he smeared with cold cream.

Wetting a fingertip on his tongue, he removed the dark brown contact lenses that hid his fiery blue eyes, put them away, and combed styling gel through his graying hair. After giving the cold cream one last blending, he donned a pair of designer eyeglasses and checked his reflection.

Soon. Very soon.

Leaving, he climbed into the other car parked in the garage—a silver Porsche Boxster—and fired up the brassy engine.

EIGHTY-FIVE MILES AWAY, Greg Walker eased off I-40 near Calypso at its intersection with US 701, turned right, and pulled up to a gas pump at a truck stop. The parking lot was overrun with tractor trailers, campers, and overnight travelers hoping to make better time driving at night. As he inserted the fuel nozzle and squeezed the trigger, he also pressed his legs together and scanned the building for a restroom. The cool air made the urgency in his bladder worse as he shuffled from foot to foot. On the opposite side of the pump, an older woman with a bold streak of gray in her hair filled the tank while a younger woman and two kids slept in their station wagon.

When the nozzle finally tripped off, Greg slapped it back on the pump, screwed the cap back in place, and loped toward the entrance holding his side. He brushed past a drifter sitting next to the door holding a sign that read *Memphis,* straightened up as best he could, and hustled as casually as possible toward the men's room at the rear of the store.

Banging into an empty stall, he gripped the handicapped bar, closed his eyes, and released his bladder. The ground shook and the building rattled. His head jerked around as multiple car alarms went off simultaneously and people began shouting and screaming. A sprinkling of dust drifted by his eyes and settled on his shoulders as he held his position until the last of the liquid dribbled from his bladder.

When he left the restroom, the screams and blaring horns grew louder and he instantly felt the heat from the enormous fire burning in the parking lot. His shoes skidded on tiny squares of glass from the windows blown in along one side of the building. Stepping out through an opening now missing its glass, he saw men struggling against the heat trying to get close to a car on fire at an exit to the parking lot, and another man running toward the fire with a large hand-held fire extinguisher. The woman driving the station wagon rammed the car behind her, shoving it out of her way while the children in the back seat screamed.

Another explosion propelled the burning car up and backward toward the gas pumps. Flames leapt fifty feet into the air and everyone scattered for cover. The attendant hit the emergency kill switch and waved everyone away. "Get back!"

Greg ran toward the spot where he'd left the Corvette, but it was not there. He turned in a circle looking for it and ran to the middle of the parking lot searching the entire area. He turned back to the burning car and his eyes fell on the silhouette of the man inside slumped against the steering wheel—his clothes on fire—then moved down to the wheels. Polished chrome wheels. *Corvette wheels.* A tire blew and Greg began to shake. Just a little at first, then an uncontrollable violent rattling of his bones. His knees became weak and his lungs spasmed. He backed away, turned, and stumbled back into the building, snatched a cold soda and a map, tossed five dollars on the counter, and walked down the road heading back toward I-40.

Looking over his shoulder, he could see the glow of the fire and thick black smoke curling into the night sky, sparks shooting upward like fireflies.

As fire trucks and police cars wailed by, he flipped his collar up, crossed the highway, and stuck his thumb out.

40

A S THE WHITE LIGHT FADED I could see the doctor and nurses working around me. I lay lifeless on my back with my arms at my sides, my pants and shirt gone. A doctor scrubbed two paddles together and placed them on either side of my bare chest. Everyone stepped back.

"Clear!"

A tone sounded and as the capacitors discharged, the lights dimmed and my body jolted off the gurney. I had the revolting sensation of being sucked through a tunnel and slammed into a concrete wall. Then it happened again.

"Clear!"

Again, the capacitors discharged. Lightning streaked through my brain and my heart vaulted. Faces and events streamed by. Mom, Dad, and me. My sister jumping in the surf at the beach. Sydney at thirteen, ducking away from me laughing and running. Martha in cap and gown crossing a stage. An ivy covered gravestone. Winston sitting in a car outside the fence at the Little League park watching my first time at bat. His face dark. His eyes peering out from under his hat giving me courage. I swung and barely hit the ball, but I got on first base and when I looked back, I could see Winston, his hands clutched together waving back and forth over his shoulders as he cheered for me.

"I've got a beat," said a distant woman's voice.

Pain flashed through my body and my eyes snapped open. White light burned into my brain. I coughed and gasped for air. A mask came down over my face and I felt the cold rush of dry oxygen burning my throat and chest. I sucked it in as deeply as I could and felt the tingle of deprived muscles coming back to life and the cold prickle of sweat breaking out on my skin.

Someone touched a hot hand to my forehead. "Welcome back, Richard."

Forty-five minutes later, I sat on the side of a gurney while a kid in a white coat shined a blinding light into my eyes and a police officer informed me that I was no longer in police custody.

The doctor, however, told me I'd have to stay until my blood pressure returned to normal. I could see Martha, Sydney, and Mom waiting anxiously in the hallway.

"Is there anything around here I could put on?" I asked him adjusting the sheet over my legs.

"I'll see what I can do."

"Thanks."

The women corralled the doctor as he left the room and I could see the relief on their faces as he brought them up to date on my condition. As she listened to what he had to say, Sydney dabbed a tissue at her cheeks, but never took her eyes off me. I winked and mouthed the words, "You look beautiful." She smiled for a second, but then her face tensed and the tears began to flow again. I blew her a kiss and she blew one back.

After the doctor left, Mom stepped into the room, wrapped her thick arms around me, and cried as Sydney wheeled Martha in behind her. "You need to stop all that snooping around and let the police take care of this."

"I'll try, Mom."

"I mean it!"

"I do, too."

Her tears smeared from her cheeks onto my bare shoulder as she hugged me again. "I love you, son."

"I love you, too, Mom."

She wiped her tears off my shoulder. "I've got to go check on your father now."

"Okay. I'll stop by later and tell you all about it."

After kissing my forehead again, she left and Martha rolled closer scrutinizing me intensely.

"You okay?"

"Still alive."

"Try and keep it that way, will you?"

I smiled. "Don't worry. I've got to take care of *you*, remember?"

She squeezed my hand. "See that you do. I'm going with Mom."

I squeezed her hand. "I love you, Babe."

"I love you, too, Richie."

Wheeling out, Martha winked at Sydney. "Later, girlfriend."

Finally alone with me in my curtain cubical, Sydney stepped closer and stood at the edge of the bed. Her face was somber and tense.

"Are you okay?" I asked.

She shook her head side to side. Her eyes got red and her jaw muscles tightened. I reached out and took her hand.

"You look beautiful."

She cleared her throat. "You do, too."

"Yeah, right. I'm covered in salve and my eyebrows are gone." She giggled. "The doctor said I can't leave until six. Would you wait here with me?"

She wiped at a tear that had broken free and run down her cheek. "If you want me to."

I swung my legs up on the bed and laid back. "I'd like it better if you'd climb up here and lay down beside me."

Sydney sat, then laid next to me. I curled my fingers into hers, touched the side of my head to hers, and closed my eyes. "This is nice." She turned her head. Her lips brushed my cheek and I felt her breath on my face. "The doctor said he isn't going to let me go until my blood pressure goes down," I whispered. "Maybe your being this close to me isn't such a good idea." Sydney started to get up, but I pulled her back. I chuckled and she giggled.

At 6:20 a.m., the doctor returned with a pair of green surgeon's scrubs, checked my blood pressure, and cleared me for discharge. I stuffed the charred remains of my clothes into the trash can, but my watch, wallet, and keys were still at the Wrightsville Beach Police Station.

Sydney pulled the van around and was waiting for me at the front entrance. "Where to first?"

"Wrightsville Beach Police Station."

I clipped the seatbelt around me, closed my eyes, and opened them again in what seemed to be only an instant later to find Sydney leaning over me brushing the hair out of my face. "Did I fall asleep?"

"Just about the time you closed the door." Her smile was radiant, her eyes glistening bright blue. I leaned forward and touched my lips to hers. The contact was electrifying—charged with hope, rejuvenation, and self-esteem. It was *delicious* and it was at that very moment that I knew I was in love with Sydney.

"Wow," I whispered.

"Me, too," she said gazing into my eyes.

"What are you thinking?"

She smiled mischievously. "I think you need to hurry."

I took her hand and kissed it. "I will."

I opened the door and spotted Scott McGillikin standing at the front of the van staring at Sydney. As I pushed the door open, he turned away and stepped into the building. I looked back at Sydney. "Are you going to be okay?"

"Just hurry."

Inside the station house, I looked for Scott but did not see him. I moved to a counter and asked to get my things. I signed a form and was given a manila envelope containing my wallet, watch, and keys, and was told where to pick up the bike. I thanked him, turned, and came face to face with Scott. His jaw was set and his eyes were cold. I tensed, expecting him to take a swing at me, but he only stared.

"Can we keep this on a professional level?" I asked. "Or will I need to get another attorney?"

He shrugged. "Sure."

"My sister used to be an investigative reporter for the *News and Observer*. About three years ago—while working on a story—she was thrown out a window and left paralyzed from the waist down."

"I remember something about that."

"They found a fingerprint on the window back then and she's been looking for the person that it belongs to ever since." His brows scrunched. "Well, yesterday, she found a print that matches it."

"And what does that have to do with your case?"

"Well, we're not sure, but *she* thinks there's a good chance our cases are related. The print came out of that house at the beach that burned."

"How did she get that?"

"I spotted someone in Ashleigh's house the other night and followed him to that house."

He studied me so hard that I wondered if he'd stopped breathing until he asked, "And she knows who it belongs to?"

"No, but it *must* belong to someone associated with that house."

"But there's nothing left of it now."

"Didn't one of the men get out?"

"Did one?"

"The one they called Fat Albert? He was outside the house at the time of the explosion. Do you think we could get a copy of his fingerprints?"

Scott looked around at the policemen in their various stations and lowered his voice. "I'll see what I can do. Call me later this afternoon."

"Thanks."

He strode away without another word and I wasted no time leaving the building, running to the van.

"Did Scott say anything to you?" Sydney asked.

"I asked him if we could keep things between us professional and he said, 'Sure.' Then we talked a minute about the case."

She cranked the engine and shifted into reverse. "I think you should get another lawyer."

The instant we hit the doorway at my house, we fell into each others arms. As we kissed, the internal train racing around my nervous system jumped off its track. Passion ignited in me like the fuse to a roman candle. My knees went weak.

"You smell like smoke," she whispered.

I stepped back and took a breath. "Oh...sorry. I'd better go shower."

She kissed me again. "Hurry."

I slipped from her arms and dashed up the stairs. "I'll be back in five minutes."

"You'd better be," she called as I hopped in the bedroom pulling at a shoe. "I'm timing you."

I started the shower, stripped, and got in even before it got warm. I rinsed my head under the cold water and watched black soot run down my body and swirl around the drain. I closed my eyes and let the water run over my head and down my back when it warmed. I shampooed my hair and had just begun to rinse it when I felt a cool rush of air.

"I've never done this before," she said slipping her arms around me, laying her naked body against my back.

I rinsed the shampoo from my hair, turned in her arms to face her, and gazed into her eyes.

"I hope you don't mind," she said. "I just couldn't wait."

Dropping my arms around her, I kissed her lips. Our slippery bodies pressed against each other's as my hands glided over her slick skin. She hung her arms around my neck, tossed her head back, and let the shower spatter her face.

"Mmmm," she moaned.

Somehow we made it from the shower to the bed where we caressed one another and tasted each other's nectars until we could wait no longer and merged our rhythms in the throws of lovemaking.

41

A SHLEIGH MATTHEWS SAT in a waiting room at Duke University Medical Center idly flipping through the pages of a dog-eared copy of Cosmopolitan. The only other person in the room—a man—surfed the channels on a TV mounted high on a wall.

Her brother David had been in surgery for five hours and she'd heard nothing from the doctor. She dropped the magazine on the seat next to her and walked to the nurse's station. "Have you heard anything about how things are going with David's operation? How much longer it might be?"

"The doctor will come and speak with you just as soon as he's out of surgery."

"Does it usually take this long?"

"What they're doing with David? Yes."

"Thank you."

Ashleigh paced to a window, stopped, and scanned the view. The TV paused on each channel just long enough to hear six or seven words before jumping to another. She addressed the man. "Do you have to keep doing that?"

He looked up surprised. "Sorry. I didn't realize I was doing it. It drives my wife crazy, too."

"Thanks." The TV had stopped on a local Durham station doing a newscast. *"An explosion and fire claimed the lives of three women in Wrightsville Beach last night..."*

The man leaned forward, set the remote on a table in front of him, and sat back. "We've only been married about a year. Last month we found out she has breast cancer."

"I'm very sorry," Ashleigh said stepping closer to the TV as video of the burned out ruins played on the screen.

"...and destroyed a luxurious three-story ocean-front house in what police believe was an attempt to eradicate evidence in the murder of a woman whose body had been found hours earlier at another

Wrightsville location. Police are seeking two men for questioning in the case—one unidentified, and one named Dane Bonner. In a related story, the body of the man killed in an explosion and fire that ripped through a 1998 Corvette less than two hours later at a truck stop along I-40 has not yet been identified. The Corvette, however, was registered in the name of Dane Bonner and police are looking into both incidents to see if they are related."

Ashleigh felt her chest tighten.

"Ashleigh?" a man's voice called from across the room.

She turned to discover Dr. Harry Tatum standing in an open doorway. He was dressed in green scrubs with slip-on covers over his shoes and a white mask dangling under his chin. As she hastened to him, the *Looney Tunes* characters on his surgical cap—Bugs Bunny, Daffy Duck, Tweety Bird, and Sylvester—eased the tension she felt in her neck.

"Everything went extremely well." His voice was relaxed and positive. "He's in recovery now. We don't know yet how well this new artificial skin is going to work, but if it goes like we *think* it will, he's eventually going to have his face back."

"Can I see him?"

"After he wakes up and we get him into a room. But," he waved a finger at me. "I'm warning you, Ashleigh, he's not going to look good. Probably not for weeks."

Her eyes reddened. "I understand."

"Now go get a bite to eat and check back around four." He flashed a warm smile.

"Okay. Thank you."

"You bet."

Dr. Tatum nodded and stepped back, the door slowly swallowing him. Ashleigh turned back to the TV News. They were now running a commercial. She got her coat and pulled it on.

"Good news, I hope," the man said.

"Yes. Yes it was." She picked up her handbag. *Yes. It was very good news.*

WHEN MARTHA GOT HOME, she called Skeeter Barnes, a former contact she'd had at the police department, and left a message saying that she needed a license plate run and asked him to give her a call. She left the plate number as well as her telephone number then unfolded the sheet of newspaper Sydney had picked up at the beach. It was dated June 22, 1986. She scanned the front and then the back, but saw nothing of any value. Her computer beeped and an instant message popped up on her screen. It was from Skeeter.

"U back in the biz?"

She smiled and typed, "Still working my case. How ya been?"

The reply came quickly. "I miss all the trouble u used 2 get me n2."

She typed, "He he! U r 2 nice. Get anything on that number?"

"Cadillac Escalade reg'd 2 Dane Bonner, Charleston, SC."

"U look for anything else on him?"

"Blank—like he don't exist."

"Thanks. IOU. CU later. ☺"

Martha pressed the "Enter" key and sat back. She missed the things she used to do—sniffing out a good story, following leads, putting the pieces together, and solving mysteries and puzzles while uncovering the crooks and their plans. Mostly, though, she missed her friends and contacts.

She missed her life!

She sighed and googled "Dane Bonner." The monitor finally displayed one, then two links. After several minutes of searching, it still had only returned a few 1986 newspaper articles from *The Journal News* of Yonkers, New York. She clicked on one titled "Yonkers Youth Sought" and began reading.

Eighteen-year-old Dane Bonner of the Methodist Home for Boys is still being sought by Yonkers Police for questioning in the death of twenty-two-year old Robert Scott McGillikin, a former resident of the home, killed in a recent car crash.

She stared at the name. *Scott McGillikin? What is this?* She read on.

Bonner is thought to have been in the car at the time of the accident, but has yet to be located. McGillikin was a 1982 graduate of Roosevelt High and a 1986 graduate of the University of North Carolina.

Martha opened the other two links and they, too, were about the same incident. She tried several more search engines, but found nothing more than the same three articles. Her eyes dropped to the newspaper Sydney had picked up at the house. The banner read *The Journal News*. Her eyes jumped to the date. *Tuesday June 17, 1986.* She unfolded the page, scanned it again, and in the lower left corner on the back side under obituaries she found a listing for Robert Scott McGillikin, 22, of Yonkers, NY.

AT LUNCH, I NOTICED THAT SYDNEY HAD CHANGED. She was now quiet, serene. Her cheeks were still flushed when we placed our orders—a house salad with ginger dressing for her, a Reuben for me.

"You look dazzling," I said, leaning forward keeping my voice low. She smiled, looking down to smooth the cloth napkin in her lap. It felt so right to be there with her—as if I'd come home after being away for half a lifetime. I knew it was love, but I was afraid to say it. Not yet. I chuckled instead.

"What's so funny?" she asked, her eyes sparkling.

"Oh. Nothing. I'm just...happy."

She reached across the table and touched my hand. "Me, too." She waited for the waitress to leave our beverages, then asked, "So why haven't you ever gotten married?"

"Man, you do get right to the heart of things. Don't you?"

"People say I'm direct."

"I almost did, once." I touched my fingers to my glass, but didn't lift it. "I dated a girl for two years right after college that I thought I was going to marry. Then one day she took off with someone else, and I haven't dated much since. Maybe I'm just too choosy. But when you've been hurt like I was, you learn to look for the warning signs before jumping back into the fire."

"Like what?"

"Like if a person is manipulative, jealous, self-centered, or critical of the things you do *before* you're married, I think you can count on that still being there *after* you're married. Probably more so."

"I'm self-centered."

"In what way?"

"I spend most of my time thinking about and working on the dance studio."

"I see that as a positive trait."

"I'm also a perfectionist."

"So?"

"You wouldn't want to be married to a perfectionist would you?"

I lifted her hand and kissed the tips of her fingers. "I'd marry you." She pulled her hand back glancing to see if anyone was watching. As her eyes came back to mine, she blushed and I could feel her trying to read my thoughts. We took our time with lunch, laughed often, and occasionally touched each other as we filled each other in on our hopes, dreams, and dreads.

After lunch Sydney took me back to the bike and headed off to work. I followed her for a short distance before heading downtown to check on things at the photography studio.

AT THE STOPLIGHT near the university's Randall Library, Sydney watched lovers walking hand in hand laughing and chatting, and thought about how different Richard was from Scott. How handsome he had become with a little age. He was gentle and considerate, positive and caring, and his eyes danced when he looked at her in a way she hadn't seen in a long time.

The car behind her honked drawing Sydney back to reality. She pressed the gas pedal, glanced at the car behind her in the mirror, and thought she saw Scott leaning over the steering wheel of his silver Porsche. She looked up at the stoplights passing over her—*still red*—and barely got a glimpse of the Lowe's delivery truck before it collided with her van.

42

MARTHA QUERIED AN ON-LINE phone directory for the *Methodist Home for Boys* in Yonkers, dialed the number it gave her, and asked to speak to someone about a former student. After several minutes, a deep, gravelly voice came on the line.

"This is Geoffrey Lord. How can I help you?"

"Mr. Lord, my name is Martha Baimbridge. I'm looking for a former resident of the home who was there back in the 1980s. A man named Dane Bonner?"

The man remained silent for a moment. "From where are you calling?"

"North Carolina."

"So Dane Bonner still lives."

"Then, you *do* remember him."

"Miss, I remember every kid that passes through here. Especially the troublemakers. Bonner came with a lot of baggage and left with a lot of baggage. Probably the most emotionally crippled child to ever leave here. Killed his own father when he was nine. Hacked him up with a Cub Scout hatchet because he took away his marijuana. I figured he'd be in prison by now. Or dead. It's scary to think he's still alive."

"I believe he might be."

"You don't sound very sure."

"The name came up in an investigation."

"You're with the police?"

"I'm—working with the police on this particular case."

"What's he done?"

Martha picked her words carefully. She knew the next few sentences would determine whether or not she got his help. "We think he may be involved in a recent murder here. Perhaps more than one."

"I figured it was something like that. And the last we heard he was in North Carolina."

"So he keeps in touch with you?"

"Oh, no. We haven't actually heard from *him* since the day of the accident."

"The accident?"

"When Dane first arrived, an honors student by the name of Bob McGillikin was assigned to him as his big brother, to help Dane assimilate into the system here. But Dane was a deeply troubled, violent young man, and was more than Bob could handle on his own. So another resident was also assigned to Dane. But Dane saw that as a weakness in Bob and taunted him even more for it until Bob finally graduated and went off to college."

"Where'd he go?"

"He did his undergraduate work at the University of North Carolina and received a full scholarship to Wake Forest Law School."

"Smart fellow."

"Yes, he was. He was valedictorian at his high school and at the top of his class at Carolina. He wanted to dedicate his life to taking care of the legal needs of orphaned kids. Bob even wrote an important paper on it while at UNC that is still the legal standard for protecting the rights and properties of children whose parents have passed on."

"You said there was an accident?"

"Yes. After graduating from UNC, Bob came back for a visit. And once again, Dane latched on to him. Bob again felt sorry for Dane and thought he could help him to see that you can't just go around bullying people and taking what you want. That there are other ways to get the things you want in life. And, for the first time since he'd been here, it looked like somebody might finally be getting through to Dane. Bob noticed it, too, and tried to do even more for him. He started taking him off campus, bought him clothes and things, and the second week he was here there was some kind of freak accident and Bob was killed."

"I saw a couple of newspaper articles about that."

"Well, the papers never knew the whole story. According to witnesses, Dane was in the car at the time, but fled the scene. The police looked for him for a while...displayed his photo on TV for months, but he never showed up and they really didn't have any reason to think it was anything more than an accident. So, they soon dropped their search."

"But you think...there was more to it?"

"Nothing was ever proven, but there's been a persistent rumor around the home here ever since that Dane was the cause of the accident."

Pearl stepped in the doorway pulling on a sweater. "I'm going back to the hospital. You need anything while I'm out?"

Martha tapped her chest and mouthed the words "I want to go, too," then spoke into the phone. "And you have no idea where Bonner might have gone?"

"Oh, every once in a while, we'd hear that someone had seen him somewhere—mostly in North Carolina—but nothing ever checked out."

Martha's mother crossed the room, rolled the wheelchair up to the edge of her bed, and pulled the bedcovers back. Martha continued into the phone, "Like where in North Carolina?"

"Someone once said they were sure they'd seen him in a nightclub on one of the beaches. Another time, he was spotted at a college basketball game. And once, someone actually swore they saw him taking the North Carolina bar exam. That alone goes to show how unreliable these sightings can be."

Pearl looked at her watch. "We need to hurry, honey."

Martha covered her open ear with her free hand. "Why do you say that?"

"Dane Bonner couldn't have passed a sixth-grade English test much less a bar exam. Believe me, I know. I taught him for three years. He was only in the seventh grade when he split."

"Would you, by chance, have a photo of him?"

"A class picture, maybe."

Pearl tugged Martha's legs off the side of the bed and tightened an arm around her daughter's back, trying to lift her as Martha continued on the phone. "That would help. Do you think you could e-mail me a copy?" she said, pushing her mother aside.

"I don't see why not," Lord said.

Martha gave the man her e-mail address, thanked him, and hung up. "Mom! I'm working on something."

"I'm sorry, Baby. I'm in a hurry. I have a lot I need to do today."

"Okay! I'm ready."

Pearl helped her twist off the bed, but as she lowered Martha onto the chair, it rolled away and before Martha could give it a second thought, her right leg caught it and pulled it back.

"Oh my God," Martha whispered.

"What?"

"My leg did something just then."

"What?"

"I'm not sure."

SYDNEY HAD NOT HEARD the crash or felt the impact. She'd only had the slight sensation that her van had slipped a little—like on a patch of ice—and felt a subtle nudge as it came to rest *backwards* between the columns in the approach to the University Library. Her window—that only a second ago had been closed—was now *gone!* She looked down and tried to make sense of the hundreds of squares of glass glittering in her lap. A warm liquid dropped off the end of her nose bursting into red mosaics on the glass in her lap. The door crunched open and the reality of what had happened began to sink in as Scott reached in and touched her arm.

"Sydney! Are you all right?"

She slumped sideways and passed out.

When she awakened, Sydney was lying on the grass near the van. A man in a white lab coat was pressing a cloth against her forehead and two fingers against her neck. A shiver bucked through her. She felt weak and nauseous. Her teeth chattered. A policeman stood nearby in the midst of a small group of witnesses telling their varying versions of what they'd seen. Scott was among them. She closed her eyes and exhaled, "Is anyone else hurt?"

"Not seriously," the EMT said.

"Did I cause it?"

"I don't know."

"I thought the light had changed."

The man lifted the cloth off her forehead and looked under it. "Shhh. It doesn't matter now."

Scott followed the ambulance to the emergency room at New Hanover Regional Medical Center where doctors removed fragments of glass from Sydney's head and put in seven stitches. An hour later Sydney handed the clerk in "check out" her insurance card and a credit card. "I can't believe I did that. How could I have done that?"

Scott leaned against the wall next to her. "Don't dwell on it. It's over and done."

"I don't have a car."

"Listen. I've come into some money lately, Sydney. And I've been thinking about what you said. I thought we could...go away together. Get married. And forget we ever heard of this—"

"What?" Sydney exhaled. "What are you saying?"

"I really need you, Sydney. Life just isn't any good without you."

"Scott! I'm sorry, but I can't." Sydney looked at her watch as the clerk examined her credit card. "Can you hurry, please? I'm a dance teacher and I'm going to be late for my first class."

Scott touched her arm. "Listen. I called Freda and told her what happened, and she's calling in a sub for you. Can we go someplace and talk?"

She jerked her arm away. "No! I can't." The clerk pushed a credit card ticket through the window and Sydney leaned to sign it. "We've got competitions coming up. They need to rehearse." She signed the charge ticket, pushed it back through the window, and slipped her cards back into her wallet. "Can you drop me off?"

"Of course. Anything you want. I'm here to help."

She folded the receipt into her purse and hurried to the exit. "I appreciate your being there for me today, Scott. I really do. I know how busy your schedule is, but this doesn't change anything between us."

"I just want you to *think* about it."

As the automatic door opened and she plodded through it, the impact of what had happened began to sink in. *All my things are in the van. What am I going to do without a vehicle?* Sydney's eyes misted over.

I STOPPED BY MY STUDIO, shuffled through a stack of junk mail, and checked email. Having nothing that really needed my attention, I headed to the hospital to check on Dad. As I down-shifted the bike and turned into the parking lot, my eyes fell on a man and a woman getting into a silver Porsche. It looked like Scott's Porsche—the one I'd ridden in once—and the couple looked like Scott and *Sydney!* As the car backed out of its parking space, I came to a full stop and set both feet on the pavement waiting for them to pass. As the car pulled forward, the woman looked up and my heart cracked in half. Even with the sky reflecting off the windshield diminishing my view, I felt sure it was Sydney. The car abruptly veered to the left and snaked through the parking lot heading for a different exit as a colossal weight settled on my chest.

43

I N THE CARDIAC CARE UNIT, I found Martha and Mom sitting in the room with Dad. He didn't look good at all—none of them did. When Martha saw me, she rolled out with her head hanging low. I bent and gave her a hug. "How's he doing?"

"Not too well. How are *you?* Things are better for you now—after the fire. Right?"

"I hope."

"That license plate number we got from the beach house belongs to a man named Dane Bonner from Charleston. Not much on him on the Internet, but I've got a lead I'm working on."

"There was a man at that house named Bonner."

"Then we might be onto something with that. Oh, by the way, I just talked to a nurse and learned that you *can* extract semen from a man by massaging his prostate gland. All you need is a rubber glove, some petroleum jelly, and a finger. She says the fertility nurses do it all the time."

"Sounds painful."

"And one more thing..." She reached into her coat pocket and removed a couple of folded sheets of paper and spread them flat. "Do you remember that case a few years ago where Scott McGillikin was sued by a client?"

I glanced over the pages. "Scott?"

"It was Ashleigh Matthews and her brother that sued him."

"For what?"

"He had represented the two of them against an insurance company following the death of their parents where they won a $1.4 million dollar settlement."

"They sued over that?"

"They sued Scott because he kept most of the money for himself. The publicity hurt his business, but he was eventually exonerated."

I handed the sheets back to her. "So? How does this help?"

"It shows how badly she needed the money."

"For what?"

"The brother had been burned, right?"

"Yes, burned badly as I understand it. Mostly his upper body."

"Then that's what they needed the money for."

"The money Scott kept?"

"And the money she *stole* from that guy that came to see you."

"The one hundred fifty thousand dollars..."

Martha rolled forward to move out of the path of a fast-moving nurse. "I've been doing some thinking and I'm willing to bet they've gone someplace where he can get reconstructive surgery."

"A burn center or plastic surgeon."

"Right."

"You, my darling sister, are brilliant!" I kissed her forehead. She winced, raised up on one side, and grabbed her leg. "Is something wrong?" I asked.

Her voice changed to a strained whisper. "I think it's what they call a 'Phantom Pain.' It feels like I've got a red-hot iron rod jammed into my ankle. I've been feeling it a lot lately, but it's getting worse." She tensed. "Would you squeeze it really hard for me?"

Dropping to the floor, I removed her shoe, gripped her ankle with both hands, and clasped down on it hard. Her head rocked back. "Ouch! Ouch!"

"Whoa, Babe! When did this start?"

"Don't stop! Please."

Her body tensed as I worked the ankle with both hands, kneading it as hard as I could. "It started four or five days ago."

Peeking out of her pants leg, I saw the tiny tattoo that she got back in college and so proudly displayed before the accident; a brilliantly colored psychedelic butterfly no bigger than a half-dollar. "Can you move it?"

She pressed her lips together, held her breath, and concentrated on sending a signal to her foot. Her head twitched to the side once, then twice, then, all at once, her five toes spread slightly.

"Oh my God! Did you do that?"

"Did they move?"

"Yes, they moved."

Still straining, she dropped her chin and concentrated. As her toes spread again, her face lit up with both pain and excitement.

"Babe!" I squeezed her foot and worked my fingers through the tissues. "Are you going to walk again?"

"They've been telling me in therapy that it could happen."

Mom stepped out of Dad's room and wiped her eyes with a wadded tissue. "The doctor says there's nothing more they can do for him except make him comfortable."

I slipped Martha's shoe back on, rose, and gave Mom a firm hug. "Maybe that's all he needs now, Mom."

She shook her head, dabbed her cheeks, and dropped onto a chair. Martha rolled up next to her and took her hand. I took a chair on the other side of her. "Mom?" I whispered. She didn't look up, just stared into the tissue. "Mama, why'd you marry Dad?"

Her eyes came up to mine and glared at me. *"How dare you!"* they seemed to say.

"I mean so soon after—"

"After what?"

"Uncle Charles—"

"Oh, Baby. Why would you bring up Uncle Charles *now?*" She rose, staggered a few steps to the window and looked into Dad's room laying her head against the glass.

"Tell me about him, Mama. What was Uncle Charles like?"

"Oh, Lord, Lord, *Lord.*" Tears filled her eyes. She wiped her nose. "Your Uncle Charles was a bright...handsome...gifted boy with big ideas. He even thought he could be President someday."

"What was he like? To be with, I mean."

She waddled back to her chair. "Charlie...was kind. Gentle. Soft-spoken." She wiped her eyes and nose. "And generous—to a fault. He'd give you his last dollar if you needed it." She sat again. "He was smart, too, and could do anything he set his mind to."

"How did he die, Mama?"

"Son, what's got you so interested in your Uncle Charles all of a sudden?"

"Just something Dad told me the other morning."

She pulled a new tissue from her dress pocket and dragged it over her face. "Your dad's been talking a little out of his head lately."

"But, how *did* Uncle Charles die?" Martha asked.

Mom waited a beat, then spoke matter-of-factly. "Uncle Charles died when the brakes on his car failed and he was struck broadside by a farmer hauling a load of fuel back to his farm. He was killed instantly and that's all I've got to say about Charlie Baimbridge."

I sat back and exhaled. *Kind, gentle, soft-spoken, and smart?* I pictured him riding around in his car with that cigarette hanging out his mouth and wondered what he'd think of the world today. How different our lives might have been if he'd lived. "I used to think I'd grow up to be President, too." I mumbled.

Mom rolled her head to the side and looked at me. "Richard Baimbridge, what's going on in that head of yours?"

I patted her hand. "Nothing, Mom. Nothing at all. Just curious."

44

SCOTT HAD SEEN how panicked Sydney became when she realized Richard had seen her with *him,* and it hurt. And it angered him. He had taken her under his wing when another love had gone wrong for her. He'd showed her how to be strong and how to get what you want out of life. He'd built up her confidence and taught her how to set goals and take the necessary steps to achieve them. The way *he* figured it, she'd have nothing today had it not been for *him.* He glanced at her. She clutched her purse with one hand and grasped the door handle with the other.

"I told you I've come into some money recently," he said, pausing to let her respond. She didn't. "It's a lot of money, Sydney, and I thought how fantastic it would be for us to just pick up and go. We could go anywhere you'd like—anywhere in the world—and you'd *never* have to work again."

"I don't want to leave here. I love my work and I *love* my studio."

"You say that now, but you'll grow tired of it. And in a few more years—"

"No, I will not!"

"Trust me. In a few more years, you're going to hate it. Then you'll be wishing you'd come, but it'll be *too late,* Sydney. This is a once-in-a-lifetime offer." The car stopped for a red light.

Sydney looked at her watch. "I'm sorry, Scott. I really am. But, I—really, I—can't."

"Why not, Sydney?" He raised his voice. "Why not?"

Sydney turned away from him and faced the side window. She knew if she didn't answer, he'd be more likely to calm down.

"Don't think I don't know what the hell's going on here, Sydney." He banged a fist against the steering wheel, and snorted, "I can't believe *you* could be that *stupid!*" Sydney checked the time on her watch. "He's a *murderer,* Sydney. He rapes young girls and then murders them!"

"No he does not!" In one swift move, Sydney unbuckled her seatbelt, opened the door, and rolled out of the car. "You're his *attorney* and this is the way you think?" The light turned green and the traffic began moving around her. She slammed the door, cut between cars, and stepped onto the median in the center of the six-lane thoroughfare. Up the road she could see her studio through the haze of tears in her eyes. The parking lot was jammed with cars and she needed to be there. Pulling her purse strap over her shoulder, she watched for a break in the traffic.

"Sydney!" a voice called behind her. She turned and saw the face of Sylvia Whitford, one of her students' moms, staring back at her from the window of a white Dodge Durango. "Get in." Sydney rounded the car amid blasts from horns and jumped in. "Going to the studio?" Sylvia asked, the vehicle rolling forward.

"Yes. Thank you."

"What happened to your head?"

Sydney had held up through the accident, the hospital treatment, seeing the stunned look on Richard's face, and Scott's proposition. But now, as her legs trembled, she placed a hand over her mouth and let the tears go.

"Hey, hey!" Sylvia piped, whipping a tissue from an overhead holder and passing it to Sydney. "You're okay now. You're with me. We're going to the studio."

IT WAS QUARTER PAST TWO when I stepped into Dad's room and stood at the foot of his bed. The room seemed darker than before. His right hand moved around as if searching for something. "What are you looking for, Dad?"

He opened his eyes, but didn't seem to be looking at anything in particular. They were weak and cloudy. The light seemed to bother him and he shut them. "Nothing," he uttered. "Just stretching out a little."

I shoved my hands into my trouser pockets, drew a heavy breath, and stepped closer. "What was Uncle Charles like, Dad?"

His chest rose high, then fell. After a minute, I took a chair.

"He was a lot like you, Richie," he said, his voice faint. "Same easy disposition, same smart looks."

The monitor over his bed wrote an endless oscillating green line across its screen jolting with each heartbeat. "You said he was my father. How did that happen?"

"Jesus, Rich." His arm swept back and forth across the sheet. "They were together for two years."

I laid my head back and expelled all the air in my lungs. "Okay. I get it."

"No, you don't." His voice was weak, his breathing labored. "Pearl and Charlie's wedding was only three weeks off when he—" His hand moved to his face and clamped over his eyes. "—when he had the accident." His dry, cracked lips moved without words as if rehearsing the story until he took a deep breath and continued. "He was getting the car ready for their honeymoon. A trip to the mountains—Asheville, I think—and I was supposed to put new pads on the brakes." He gulped a breath and swallowed. "He left me the car that morning and told me I had to be finished before three 'cause he needed it after that. I set it on blocks, pulled all the wheels, and was about to install the new pads when Buster Diggins came by with a gallon jug of moonshine whiskey and a girl he'd picked up hitchhiking. He said she needed a ride to Raleigh and he'd give me a hand with the brakes if I'd go with him and drive."

The beep on the monitor sped up. His head flopped left and right. "The two of them had already made a dent in that jug and by the time we finished the brakes, it was more 'an half gone and not one of us was fit to drive. We took off anyway and when I got back home late that night, I learned about the accident."

I stayed quiet when he paused, not wanting to interrupt the flow. His hand continued to whip back and forth as he told the rest of the story.

"The investigators said it was caused by brake failure—that the brakes had been installed wrong and everyone blamed me for what had happened." His head flipped to the other side. "Charlie was dead and it was *my* fault and nobody was going to let me forget it." His moist eyes opened, rolled in a circle, and closed. "I couldn't take it no more. I ran off and stayed drunk for more than a month—until my mama found me and told me Pearl was pregnant with Charlie's baby. With *you.*" His voice now a whisper.

I reached out and laid my hand on his arm.

"You don't know how it *was* back then, Richie. In those days, a woman with a baby and no husband had *no chance* of a normal life. I'd taken that from her. Mama said I had to do something to try to make up for it. She told me I had to *marry* Pearl, to make things right for her. So I went to her and told her I'd marry her and take care of her and the child, myself, as best I could. I don't think she wanted to, but she married me anyway. But she never loved me—least not the way she'd loved Charlie."

A tear appeared on his cheek. I leaned forward and kissed his forehead. "Thanks, Dad."

He grabbed my arm and pulled me down close. "Don't you be pressing your mama on that."

I nodded. "I won't."

There was a brief moment as we stared into each other's eyes that we *connected.* Man-to-man, friend-to-friend. Something passed between us—something *real.* I felt clean, fresh, energized. We just stared at each with tears in our eyes. *Why could we not have had this moment twenty years ago?*

As I left the room, I paused in the doorway and looked back. His eyes were still watching me and I felt for the first time in my life that I really knew him. I nodded, turned away, and left.

Scott had told me to call him later, so I went looking for a phone.

Finding a pay phone in the lobby, I rang Scott's office. When I got him on the line, I asked him if he'd gotten a copy of Albert's fingerprints.

"You know I can't do that, Mr. Baimbridge." His answer surprised me, but then he added, "but I do have something here you need to see. Can you run by here? Now?"

"Sure. Be right there."

WHEN I WALKED INTO HIS OFFICE, Scott stood with his back to me looking out a window at the Cape Fear River. He had a drink in his hand. "What is it that you *want,* Richard Baimbridge?" He sipped from his drink.

"Didn't you have something you wanted to show me?"

He turned toward me. "Out of *life,* man. What do you want out of life?"

I had to think about that. "I...want...my sister to walk again. I want to get the police off my back. I want to direct theatre on Broadway. I want my dad to get better and come home."

He took a sip of his drink. "What do you want from Sydney?"

The question caught me off-guard. I wasn't sure how to answer. "I just want her to be happy."

He chuckled under his breath, then tossed the rest of his drink down. "Women can be awfully fickle, Mr. Baimbridge."

"I suppose."

"And exactly what is it that you want from Mr. Willett?"

"Who?"

"The man from the beach house. Albert Willett."

"Just his fingerprints."

He continued to gaze out the window. "His fingerprints?"

"I told you. It's for my sister. She's looking for the guy that shoved her off that window ledge and left her paralyzed."

He lifted a file folder from his desk and waved it in the air. "And she thinks it might have been Willett?"

"A fingerprint from that house matched one from her assailant."

"I see." He rotated the folder around, tossed it back on his desk, and turned back to face the window. "Well, you know I can't be involved in anything like that."

There was a yellow sticky-note attached to the folder. I leaned closer to read it. "I understand."

He didn't turn around. "That's the kind of thing that could get a lawyer disbarred."

I leaned further over the desk toward the note. "Certainly. I understand."

The note read, *McLeod Hotel. 8 p.m. Room 306.*

45

A S THE LAST STRANDS of pink faded and the sky turned steel gray, I drove past the McLeod Hotel and parked several blocks away. It stood tall and proud at the center of the seediest part of Wilmington. Built in the late 1800s, it had not had a coat of paint since Hitler marched on France. A few windows on the bottom floor had been covered with plywood that had since grayed and curled, threatening to fall off. One window on the second floor was covered by cardboard. I got more than a few strange looks as I walked past the neon signs and cheap bars back toward it.

The prostitutes propositioned me, and the men kept an eye on me. The entrance to the hotel was too narrow and too congested with people I wouldn't dare ask to move, or try to slither through. I lowered my head and walked on by, disappearing into a narrow alley a few doors farther. Stepping over broken bottles, drug vials, and piles of excrement, I made my way to the back of the buildings.

Night was falling quickly. The interior of the block was a menagerie of fire escapes, sagging porches, broken windows, and dilapidated sheds. There was an equal amount of cracked pavement and tall weeds with clear open dirt paths squirreling around the garbage containers and outbuildings. I could feel the presence of people all around, but couldn't see any. I heard a whisper from one direction, a grunt and a moan from another. In the distance a police siren wailed and a woman screamed at a whimpering infant.

I followed a path toward a rotting wooden stairwell at the rear of the McLeod and came upon a man leaning back against a telephone pole watching me. I paused to see what he was going to do, but when I realized there was female down in the shadows in front of him with her face in his crotch, I moved on. Stepping around debris, I entered the stairwell and looked up. The only light came from a bare bulb just inside the door. The stairs had broken treads and missing boards, and grew darker as they went up but still felt safer than going through the front.

It was 7:56 p.m. I presumed room 306 would be on the third floor and began my ascent. Avoiding abandoned toys and beer cans, I had to step carefully as the light grew dimmer. At the third floor, I held my breath and pulled the door open. To my surprise I found the interior clean and well lit. Down the hall someone practiced a classical piece of music on a well-tuned piano and children laughed. I moved quickly to room 306 and although I had no idea what I was going to say when he came to the door, I knocked. Getting a fingerprint might not be that easy. I knocked again—harder—and the door opened ajar. The room inside was dark and I wondered if he was out—or worse—*had checked out?*

"Mr. Willett?"

Looking around for a glass or bottle or anything that would hold a fingerprint, I heard shuffling in the next room and saw light coming around the edges of the door. Stepping closer, I peered through the tiny gap. There was a man sitting at a metal table. As I cranked my head to see if I could tell who he was, a gun discharged, and the door to the room banged open.

Stumbling backward, I was confronting a man in a black ski mask holding a pistol in his hand, smoke curling from its barrel. Behind him sat Fat Albert, gagged and bound to a chair. There was a hole in the center of his forehead with a column of blood sprinting from it. As the gun flashed up, I lunged for the entrance and a shot whizzed past my head. Bolting up the hall, I burst through the door to the stairwell with bullets zipping by me. Through a crack in the wall of the stairwell, I saw police vehicles with flashing lights skidding to a stop behind the hotel and men scrambling from them.

I clambered down the steps three and four at a time, banged through the door to the second floor, and barreled down the hall with voices behind me shouting, "Stop! Police!" A door swung open in front of me and I dodged past a screaming woman into her apartment, tugged at a window that refused to open, smashed a chair through it, and leapt from the second floor.

I fell to the ground hard, pain shooting through my left ankle as I tumbled backward and—for an instant—I considered the game over. *I give up!* But the sounds of more police cars screeching to a halt on the street got me going again. I hobbled along the narrow alley to the front of the building, merged into the angry sidewalk crowd squeezing between hookers and addicts, and entered into the darkened interior of the building next door. It was some kind of club.

The air was thick with tobacco, reefer, and stale beer. The only light I could see came from dim colored bulbs in the ceiling aimed at erotic art and life-sized nude statues recessed into the walls. A heavy bass and drums rhythm thumped loudly amid a celestial tinkling of music lacking a melody. I pushed forward through the sweaty bodies and felt a hand grab my crotch.

"Oh, darling," a man purred. I twisted free and limped on. "Over here, lover," another beckoned. The air was hot, musty, and hard to breathe. Beads of perspiration trickled down my sides. My ankle throbbed with pain. I had no idea where this would lead, but knew it was safer than being outside. I moved my wallet to a front pocket and hobbled on blindly, my legs trembling. I could feel my heart beating in my gums as my eyes adjusted to the darkness.

Farther in, the crowd in the aisle thinned and the room angled to the left. Voices whispered and giggled from dark alcoves around me and I could smell the odors of sex—male and female.

What lay behind me was life in prison and possibly death. *What lay ahead I could not have imagined.*

I N SPITE OF THE RECENT WARM WEATHER, Scott McGillikin pulled the collar of his wool overcoat up around his ears, hunched forward with his shoulders high, and slunk along the street Martha and Richard had played on as children. As he approached the Baimbridge home, a Saint Bernard across the street reeled off a string of low-pitched barks that sounded more like a car being started with a dying battery than any kind of living creature.

The neighborhood was actually safer now than it had been twenty years earlier. Transplants from the north were buying up all the older homes, restoring them to better-than-original condition, and adding decks, brick walks, outdoor lamps, and herb gardens.

As he turned up the Baimbridge sidewalk, a young girl next door leaned out over a porch railing to get a better look at him. He lowered his chin, mounted the steps, and had raised a gloved hand to knock when the door abruptly swung open.

Before him sat a startled woman in her wheelchair bundled in an overcoat with a scarf around her neck. Shocked at the unexpected sight of a man on the porch, she recoiled and slammed the door. The Saint Bernard across the street again cranked his engine.

Stepping back, Scott called out. "Hello? Is this the Baimbridge home?" The porch light came on. "My name is Scott McGillikin. I'm Richard's attorney. Are you Martha?"

The door opened and Martha spoke through a narrow crack. "I'm sorry. You startled me. Yes, I am."

"I apologize. I should have called first. You're obviously headed out."

"I was just going for a stroll. The night air and the exercise help me sleep."

"I see. Well, mind if I join you?"

"Who is it, Martha?" Pearl called from upstairs.

Martha wheeled around and called back to her. "It's for me, mother."

"All right, darling."

Martha kept one hand on the doorknob. "What's this about, Mr. McGillikin?"

Scott cleared his throat. "Your brother told me that you had some information that might have something to do with his case."

She studied his face wondering if he could be the imposter named Dane Bonner. "It's a fingerprint from that house at the beach that blew up."

"What about it?" he asked.

"It matches one belonging to the man that pushed me off a ledge a few years ago."

"And how does that affect your brother's case?"

"Richie followed a man he spotted in the Matthews house to that beach house."

"So, *you* think the cases *could* be related."

"Yes, I think there's a connection. The problem is that the prints the police found have never been identified."

Scott scanned the neighborhood. The girl next door had faded back into the shadows and a dog in the next block now bayed incessantly. "So, basically what you have is a set of matching fingerprints, but you have no idea to whom they belong."

"Right."

"Well, that's interesting, Miss Baimbridge, but not very helpful. However, I do appreciate your sharing that information with me. You never know what might turn out to be important."

"Of course."

"You're close?" he asked, then seeing her confusion added. "Your brother and you?"

"Oh, yes. Very."

"He's lucky to have a sister like you. Thank you. And again I apologize for interrupting your stroll."

"Not a problem. Thanks for stopping by."

"Anytime you have anything you think might be of importance to his case, feel free to call."

"Thank you. I will."

Scott nodded. "Well, good night, Miss Baimbridge."

Martha rolled the chair back. "Good night, Mr. McGillikin."

She watched him step off the porch and waited to see which way he went before closing the door. Knowing that he might be a murderer gave her the creeps. She waited fifteen minutes before opening the door again and looked carefully as she rolled out onto the porch. Seeing no sign of him, she closed the door, took the ramp down, and checked the street before heading toward the abandoned warehouse.

MY EYES ADJUSTED SLOWLY to the low light as I penetrated deeper into the interior of the club. I could make out couples in booths kissing and pawing at one another—men with men, men with women, and women with women. With every step I searched for a bottle or other weapon to grab should chaos suddenly break out. There was a commotion at the front doors and I knew from the shouting and groans that the police had arrived. Beams of light circled into the smoky darkness lighting patrons that hid their faces and cursed.

I crouched, feeling my way along a pathway when a hand hooked the back of my belt and flipped me up into a booth. A woman, nude from the waist up, ripped the front of my shirt open, flipped it off my shoulders, and whispered, "I hate pigs." She thrust her tongue into my mouth, pressed her chest against mine, unzipped my fly, and forced her hand inside my trousers.

With my face against hers, I watched the cops as they shined their lights into every nook and corner and saw that some of the nude statues weren't statues at all, and some of the women weren't women. As one of their lights fell upon me, I closed my eyes and held my breath, the hammering in my chest drowning out the beat of the music. When the light moved away from me, I pulled back and examined the woman fondling me. Her breasts were high and well-formed, and her face certainly looked female. But if she wasn't, *I sure as hell didn't want to know it.* As the cops approached, I shoved her against the rear of the booth and kissed her passionately. She arched her back, moaned, and gyrated against me.

As the police moved past our booth, someone in the next stall screamed and a scuffle broke out. One cop leaped into our booth, his large shoes kicking and stomping me while he grappled with the suspect in the next booth until they managed to get him to the floor and cuff him. My chest was clinched so tightly, I could hardly breathe. Sweat poured off me.

A moment later, they stomped out a back door dragging the naked man kicking and screaming with them. When they'd gone, I exhaled and waited for my nerves to calm before flipping my shirt back onto my shoulders and thanking the woman for her help.

"My pleasure," she trilled, her voice deep and throaty blowing smoke from a long slender cigarette into my face.

I zigzagged back to the front of the building, tucked my shirttail into my pants, zipped my fly, and stumbled out into the crowd on the street—and the cool, refreshing night air.

ACROSS TOWN, MARTHA INCHED back into the recesses of a row of bushes and switched the safety off on a can of pepper spray as two teenage youths headed up the sidewalk toward her. Laying her index finger on the trigger, she sat motionless in the shadows as they passed within inches of her, then waited for them to get well down the block before resuming her trek. Several blocks farther, she turned toward the river.

As the warehouse came into view, the palms of her hands grew damp. Concentrating on the upper floor of the abandoned building, she failed to notice the car following her from a block away with its lights off. Nor did she notice the driver park and get out when she maneuvered into a hidden berth not far from the spot where she'd parked on the night of her accident.

Pulling a pair of binoculars from under her coat, she raised them to her eyes, located the window in them, and saw that the room was dark. She lowered the angle of the lenses and scanned along the bottom of the warehouse as a sharp pain ripped through her right leg from her hip to her ankle. Gritting her teeth, she shifted her weight onto her left hip.

Movement in the shadows behind the warehouse drew her attention. *What is that?* Rolling the wheel with her finger, she brought a silhouette into sharp focus just as it disappeared behind the corner of the building. *My God, there's someone back there!*

Martha pushed back to the sidewalk, looked up and down the street, and rolled toward the warehouse for a better look behind the building.

Again something moved back there.

Slipping into a thicket off the sidewalk, she drew the binoculars to her eyes, focused on a light moving about behind the building, and realized she'd been watching a boat maneuvering on the river beyond the warehouse. *Rats!* Taking a deep breath, she glanced back at the window and jolted upright in her seat. Above and to the left of the window from where she'd been pushed—in the room at the top of the stairs was a faint glow of bluish light.

Her body tensed and her breathing grew shallow as she pulled the cell phone from her coat pocket and dialed Sam Jones.

"Sam, it's Martha."

He hesitated. "Martha?"

"Baimbridge," she muttered, her right leg twisting painfully outward.

"Yes. Martha, how've you been?"

She massaged her thigh as she spoke. "I'm sitting across from the warehouse right this second and—"

"What warehouse?"

"What warehouse do you think, Sam?"

He sighed. "I'm sorry. There's a lot going on tonight. The *railroad* warehouse, of course."

"Sam, there was a light in the top window of that warehouse just a second ago. I saw it." He did not answer. "Did you hear me?"

"Yes, I heard you."

"I saw a light coming from that room, Sam! Can you come and check it out?"

"It's been three years, Martha. Aren't you ever going to let it go?"

"Please, Sam. Come check it out. You owe me that."

After a brief pause he gave in. "Okay. I'll be right there."

"Thank you, Sam."

"Sure."

With the binoculars still to her eyes, Martha closed the phone and dropped it back into her coat pocket. Behind her, a twig snapped. Lowering the binoculars, she held her breath and listened, looking up and down the sidewalk, hearing only the beat of her heart and the sounds of the city. Grasping the wheels of her chair, she moved one forward and the other backward to rotate the chair, but the chair resisted. Looking over the side, she saw that an exposed root had snagged in the spokes of the left wheel. She tried to roll backward, forward, to the left, and to the right, but the root held. Leaning, she grasped the two-inch thick tentacle and twisted it upward straining to free it from the wheel.

The root flexed, but not enough. She leaned farther, took hold of it with both hands, jerked a bit more of it free from the ground, then curled the loose end up out of the spokes. As she held it back and tried to move the chair, a man's shoe stepped on the root jamming it back into the wheel.

Startled, Martha's heart jumped into her throat as she fumbled to locate the pepper spray in her pocket.

"Need a little help, Miss Baimbridge?" the man muttered, his hands deep in his overcoat pockets.

Realizing it was Scott McGillikin standing before her, she pretended to relax. "Jeez! You scared the devil out of me!"

"Looks like you're hung up on a root," he said grasping the two handles on the back of the chair, lifting it off the ground, shifting it to the right freeing the wheel. "You should be more careful. This is a dangerous neighborhood to be in at night."

With her heart racing, she tried to sound calm. "You never quite get used to the limitations."

"No, I wouldn't think so."

Scott turned the chair around, rolled it out onto the sidewalk, and headed up the street away from the warehouse.

Martha placed her hands on the wheels and tried to take control. "I'll be fine now, Mr. McGillikin. Thank you."

Scott ignored her efforts and continued to push the chair before him as he walked along. "Have you ever thought about being in the movies, Miss Baimbridge?" His voice was calm, almost musical.

She attempted again to grip the wheels, to slow the chair. "Please, I can handle it from here."

"A smart girl like you with a cute figure like yours? Crippled or not, I'm sure I could get you a job in the movies."

As the chair abruptly gained speed, Martha gripped the side rails and took inventory. *What do I have? Pepper spray, cell phone, and a pair of binoculars.* Slipping her right hand into her coat pocket, she closed her fingers around the spray. "What kind of movies, Mr. McGillikin? Porn? Or should I call you *Mr. Bonner?*"

A chuckle gurgled up from deep in his throat. "Bonner?" His pace quickened. "I don't believe I know anyone named Bonner."

She laid a finger on the trigger of the pepper spray. "Scott McGillikin is *dead.* He died in an accident up north. You were there."

"Well, well." Scott snickered. "Aren't you the brilliant little investigator?" Lengthening his stride, he turned a corner onto a dark, tree-lined sidewalk that dropped steeply toward a busy four-lane intersection a block away. An eight-foot tall ivy-covered brick wall ran the entire length of the block. Sensing the danger ahead, Martha looked back just as a patrol car crossed the intersection behind her. *Sam?*

"*Heeeelp!*" she screamed. "Somebody! Help me!" A gloved fist whacked the back of her head stunning her momentarily. Whipping the canister out of her pocket, she twisted to her left, pressed the trigger, and aimed the stream of irritant directly into Scott's face.

He recoiled, then lunged at her slapping blindly at her head and shoulders, ripping the spray out of her hand, whacking the back of a gloved hand across her mouth. "You little bitch!" Flinging the canister over the wall, he gripped the chair and yanked it sharply to the left, charged forward, and rammed it hard into the wall slamming Martha head-first into the bricks, shattering a lens in the binoculars and ripping away a piece of one eyebrow.

Laying on the ground racked with pain and fear, she grabbed hold of the chair and used it to fight him off, keeping it between the two of them. "Somebody *pleeease!* Help *meeeeeee!*"

Ripping the chair out of her grip, Scott one-armed her back into the seat and, with tears streaming from his stinging eyes, galloped toward the intersection below—the chair jangling as it bounced over broken sections of sidewalk lifted by the roots of century-old oaks. Struggling to hold on, Martha reached into her pocket, thumbed the phone open, and pressed the "send" button knowing it would redial Sam's cell phone automatically. But the right wheel struck a raised section of cement flipping the chair up on its side, wobbling, threatening to topple over. Martha's reflexes whipped her hand from the pocket to grasp hold, and the phone went tumbling off into the grass.

"Please! Somebody help me!"

Careening toward the busy intersection, Martha twisted to her left, locked an arm around his, and bit down on his sleeve. Failing to get his arm free, Scott smashed his other elbow against the top of her head three, four, five times. Still she held on, her teeth closing through his flesh. Grappling to get loose, Scott fell back dragging the chair to a halt, grabbed the binocular strap wrapped around Martha's neck, and yanked it tight cutting off her air supply.

Panicked and fighting for breath, she lunged over the side of the chair toppling to the ground, writhing to get her fingers under the strap, gasping for oxygen. Twisting the strap tighter, Scott dragged her across the ground until the strap broke and she rolled free, blood spraying from her mouth as she coughed and screamed. *"Please! Somebody! Help!"*

Martha had never backed down from anyone in her life and as he lifted her off the ground and tossed her back onto the chair, she punched and clawed at his head, digging her nails into his skin. *"Scott McGillikin's trying to kill me!"*

Exhausted, he slapped a hand over her mouth, circled the chair, and pushed on toward the streaming traffic. And again Martha locked onto his arm. But this time, he wrenched his hand from the glove and punched the side of her head with his bare knuckles.

Capturing his arm again, she sank her teeth into his bare skin ripping a chunk out of his arm. Jerking and twisting to free himself, Scott stumbled to his knees dragging the chair to a stop just before the end of the wall. An eighteen-wheel tractor-trailer rumbled past blasting Martha with a powerful gust of wind.

"Hey!" she screamed waving at oncoming traffic. *"Somebody! Help me!"* But the traffic was moving too fast and the chair was hidden by the darkness and the wall.

Striking a demobilizing blow to the side of Martha's jaw, he yanked his left arm free. As her head snapped back, her eyes caught the refraction of headlights in the *aqua* stone of the ring that sailed off his left hand and—for the second time in her life—she saw a *blue* flash and the letters "N3."

Regaining her senses, she lunged at him grasping the tail of his coat. *"It was you!"* she cried leaning over the back of the chair. *"I found you, you friggin' bastard!"*

Falling to the ground, Scott kicked at her face, set his feet against the back of the chair, and in one powerful thrust, launched her off the sidewalk and into the intersection.

For an instant, Martha was back on that ledge, dropping away in slow motion, seeing the gloating in his eyes as she floated off.

The chair bounced over the curb into the path of a red Chevelle that swerved over the curb—its brakes squealing—to avoid hitting her, but the man in the yellow rental truck hauling his shattered life to a storage bin on the other end of town had nowhere to go. He stomped the brakes and turned the wheel, but the truck was too heavy and could not be stopped. The fully-loaded vehicle slammed into her wheelchair and—like Pélé kicking a soccer ball—sent her careening into the third lane where a bus returning alcoholics to the Wilmington Treatment Center from an AA meeting at St. James Episcopal Church struck the wheelchair head on.

47

A S I PULLED UP TO MY PARENT'S HOUSE, I saw my mother flailing about the front yard flanked by two policemen and two neighbors attempting to console her. My first thoughts were that something had happened to Dad. I left the engine running and jumped out. "What happened?"

Mother surged toward me screaming and crying, but her cries concealed her words. I took hold of her hands. "What? Slow down."

She tried to say something, but instead collapsed against me, her weight sending both of us against the side of the car.

"What is it, Mama? Has something happened to Dad?"

Like a wounded animal, she thrashed about sliding down the side of the car to the ground.

"For Heaven's sake, can't someone tell me what's going on?"

The woman living next door stepped forward. "Your sister's been in an accident."

"An accident?"

Mom rolled to the ground, threw her head back, and let out a shriek that all of nature would recognize and I knew it was bad. "What? What happened?"

The woman pointed up the road. "We were standing here talking about your dad when somebody ran up and told her that Martha had been hit by a bus."

I saw a faint flashing in the distance. A vice clamped down on my chest. I couldn't breathe. My blood pressure soared. I could feel my heart pounding in my fingers. Muscles I never knew I had twisted into a knot. As I spun to turn, my right leg gave way. I caught myself on the car door, bumbled into it, dropped the shift into "reverse," and stomped the accelerator. The car wheeled backward squealing as it spun around and raced off to find the scene of the accident.

It wasn't hard to find.

When I got there, they had Martha on a gurney and were lifting her into an ambulance. I ran to her but was held back by Sam Jones as they closed the doors.

"They're taking her to the hospital," he said.

"What happened?" I gasped.

"I got here right after it happened. They say she just came out of nowhere. She just shot out into the street without even trying to stop. Like she meant to do it."

I felt the blood leave my head and my limbs began to tingle. "That's ridiculous! She wouldn't do that."

"Maybe not."

I bent forward and grasped my knees, my pulse suddenly weak. "Maybe, *hell!* She would never do that, Sam!"

The ambulance let go a yelp from its siren and pulled away exposing one of the metal arms broken off the wheelchair lying in the street. I turned away and grabbed hold of a sign post. My chest rattled and my legs shook. "Jesus! How could this have happened?"

"You don't look so good," Sam said. "Maybe you should sit down." He took my arm and walked me toward my car. "There's something else, too, Richard."

I panted. "What?"

"She called me about ten minutes before the accident and told me she'd seen a light in a window at that damned warehouse. She told me she'd wait for me. I was coming to meet her."

"So how'd she end up here? Three blocks away?"

"I was on the way when I came upon the accident and when I realized who she was, sent another car around to have a look at the warehouse. There was nothing there."

"Well, there must have been *something* there or *she'd* still be there waiting for you right now." I felt lightheaded. I leaned against the side of my car, bent low, and vomited in the gutter. "Damn it, Sam." I cleared my throat and spit. "Some goddamned body did this to her."

"We'll see." He patted my shoulder, then headed back toward the scene of the accident.

"*You'll* see!" I got in the car, laid my head against the steering wheel, and let the tears come.

MOTHER AND I ARRIVED at the emergency room about the same time and were told they were doing x-rays and prepping Martha for surgery. They sent us to the surgical waiting room and told us they'd let us know something as soon as she was out.

Just before 2 a.m., a doctor in a blue gown and paisley head-cover came and told us that she'd suffered multiple fractures and broken bones, internal injuries, and a concussion. He said she was a very lucky girl, but that it was too early to tell if there would be any permanent damage. He said they would be moving her into an intensive care unit shortly and that we could see her for a few minutes then, but that she would not regain consciousness for days.

When I first saw her, I gasped. Practically her entire body was wrapped in bandages. There were two holes for her eyes and a hole for her mouth and a tube running into her nose. Her left leg had a cast to the hip and the right had one to mid-calf. It was three years ago all over again. I leaned close and whispered that I loved her.

An hour later I took Mom home and sat in the dark in Martha's bedroom trying to figure out what could have happened. Nothing made any sense. I picked up her writing tablet and there was Sydney's number she'd written down when I was at the beach house.

Sydney! I'd forgotten about Sydney.

I picked up the phone and dialed the number. It rang several times before a sleepy voice answered, "Hello?"

"It's me."

"Richard? What time is it?"

"I know it's late, but I had to talk to you."

"What's wrong?"

I dragged a hand over my face. "Martha was in an accident."

"Oh, Richard, I'm sorry. Is she...all right?"

My voice dropped to a whisper. "She's in the hospital."

"Is it bad?"

"Yeah, it's pretty bad. She might have brain damage. They said they may not know for sure for weeks, or even months."

"Oh, Richard. I'm sorry. What happened?"

"She was..." My eyes burned again. "...hit by a bus."

"Oh, no! How?"

"Nobody knows what happened, Sydney." I tried to hide the quiver in my voice. "She had gone back to that warehouse after I asked her not to go there anymore without me."

"Where are you now?"

I sucked in a deep breath and wiped my eyes. "I'm at Mom and Dad's."

"Come get me."

"What? Now?"

"I'd drive myself, but I wrecked my van. I just need fifteen minutes."

I took down the directions and fifteen minutes later pulled into Sydney's drive. As I stepped out of the car, she pulled the front door shut behind her and ran to me throwing her arms around me, drawing me into her as tightly as I drew her into me. For a while we just stood there in the dark and held each other. Finally, the fragrance of her hair and the touch of her cheek came through and all the years of pent-up angers, fears, and frustrations came spewing out of me. I withered into a mass of sobbing spasms. I tried to pull away, but her arms tightened around me and a tender hand cupped the back of my head.

"I'm so sorry," she whispered.

I pulled her to me and buried my face into her neck, and there—in the wee hours of the night—we wept together and our hearts fused. Together, we said good-bye to our pasts.

It was humiliating and disgraceful, but when it was over I felt cleansed.

I drove Sydney back to Mom's house where the two of us stretched out side by side on Martha's bed and laid in the darkness talking. We talked about Martha's accident, Sydney's accident, and the stitches in her head. And how she happened to be with Scott when I'd seen them at the hospital. Then we lay in silence wrapped in each other's arms until she turned her face upward and kissed me. It was a tender kiss, but one that swept through me like a great wave knocking me down and pulling me under. Out of control, breathless, tumbling in a sea of passion, we made love.

Afterward, we lay in the darkness holding on to each other as if afraid that if we let go, the other one would vanish and we'd end up back in our old lives. I never felt more attached to anyone in my life. Even our hearts read one another's rhythm and merged together. Lying next to Sydney staring at a faint green glow on the ceiling, my mind felt more alert than it had in years. I could see clearly how hard things must have been for my father and mother and understood for the first time the difficulties they must have faced in those early days. I doubted that I could have done it.

I lay in Sydney's arms staring at that green glow on the ceiling until I began to wonder about the glow itself and realized it was coming from a tiny light on Martha's laptop computer. I pressed the switch on the arm of her bed and raised the head high enough for me to read without awakening Sydney. Lifting the lid on the laptop, I found that it was on and that Martha had been working last on her novel. There were now one hundred seventy three pages. I pulled the computer stand closer to me, shifted back to the beginning of the story, and began reading.

It was titled *Down in Flames* by Martha Baimbridge. It opened with a shy teenage girl named Chelsea who, when invited by a popular boy in school to go on a trail ride with him and his friends, had been thrown from the horse and left paralyzed from the waist down. I read on.

From there, it was a heart-wrenching resemblance of many of the problems Martha had faced and the girl's struggle to accept her fate and put her life back together. It was at times difficult to read as I saw it more as Martha's story than Chelsea's, but I read on, feeling that at that moment my sister was speaking to me and that I was as close to her as I could get.

With Sydney sleeping quietly beside me, I accompanied Chelsea as she buckled down hard, did exactly what her therapists said, and struggled through the pain and frustration of striving to become whole again. But after much pain and little progress, she became angry and bitter. She was difficult to deal with and cruel to her doctors and therapists—even Andrew, who had fallen insanely in love with her. Turning inward, Chelsea became obsessed with the challenge of finding a better medicine, a better doctor, a better therapist, and fired them all.

Her friends stopped coming and her family gave up on her, yet she was determined to find a way. But one failure led to the next and frustration led to devastation, and finally to the crushing reality that she would never walk again. As Chelsea sat in her wheelchair perched high on a ridge overlooking the sea below and pondered suicide, my heart ached for her and I cried for her, and as dawn broke and Chelsea searched for some thread of hope to hold on to, the pages stopped abruptly and Martha left me hanging.

Oh, God! Maybe her suffering had been worse than I'd thought. Maybe she did throw herself out into that traffic. Maybe she'd lost all hope like Chelsea and needed relief—one way or another. Oh, Martha! Why didn't you tell me?

48

A MISTY RAIN WAS FALLING as Ashleigh crossed from the parking garage to the lobby of Duke Medical Center in Durham. A clock high on a wall read 7:39 a.m. Collapsing her umbrella, she stepped to the main information desk where an elderly woman stared at a computer monitor.

"Could you tell me which room David Matthews is in, please?" Ashleigh asked.

Leaning forward, the woman clicked a few keys on her keyboard and squinted at the monitor. "Let's see... Hmm. Is he a patient here?"

"He was in surgery all day yesterday."

"Matthews...Matthews...Okay, here he is. Are you family?"

"Sister."

"Well, he spent the night in Intensive Care, but he's being moved to another room right now and I don't have that number yet. Give me your name and I'll page you when I have it."

"How long is that going to take?"

"I don't know, honey. Usually not more than half an hour. I'll keep checking and will call for you when I get it."

Ashleigh gave the woman her name and stepped into the almost-empty waiting room. Picking up a recent issue of *People Magazine,* she settled into a padded chair. A TV on the wall above her softly chattered with *Good Morning America.* During the next fifteen minutes, visitors began lining up for passes and the waiting room filled with spouses, parents, and noisy children. As two women across from Ashleigh exchanged graphic details of their recent hysterectomies, a well-mannered, well-groomed eight-year-old boy sitting next to the women, placed his feet together on the floor, folded his hands in his lap, and stared at Ashleigh. Ashleigh checked the time and turned her attention back to the magazine.

"Look, Mama," the well-manner boy whispered loudly. "It's the woman on TV." Ashleigh felt a change in the mood around her.

Looking up, she realized that the entire section was staring at her. On another TV screen across the room she saw her own driver's license photograph.

"Miss Matthews," the receptionist called.

Ashleigh dropped the magazine in the seat next to hers, rose, and marched quickly out the front door slapping her sunglasses on as she left the building. Outside, she raised the umbrella and ran through the light rain toward the parking garage.

AS THE SOFT GRAY LIGHT of a rainy morning filtered into Martha's bedroom, Sydney opened her eyes and gazed into mine. I brushed a lock of hair off her forehead. "Good morning."

She smiled and tucked her face a bit lower into the covers. "Good morning."

"You look beautiful."

"Did we just spend our first night together?"

"Looks that way."

Sydney rose on an elbow. "I don't think I should be here when your mother comes down. Could you run me home?"

"Can I trust you to take my car and not wreck it?"

She smiled sheepishly. "What time do I need to be back?"

"I'll ride with Mom today if you'll promise to bring it back tonight."

She smiled. "Okay."

We kissed and just when things seemed headed toward a repeat of the night before, we heard mother stirring upstairs. Sydney jumped out of bed, dressed, took the keys to my car, and kissed me goodbye.

After she'd gone, the house felt hard and empty. My footsteps echoed off the walls and I became acutely aware of the pain in my swollen ankle as I limped upstairs to check on Mom. Through the door, I could hear her crying and it crushed my heart. I knocked twice, but after hearing no response opened the door ajar and looked in. Mom was seated at a window in her robe with her head down on a table. I pushed the door back and entered.

"You okay, Mom?"

She raised her head, covered her eyes with a hand, and sobbed. I dragged a stool up next to her and rubbed her back.

"Why?" she cried. "Will somebody *please* tell me *why?*"

I looked out the window at the backyard below where Martha and I had played together as kids. "I don't know, Mom. God works in mysterious ways."

"Don't give me that...*crap!* If there was a God in heaven, he would have taken better care of that child. She never did anything bad to anybody. She is an *angel*. One in a million!" Her voice dissipated into babbles and sobs.

"I know, Mom. I don't understand it either." I wrapped both arms around her and held her.

"I used to sit up here and watch the two of you out there playing in the yard when you were little. Chasing each other 'round the yard, climbing trees, and swinging from the branches. I can see it just as clearly as if it had happened yesterday." She sniffled and wiped her nose. "But I knew it wouldn't last. Nothing turns out good for me."

"What are you talking about, Mom?"

"I've always had a dark cloud hanging over my head, Richard."

"Now, Mom, you know that isn't so."

"No, I mean it. My life has been cursed from the beginning."

"Mom!"

"If I got a new dress, it would snag on something and get torn first time I wore it. If I got a dog, it'd get run over. Every good thing that ever came along in my life has turned bad."

"It's not true, Mom. You stop thinking like that."

She sniffled and wiped her nose. "Charlie's wreck, Martha's first accident, and now *this* one. She could be brain-dead." She pressed a tissue to her eyes. "Gus is dying and you're in all that trouble."

I sighed. "Look, somebody needs to be there when Martha wakes up. Don't you think we should get dressed and get back over there?"

"*If* she wakes up."

"She's going to wake up, Mom, and things are going to get back to normal. You'll see."

She turned to the window. "Yes. Back to *normal*." She dabbed the tissue into each eye.

I closed my arms around her, kissed her forehead, and helped her into the bathroom where she blew her nose and wiped her face with a wet cloth. I left her there, took her car, and ran over to my house for a shower and change of clothes. The swelling in my ankle was getting worse and it killed me to walk on it.

When we arrived at the hospital, we looked in on Martha first. She was still unconscious. Blood had soaked through her bandages here and there, but her breathing looked strong and steady. The doctor stopped by and told us that she had a serious concussion and that they'd given her medication that would keep her unconscious until the swelling went down.

"How long's that going to take?" Mom asked.

The doctor gripped Mom's shoulder. "Could be weeks."

After we'd spent a few minutes with Martha, Mom asked me to go upstairs and tell Dad what had happened. "Ain't no way I could bear to tell him myself," she said. "Couldn't get the words out without balling like a baby. He'll just get mad and upset if I do it."

FROM THE FOOT OF HIS BED, I watched the peaceful rhythm of his sleep and questioned the logic of telling him anything at all, knowing it could possibly kill him. *But what if she dies?* I had to tell him. I owed him that.

I moved cautiously on my swollen ankle to the chair next to the bed and sat with my head bowed. All of a sudden my exhaustion caught up with me. I couldn't get things organized in my head. I didn't know where to begin.

"What are you doing here this time of morning?" he asked, his voice smooth and gentle.

I leaned forward resting my elbows on my knees. My head hung low and my voice was hoarse. "I came to bring you some very bad news, Dad."

"They've arrested you for the murder of that girl?"

I sighed. "Worse than that."

The slow beeping of his heart monitor skipped a beat. "What then? Have I been fired? Ha! That sounds like something that jackass would do." I covered my face with my hands while he babbled on. "Call the house and fire me while I'm on my deathbed so he won't have to send flowers to the funeral. What a tight-ass. I made that air-head a millionaire. For what?"

"Dad..."

He breathed heavily. "Shit, maybe you got the right idea after all, boy. Work for your damned self. Can't get fired if you work for yourself."

I drew a deep breath and sighed. "Martha's been in an accident, Dad."

His head rose off the bed. His red-rimmed eyes bore into me. The beep on the heart monitor sped up. "What kind of accident?"

"Her wheelchair rolled out into the road. A bus hit her."

His mouth fell open and his head plopped against the pillow. He drew the back of his right hand up against his thin gray hair. The heart monitor began to gallop and his left hand began pounding angrily against the mattress. "Is she..."

"She's in a comma."

"Damn!" A tear trickled from his eye. His voice grew louder. "How much more will that baby have to endure, for Christ's sake?"

"She went through surgery last night and she's in intensive care now."

His hand slapped harder and his heart rate climbed above one hundred thirty beats per minute. "Hasn't she had enough, goddamnit? What the hell's it gonna take?" When his heart rate hit one-sixty, an alarm sounded on the monitor.

My voice cracked as I choked back tears. "Dad?"

A nurse rushed through the door and tried to calm him as he flailed about pounding his fist. "God-almight-damn!"

She pressed a button on the wall and a half-minute later, another nurse entered with a syringe. I didn't have to be told he'd be out for the rest of the day.

THE BANK CLERK held out her hand. "Your key, Mr. McGillikin?" She was youthful with long curly hair streaked with highlights, an early tan, and thick eyebrows. Scott's eyes dropped to the gap in her blouse—open just enough to expose the top of a breast—then to his billfold. Digging into a hidden slot, he extracted a small brass key and laid it in the palm of her hand. Her eyes rose to his. "Aren't you the McGillikin that my daddy's built that new yawl for?"

"Is your daddy named Walker?"

"Lenny Walker."

"Then I guess I'm the one."

She smiled. "That's—by far—the best sailboat he ever built."

"Is it?"

"Oh, yes. It is. And I should know. I take them all out for their maiden voyages and I took yours up the river a couple of Saturdays back. It handles like a dream. Best boat I ever sailed."

"That's good to know. I'm taking it out for my first run today."

"God, I'd love to go with you. I'd rather be sailing than anything." She leaned closer and whispered. "Especially this."

The fragrance of her perfume filled his head. "I know exactly what you mean, Miss Walker?"

She nudged him with her shoulder and winked. "You can call me Tiffany."

A thin smile cut across his face. "Tiffany. I like that. How old are you, Tiffany?"

"Old enough to handle that big toy of yours." She cut her eyes at him, flipped her hair back, and inserted the keys into a pair of locks high on the wall. His eyes roamed to her breasts then to the back of her skirt as she reached up with both hands, turned the keys together, and withdrew a large safety deposit box from its vault. "Hey, this is heavy," she groaned. "What've you got in here? Gold bars?" He smiled in spite of the pain that shot up his left arm when the box pressed against an open wound under his sleeve. "Take your time, Mr. McGillikin. Just let me know when you're finished. And if you ever need anyone to crew with you, just give me a call."

"Thanks. I'll do that."

When she'd gone, he carried the box into a private chamber, set it next to his briefcase, and locked the door. From the box he removed three passports—each with his photograph, but a different name—a Beretta 9mm semi-automatic pistol with a silencer, a full box of ammunition, and close to two hundred thousand dollars in cash. He stuffed it all into his briefcase on top of a photograph of Ashleigh Matthews, the one person to have pulled one over on him—a score he intended to settle if it took him the rest of his life.

He locked the briefcase, signaled Tiffany that he'd finished, and crossed the street to another bank where he transferred $2 million dollars from his clients' trust accounts to an offshore account in the Cayman Islands along with several million more from his lucrative Internet porn business.

He returned to the first bank, asked Miss Walker if she'd like to join him on a year-long cruise to Central and South America, and waited as she grabbed her purse and walked out on her job.

49

D ETECTIVE SAM JONES and his partner Crabby Staten
stepped from their car and were met by a pudgy fifty-year-old
with a two-day beard and a jaw full of chewing tobacco.

"We jus' put this asphalt down Monday," the man slurred
in a deep southern drawl. "And a piece of it caved in t'day when
somebody drove over it. We figur'd we had us a water leak, but when
we dug in, this is what we found."

The two detectives stepped to the edge of a hole that had been cut
into the asphalt, looked down, and saw the crown of a man's head
exposed in the bottom. A wisp of water misting behind it washed a
trench around the body.

"Anybody missing on your crew?" Sam asked the man.

"Nope."

"Where's the cutoff to that water line?"

"Got no idea. We jus' do the paving."

Sam pulled the tail of his long coat up around his waist, stepped
into the hole, slipped on the wet clay, and stumbled down to the
body. Regaining his footing, he snatched a ball-point pen from his
breast pocket, bent over the exposed head, and dug the dirt back
from the man's face. *Dark complexion. Thin mustache. Mexican?*

Sam scaled back up the slope and—with the help of the foreman's
beefy hand—climbed out. "Notice anything unusual around here the
last few days?"

The man spit a stream of tobacco juice toward the curb and
adjusted the wad in his cheek. "One of the guys said somebody'd
messed with his backhoe over the weekend."

"Where is it?"

"That's it down yonder." He indicated a machine parked two
blocks away.

"And the man that runs it?"

He pointed to a crewman propped nearby with his arms folded
across his chest. He wore dark wraparound sunglasses under a

Caterpillar baseball cap, and his hair was pulled back in a three-inch ponytail. "Thanks," Sam replied, stamping the mud off his shoes as he walked toward the backhoe operator. While Sam took a look at the machine, a public works superintendent showed up, studied a survey map, and backtracked to the nearest water turn-off valve. Shortly thereafter, the misty spray ceased and the forensic team arrived to begin the work of extracting the body.

WHEN SCOTT AND TIFFANY arrived at the docks, *Steal Away,* the sleek, black, fifty-five-foot Lenny Walker original, pulled anxiously at its mooring lines at the far end of the dock. Its two masts towered above all other sailboats in the marina reaching for the sky. The crowd in the bar had moved to the windows just to admire it and take bets on to whom it belonged. Scott could feel the jealousy in their eyes as he and Tiffany headed down the pier.

Although he'd learned to sail smaller boats, Scott was not capable of handling this one by himself. He'd assumed he'd have a few months to spend on the Intracoastal Waterway learning to sail it with Sydney's help before taking it out into the Atlantic. But now, with Tiffany handling the boat, they could be in Abacos—their first port of call—within a few days. He would be a multi-millionaire *free* to come and go as he pleased, to live life to its fullest, to explore the world the way man was intended—seeing, tasting, touching, and taking whatever and *whomever* he pleased. He'd slip away under the cover of darkness dumping his garbage at sea.

And, for now, he had Tiffany.

Like a panther lurking in the grass, he could taste her already as she ran ahead of him and stepped over the railing onto the wooden deck. She would do for now. She'd teach him to sail and he'd teach her how to please him. And when he grew tired of her, he'd pick up another.

As he climbed down to the galley below deck, Tiffany threw her arms around him bouncing up and down. "Thank you. Thank you. Thank you, Mr. McGillikin. I can't believe this is really happening."

"Please, call me Scott."

She slid off him and saluted. "Aye, aye, sir. Mr.—Scott."

"Good. Now, we need to get a few things straight. Can you cook?"

She wrinkled her nose. "Some."

"Very well. Your job will be to keep the boat clean, afloat, and on course."

"No problem. I can do that."

"My job will be to plan the trips, pay the bills, and teach you to cook."

"Great. When do we sail?"

"Tonight."

"Seriously? I'll need to run home and get some things."

"No. If you go home, somebody's going to want to know why you're not at work." Scott opened his billfold and handed Tiffany five one-hundred dollar bills. "We'll shop in every port. There won't be room for it all. But today, just buy what you'll need to get underway and be back here by one o'clock."

"Yes! Wow! This is going to be so much *fun!*" She gave him a daughterly squeeze, then climbed out. When he was sure she was gone, he moved the passports and one-quarter of the money from the briefcase to a combination safe he'd had built-in, then hid the gun, the cartridges, and the rest of the money around the boat.

He tuned the satellite TV to the *Weather Channel* while checking the rest of the equipment to see that it was all working. VHF marine radio, GPS receiver, single sideband LORAN radio, depth finder, radar, and NOAA weather radio.

The forecast for the tropics called for no disturbances during the next seven days. He switched the TV to the local antenna and flipped through the Wilmington stations. Everything seemed to be working perfectly. *Plan the work. Work the plan.*

As he checked items off his list, the TV station interrupted its scheduled program with a news bulletin. "*Twenty-three-year-old Ashleigh Matthews has been found alive and well.*" Scott's eyes shifted to the TV. "*She was spotted this morning at Duke Medical Center in Durham where, according to eye-witnesses, she was seated in a hospital waiting room when photos of her were aired on television. Recognized by others in the waiting room, she fled the hospital.*" While the reporter interviewed an elderly woman who said that Ashleigh seemed alert and aware of what was going on around her, they showed still shots recorded by hospital security cameras of Ashleigh as she fled. "*Anyone with any information as to the whereabouts of Ashleigh Matthews is asked to contact the Wilmington Police Department.*"

Spreading a nautical chart on a table, he used a pushpin to mark the location of a farm on the south side of the Cape Fear River and dropped a key on the pin. He then wrote a note telling Tiffany to take the boat to the location marked by the pin, to transfer the boxes she'd find in the barn to the boat, and that he'd meet her there after dark.

50

S YDNEY PICKED ME UP at the hospital and drove me to the site of Martha's accident. A southwesterly breeze had brought in warm tropical air and with it, the scent of the Japanese Cherry blossoms lining the other side of the road. As we stood at the corner with cars and trucks streaming past, I closed my eyes. *Martha, what happened? Talk to me, Babe.*

Years of memories popped into my head, one on top the other like a Fourth of July fireworks show. Things I'd long ago forgotten. The time Martha went to Donald Wolfe's house and punched him in the nose because he'd punched me at school. Martha pressing a towel to my bleeding leg after I fell over a chain-link fence and split my calf open. Martha lifting a neighbor's dog off the street and carrying it all the way home after it had been hit by a car.

I followed skid marks in front of me to the right where they jumped the curb. Tiny bits of glass, plastic, and metal lay in a ribbon of sand that stretched along the gutter. They meant something, but I'd had no sleep. I couldn't think. My mind was only clicking on one cylinder.

"See anything?" Sydney asked.

I looked back up the steep hill and shook my head. "I don't understand how she could have just rolled off into the street."

"That's a steep hill."

I tried to imagine that—her coming down that hill not being able to stop, bumping off the curb into that steady stream of traffic—but it didn't work for me. No way could that have happened. "I don't think she would have come down that hill in the first place. It's too rough. The sidewalk's all pushed up by the roots in places."

"Unless she did it deliberately."

I didn't want to think about that. I'd read her story. I knew where it had stopped with Chelsea poised on the brink of suicide and I told Sydney about it. "But I don't think Martha did this to herself. Not now. The timing's all wrong."

"Which means you think somebody had to have pushed her."

I didn't want to think about that, either. The thought of Martha being shoved into traffic and knowing what was going to happen was just too difficult to consider. My throat closed up on me as I felt the fear she must have felt and I grunted to clear it. "Who would have done that?" My eyes stung again.

"A mugger maybe?" I pondered that, but didn't reply. "Or someone from the warehouse."

I wiped my eyes, turned away from the corner, and looked up and down the street. "This is not on the way to the warehouse, so what was she doing here?"

"Looking for something?"

"Minutes earlier, she'd called Sam from the warehouse and surely had intended on waiting for him. So I think she must have either followed someone here...or was *brought* here."

"So—either way—there had to be someone else here."

"And she could only have come from that direction," I said, looking east. "—or down that hill."

Sydney and I walked eastward for two blocks looking for some kind of clue, but found nothing that seemed to be connected. We returned to the corner and started up the hill when something caught her eye. She reached into the ivy next to the wall, pulled back a large class ring, and held it out on her open palm. "Some guy lost his class ring. UNC. Sigma Nu. He shouldn't be too hard to track down." She looked inside the band turning it slowly. "It's—" She gasped.

"What?"

"It's Scott's. Scott McGillikin's."

"You've got to be kidding." I looked inside. There it was. *Robert Scott McGillikin.* It looked clean; no dirt or film on it anywhere. "Wonder how long it's been laying out here?"

"It couldn't have been very long anyway. I've never seen him without it."

I bounced it in the palm of my hand. It was heavy. Not the kind of thing that would drop off your finger without your noticing. "Does he live around here?"

"No. Not unless he's just moved."

"What's it doing here? What was *he* doing here?"

"He's a lawyer. Maybe there was another accident here—before Martha's."

"Even it that's true, don't you think he would've noticed it when it fell off?"

"I would think," she replied.

"I'd like to give it to him, myself, if you don't mind. I'd like to know what he was doing here."

"Sure. I'm not going to be seeing him—I hope."

I pocketed the ring. "Have you got time to stop by Mother's? I want to take a look at Martha's notes."

"An hour."

"Let's go."

WE SCANNED THE FILES in Martha's computer concerning *her* case, but didn't find anything new. I noticed, however, that she'd been working recently in a file called "Richard." Opening it, we found most of the things she and I had talked about since Ashleigh disappeared as well as a few things I knew nothing about. Sydney sat next to me and together we read a clipping about a man named Bob McGillikin who had died in an auto accident back in the 1980s and a man that police were looking for named Dane Bonner.

"There was a man at that beach house they called Mr. Bonner," I said. "And Martha told me she was looking for more information on him." Scrolling down the file we came across a picture of a redheaded, freckle-faced boy labeled *Robert Scott McGillikin at UNC* along with it was a summary of his rather outstanding scholastic career.

Sydney shook her head. "The name's the same, but that's not the Robert Scott McGillikin we know."

"So, what's she onto here?"

There was a link to a Wake Forest University webpage. I clicked the link and a page entitled "Robert Scott McGillikin" opened. First came the text then, as a picture began to appear in the top left corner of the screen, I scrolled down the page. It was another summary of McGillikin's education and background, much of it a repeat from the UNC site. "I don't get it. Why would she care about this guy?" I scrolled back to the top of the page and the picture leapt out at us.

Sydney gasped. This was definitely a photo of *our* Scott McGillikin. "What's going on here? Are there *two* Robert Scott McGillikins?"

I jumped back to the newspaper article. "I thought he was killed in a car wreck."

"According to that clipping, he was. But according to that transcript, he went on to finish law school."

We searched through the file again, but found nothing else about either of the two men. "Somehow Scott's tied into this thing besides being your lawyer."

I sighed. "Do you think he could also be working for Bonner?"

"Nothing would surprise me about Scott. What do we *know* about him?"

"We know he's my attorney and that he graduated from Wake Forest Law School."

"And he once told me he was raised in an orphanage."

"But the article said that the McGillikin raised at that orphanage died in a wreck."

"And he doesn't look like the man in the photo, either."

The computer dinged and a message appeared on the screen. *New mail has arrived. Would you like to read it now?*

I clicked the "yes" button and it opened a piece of new mail with the name *Dane Bonner* in the subject line containing a couple of photographs in the body.

"Richard! That's a photo of Scott!"

"But the sender says it's Dane Bonner."

"Well, I've been with him for five years. That's Scott."

The photo was fuzzy, but it looked exactly like a younger version of Scott. "Didn't that article say McGillikin was killed and Bonner disappeared after the accident?"

"Yes. The police wanted to question him, but could never find him."

"Yet someone showed up at Wake Forest and used the scholarship."

She pulled at my arm. "You don't think Bonner took the real McGillikin's place, do you?"

"Can a person get away with that?"

"What better way to hide from the police than to become someone else?"

"So, my attorney, Scott McGillikin—the very person I'm expecting to clear my name—could actually be the same person Ashleigh was running from. I withdrew the ring from my pocket and held it in front of me. "So this ring must have belonged to the original Robert Scott McGillikin and was stolen at the time of the accident. Which tells me that the sly son-of-a-bitch might have had this plan in his head even *before* the wreck that killed the real Scott McGillikin." As I rotated the ring in my hand, sunlight streaming in the window caught in the stone. There was a brilliant blue flash that left the image "N3" lingering in my eye for an instant. I looked again and the Greek letters ΣN were upside down forming a rough "N3."

"Oh, my God!" I looked at Sydney. "It was Scott all along!"

"What was Scott?" she asked looking at the ring.

"Martha always said that when she was thrown out that window, she saw a flash of blue, the letter N, and the number three." I handed her the ring. "Turn the ring upside down and tell me what you see."

Sydney rotated the ring. "N3?"

"Right! That ring was there when she was thrown off that ledge and now it shows up in the same place where she was hit by a bus."

"Scott?"

"This *cannot* be a coincidence! The son-of-a-bitch tried to *kill* her—*twice!*"

"Oh Richard!"

I disconnected the connection cable and tucked the laptop under my arm. "Come on! I want to see what Sam Jones thinks about this."

SCOTT MCGILLIKIN BOUNCED onto the sales lot at Wilmington Foreign Cars, parked his one-year-old Porsche Boxster at the front door, dropped the title on the desk, and got about half of what it was worth in cash. He took a cab to the airport, rented a Mercedes-Benz SL550 Roadster, and walked into Duke Medical Center in Durham two hours later.

"Aye'm Scott McGillikin, attorney for Miss Ashleigh Matthews," he drawled with his fake accent to a steely-eyed woman in administration. "Aye have the papers authorizing me to act in her behalf and to secure the release of her brother, David Matthews." It only took forty-five minutes for Scott to muscle his way through the system and have a heavily bandaged, heavily sedated David brought to his car. When David saw Scott, he raised his head and spoke in a slur. "Where's...Ashleigh?"

Scott tossed David's bag behind the seat and helped him into the car. "She's waiting for you, David. She asked me to take you to her."

"Why...isn't...she...here?"

Scott fastened David's seatbelt, thanked the hospital volunteer for his help, and got behind the wheel. "Ashleigh was identified at the hospital this morning and the local police are out looking for her." He opened the packet of information the hospital gave him and found a telephone number for Ashleigh. "But she's going to join us later." He set the page to the side and fired up the car's engine.

David's tongue was thick and his mind sluggish. "When?"

Dropping the faked accent, Scott replied, "Tonight, I suspect." He pulled the gearshift back and the car rumbled off.

ASHLEIGH PACKED A FEW BOXES and placed them into the Honda Civic she'd picked up for six hundred dollars, then called David's room to tell him what was going on, but got no answer. She called back, got through to the nurse on duty, and was told that David had checked out.

"What? He just had surgery yesterday! He's not supposed to check out until day after tomorrow. Please check again."

The woman on the line assured her he had checked out.

Ashleigh tried not to lose control. "When? How?"

The nurse transferred her to an administrative clerk and when she put her on hold, Ashleigh got beeped and switched to the other call. "David?"

"Hello, Ashleigh." The man's voice sounded familiar.

"Who is this?"

"I think you know."

"What do you want?"

"Would you like to speak to David?"

Ashleigh grasped the edge of a table to steady herself.

"Ashleigh?" The voice was sleepy.

She dropped into a chair. "David? Are you all right?"

"What's...going...on?"

"I don't know, Sweetie. Just—"

"As you can see," Scott said, "he's fine...for now."

"What do you want?"

"There's that little matter of one hundred fifty thousand dollars."

"I don't have it anymore! I spent it!"

"Come on, Ash. All of it?"

"I've got..." she exhaled, "...maybe a third."

"Fifty thousand? That's like a million dollars in some parts of the world."

"Fine. It's yours."

"Good. Bring it to Wilmington tonight and keep your phone on. I'll let you know where to meet me."

"I'll never make it. My picture's all over the TV."

"That's your problem, darling." The line went dead.

"Dane? *Dane!*"

51

I DROPPED SYDNEY OFF at her dance school and found Sam Jones in his office picking through a muddy stack of canceled checks and file folders. There were several more mud-caked boxes on the floor around him. He leaned back in his chair. "I'm sorry about your sister, Richard. I never expected Martha to do anything like that. She must have been a lot worse off than everyone thought."

"She didn't do that to herself, Sam. Somebody pushed her."

"I know it's hard to believe she'd—"

"No, really, Sam. That's what I came to see you about. I found some things on her computer I think you need to see." I set the laptop on his desk. "And I think I know who did it."

"Did what?"

"Who tried to *kill* her."

"Oh, for Christ's sake, Richard. Now you're as bad as her—trying to play detective."

"Please. Just give me a minute. One minute." I dug the ring from my pocket and handed it to him. "Look at that and tell me what you see."

"It...looks like a class ring to me. UNC. There's a million of them around Wilmington."

"Look at the name inside."

He sighed, propped his elbows on his desk, and looked inside the ring. "Robert Scott McGillikin. The attorney?"

"I believe so."

He handed the ring back to me. "I'm sure he'll be glad to get it back. Now if—"

"Sam, Sydney Deagan found that ring this afternoon on that corner where Martha was hit."

"And I found all these boxes buried in a hole in the ground today along with a dead body and a 44 magnum. And it's all connected to that house that blew up. *Dane Bonner's* files." He grasped a handful of checks and waved them at me. "These checks have his signature on them. I have a record of his whole life here. So if you'll please let me get back to it, I'd like to see what I can make of it before another body shows up."

"That's the man! Please, Sam. Let me show you this one thing." I brought up the photo of Bonner and spun the computer to face Sam. "That's Dane Bonner." Sam stared at the monitor. "He was raised in the same orphanage as Scott McGillikin, only McGillikin died in a car wreck after finishing his undergrad work at UNC." Sam sighed, but I continued. "...and I think this man—Dane Bonner—took his identity. Went on to Wake Forest and used his scholarship."

Sam slumped back. "Are you out of your mind?"

"Damn it, Sam. I know it sounds crazy, but I believe McGillikin *is* Bonner." Sam picked up a document in front of him and began scanning it. "Remember what Martha said about a blue flash and an 'N3?' And how she had you try to figure out what that meant? Sam, look at the ring. Please?" I handed it back to him. "Turn it around." Sam sighed loudly and rotated the ring. "You're looking at it."

"Looking at what?"

"Upside down it becomes N3."

"If you use your imagination, you might be able to make an N3 out of it." He tossed the ring back at me.

"Sam, this ring was there the night Martha dropped from that window and it was at that intersection last night. Look at her computer files. Please. She figured out that Scott was Bonner. It's all right here. Look at it."

"I see it, Richard. I'm sorry about your sister, and I know you're just trying to help. But there is nothing here that *proves* anything."

"What about the pictures?"

"I'm sorry, Richard. You're going to have to come up with more than that."

My eyes dropped from his face to the checks on his desk. One stack had toppled over and were spread such that the signatures all lined up one on top the other. But one in the group was different. "Did you say these were Bonner's?" I reached for one of the checks.

"Don't touch that!"

I withdrew my hand and pointed. "I couldn't help but notice that the signature on *that* one is different from the rest."

Sam leaned forward and, using his pencil eraser, slipped the check out of the stack. It was signed Scott McGillikin. He compared the signature to a few of the others. "Well I'll be damned. Looks like Mr. Bonner forgot which checkbook he was using."

My cell phone rang. It was Mother.

"Hello?"

"Richie, you need to come now. Martha's taken a turn for the worse."

52

TIFFANY FOUND THE NOTE and the key and immediately ripped the tags off a new string bikini her mother would never have allowed her to wear. Strutting about under the watchful eyes of every man on the dock, she cranked the engine, brought in the lines, shoved the magnificent sailboat off, and motored *Steal Away* out to the channel where she found a strong southerly breeze—perfect for a reach down the river.

Bringing the vessel about, she headed directly into the wind, set the brake on the wheel, and raised the mizzen to steady the boat. Electing to keep the mainsail furled, she climbed barefooted onto the roof of the cabin, sidled toward the bow, and—bending her knees as the vessel rose to meet each wave—reached to the low side and tugged the line to release the jib. As the massive sail unrolled like a window shade, its bitter end flapped loosely in the wind, snapping and popping against the mainmast, sending her heart to racing.

Releasing the brake, she steered the boat away from the wind letting the loose end of the jib flap out to the side as she expertly wrapped the sheet around a wench. Then, with the wind in her face and the sun on her back, she cranked the massive sail in. As it filled with air and caught the wind, the boat leaned and she felt a surge of power.

Back at the helm, she turned the switch and the putter of the engine died, replaced by the sound of water swishing along the side of the hull.

For Tiffany, this was *heaven*. There was nothing better than sailing and the best life she could imagine would be to sail about the world forever.

She'd admired the boat's sleek lines as it came together on its construction frame at her father's shipyard with its golden teak deck, lacquered black hull, and brass fittings—a beauty to behold. But it was on its maiden voyage that she'd really fallen in love with it. It was the majestic way that it sat in the water and the ease with which it handled that she loved. 'A pussy to sail' as the men in the yard would say. And she loved the name. "*Steal Away*," she whispered into the wind.

It was a quick ten miles to the farm—too quick—and she had time to spare so she marked the location on the global positioning system and sailed on for another ten miles before coming about and returning to the farm.

After tying the boat off at the end of a twisted weather-grayed dock with boards missing here and there, Tiffany went for a quick swim, changed into Bermuda shorts and a T-shirt, and took the short walk up the dock. Keeping a sharp eye out for snakes, she followed a dirt path through long-shanked reeds to a hundred-year-old barn that had long ago given up holding back nature. Tallest at the center, it spread wide at the bottom including an open shed on each side. Its rusting tin roof lay folded back on one corner exposing a sagging, black skeleton of a roof underneath. The boards that made up its skin had over time been bleached gray and warped by the sun, a few breaking free and hanging by a single nail. The three openings on the back side—two ports near the top and a tall narrow rectangle at the bottom—were black in shadow and reminded Tiffany of the terrifying mask used in the "Scream" movies.

There was a pair of doors on the far right held shut with a padlock that opened with the key. Inside she discovered a cache of cardboard boxes and wooden crates, some closed and some open. There was food of all kinds, enough to last at least a month. There was water, wine, paper products, pots and pans, utensils and dishes. There were towels, pillows, life preservers, and a broom.

Starting with the heaviest boxes, she lifted a case of wine and stumbled out the door struggling to carry it. The bottles clinked against each other with each step and she had to stop twice to rest before getting it on deck and into the cockpit. The boxes of canned food seemed even heavier. She found a loose board in the reeds and dropped it across the span between the boat and the dock to use as a ramp, and pushed the seventh box—a wooden crate—across it to the boat. As she maneuvered the box toward the galley, it fell open exposing the butt of a pistol wrapped in newspaper.

Taking the gun in her hand, Tiffany raised it, looked down the sight, and aimed it at the barn.

"Bang. Bang," she whispered.

Digging through the crate, she also found five boxes of bullets buried among a hammer and various tools. She took the pistol and the bullets down the ladder to the galley, dropped them in a black plastic garbage bag, and lifted the bilge hatch in the floor with the intention of placing it in the narrow space below the floor. But the space was filled with other plastic bags. Opening one, she found it stuffed with hundred dollar bills. She checked another and it, too, was stuffed with money. Jamming the gun in with the other bags, she replaced the bilge hatch, climbed the ladder, and spent the rest of the afternoon loading the boat and stowing the cargo away.

IN THE SEMI-DARKNESS OF MARTHA'S HOSPITAL ROOM, Mother filled me in on what the doctor had said. They were having trouble bringing the hemorrhaging under control and that there was more swelling in her head than they'd expected. She said they took her back into surgery and opened another hole in her skull in an attempt to relieve the pressure, but the prognosis was not good. We hugged each other for awhile and for awhile I was strong for Mom. But left alone with the monotonous rhythm of a life-support system that neither knew her nor cared, I lost my composure.

She'd spent her whole life looking out for me, fixing the things I'd broken, trying to keep us together as a family. She had the biggest heart of anyone I knew and while I seldom told her, I loved her. I never imagined there could come a time when she wouldn't be around. Now, as she lay at death's door, I feared that she'd die never really knowing how much I loved and needed her.

Moving to her bedside I laid my head next to hers, my mouth at her ear, and sobbed shamelessly. "Oh Babe, I'm so sorry. Why did you have to go back down to that warehouse? Why didn't you call me to go with you?" I choked on the words as they poured out of me. "You were right, you know." I wiped my tears on the sheet. "It was Scott. I found your notes and showed them to Sam. And the ring. Sydney found his ring, Babe. At the scene of the accident, in the grass. We saw the flash of blue and the 'N3' just as you did. But they're on to him now, Babe. It's finally over. You did it! He'll get his, I *promise* you."

She flinched as though shocked by a jolt of electricity.

"That's right, Babe. Fight this thing. Fight it, girl. I swear to God I'll take care of you for the rest of your life. Just don't die. Please. I'll never forgive myself if you die. I love you, Babe. You are the best sister in the world."

Her body jerked again and this time the monitor skipped a beat. I raised to look at her face. Behind the holes in the bandage her eyes stretched wide. One stared to the upper right, the other down left.

"Yes, Babe! Fight it! Stay with me, girl!"

The beeping stopped. She tensed, then exhaled a long, slow breath.

"Babe?"

Her eyes rolled up, the lids relaxed, and her body fell limp.

"*Babe!* No. No, please. *Babe!*"

I lunged to the door and flung it back. "*Somebody! I need help!*"

They must have already known. They were running toward me and shoved me out of the way as they crowded around Martha's bed and began CPR. One of nurses pulled the curtain around them blocking my view. Ten minutes later, the doctor stepped out pausing at the door to gather her thoughts before giving us the news. "We got her back—for the moment."

Mom grabbed her arm. "She's going to be all right, isn't she?"

The woman took Mom's hand in hers and squeezed it. Her eyes revealed the truth. "Unless the swelling goes down pretty soon, it's impossible to say what's going to happen. She has massive internal injuries including substantial damage to her one remaining kidney." Mother's hands went to her mouth and tears filled her eyes. "If she lives, she could end up on dialysis for the rest of her life. It's really up to her now. We'll know more in a few days."

The doctor told us we'd have to leave, that they'd call if there was any change, but Mom refused to leave choosing instead to wait in the chapel down the hall.

I left in a daze. Nowhere to go, nothing to do. Afraid of what would happen to my mother if Martha died. And to *me!*

I stood in the parking lot waiting for instructions; where to go, what to do. It was a glorious spring day. The temperature had warmed into the low 70s and the world moved about as if nothing had changed—and I guess it really hadn't.

But *I* had.

For once, it all made sense. Trucks rushing here, there, and yonder. Women pushing baby strollers. Birds circling overhead. A man hammering a steel beam into place. Another man on his knee scolding a little boy.

Life just isn't that complicated.

I'd spent mine in a speeding car with an unpredictable fun-house steering wheel and no brakes while the world was moving in the opposite direction. *What had I been focused on? What had I been trying to achieve? Why had I been so out of sync?*

Martha's life may have been short and difficult, but it had been filled with love and friends and *purpose*. She gave and gave of herself and asked for so little. The pressure intensified across my chest and tears distorted my vision. My heart was beating much too fast and my head felt light.

I got in the car and drove around until dark. Nowhere to go. Nothing to do. I pulled into the parking lot at the dance studio an hour early to wait for Sydney to get off. Time seemed to stand still. I called Mom to see if there'd been any change. She said no and added that Dad was asking for me. I told her to tell him I'd be by tomorrow.

My mind wouldn't stop thinking about the accident. About how terrifying it must have been for Martha when Scott shoved her out into that street. I laid my head on the steering wheel and wept while people going and coming from the dance studio eyed me cautiously.

After the last of the cars had pulled away, Sydney opened the door and got in.

"How's Martha?" she asked dropping her bags on the floor.

I wanted so badly to keep my composure. I'd rehearsed what I was going to say, but instead shook my head and could only say, "It's bad." Afraid that I'd break down if I said too much, I spoke very little on the ride to her house and let Sydney ramble on about how good doctors are these days and what they can do. At her house I cut the engine and stared out into the darkness.

"Have you had anything to eat?" she asked. I shook my head. "Come on in. I'll fix you something."

I wasn't hungry and didn't think I could hold it down if I did eat, but I didn't want to be *alone*. Not this night.

Her house was like a garden inside. Flowers and plants everywhere. Green, orange, blue, yellow, billowing, hanging, standing. It smelled more like a florist than a home. It was nice. Martha would love it.

Sydney warmed a bowl of home-made soup and made me a peanut-butter and jelly sandwich to go with it.

The more I ate, the more talkative I became. "She wanted so much to have children of her own," I said, my words sounding like fingernails on sandpaper. "But the first accident took that away from her."

"She would make such a good mother, too."

"Yes, she would."

Sydney saw tears come to my eyes and slipped her arms around me. "What are you thinking about?" she asked.

"How that son-of-a-bitch Scott just sat in that chair with that smug-ass look on his stupid-ass face acting so damned concerned and the whole time *knowing* he was the one that pushed her off that ledge."

"I still can't believe Scott did that."

"Oh, he did it all right." Leaning forward, I covered my face with my hands. "Jesus Christ! Can you believe all the things he's gotten away with? How the hell can somebody go directly from Jr. high to law school and pull that off?"

Sydney stroked my back. "He *is* clever, I'll give him that."

"Oh no!"

"What?"

I slammed my hands on the table and grasped my head. "I told him everything. What Martha was doing and what she'd found out." I pressed my clinched fists against my temples. "I think I even told him she was going back down to the warehouse at night looking for a light to show up in that window. *Damn! I set her up!*"

Sydney laid her head against my back. "Shhhhh." Her voice was like fingers sliding across satin. "Don't say that. It's not your fault."

"That...son-of-a-bitch!" I couldn't hold back the tears. "Oh, Babe, I'm so sorry."

Sydney squeezed her arms around me. "Shhhh."

"Damn it!" I rose from the table breaking her hold. "I can't let him get away with this!"

"Come on." Sydney took my hand and pulled. "Let's go get a shower."

Tears streamed down my face. "Oh, God!"

She pulled me stumbling into a nearby bedroom, shoved me onto my back, and took *control* of my mind and body. Falling on top me, she redirected the storm raging inside me re-channeling my pain and fury into passion and desire. *Icy hatred* melted into *flaming love.* For the next hour the fire and the cold swirled through me ripping me apart as she held me down, kissed me, and took me to a final release that shattered every obstacle I had left to becoming the man I was born to be.

As I lay spent listening to the quiet sounds of a radio I never knew was even playing, I realized I couldn't live without Sydney. I *had* to have her.

"I love you, Sydney."

"I love you, too, Richard." She laid her head against my chest. "I think I always have."

ASHLEIGH SLOWED HER CAR and peered up the dark driveway to the pool house in the backyard. Seeing no lights, no people, and especially no police, she eased down the street and pulled into the shadows of a huge live oak dripping with Spanish moss. Emerging from the car, she kept to the shadows running alongside a line of azaleas into a neighbor's backyard. Clutching her house key in her hand, she dashed across several backyards then cowered behind a row of bushes to avoid Mrs. Winslow's hawkish eyes.

With a sliver of moon twinkling off the lake, Ashleigh crawled through the shrubs and sank into the darkness at the side of her house. Seeing no one around, she moused across the porch, inserted the key, pushed the door back, and was immediately overcome by the foul odor of decaying blood. Bumbling back to the edge of the porch, she caught her breath, held it, and sprinted through to the bedroom where, even in the dim light, she could see the black stains on the walls, bed, and floor.

Working quickly, she swung the dressing stool into the closet, raked the boxes on the top shelf to one end, pressed a finger into a tiny indention in the sheetrock, and jiggled it back and forth. But the sheetrock didn't move. She jiggled harder and still the section of wall held tight. With her lungs bursting and perspiration dampening her skin, she retreated back to the front porch, and—checking to see if all was clear—leapt into the shadows around the side of the house.

Landing on her hands and knees, she gasped for air trying desperately not to throw up. When her wind returned and the shivering had diminished, she took a chunk of brick from the flowerbed, charged back into the house, stepped back up on the stool, and bashed a hole in the sheetrock.

Feeling around inside the cavity in the wall, she grasped the only thing she'd left behind—the one thing she figured she'd never need again—a loaded 25-caliber pistol.

53

MARTHA HELD ME TOGETHER all through high school when my relationship with Dad had totally come apart. What a blessing that was. No person should have to live without a sibling. If I ever have children, there'll be at least two. But even with Martha there supporting me emotionally, I'd not been complete.

Until Sydney.

With Sydney, I felt I'd come full circle. As if she'd taken hold of my spine and given me some sort of adjustment. A spiritual realignment. My breathing slowed. My muscles relaxed. I felt a presence within me that had long been missing—a thousand voices singing.

Looking at her leaning against the carved headboard of her bed holding a sheet to her breasts, I felt I was looking more *into* her than *at* her. I wanted her heart more than I wanted air to breathe.

"Come home with me," I said. "Have dinner with me. Have breakfast with me. Bring a plant if you like. I don't care, just—come home with me." I couldn't help myself. I *needed* her and I was afraid if I didn't say so then, I might not get another chance.

Thirty seconds is all it took. For thirty seconds, she thought it over. After thirty seconds, she flipped the sheet off, gathered the things she'd need, and packed an overnight bag.

As I slipped back into my clothes, those thousand voices rose in pitch and intensity—the voices of angels.

I took her hand on the drive back to my house and held it, afraid that if I let go, I'd turn and find her gone. As we slowed near my house, the headlights spotlighted a woman moving toward a parked car up the street.

Instead of turning into my drive, I continued forward. "That looks like..." As I approached her, the woman turned her back and as she struggled to get a key into a car door, I passed within a few feet of her.

"My God," Sydney whispered. "Isn't that Ashleigh?"

I slammed on the brakes. "Yes. It is."

Sydney rolled her window down and leaned out. "Ash?"

The woman jerked her door open, dived in, started the engine, and backed the car away without even closing her door, then whipped the car around and headed up the road to her right.

I swerved into a driveway, turned that heavy wagon around, and floored the gas pedal. "Reach behind your seat and get that black bag. There's a camera in it," I told Sydney.

Sydney grabbed my arm. "She has a gun. I saw it."

I handed her my cell phone. "Call Sam. The number's in the directory. Tell him who we've just seen and that we're following her."

I turned my lights off and rounded the corner after Ashleigh. Her car had a section of red lens broken out of the right-rear taillight that made it easy to follow from a distance. After a few turns, I switched my lights back on and stayed well back. She drove fast and erratically, but I managed to keep her in sight. Sam's voice-mail picked up and Sydney handed me the phone.

"Sam, Richard Baimbridge. Sydney Deagan and I have just seen Ashleigh Matthews. She was parked just up the street from her house and we're following her now. I'm hoping to get a few photos of her so I can prove she's alive. She knows we saw her and she's running pretty hard. I'll let you know how it turns out and where she goes...if I can keep up with her."

Ashleigh turned onto US 17 North and headed toward Jacksonville for about eight miles, then doubled back and meandered aimlessly about Wilmington for another half-hour. With that taillight out, I was able to keep a great distance between us and pick her back up if I lost her. Once when I *did* lose her, I looked to my left at a stoplight and realized we were sitting right next to her. She was engaged in a frantic telephone conversation and didn't notice us, but the light changed before I could get the camera ready.

Shortly afterward, she headed south on US 17, crossed the Cape Fear River, and turned southeast on NC 133 toward Southport. We kept our distance, following down the narrow two-lane road past intermittent patches of farms and forests until she slowed well below the speed limit and used her brakes often.

There was little traffic along the road and I feared that if I continued to follow at her slow speed, she'd realize she was being tailed. I let her get out of my sight briefly on a curve, turned my headlights off, and followed as best I could in the dark avoiding any use of the brakes. A minute later, she turned left onto a narrow overgrown trail that threaded back into the trees. Coasting toward the turnoff, we watched her headlights as she drove deeper into the forest.

"What do we do now?" Sydney asked as we rolled to a stop just beyond the turnoff.

"Hit redial and let Sam know where we are. Tell him to look for my car and that she went up a dirt road across from it." I dropped the strap to the camera bag over my head. "I'm going in on foot. You wait in the car."

"You just hold on," she said punching the redial key on the phone. "You're not leaving me out here alone."

And I didn't.

As we stepped into the trail Ashleigh had taken, darkness engulfed us as though we'd walked into a mine. The air was pungent with the scent of earth, pine needles, and decaying plants and my swollen ankle throbbed with each step. Sydney took hold of the back of my belt and held on tightly. Well up the dirt path, Ashleigh's car appeared to be moving through a tunnel lit by her headlights. It gave us a heading as well as a look at the path in the distance. We used her lights to avoid trees until she turned sharply to the left and headed toward the only other light we could see—a faint glow far in the distance. Without light, following the path became nearly impossible so we opted for the shortest route. Stepping over a soft, decaying log into thick brush, we waded through swishing leaves in the direction of the faint glow.

Briars and sticks tore at our clothes and skin. Fallen trees lay in the darkness waiting to trip us. Three quarters of a mile in, Ashleigh's lights stopped moving and went out leaving us blind except for the faint glow. With that as our compass, we stumbled through the wilderness brushing away spider webs, slapping at insects, and pausing for an occasional animal to rustle from our path.

Pushing branches away from our faces, we emerged from the trees, crossed a shallow ditch, and came upon a freshly turned field. A break in the clouds gave us a sliver of moonlight by which to see. The field would take us most of the way to a house and barn a half mile in the distance, but the ground was soft. Disked into high mounds and deep furrows, it was as difficult to walk on as sand dunes—but was far better than the briars, insects, and sticks in our eyes.

I shifted the camera on my shoulder and took hold of Sydney's hand marveling at how tiny it was, and how well it fit into mine. Holding her hand was like taking hold of her heart. There was something there that coursed back and forth between us. I was certainly getting something from Sydney. I hoped she was getting something back.

What we were doing was crazy. Chasing a girl with a gun. Running across a field blind and defenseless. Sneaking up on God knows what. It was stupid. Like holding a flame over a bucket of gasoline. And it was *invigorating*. I hung suspended between hysteria and devastation in a world turned on its side.

As we panted to a stop midway the field, another car turned into the lane and snaked through the trees.

"Do you think that's Sam?" Sydney asked, catching her breath.

I bent low and massaged my ankle. "Let's hope."

"Come on," she grunted dragging me behind her. The vehicle wound its way along the length of the path finally stopping short of Ashleigh's car. After a moment, the driver's door opened and a man stepped out silhouetted against the light of his headlamps. He shined a flashlight around him—even pointed it our way. I waved a hand high over my head and shouted, "Sam!" But we were too far away and there was a fawn grazing at the edge of the field between us that raised its head as he shone the light on him. The man neither heard us nor saw us in the distance. The flashlight turned away, the headlights went off, and the light inside the car went out.

Stumbling over mound after mound, we hurried forward as the beam from the flashlight moved toward the barn and eventually disappeared.

As we approached the far side of the field, a shotgun blast lit the front of the barn like a camera flash, scattering a buck and three does grazing at the edge of the trees. The booming echoes rolling back from distant forests turned the deer in flight and brought them galloping back toward us, the buck leaping right over our heads.

Dropping into the dirt, we held our breath and listened, but heard only the wind flittering lightly through the trees, and mosquitoes buzzing around our ears. Seeing nothing, we advanced to the edge of the trees, then to the cars, and up a lane bordered by giant pecan trees. To our left we saw the silhouette of a sagging two-story farm house—dark, heavy with the sorrow of a century of tears, a porch stretching across its front.

Straight ahead, there was a wide barn, easily forty feet high at its peek, its roof sloping nearly to the ground on each side. The light we'd followed came from a tiny square window in the lower left corner of the barn.

Feeling the first gnawing of fear, I tightened my grip on Sydney's hand and ran with her swooshing through high weeds to the left of the house where we squatted in deep grass. I took her by the shoulders and whispered. "I want you to wait here no matter what happens."

She clutched my arms. "What are you going to do?"

I could hear the fear in her voice and tried to conceal it in mine. "I'm going to look in that window, try to find Sam, and maybe get a picture of Ashleigh." In an instant of fleeting moonlight I saw both love and fear in Sydney's eyes. It was a look I'd never seen on any face other than my mother's. I kissed her and turned quickly, her hands pulling at my shirt as I slipped away before she could change my mind. I negotiated the creaking porch with its rotting cavities and spongy boards stopping at the other end to remove my Nikon from the bag. Looking over my shoulder, I saw Sydney watching, motioned for her to get down, then dashed across the open yard to the barn. With camera in hand, I crept to the lighted window and looked inside.

A kerosene lamp hung from a nail on a post amid a storehouse of rusty tools, tractor parts, bags of fertilizer, large opaque polyethylene drums, and a stack of empty burlap sacks. Ashleigh lay motionless on the dirt floor, her right shoulder a bloody mass. By her hand, a western-style pistol. At the back of the barn, wide doors stood open.

I turned off the flash and raised the camera, steadying it against the milky glass. Pressing the shutter, I made a one-second time exposure. The camera beeped and stored the image. I made a second exposure, this one for three seconds then, moving to my right, crossed the front of the barn to a shed at the other end where round wooden posts and rolls of fencing had been stacked.

Something heavy hit the ground inside the building. Stepping over coils of barbed wire and fence posts, I crept to the right rear corner of the barn to a stack of dried firewood split decades ago for a wintry night that never came.

There, a man, barely visible in the light from the doorway, was bent over one of the polyethylene drums struggling to roll it away from the barn. Beyond the man there was a wide gap in the trees and I could see the silhouette of a sailboat at the end of a tall pier with the lights of Wilmington twinkling behind it. To the right of the pier, a rectangular canal had been cut in from the river to within fifty feet of the barn with a short pier jutting out into it.

Laying against the tank, he pushed with his feet slowly rolling it through thick sand to the edge of the canal where he lifted it onto the short pier one end at a time, then maneuvered it down the dock, its contents thumping with each revolution. At the end, he shoved it with his foot and the drum splashed into the canal, bobbed, and floated with a third of it above water. Pulling a pistol from his belt, the man fired five rounds into the tank; two above the waterline and three below. As hot lead thumped holes into the hard plastic, the container began to sink.

When the man turned and started back toward the barn, I dropped behind the dried firewood and watched as he lumbered back toward the lighted door breathing heavily with gun in hand. I gently eased my foot to the left and had risen slightly to get a better look at his face when a terrified creature pierced the silence with a heart-stopping screech just above my head. Dropping to the ground behind the woodpile with my heart hammering in my chest, I looked up into the face of a long-eared owl bobbing on a low-hanging branch above me, its enormous yellow eyes blinking independently. In its talons it clutched a young rabbit screaming, fighting to get free, pumping its feet uselessly against the air beneath it.

The owl turned its head backward, leapt from the branch, spread its enormous wings, and carried its screeching prey off. A few seconds later the screeches ended in a shrill squeal, but the pounding in my chest remained. Shaking violently, I looked around the edge of the logs and saw the man's face more clearly now.

It was Scott McGillikin!

As he stared in the direction of the owl, more adrenalin flooded into my bloodstream. My muscles flexed. My heart raced. My mind became the puppeteer seeking to force my body to do its will.

Kill him! Kill the bastard!

54

I N MY MIND, I SAW MYSELF LEAP from the shadows and lock my hands around his neck. I saw the shock in his blood-streaked eyes as I choked the life out of him with my bare hands. I felt panic ripple through his body as he realized that he was going to die and there was nothing he could do to stop it. In one glorious flicker of thought, I watched him die in my hands. *But death would be too good for Scott—or Dane Bonner—or whoever the hell he was.* I wanted him to suffer as my sister had, to know her pain, to curse my name every time his cell door closed for the rest of his tortured life.

As his shadow followed him into the barn, I grasped a chunk of firewood, flattened myself against the rear of the building, and treaded on quaking legs to the edge of the doorway. Drunk on hate, I didn't care about the law. I didn't care about the other lives he'd torn apart. He had destroyed my sister and I wanted to punish him for it. I wanted to be the one that did it, to be the one to tell her, to see the sparkle return to her eyes when I gave her the news.

I could smell his sweat and the burnt gunpowder that lingered in his wake. I listened to his footsteps as he moved about on the dirt floor inside, dragging something, bumping something, and another heavy thump. My heart pulsed in my neck as his steps came near the door. I waited with the wood cocked, ready to swing. It would be quick and there'd be no compassion as he'd given none to Martha. Wind blowing in off the river chilled the perspiration on my skin as I waited, until his footsteps faded off in another direction and a door elsewhere squeaked and bumped.

I dared to peer into the room, into the stabbing silver light from the lantern consuming its fuel in a perpetual inhale. Scott was gone and so were Ashleigh and her gun. I leaned farther into the room and heard a frightened scream.

Sydney?

Running past the door as fast as I could on my swollen ankle, I rounded the other end of the barn and tripped over a body in the grass landing face down in the dirt, my camera under me.

Clutching my hip, I rolled to the side and bent low over a warm body. It was Sam. There was a dark stain in the dirt beside his head. I laid an ear to his chest, detected a slight heartbeat, and shook him. "Sam." He didn't respond. I searched him for a gun, but found only an empty holster and a flashlight. I left the camera, took his flashlight, and ran beyond the house to where I'd left Sydney.

I whispered in the dark, "Sydney?" There was no answer. "Sydney!" I switched the light on and I could see that there'd been a struggle. One of Sidney's shoes lay in the grass and there was a distinctive odor in the air that I recognized from having my tonsils removed as a child. *Ether!*

I felt a clamp squeeze down on my chest. I clutched the shoe. The heat of her foot was still in it. I tracked footprints around the back of the house, through waist-deep weeds and soggy earth, ending in standing water that seeped into my shoes. I hobbled back toward the barn spotting a young woman frozen on the pier, her eyes wide with fear as she gazed toward the light coming from the barn. Turning the corner, I glimpsed Scott lugging an unconscious Sydney into the back door of the barn.

I bent forward gasping for air, trembling. *I had to do something, and I had to do it now!* I took a deep breath, tightened my grip on the flashlight, and charged through the doorway throwing every ounce of weight and strength I could muster into Scott as he held Sydney over one of the polyethylene tanks. Knocking him forward, I fell on him beating him relentlessly with the steel light. I swung with both hands chasing after him as he tried to crawl away on his back, drawing blood from his face with every blow. Insane with rage, I unleashed a vicious barrage onto him—a blow for every bully that had ever taunted me. I kept banging and smashing until he locked my arms with his legs and wrestled the light out of my hands. Dragging me to the ground, he rolled on top of me crushing the air out of my lungs, jamming an elbow into my throat cutting off my air.

Struggling against his incredible bear-like strength, I tried to roll out from under him, to snatch a quick breath, but his fist smashed into my face. I heard my nose crack and tasted blood in the back of my throat. I twisted and yanked at his arm feeling the energy leaving my oxygen-starved body. I thought of my mother trudging back and forth between hospital rooms comforting a dying husband on one floor and begging her only daughter to wake up on another. I saw the tortured wail form on her face when told that her only son was dead. I saw the light fade from her eyes, heard her agonizing sobs, and felt her slipping away from reality as I drifted toward unconsciousness. *God, have mercy on my mother!*

My hands clawed at Scott's head seeking a hold. My nails ripped at his ears and skin. My right thumb found his left eye and I dug the nail in with all my remaining strength. He rattled his head and bashed his elbow against my arm, but I refused to let go forcing my nail deeper into his eye. He whipped his head from side to side lessening the pressure on my neck and I gasped a lungful of air. He pummeled my face with his fists and whacked my head against the dirt floor, but I could breathe and with every breath my grip got stronger.

I saw the color rush back into my mother's face as the tip of my thumb slipped behind his eyeball. He grabbed my wrist with both hands and wrenched my hand away; his bloody eye falling against his cheek dangling from muscles, sinews, and nerves.

Reeling back, he held his eye with one hand and pointed his gun at me with the other—the white of his good eye stark against his bloody face, agony contorting his features.

"You fuck!" He pulled the trigger and I saw the bullet leave the barrel in a puff of white smoke. I felt the impact as I spun to my left and came face to face with Sydney. Gazing upon her slumbering eyes, I felt a burning in my right arm and a tingling in my fingers. Reaching up, I touched those tingling fingertips to her lips.

Life is a journey of chance and choices; a maze of paths each leading to a different venture and each holding a lesson to be learned through pain and consequence. There's no way to know what lies at the other end of a particular path before you start down it. *And there's no way back.*

My pilgrimage had brought me to Sydney, and hers to me. Our lives had intertwined for a brief moment in time, but I knew I could never be the man she needed, or give Sydney the life she deserved. I knew, too, that I would not be able to live without her. I tasted the salt as tears dripped into my mouth.

"Let her go, please," I uttered.

"You...ripped...my...fucking...eye...out!" he screamed attempting to push it back into its socket.

"Please. Let her go."

He jammed the pistol against Sydney's temple.

"No, please!"

"Kiss my ass!" His finger squeezed the trigger. I shut my eyes and heard the hammer click, but the gun did not fire. I opened my eyes and saw Sydney still sleeping quietly.

I grabbed his pant leg. "Please—"

He kicked me in the throat with his shoe. "Get up, damn it!" Grasping the back of my collar, he lifted me off the ground and swung me against a wooden bench loaded with steel tractor parts and chains that gouged my face and tore my right ear. "Get up!" The burning in my arm flared with hot pain. I clenched my teeth and rolled facedown onto the dirt floor pulling my knees up under me.

"I said 'Get up!'" He whipped the barrel of the gun against my head, the sight cutting a gash behind my ear. Heaving me off the floor, he bowled me into the plastic drums sending them toppling and crashing above and beneath me. Pain ravaged my right arm as blood saturated the sleeve. Pushing up on my left hand, I rolled to the right, propped my back against the wall, and was reaching for the top of an upright drum when I spied Ashleigh's pistol lying under an overturned tank. It had a thick barrel and finger grooves in the grip. I could see that at least some of the bullets in the cylinder had not been fired.

"Okay! I'm coming," I groaned, clenching my teeth against the pains as I struggled to rise from the ground. As I got to my feet and turned to face him, a powerful punch landed on my right cheek.

I AWOKE A SHORT TIME LATER lying face down on the dirt floor. Scott was leaning over Sydney with his back to me folding her arms over her chest. I twisted my head and looked for Ashleigh's gun, but did not see it. Grunting as he lifted her, he carried her to an open, upright tank, and lowered her into it. The eye dangled against his bloody cheek jerking grotesquely whenever his other eye moved. Releasing her, he whipped his gun from his belt and aimed at me as she settled with a thud against the bottom of the barrel.

"Yes," he said, his eye swinging. "I reloaded while you slept." To prove his point, he fired the gun into a barrel behind me, the percussion ringing in my ears long after the bullet stopped spinning around the empty drum. "How do I look, Baimbridge?" he said leaning over me holding his eye in place. "Huh?" He fired another round that pinged off a piece of iron, ricocheted off a wall, and rolled across the dirt to his feet collecting dust. "Do you think that little girl on my boat is going to want to screw me tonight? Huh?"

"She can thank me later."

"Fuck you!" He kicked me in the kidney. "Get up!"

As I struggled to my feet, he moved around me, stuffed his gun in a holster, then lowered his head and charged me, striking me hard in the chest, knocking me backward against the barrels, flipping my legs high in the air. Tumbling headfirst into a tank, I slide down against Sydney with my legs folded painfully under me. I couldn't budge. These tanks surely held at least a hundred gallons, but there was hardly enough room for one person, much less *two*. Blood settled in my head. I couldn't get my weight off Sydney. I felt I was crushing her. There was nothing to grab hold of, no way to pull up. I was as helpless as a turtle on its back. It was suffocating.

"For God's sake, Scott, don't do this to Sydney. Let her out!"

I squirmed and rocked the tank pushing with my one good hand trying to back out, to take the pressure off Sydney, but my movement only wedged me in tighter. He hammered my knees with the lid, compacting me deeper into the cylinder, and laid his weight on top of it to set the latches, casting us into near total silence. The sound of the metal clasps snapping into place around the container reverberated through the drum like a nail-gun sealing the lid of a coffin.

55

THE TEMPERATURE INSIDE THE DRUM instantly began to rise and my claustrophobia drove me into a panic. Without air, we would suffocate in minutes. There was light coming through the opaque sides and I could see shadows moving around it as the drum tipped and fell on its side slamming us against the hard shell. My heart pounded so loudly I could hear it. A drum within a drum. Fear gripped me, its sharp spears ripping my senses. I pressed my knees against the lid and pushed. My muscles cramped, but nothing gave way.

Scott's shadow fell over the barrel and I could hear his clothes rubbing against it as we began to roll—the heavy container crunching the ground like shoes on soft rocks. "This is what you wanted, isn't it, Baimbridge?" he grunted. "You and Sydney together forever? Is that what you wanted, Baimbridge?"

The tank turned another revolution. My right arm was locked behind my back, and I could barely move my left. The temperature in the cylinder climbed rapidly and perspiration poured from me. "Please, Scott. Let her out! She's never done anything to you!"

"You don't know the first goddamned thing about Sydney and me!" His body rubbed the barrel as he lay against it, pushing with his feet, grunting, forcing it to roll in the soft dirt. Sydney's knees were crammed against her chest and my chin jabbed her shoulder. As we tumbled, Sydney rolled on top of me, moaned, and tried to move. We rolled again and I fell into her and I heard the air press from her lungs. Sweat burned my eyes.

"Richard?" she whispered near my ear. "I can't breathe."

I could hear my weight forcing the air out of her as we rolled. "I'm trying to keep my weight off of you."

"It's hot." She panted, then screamed. "Let us out! We can't breathe!"

Her cries pierced my ears and gave me strength. I tensed my body and swelled in size trying to burst the thick plastic container open like Superman, but I was not Superman.

Scott pounded his hand against the drum. "I love it!"

"Shhh. Try to relax," I whispered to Sydney as sweat rolled around my neck as the tank tumbled. "Take slow breaths." The light in the tank grew dimmer as it rolled away from the lantern until there was none. I forced my muscles to go limp and exhaled as her lungs expanded against me. When she exhaled, I inhaled. "We're going to have to take turns breathing."

"What's he doing? Why are we rolling?"

"He's going to drop us in the canal."

The barrel bumped something and tilted up at one end.

Sydney quivered. "What are we going to do?'

"He's just trying to scare us," I lied. I knew what was going to happen.

I felt her body quaking with silent sobs. "I'm sorry, Richard."

"For what?" I gasped.

"For getting you involved."

I panted. "You just gave me the best two weeks of my life." As the tank began to move again, it bumped every few inches and I knew we were on that short pier. As it hit each plank, it pounded us against each other, knocking the last of the air from our lungs. With every bump a new image flashed through my mind. Martha and I lying on a hill picking out rabbits and foxes and elephants in summer clouds. Dad on a tirade, his fingernails cutting into my jaw as he screamed and spit into my face. Martha fading away in that hospital bed while nurses worked to pull her back. Sydney laying naked against my back in the shower her arms moving over my chest and abdomen.

Our bodies were slick with perspiration, our breathing accelerating, gasping at the thin traces of oxygen left in the air. I could feel my heart pounding throughout my body. Tears spilled down my cheeks then back up into my eyes as the cylinder came to rest with me upside down.

What was it all about? Why was I even born?

"If only I could have gotten that *gun*," I sighed.

"It wouldn't have mattered," Sydney panted. "It didn't w—"

Our vessel abruptly lurched forward and plunged several feet before smacking the water of the canal bashing us against the walls of the drum like a baseball meeting a bat. The centrifugal force of our weight carried the tank deep into the water before it popped back to the surface bobbing like a cork. The side of the drum became cooler giving me a trace of comfort, a smidgeon of hope.

"Hey!" Scott called from a short distance away. "You say it's getting a little hard to breathe in there, Sydney darling?"

"Don't answer him," I panted.

"Maybe you could use a couple of *air holes*." He sounded delirious.

The first shot caught the corner of the drum ripping through the thick plastic creating a circle of light near my face, the impact reverberating through the drum. The glowing, red hot lead buried itself in the wall melting the plastic and sliding down the wall burning the flesh on my arm.

"Go ahead! Shoot me! Please!" Sydney screamed wrestling for room, for air, for cool. "I can't take it!"

The second bullet thumped into the drum and Sydney flinched. "Oh, God, that hurts," she moaned holding her breath.

I felt trapped. Powerless. *Castrated!* Rage swept through me like a hot wind on a wild fire. "You hit Sydney!"

"Don't," she hushed me as she drew short labored breaths, her body trembling against mine.

A volley of four more rounds smashed into the barrel and molten lead seared into our flesh as cold water mercifully spewed in behind it—so cold that it, too, burned.

"Oh, Sydney, I'm so sorry. I just wanted to get a picture. I thought that maybe for once something would work out in my favor." I choked back tears. "If I'd just...gotten my hands on that...gun."

"I told you," she panted, her voice growing faint. "The gun didn't work. I tried it."

"The gun under the barrels?"

"Yes."

"When?"

"Right after he knocked you out...when he reloaded his gun. I pointed it at him and pulled the trigger, but it wouldn't work. I tried it three times before he turned around."

Outside, we heard shouting. "Shhh. Listen." Men's voices, shouting. Through the hole in front of me I could see lights flickering through the tree tops. Blue, red, white. "Sydney, the police are here!" We shouted and beat the drum. A shot rang out, then more shots. Hand guns. Shotguns. Tear gas launchers. As the tank bobbed in the canal, I watched the scene unfold through my tiny window and relayed it to Sydney. I saw an officer take a hit, heard the faint crackle of fire igniting, and watched the barn as it went up in flames.

They couldn't hear us and no one knew we were there.

As the oxygen diminished, I had difficulty thinking. I tried to get my mouth closer to the hole in front of me to suck air through it, but couldn't reach it and choked on what filled my lungs. The cold water had reached my knees and the euphoria I'd felt when the police arrived evaporated.

Sydney whispered, "We're going to die, aren't we?"

I shuttered and gasped for air. "Ironic isn't it?"

"What?" she breathed.

"I finally have something to live for."

She whispered, "Me, too."

Of all the unjust tragedies I'd witnessed in my life, this was the most unjust. Sydney was so *innocent.* She had molded a fabulous life for herself...had a...successful...business...and...

Starving for oxygen, I drifted in and out of consciousness.

Think!

"Sydney? What'd you do with that gun?" I coughed.

She panted rapidly. "I...hid it...in...my..."

"Where?"

"It's..." She fell silent.

"Sydney, where is it? Where's the gun?"

"It's...it's..."

"Do you have it? Is it here?"

"What?"

I must have been getting some oxygen through that hole. I wasn't thinking too well, but at least I could still think. "The gun. Is it here?"

"It's..."

"Where, Sydney? Where's the gun?"

Her voice was faint. "Under...my...shirt."

THE FIRE NOW CONSUMED the barn and licked high into the air. The cold water slowly filling the barrel helped to cool our brains, but I knew it was only a matter of time before it would eventually drown us. Ten minutes tops. Our only hope was a gun that wouldn't fire even if I could get to it. And *what* would I shoot to get us out? More holes and we'd drown quicker.

My right arm was pinned, but I could move my left...slightly. Sydney's legs were wedged back against her chest and I was squashed against them upside down. Our heads rested near one another, mine bent under with my abdomen pressed against the back of her calves. I worked my hand down my left side and tried to find a way to get around her legs to her waist. The water was now midway up my thighs. Sydney had gone quiet—passed out from pain, heat, loss of blood, or a lack of oxygen. But she was still alive. I could feel her expand...occasionally...to take a breath of the rancid air...such that it...such that...

Think! Where's the gun?

I curled my back and drew in my abdomen and managed to work my hand through to my right side. The barrel rolled a half-turn in the water shifting more of Sydney's weight against me. I squeezed my hand between her thigh and abdomen just below her breast and heard the air escape her lungs as I forced my arm through. The barrel rolled another half-turn and I felt the punch of cold water hit my upper back. Air trapped in our clothing began bubbling through the water popping around us, bringing a trace of oxygen with it. I realized we were sinking faster and felt a surge of energy sweep through me. I forced my hand farther into the space between her thighs and touched something hard and cold beneath the cloth.

I raked my nails across the wet fabric and tugged at it, but it refused to move as the water rose to cover the gun. I could feel it—its hammer, cylinder, and grip. My energy was gone. My mind could no longer focus.

One minute!

My hand worked frantically as a new stream of cool water trickled down my neck and the bubbles began to fade. My fingers found a button and the opening it secured. I felt the smooth cold metal beneath as the water, rising faster, swallowed my elbow.

Thirty seconds!

I pulled at the gun, but it would not budge. Panic overtook me. Fighting the urge to give up, I closed my fingers around the grip afraid to touch the trigger and gave it a yank. Sydney gasped, sucked a deep breath, then emptied her lungs completely shrinking the size of her chest cavity and the gun slipped *free*.

I could hold it in my hand, but it was still lodged between us. As the water rose above my shoulders, I tried to pulled the gun through the tiny space behind her leg.

Suddenly the drum sat straight up, dropped, and sank beneath the water!

The remaining air bubbled out through a hole in the top as the tank struck the bottom of the canal with a thump. Cold water washed up my neck and I gulped a final lungful of air as the cylinder rolled slowly and fell onto its side. As water covered my head, I jerked the gun frantically up and down working it back and forth; edging it slowly through the opening until it finally came though.

Exhausted, trembling, starving for air, I pushed the gun down under my knees and slid the end of the barrel along the rim of the drum hoping to feel the bolts that held the latches in place. I worked back and forth along the edge of the lid until the gun bumped a rounded brad. I pressed the muzzle against the brad and pulled the trigger. I felt the gun click, but there was no explosion.

My fingers searched the gun for a lever or safety button. My lungs screamed for air. I pulled the trigger again, and again there was no sound.

I could hear nothing but the sound of water lapping the top of the tank.

I pictured my funeral. *What's it all about, Alfie? Is it just for the moment we live?* That's the song I want them to play. Not *Amazing Grace* or *Nearer my God to Thee*. *Alfie* is the song for me.

I felt Sydney twitch. Using both thumbs and all the strength I had left, I cocked the hammer locking it back to its farthermost position. *A shot in the dark.* That's all life is—or in my case—the lack of one. I smiled and air gurgled from my nose. My lungs spasmed, as if to laugh, then my throat opened and I involuntarily gulped water that set my chest on fire.

I squeezed the trigger and the cartridge exploded. For an instant it didn't register. When it did, I frantically locked my thumbs on the hammer and cocked it again. I pulled the trigger, and again there was an underwater explosion. I tried to push the lid off, but it remained tight.

Where am I? Think!

I cocked the hammer again, slid the barrel of the gun along the rim, hit a brad, and fired. I heard bubbles. I jammed my knees against the lid, but it held. I wrapped my thumbs around the hammer and struggled to cock it again. My thumbs aching. The hammer spring resisting. *Oh, Sydney!* I forced the water from my chest as I squeezed back the hammer with all my strength. *Our Father, who art in heaven...give us this day our daily strength...* I felt the hammer lock back, touched the trigger, and barely heard the explosion, but felt an instant release of pressure as the lid sprang away. I groped through my knees for the edge of the tank, turned the gun backward, and hooked the grip on the lip and pulled.

As we floated weightless out of the drum, Sydney grabbed hold of me clutching me hard against her. My legs were numb and did not respond when I tried to stand. Her arms pulled at my head and shoulders. Through the murky water, I saw the end of the pier against the raging fire. Reaching for the piling that supported it, I grasped hold of it and climbed it like a greased pole.

When I burst out of the river with Sydney on my back, my lungs locked. I heard Sydney cough and suck in air, but my lungs failed to work. I gagged, threw my head back, and vomited, but still there was no air going into my lungs. Panicked, I flung myself back into the water fighting to get my feet planted on the muddy bottom, but my energy had disappeared. I had nothing left. I sank below the water and settled slowly to the bottom as my arms and legs fought to get hold of something solid. As I came to rest in the mud, peace settled over me and my pains faded. My arms and legs fell to my side.

Through the mist I saw Dad reach out for me. His eyes were red and his tongue was black. In his hand he held a whip from the hickory tree that grew in the corner of our backyard and I knew I was headed to hell. He swung the branch and pain exploded up my back. I saw Sydney above me, straddling me, her hair on fire, bending to kiss me. He swung again. Pain wracked my legs. I was with Martha. We were pedaling our bikes in an undeclared race to old man Jenkins's private pond where we stripped to our underwear and swam with the wild ducks and geese to a tiny sandbar in the center. It was on that sandbar that we saw each other naked for the first time. The whip swung again and my body burst into flames. Sydney reached for me and as my skin turned black and cracked open, she pressed her lips to mine and forced her breath into me.

The whip smashed across my chest and I felt seawater ooze out of my mouth and run down my neck. Flames licked high into a black sky and I felt myself being sucked through a tube. Mom reached out for me as I swept past her, but disappeared in the smoke. My body swelled like a balloon as air rushed into me and Sydney appeared pressing her hands against me to force it out. As air gurgled up through the water in my throat, tears streamed down her checks. She slammed her fists against my chest and seemed to scream, yet I heard no sounds. She kissed me and her cold wet hair fell softly around my face and neck as my chest expanded. I had a vision of a helicopter overhead beaming its spotlight directly into my eyes.

Sydney placed her mouth to mine and my lungs again expanded and burned. The spotlight blasting into my face suddenly hurt and I heard the thump—thump—thump of its rotor blades. I tasted water in the back of my throat. It gagged me and I coughed. It ran down the sides of my neck. I coughed again. Sydney's hot tears dripped on my cold skin as my lungs sucked in air and I tasted smoke.

As I drew another breath, she burst into tears. "I thought you were gone." I could feel her trembling.

I coughed again and drew another breath. Falling against me, she locked her arms around me and we held each other weeping and laughing until they came and took us away.

57

S YDNEY AND I were taken by ambulance to Cape Fear Medical Center where we were x-rayed, probed, stitched up, smeared with ointment, and admitted for observation. They told me I had a broken ankle and sealed my left foot in a cast. The D.A. stopped by to tell me that all charges against me were being dropped. I also learned from him that Sam had been transported by helicopter to Duke University Medical Center and that David had been found alive, bound and gagged in another room of the barn, and had been rescued before the fire, but that Ashleigh didn't make it. They found her body in the other tank that had been sunk in the canal. He also said that although Scott had been severely wounded in the shootout, he was expected to live to stand trial.

After two days in the hospital, Sydney and I were released, but refused to go anywhere without each other. After getting a change of clothes and a bite to eat, we returned to the hospital around 4 p.m. that afternoon to spend some time with Martha. It was still touch and go for her, but the nurses said the doctors were encouraged by her most recent signs.

They told us that Dad didn't have long and Sydney stayed with Martha while I went in to see him. From the door, I could see that his skin had turned sallow. He was loosing weight and his eyes appeared to have sunk deeper into his head. He sensed that I was there and when he opened his eyes, I was amazed to see a light actually coming from within them. They were glowing from the inside. It's something I'd never seen before nor seen anything like it since.

He raised his hand. "That you, Martha?"

"No, Dad. It's Richard."

I stepped in and let the door close behind me.

"I heard you were shot," he mumbled, his mouth tight and toothless.

"I'm fine."

"They called you a hero."

"They weren't there."

"You did good, son."

"Thanks, Dad."

His shriveled hand tightened into a fist that seemed so much smaller than I remembered. I laid my hand on it. It was cold like the sunfish Martha and I used to catch on worms that we dug up in the back yard when we were kids. His skin felt dry and rubbery—not at all real—like our relationship. I traced the veins on the back of his hand. Touch is important. A son needs a father's touch. I imagined what could have been, what *should* have been, what our lives might have been if things had gone differently that tragic night some thirty odd years ago when Uncle Charlie's brakes failed. Would Dad have thought more of me as my Uncle Gus? How much disappointment and pain had *he* endured? I squeezed his hand. It was hard and boney like the rest of him—no tenderness inside.

Shortly after 5 a.m., he opened his eyes and I saw that the light in them had gone out. He moved his hand away from mine, drew a deep breath, and as it slowly exhaled, the beep on the monitor changed to a solid tone.

And that was it. It was over.

AT HIS FUNERAL I stared at the casket and wished I could have gotten to know him better. Wished we'd had more time at the end. Wished I'd known the truth earlier. At the wake afterward, I smiled and nodded as friends and family politely recited their rehearsed phrases. *"He did good by your mother,"* many said as if they'd called a meeting and prepared an official family response. I left the house before the plates were passed around and sat in the darkened hospital room with my sister—or rather my *half*-sister.

It didn't bother me to know there was no part of Gus in me, but I hated the fact that Martha and I were less related. There had always been some comfort in knowing that someone else in this world had the same genes as me and that they were still sane and functioning.

A nurse came in to change the IV drip and checked the tube coming out of the side of her head. "Swelling's going down," she said making a note on Martha's chart. I didn't reply. I knew it was good news, but there was still a lot that could go wrong. The nurse placed Martha's chart back on a hook at the foot of the bed and left saying that she might wake up soon.

I pulled up a chair and took Martha's hand. People can tell how much you love them by the way you touch them. There were cuts and bruises on all her fingers and her nails were chipped and ragged, but her hand was soft, and warm like her heart. I kissed her fingers.

"We buried Dad today," I said in a near whisper. "You should have been there. Mom needed someone to cry with her. Listening to her sobbing almost did me in. Winston was there and he cried too, but I think he was crying for Mom, so he doesn't count." I rolled her hand over and examined the palm. She had a long life line and a complete "M" in her palm that I'd always heard meant you'd have money.

"Babe, you need to wake up, get well, and come home. I don't think Mom could take it if you died, too." I tried to keep them back, but tears still formed in the corners of my eyes. "And I don't know what I'd do if I didn't have you to look out for me."

Martha tightened her fingers around mine and it felt deliberate. "That's good, Babe. Come back to us. We need you." She took a deep breath and her right leg shifted under the covers, bending at the knee.

But, that was it.

I stayed another two hours hoping to be there when she did awaken, but the nurses finally ran me off so that they could give her a bath.

At the elevator, I spotted Winston in a waiting room. He had his hat pulled well down over his face and I wouldn't have noticed him if he hadn't had a photograph in his hand that I recognized—a school photo of Martha taken when she was in fourth grade.

"Winston?"

He jumped up expecting someone from the hospital staff, I think, and I saw tears on his scarred cheeks. He tilted his head and the brim of his hat covered his eyes. "Hey, Rich," he said clearing his voice. "Have you been in to see her?"

"Yes. She's—" I hesitated as a tear dropped off his chin. He and Mom had a special kind of relationship. He was obviously in love with her, and Mom was going to need all the love she could get for a while. "Martha's like family to you, isn't she?"

He nodded. "Yeah."

"I think she's better. The pressure's going down and she might even wake up in the next few days. She squeezed my hand a while ago and I'm sure she meant to do it."

He wiped his chin and lash-less eyes. "Thanks for letting me know. They don't give out information unless you're family."

I squeezed his shoulder. "You bet."

"I saw in the paper how you helped the police catch that serial killer. He was something, huh?"

"It was Martha. She's the one that figured it out."

"Paper said that if it hadn't been for you, he would have gotten away. Your dad would have been mighty proud of you."

"He would have found a way to shoot holes in it. He'd think I was guilty of something and simply got away with it."

"Don't you go around thinking like that, Rich. It'll eat you up inside and turn your heart to stone."

It was too late. My heart had already turned—at least as far as Dad was concerned, but there had been something there at the end I could hold on to. I patted his shoulder. "Yeah. See you later."

I pressed the button for the elevator.

DURING THE NEXT TWENTY-FOUR HOURS, the swelling continued to go down in Martha's head. She became more active during the night and the next afternoon opened her eyes, but seemed puzzled by her surroundings and unsure of who we were. We spent the afternoon talking and laughing, trying to bring back memories, but it didn't seem that we were getting through. We were strangers to her. She didn't even know who *she* was.

Though she spoke rarely, when she did speak, she mostly repeated what we'd just said. The doctor told us that it was normal for her to do that considering the severity of her injuries. He said that talking to her about her past could help to reconnect her to her memory. She said that it could take anywhere from a few hours to a few *years* for her to recover, and that there was even a possibility that Martha may never recover.

Mom managed to be strong and cheerful at first, but eventually went to pieces. The doctor gave her something to help her sleep and Sydney took her home. I stayed behind and sat up with Martha all night. If talking about her past could help, then I was going to tell her everything I could remember. I started at the beginning, the day they brought Martha home from the hospital. I told her how tiny I thought she looked and how Dad had beat me after I kissed her and made her cry. I talked about all the crazy times we had growing up and all the friends she played with in the neighborhood. I recounted how we used to bum rides down to Carolina Beach so she could spend time with Todd, and how she would take up for me when Dad got mad. She slept through most of it, but I just kept on talking. I recalled things I hadn't thought of in years. I laughed about some of it and cried on occasion. I told her how much Dad had loved her, how she was his favorite, and that I was ashamed to admit I felt relief when he died.

I talked to her about her accident, what had been going on with the investigation, what she'd discovered about Scott McGillikin in her files, and what had happened at the farm across the river. I had grown stiff in my chair and run out of things to talk about by the time the sun came up. My foot itched down inside the cast and my shoulder ached.

I hobbled to the window, opened the blinds, and let the glorious golden-orange light fill the room. "Look, Babe," I said looking out at the mist lingering over the waking city. "It's going to be a beautiful day. A fabulous day for the beach. Remember the beach? You always loved the beach, Martha. You even had a house down there for a while. Remember?" I stretched my back twisting left and right and noticed that her eyes had opened and were following me. I smiled, "Good morning."

"Good morning," she repeated.

The cast on my foot thumped when I took a step. "Guess who's been asking about you," I asked lowering myself back into the chair. "You remember Winston, Babe?" The great white gauze ball on her head moved and I took it as a nod. "He was burned in a fire." I wiggled my toes trying to relieve the itching under the cast. "We used to go out to his farm with Mom and chase the chickens and the baby goats. You remember that, Babe?" Her eyes studied my face. "Now that Dad's gone, I hope Mom spends more time with Winston. He brings something out in her that I've never seen with anyone else. A kind of shy silliness that makes her seem younger somehow. Mom's going to be fifty soon. She deserves to have a little silliness in her life for once. Don't you think?"

"Richard?"

I sat forward and laid a hand on hers. "Yes, Babe. What?" All I could see of her was her eyes and they looked frightened. "Did you sleep well? Are you waking up now?"

She coughed and rolled her head to the side. "Where am I?"

"Oh, Babe, you're in the hospital."

She moaned. "What happened to me?"

I squeezed her hand. "You were hit by a bus."

And so began my sister's recovery.

58

M ARTHA WAS BACK TO BEING her old self with her memory fully restored a few weeks later. They replaced the bandage on her head with a smaller one and we got our first look at her face through a plastic shield she would wear for another six weeks.

After they removed the tubes from her head, the primary area of concern shifted to her one remaining kidney which was growing worse by the day.

Winston continued to stop by for progress reports and was allowed to see her after the third week. He cried like a child and I wondered if seeing her like that brought back painful memories of his own recovery.

I was proud of Mother for not only shopping for him and spending time with him all those years, but for bringing him into the family and giving him the opportunity to love and be loved. People are just not people at all until they have someone to love and be loved by. Without love, people are more like animals taking care of their basic needs and living in seclusion. Believe me, I was a perfect example.

Winston and Mom began spending more time together and he often ate meals with us. But he and Mom weren't the only ones falling in love.

Sydney and I were now inseparable, when we weren't working. The photography studio had begun to recover. Most of the agents had come back and the publicity had brought in lots of new customers. Students from Sydney's dance studio went to national competitions and came back with arm-loads of trophies including a few first overall awards and a couple of national championships.

The casts on Martha's arms came off first, then the one on her right foot. After five weeks, she was allowed to go home.

"I want to show y'all something," she said as she steered her new electric wheelchair into her bedroom.

"What?" Mom asked pulling the bed covers back.

"Watch." Her left leg was still in a cast to the hip. She moved the footrests aside, took hold of the edge of the bed, and pulled herself up on her feet. We all applauded and praised her. Mom, Winston, and me.

"Now watch," she said looking down at her feet. We hushed and waited. After a brief pause, she shocked us all by moving the toes on both her feet.

DURING THE NEXT SEVERAL MONTHS, authorities recovered the money McGillikin had transferred offshore. It was divided by the courts among the thirty-seven clients whose funds he had stolen along with the insurance money from the beach house. Sydney received about 80% of what she figured Scott had taken from her savings.

In a statement to police, David Matthews described how Ashleigh, after taking a few courses in nursing, had drawn her own blood and stored it in her freezer until the night of the robbery hoping that by pouring it all over her house, everyone would assume she was dead and that Bonner would not go looking for her. He said that she'd picked Richard because he was right next door and always alone, that she learned about the beach house by following Scott, then only took what she figured he owed them from the insurance settlement. As the only heir to the Jackson's estate, David took over his uncle's turkey farm at Lake Waccamaw and shortly afterward began dating a girl that lived up the road.

The check Scott had written to pay for the sailboat had bounced and the title had never been transferred. Tiffany sent her father a post card from Greece and told him she was having a great time, that the boat was performing beautifully, and that she'd try to get home by Christmas—the following year.

By the end of summer, Martha's recovery seemed to come to a halt as she became overwhelmed with fatigue, fluid retention, frequent headaches, and shortness of breath. She began dialysis every few days and was placed on a transplant list. We packed a bag for her and waited by the phone for word that a match had been found. Mom and I had both been tested and ruled out as donors, but as Martha's condition worsened, Winston insisted on being tested, and—to my astonishment—was considered an exceptional match.

Martha's surgery was performed at the *University of North Carolina Comprehensive Transplant Center* in Chapel Hill and went well. She recovered quickly and was soon back to rigorous physical therapy and working on her novel. Mom rebounded from the loss of her husband and life for the Baimbridge family was gradually returning to normal.

On a rainy Tuesday night in October, with all of us sitting around the TV keeping an eye on Hurricane Isabelle as it churned up the Atlantic coast, the investigative reporter in Martha surfaced again. "Mama, Daddy told Richie that Uncle Charlie was his father, but at the time you didn't want to talk about it. Was he right? Was Uncle Charlie his father?"

Before she could answer, the power went off and the house got deathly still. Mom quickly rose. "Stay right here. I'll light some candles." A moment later she was back with a box of kitchen matches and—as wind whistled under the door and thunder rumbled in the distance—Mom gathered three large candles from around the room and moved them to the coffee table in the center of us.

"So..." Martha began again. "Was Uncle Charlie really Richie's father?"

Mom struck a match and held it to the first candle. "Yes, Sweetheart. Charlie Baimbridge was Richie's father."

"And then he was killed in a car wreck just before you were to be married."

Mom cleared her throat. "That's right, Sweetheart."

"Gosh, Mom," I said. "You must have been devastated."

Mother exchanged glances with Winston as she moved to the second candle. "Charlie and I were...deeply in love...so *very* much in love." Her eyes glossed over and I could see the reflection of the flames in them. "After the accident, I stayed in bed and cried for weeks. There was nothing anyone could do. Charlie was gone and I had nothing to live for."

"What did you do?" Martha asked.

Normally, Mom left the room when she was about to cry, but as she struck another match and touched it to the third candle, a tear rolled down her cheek. "The doctor left some tablets to help me sleep," she said, her voice low. "And on the morning of June seventeenth—what was supposed to have been our wedding day—I took them. I took them all."

"Oh, Mother!" Martha gasped. "You didn't!"

Mom waved the flame off the match and tossed the burned stick into the fireplace. "My heart was broken. I couldn't imagine ever being happy again. Not without Charlie."

As she took her seat, Winston wiped her tears away with his fire-shortened thumb. She took his hand and clutched it for support as a powerful wind whistled through the trees outside. We'd never heard this part of our mother's history and I wanted to hear the rest.

"But you lived," I said.

"Yes," she said gazing into the candle flames. "Mama rushed me to the hospital where they pumped my stomach. And that was when I found out I was pregnant." She dabbed a tissue at her eyes.

Martha's mouth dropped open. "You didn't know?"

"Oh, the signs were all there. I was throwing up every day, but I just assumed I was upset over Charlie. I never imaged I was pregnant. But, there was never any doubt whose baby it was. Charlie was the only boy I'd been with."

"Oh, Mother," Martha sympathized. "What did grandmother and granddaddy say when they found out?"

Mom chuckled nervously. "Mama and Daddy were as mad as ground bees run over by a plow. They wanted me to get an abortion, which was against the law in those days. But they said they knew someone that could do it, but *I* wouldn't do it. I didn't give a hoot about what people would say. It was Charlie's baby and I was not about to let it go."

"Thank goodness," Sydney said, planting a kiss on my cheek.

Winston smiled.

Martha leaned forward in her chair. "So when did Daddy come into the picture?"

Mom sipped her iced tea and, as our shadows danced on the walls around us, I could see the pain of remembering in her eyes. She swallowed and took a deep breath before responding. "I was about four months along when Gus and his mother showed up at the house. He looked awful. His beard was all grown out. His eyes were bloodshot like he'd been crying. His hair down over his ears. With his mother there holding his hand, he sat down before us and told us it had been his fault, that he'd messed up the brakes on Charlie's car the day of the accident, and that he was sorry. He said he wanted to make things right, knelt down on one knee in front of me, his mother, and both my parents, and asked me to marry him. I was eighteen years old, pregnant, and had disappointed Mom and Dad enough. They all thought it was the right thing to do—and, truthfully, it guess it was. As far as I was concerned, if it couldn't be Charlie Baimbridge, it didn't matter *who* it was. At least with Gus I'd be *Mrs. Baimbridge*—and I liked that.

"A few days later, on August 26th, we were married at Mother's house with only our parents in attendance." Mother blew her nose and wiped it oblivious to the sound of a shutter banging intermittently against the side of the house.

"It sounds beautiful. What did you wear?" Sydney asked.

Mother wiped her nose. "I wore my Sunday School dress. It was...white with pink and blue crocheted flowers on it. And he wore a new brown suit his mother bought for him."

"Did you carry a bouquet of flowers?" Martha asked.

Mother crushed the tissue in her hand, closed her eyes, and rested her head against her fist as if it would help her remember. "The next door neighbors—the Cramptons—had a pink rosebush that grew along the fence between our yards. Daddy went out to it and cut every flower off it that came through the fence and made me a bouquet to carry. Mama added some honeysuckle blossoms, wrapped the stems with a piece of white ribbon she'd been saving for my wedding dress, and then pinned some honeysuckle in my hair."

"I'll bet you were beautiful," Martha said.

"I was sick all morning and the air conditioner quit before noon. It was too hot to stay inside so we all walked out to the front porch where there was a little breeze and did it. Right out on the street with all of Carolina Heights looking at us. When it was over, Gus kissed me and then we went into separate rooms, changed clothes, and sat out in the back yard under a shade tree."

The rain, which had paused briefly, began pounding the window glass again as if the house was being washed by a fire hose.

"Where did you go when you left?"

"We didn't go anywhere. Not together. Gus went back to his mother's house and I stayed home. We hardly saw each other until Richie was born and then we didn't move in together until Gus got a job selling cars and rented a house for us."

"Then four years later I came along," Martha said. "Which explains why Richie wasn't all that good of a match for the kidney transplant. We're only *half* brother and sister. But what I want to know is, how in the world could *you* have turned out to be the perfect donor for me, Winston? What are the chances of that happening? My mother's boyfriend being a better donor than my mother or my brother—even if he is my *half*-brother? Are we related in some way?"

Winston looked to Mom for help. "What do you think, Pearl?"

A clap of thunder rattled the windows and as it faded into the distance, Mom massaged her temples with both hands. "There *is* a logical explanation, but you three have to promise me that you will *never* tell a soul." She looked at each of us as she awaited our responses.

Martha looked at me, then back at Mom. "Okay! Of course. Tell us."

"I want to hear each of you *promise*. Sydney?"

Sydney slouched a bit lower in her seat. "Yes. Sure. I promise."

"Richie?"

"Yes. I promise."

"Martha?"

"Mother! For heaven's sake, I promise. Now tell us!"

Mom took Winston's hand and flashed him a smile before turning back to face us. "A few years after Richie was born, I got a call from the church secretary. She told me that one of church's mission cases happened to be the farmer that had been driving the truck that hit Charlie's car. She said he'd suffered burns over seventy percent of his body and said that he'd asked for me by name. That he wanted to know if I'd pay him a visit. I had no idea why he'd asked for me, but I thought maybe he wanted to say he was sorry for what had happened. So I went.

"I drove up to the farm where he lived and...when he opened the door..." Mom's voice cracked and a tear rolled over her cheekbone. "...I couldn't believe my eyes."

"What?" Martha uttered.

Mom turned to Winston, who nodded and flashed a reassuring smile.

Martha slapped her hands on the table. "Come on, Mama. Tell us!"

Mom cleared her throat. "When he opened the door, I knew instantly who he was. Even with the bandages and scars, I could tell he was Charlie Baimbridge."

59

I THOUGHT MARTHA AND I HAD FIGURED every possibility, but we *never* considered this one. *Winston is Uncle Charlie?* My heart skipped a beat. *Dad?* Goose bumps rose on my arms. I've often heard that the first time a man sees his newborn child, an emotion of unconditional love sweeps through him like a flame on spilled gasoline. I was meeting my father for the first time and I felt something powerful sweep through me.

Sydney stammered like a child who'd just been tricked by a slight-of-hand magician at the county fair. "W—What did you do?"

Mother dabbed a tissue at her eyes, but looked as if she'd been relieved of a load she had carried her whole life. "All the feelings I thought I'd stowed away forever came rushing back. I went to pieces, burst into tears, and collapsed in the doorway. When he lifted me up, I grabbed hold of him, kissed him, and wouldn't let go." That loose shutter banged again against the side of the house. "We held each other for hours crying and laughing, and then made love. It was the most wonderful, most *magical* day of my life. And when it was time to go, I didn't want to leave, but Charlie insisted that I had to go home, that I had to keep his identity a secret."

"What? Why is that?" I asked Winston.

Winston—No, Charlie—No. My God! *My father*—my *real* father took over the story. I stared as if seeing him for the first time, hanging on his every word, looking for pieces of myself in him.

"The first few months in the *North Carolina Jaycee Burn Center*, they kept me so doped up that I was seldom conscious. And when I was, the pain was so intense that all I wanted was to be knocked out again."

Mom watched him just as I did and his pain showed in her face.

"I'd been there for months before I realized that they thought I was somebody else. I told them my name was Charlie, but they just ignored me and kept calling me Winston. Then people that had known Winston before the accident began coming up from

Wilmington and little by little I learned about Pearl—that she had married my brother Gus and that they'd had a child." The pain in Winston's voice brought tears to every eye in the room.

"After that, I didn't care what they called me. Or whether I lived or died. I just laid there and cried. The nurses thought it was because of the pain caused by my burns."

"I didn't know," Mom said sliding an arm around Charlie, laying her head against his shoulder.

"Then, after being there for a year and a half, they released me from the hospital. But I didn't have anywhere to go. So I did what everyone around me expected me to do. I let them bring me back to Wilmington and set me up at the farm."

"Why didn't you tell anyone who you were when you got back to Wilmington?" I asked.

"I didn't want to be pitied," he said looking down. "And people said they thought things had worked out pretty well for Pearl. They said she looked happy and I didn't know that you were *my* son."

Hearing those words caused my chest to tighten. I could feel the love in his eyes as they peered at me through his scarred slits. I felt dizzy. My legs shook nervously and my face felt as if it was on fire.

"And the biggest reason I kept my identity a secret is that I didn't know how Pearl would react if she saw me. Winston had never been married and his parents were dead, so I figured the best thing for me to do was leave well enough alone."

It was a powerful moment and in that moment my universe turned right-side up. Suddenly, everything made sense. My conflicts with Dad. The bond I had with Martha. *Life!* I was conceived by their love and I could feel that love flowing from him to me and back from me to him. I didn't have to think about it. It was as if someone had turned on a light switch inside me. Sydney tugged at my arm. "Are you okay?"

Something inside me that I'd held in check all my life had broken loose and was now running rampant. I was awash in peace, love, and happiness. Although I had tears in my eyes, I laughed. "Hell yes I'm okay! That's my dad!"

But Martha wasn't smiling. Her teeth were clinched, her eyes cold. "All these years, the two of you kept your little secret and you stayed married to Daddy while you had your fun?"

Mother's face turned a shade darker. Wind swished down the chimney and the candle flames waved about nervously. "It wasn't easy, Sweetheart," Mom said. "People didn't run out and get a divorce in those days like they do now."

"God, Mother! What did you do? Run up to that farm every week and cheat on Daddy?"

"No! It wasn't like that."

"Well, how was it, Mother?"

"That was it! That was the one and only time." A Venetian blind buzzed as wind passed through it.

"Oh, come on, Mother. Don't lie about it. Not now."

"It's true," Winston said leaning forward where the light from the candles reflected off the smooth skin of his face as if it was a plastic mask. "I told her not to come back. I only invited her there to begin with so I could see for myself that she was doing okay. What wasn't covered in bandages looked hideous. I never dreamed she'd recognize me. Or that things would go the way they did. Yes, it happened. But, I couldn't let it go on. I told her she had to go home to Gus, that things happen for a reason, and that God had not intended for us to be together."

"But you did go back," Martha snapped.

Mom wiped a tear. "Not until I found out I was pregnant again." That loose shutter slammed against the side of the house.

"And why would that matter to Charlie?" Martha screamed. "What business was it of his?"

Mom's chin trembled. Her eyes darted around the floor. Our reflections quivered high on the walls as a draft blowing through the room passed over the candles.

"Oh, Mother! What did you do? Get an abortion? Give it up for adoption? What?"

"No! Yes, I was pregnant. Yes, it was Charlie's. But I carried that child full term and raised her."

"Who—? Me?" Martha's eyes moved from Mom to Charlie. "Are you saying—?"

The secret was finally out. And Mom's reply had a hopeful, proud resonance to it—much like the storyteller's at the children's library confirming a child's sudden revelation. "Yes, Darling."

Martha's eyes jumped from Mom to me, to Charlie, and back to Mom. She exhaled, snatched up a candle, slapped the electric lever on her wheelchair, rolled back from the table and sped from the room bumping the door casing on her way out.

"That was a bit of a shock. For all of us." I said. "I'll go check on her."

I found Martha in her room, her face buried in a pillow she'd pulled off her bed. I stepped in and closed the door. "Hey. You okay?"

"Why did she have to tell us that? Why couldn't they have kept their dirty little secret to themselves?"

"I don't know, Babe. Maybe it's not the right time...and maybe it's long *past* time."

"My whole life has been one big, fat *lie? Why?* So they could have their fun?"

I sat on the edge of the bed. "Hey. You know Mom's not like that."

"I *loved* my daddy and my daddy loved *me.*"

"Yes, he did."

"And now I find out my daddy is *not* my daddy?"

"No. You're wrong. Gus *was* your daddy. He adored you. He looked out for you, spent time with you, bought you things, and taught you things. He did all the things for you that I wished he'd done for me. And this doesn't change any of that, Babe. None of it! Do you hear me?"

Tears flowed down her face. "God, I can't believe they did that to him. Don't you think Daddy deserved better than that?"

"Yes, Babe. He deserved to know the truth, but it couldn't have been easy for them, either."

"Oh, stop it! Why do you always take up for Mom?"

I reached under her and raised her out of her chair—pillow and all. "I know it's a shock, my darling sister. But do you have any *idea* what this means?"

"Put me down!" she shouted kicking her legs.

I spun around in circles, stumbling as we turned. "That-a-girl! Keep it up! It'll strengthen your muscles. You'll be walking again in no time."

"I mean it! Put me down!" She pounded my back with the side of her fist.

"Not until you grow up."

"Grow up yourself!" I became dizzy and tossed her onto her bed.

She rolled to the other side facing away from me. "You shit!"

I leaned on my hands panting to catch my breath. "I don't know about you, Babe...but I *like* the idea that we're brother and sister again."

"But—" she sniffled.

"But *what?* Yes, Daddy loved you. You were his reason to live. He would have given his life for you. When you had your accident and they wouldn't let anyone in to be with you, he disappeared for two days and I found him in Oakdale Cemetery. He was passed out drunk draped over Charlie's grave. It took Mother and me both to get him home."

She rolled over to face me. "Why haven't you told me this before?"

"Everyone has secrets, Babe."

"Well, *I* don't." She rolled back on her side facing away from me.

It seemed wrong for me to be lecturing her. It was usually the other way around. She was the stronger one. She was the logical one. It felt good to be needed for something besides a pair of legs, but I had no idea what to say. "Daddy knew the truth about me and hated me," I said searching for the right words. "Would you rather he'd known about you, too?" She didn't answer, just sniffled. "Do you think it's easy giving up a child? Not being able to hold it? Not being able to tell it who you are?" I waited for a response, but none came. "It takes a lot of love, little sister, to give up *not one*, but *two* of your children."

"I would *never* do that."

"Of course you wouldn't. And maybe Charlie Baimbridge didn't want to either. But he had to. He knew that he would never be able to give us much of a life. That he would never be able to take us places and be the kind of father that he wanted to be."

"He could have done *something*."

"Did you know he was there at the hospital every single day both times you were there?"

She turned back to face me. "I didn't see him."

"Yes you did. He came in the room many times with Mom."

"I just thought..."

"I know. So did I. I thought he was there for Mom. But he stopped me every time I left and asked how you were doing. And how Daddy was doing, too. And he listened to every word I said. I could tell he really cared, I just didn't know how much."

Tears welled up in her eyes. "Why didn't you tell me?"

"I don't know. Didn't I?"

"Maybe."

"And all those times we went out to the farm with Mom, don't you remember how he always wanted to know everything we were doing? How we always had to take our report cards? Charlie Baimbridge had to let his brother raise his children because he knew it was the best thing for them. But he stayed in touch the only way he could."

She sat up and laid her head against mine. "What do we do now?"

"He's our father. Let's get to know him. Give him a chance."

"I'm so ashamed."

I put my arms around her. "Believe me, he'll forgive you."

As Hurricane Isabelle churned up the coast and changed the history of Ocracoke Island that day, so too were our lives changed forever. Secrets and lies gave way to truth and understanding. Charlie Baimbridge could never replace Gus in Martha's life, but she agreed to open her arms and her heart to him. And although my father's existence created new questions that needed answers, it answered quite a few that had haunted me for years.

Epilogue

OVER THE NEXT FEW MONTHS, we would come to know ourselves, Charlie, and Mother in ways we never imagined. I looked behind the disfigurement of my father and discovered myself within him. His love of the arts, his passion for the theatre, and his gentle manner mirrored mine, and made me as proud of him as he was of me. The tension in my life disappeared. Whatever I'd been running from no longer chased me. I'd been set free.

Charlie and Mom married the following spring and she became Mrs. Winston Gaylord. She sold her house and moved to the farm. I've never seen her happier.

Dane Bonner was eventually found guilty of the murders of Scott McGillikin and Ashleigh Matthews as well as two of the missing Wilmington girls. He was sentenced to death.

I did make it to Broadway, after all. Twice in fact. Sydney and I went to New York on our honeymoon that first Christmas after Gus died where she took dance classes during the day at *Broadway Dance Center,* then saw many of her instructors performing in the shows we took in on Broadway at night.

We were back in New York again just last month to accompany Martha to a book signing at *Barnes & Noble* for her new bestselling novel, *Down in Flames.* When she arrived, the line waiting for autographs stretched out the front door to the sidewalk. Everyone applauded when she arrived and walked in on crutches.

After returning from the book signing in New York, I sat on the back deck and watched the sky grow dark in the west stroking the long black and tan fur on the feline curled in my lap. She nudged her head against my palm and closed first the blue, then the brown eye as she practically caressed herself with my hand.

Mrs. Winslow scurried around her back yard folding chairs and putting them away before the storm arrived.

I waved. "Evening, Mrs. Winslow."

She turned and waved. "Good evening, Mr. Baimbridge. There's a storm coming!"

"Yes, I know," I called back. "I'm looking forward to it."

She shrugged her shoulders, wrapped her housecoat more tightly around her, and scampered back inside. Flags along the lakefront snapped and popped while boats tugged at their lines as the wind rose. I laid my head back, closed my eyes, and tuned in to the distant thunder.

"You too busy to see an old friend?" a voice called.

I opened my eyes and looked around. It was Sam Jones coming up the walk in an electric wheelchair. He looked a little grayer than I remembered, but his eyes were still piercing under those thick eyebrows.

"Hey-Hey! The man is back! Can I get you something to drink?"

"Nope. On duty—sort of."

"I thought you retired."

He steered the chair along the brick walk toward the steps. "Yeah, my body retired, but my mind didn't. I'm doing private-eye work now."

I put the cat down, stepped down the stairs, shook his hand, and sat on the bottom step. "That's good isn't it?"

"Well, it pays okay, but the hours stink." He leaned forward and rose to stand in front of the chair. "Look, the reason I stopped by is that I need your help with something." He carefully turned and sat on the step next to me, stretched his legs, and leaned back on his elbows.

"Okay, shoot."

"I need a photographer."

"For what?"

"I'm trying to get a part in a movie."

"Forget it! I don't do nudes anymore."

He laughed so hard, his eyes watered. I laughed, too. When he settled down enough to speak, he continued. "My granddaughter's coming to town next month and I want a good portrait of her."

"Who does she look like?"

"Looks like her granddaddy, of course."

"Save your money. Take her to Wal-Mart."

He cracked up in another huge belly laugh. "Well, she looks like me, only prettier."

I slapped his knee. "Call the studio and make an appointment. This one's on me."

The door behind us opened and Sydney leaned out as Tux bolted out through her legs. "Hey, Sam!" she said.

Sam twisted around. "Well, hello there, Miss Sydney."

"You two mind a little company?" she asked.

"'Course not," I said.

She held the door back and little Charlie toddled out. Thunder boomed a short distance away and Tux bolted back in the open door.

"'Torm coming," Charlie shouted.

"You got that right, Buddy!" I said clapping my hands together. "Come here, Tiger."

The toddler bobbled along with Sydney bent forward holding his hands to help him keep his balance. I reached out, lifted him, and set him on my lap. "Say hello to Mr. Sam, Charlie."

Charlie just sat and looked at Sam.

"Growing up, ain't he?" Sam said pulling at Charlie's toes.

"They do that."

As thunder clapped and leaves fluttered across the ground, my son bobbed up and down on my knee slapping his hands together.

"I don't understand," Sydney said. "Most children run from storms, but Little Charlie wants to be right in the middle of it."

"Takes after his daddy," I said.

Sydney leaned down and kissed my forehead, her long hair spilling around my face until thunder exploded nearby sending her racing back inside.

Charlie laughed and clapped his hands together.

"'Torm coming!"